the paternity test

the paternity test

michael lowenthal

terrace books
a trade imprint of the university of wisconsin press

Terrace Books, a trade imprint of the University of Wisconsin Press, takes its name from the Memorial Union Terrace, located at the University of Wisconsin–Madison. Since its inception in 1907, the Wisconsin Union has provided a venue for students, faculty, staff, and alumni to debate art, music, politics, and the issues of the day. It is a place where theater, music, drama, literature, dance, outdoor activities, and major speakers are made available to the campus and the community. To learn more about the Union, visit www.union.wisc.edu.

Terrace Books
A trade imprint of the University of Wisconsin Press
1930 Monroe Street, 3rd Floor
Madison, Wisconsin 53711-2059
uwpress.wisc.edu

3 Henrietta Street
London WC2E 8LU, England
eurospanbookstore.com

Printed in the United States of America

Library of Congress Cataloging-in-Publication Data

Lowenthal, Michael.
The paternity test / Michael Lowenthal.
p.   cm.
ISBN 978-0-299-29000-9 (cloth: alk. paper)
ISBN 978-0-299-29003-0 (e-book)
1. Gay men—Fiction.   2. Surrogate mothers—Fiction.   I. Title.
PS3562.O894P38   2012
813'.54—dc23
2012009962

for my father

abraham lowenthal

cape codder by birth,

and for

mitchell waters

the paternity test

one

It's not too late," I said. "You could still change your mind."

"What?" said Stu. "Now?" He glanced down at his watch. "Quarter till. They might already be there."

We'd rumbled down the hill in our rust-corrupted Volvo, my parents' "summer clunker" we inherited with the cottage. Now Stu turned and steered us through the narrows of 6A: past the shuttered ice-cream stand ("C U all next season!"), the barns with empty clam-shell drives and sluggish whale-shaped vanes. Weathered shingles, the gull-gray sky, the browned, static marsh—the sober shades of Cape Cod in December.

But this was what I'd longed for: a hushed and dullish outback. I hadn't set foot in New York since we'd moved.

"So call them," I said. "Say you thought of a better place. It's fine."

With one sure hand, Stu veered to dodge a road-kill squirrel; the other hand was fidgeting with his scarf. "What kind of a first impression is that?" he said. "We can't even commit to a *restaurant*?"

The Pancake King, where we were headed, had been his bright idea, overriding my suggestion of the Yarmouth House or one of our other surf-and-turf standbys. Someplace less expensive, he'd insisted: "Cheap enough so they'll feel at home if they're not used to fancy—or, if they are, maybe they'll think it's witty."

3

He'd made a decent case, but it was just conjecture. We knew so very little about Debora and Danny Neuman, certainly not enough to safely judge what they might like. And yet here we were, crossing the Cape to meet them, to see if she'd agree to have our baby. Had ever there been an odder double date?

While Stu tossed and turned about the question of where to meet, I was trying to float atop the waves of my own worry: Would Debora and her husband see the patched-up, worthy Stu and Pat? Would any of our old frayings show?

I didn't remind Stu—not in so many words—that it was he who'd pushed us toward a restaurant so silly. What I said (too carelessly) was, "Well, there's always the Yarmouth House . . ."

"Perfect," he said. "I knew you'd say 'I told you so.' I knew it!"

With a stagy crunch of gravel, he pulled to the shoulder and stopped. He stabbed the hazards button, got them clacking.

Stu was that incongruous thing, a Jewish airline pilot, and his manner could be just as oxymoronic. Forcefully indecisive, authoritatively whiny. With me, at least, in private, that could be his way. Strangers noted his rinsed-of-accent speech, his stringent crew cut, a gaze that seemed to own the whole horizon—the earned-in-sweat antithesis of a nebbish (a word he'd taught me). But late at night, or during sex, when Stu let down his guard, I could see his impressive eyes inch a smidgen closer, as though he wanted to stare at his own nose.

His eyes were like that now. I guessed they were, behind his Ray-Ban shades.

"Patrick," he said. "Pat, hon. Be honest. You're not nervous?"

The quaver of his humbled voice disarmed me. "Kidding?" I said. "Of course I am. I almost puked this morning."

"Okay. And Debora and Danny—you think they feel the same?"

Considering what we'd ask of them, how could they not? I nodded.

"Right," said Stu. "So, please, can't you let *me* feel that, too?"

The world at large got Captain Stuart Nadler, at the stick. Who did I get? Someone neurotic about his choice of lunch spots.

4

"Just let me spaz a little," he said. "It's nothing. It's routine turbulence. I mean, look at us. Look where we finally are!"

Where we were was a cattail-shaded stretch of silent road. Not a single car had passed since Stu had pulled us over.

I thought of an evening shortly after we had made the move, when I still worried he might quit and head back to the city; I had feared that our new life wouldn't—that *I* wouldn't—be enough. We went to see *Shrek 2* at the theater down in Sandwich, the lobby empty except for the wizened lady who took our tickets, who offered also to make a batch of popcorn. Stu, as the trailers started, looked around and whispered, "We can't be, can we? The only people here?" He flung a kernel of popcorn at the screen. But then, after the lights went dark, seeing that we were indeed alone, he jumped up and took my hand and skipped us down the aisle, belting out the soundtrack in falsetto. Our own Kingdom of Far, Far Away!

Now, in the car, he removed his aviators. "Kiss me," he said.

There was the Stu I craved: my own top gun.

I followed his order, and tasted his familiarly foreign tongue: still, after a decade-plus, surprising in its saltiness.

"Ready?" he said, and revved the engine.

"I've *been* ready," I said. "You know that."

And so into the brackish Cape Cod bluster we charged, back on the road and off to the Pancake King to meet our womb.

two

A surrogate mother, at last! A woman who could give us what we couldn't give ourselves.

I was thrilled, even if I'd hoped we'd get here sooner. How could we have wasted nine full months since we had moved?

Our first excuse for stalling—the one we'd dared to voice—had to do with all the stresses of taking over the cottage. On a ridge in West Barnstable, above the stylish dunes of Sandy Neck, the home was where we Faunces, for thirty-some years, had summered. Or, to follow Stu's edict that *summer* was not a verb, the cottage was my family's "summer home." (Stu had tried, less successfully, to wean me off of *cottage*: with four bedrooms, two baths, a two-car garage, the house would be a mansion in Manhattan.) I had stayed at the cottage every school break as a kid, and since my parents had died, had co-owned it with my sisters, but suddenly it was mine alone—actually, mine and Stu's—and suddenly, too, was meant to be the scene of our redemption.

All we'd known together was a queered-up city life: a life of sexual license, of looking the other way, our love stretched so thin it almost snapped; now we were nesting in this tranquil bayside home, having convinced each other that a baby would be the answer . . .

. . . and every domestic mishap gave a little karmic poke: *You really believe in happily ever after?*

A clogged oil-burner nozzle. A leak in the chimney flashing. A bombardiering blue jay that mistook our picture window for the sky and left it smithereened with cracks.

The old poetry major in me couldn't help but see the cottage in metaphorical terms. My answer was to make of the place a bold "objective correlative": an external framework to stand in for—and influence?—our emotions. Thus came my compulsion to de-bramble ancient blueberry bushes that never, till just now, had called for rescue, and my early-morning passion for repointing decorative garden walls (the ones now made more visible by de-brambling).

In order to prove our readiness to raise a child together, I would get the place—and us—in unimpeachable shape.

Not that I minded the effort. In fact, I sort of loved it. As someone who wrote textbooks, shuffling words and phrases, getting the chance to grapple with actual objects pleased me greatly. More than that, I liked the work because it now was my work. At thirty-six, at last I had my private patch of earth.

My work, *my* private patch of earth. But the house was also Stu's now—or should have been, and had to be. And that required additional adjustments.

Stu insisted, rightfully, that he should make his mark upon the house, which basically hadn't been touched since Mom had died. First to go was the sign—routered driftwood dangling from rusty chains—that had touted the property, ungrammatically, as "The Faunce's." Also tossed away were some dozen wall-hung photos, depicting scenes a great deal like (or maybe they were) our deck's bay view; Mom had bought them, as if to claim her view as pictur*esque* she needed actual pictures for comparison. In their stead, Stu put up his raft of vintage travel posters. "Come to Ulster, the Holiday Wonderland, for a Real Change and Happy Days"; "Visitez L'Afrique en Avion." He also set out keepsakes to remind him of New York: a coffee table whose surface was made of inlaid subway tokens; a sign from Yonah Schimmel's: "Eat Knishes!"

Better, then. Much better. But still, sometimes, he told me, he felt like a hermit crab in some other creature's shell. (It took all I had to keep from noting that his simile was proof of his becoming a Cape Codder.) "I watch you," he admitted, one April Sunday morning, when I was sprawled on the living room's shag carpet, doing a crossword. "The way you walk around from room to room. It's like you've got your memories, this massive *net* of memories, throwing it over every inch, to claim things."

True enough, and I wasn't about to block those recollections. Even if I'd wanted to, I couldn't.

The answer was to work on making memories now together, to co-star in our own all-new show.

Here we are, planting a row of rhubarb in the yard, dreaming aloud about the jams and chutneys we'll cook up. In the house, we take the muslin, mollusk-patterned curtains down, replacing them with sleek bamboo shades. And, acceding to beachy norms, but also being camp, we park a homely trinket on the lawn: a whirligig whose plywood fisherman forever hooks a big one.

For my birthday Stu surprises me: a flight in a rented Skylane. We skim over glacial ponds and purple fallow cranberry bogs: a chain of gems along the Cape's thin neck. Stu says, "You know, when we first started coming here, I couldn't help but see what was missing: no decent theater or Chinese food, no *oomph*. But living here"—he swoops above a pond, whose surface shivers—"now I can see what *I* was missing."

Next we're at the Cape Cod Mall, a nor'easter banging away outside, the halls packed with prepubescent girls. Mrs. Rita, the fuchsia-nailed proprietress of Mrs. Rita's Rice, bodily—almost violently—accosts us. "Write your name on a piece of rice," she importunes redundantly (the awning above her booth bears this slogan). She offers me a magnifying glass to glimpse some samples. *World's Best Dad. Class of 2004. Your Name Here.* I muse about how long this place would last in

New York: not long. "My specialty is guessing who people are to each other," she says. "You two guys—a couple, right? I think that's just fantastic. Anyone tells you otherwise, then screw 'em! Newlyweds, I'm willing to bet: the both of you've got that glow. How about two grains that say 'Till Death,' one for each? Put them in glass beads, on a necklace?" Stu looks at me. What would be the point in disabusing her? She has stretched a hand across the great divide of strangerdom; better to endorse her endorsement. "Sold," he says, and asks her to engrave the matching grains, but the glass beads? Thanks, we'll take a pass. "Really? Just the rice?" she says. "Aren't you going to lose them?" But here she goes, doing her nifty Lilliputian trick, as solemn as a sapper with a bomb. A minute later, finishing up the grains, she gives it one more try: "Can't just hand them off like this—naked! Are you serious? Okay, then, you're well and warned. The customer's always right . . ." We thank her, and pay, and deep-kiss right in front of her: let her take some credit for our romance. And then, when she lunges for the next passing couple (sixty-somethings in matching madras slickers), we turn and, with laughter in our eyes, without the need to ask, count to three: the grains go down the hatch.

But even on the best of days, our happiness felt fragile. Every forward step, if set down wrong, could remind me of the hurt Stu'd caused, could flare that sprain again.

The day we gobbled Rita's rice, we went next to Filene's. I'd seen their ad in the *Cape Cod Times*: boxer shorts, all brands, two for one. I picked up some Jockey packs, but Stu splurged on Calvins. "That way," he said, "simpler to tell, in the laundry, whose are whose."

"Yuh," I said, "as if *you* do the laundry."

He pinched my butt. "Just watching out for you, my love. As always."

After we'd paid, and browsed the bedding aisles for duvet covers (Stu was still chipping away at my mother's old décor), I had a thought: "Hey, let's look in Baby."

"Now?" he said, and then, "Why not? The power of positive thinking."

Even during these early days, adjusting to our new life—assuring each other, "Once the *house* is dealt with . . ."—I'd been getting ready for a baby. I read Dan Savage's book *The Kid*, and pored through old issues of *Gay Parent*. I boned up on breast-milk facts, theories of early learning. Cloth or plastic? I could have penned a tome.

But still, almost three months gone, we had yet to even start to try to find a surrogate.

I tried to push Stu along, but never to push too much. He would be ready when he was ready, and not a second sooner. (I'd asked my buddy Marcie, once, how she'd known she was ready to be a mom. "Pat," she said, "if we waited till we were *ready* for having kids, there'd never be another baby born.")

"Ooh, look at this," I said now, holding up a onesie, blue-striped like a French sailor's shirt.

"Huh," said Stu. He shrugged.

"All right, how 'bout this?" The second one was brown, and showed a tiny trumpet, below which were the words: Little Tooter.

Stu ran the fabric hypercritically through his fingers, a spoof of a Jewish garment broker. "Feh," he said. "Not that junk. For *our* kid? Only silk!"

I wanted to be cross with him, for being so blithely pie-in-the-sky. But then, without his humor, we never would have gotten this far. And what was having kids about if not pipe-dream ambitions?

I'd moved on to baby shoes. How cute! Mini One Stars! "But Christ," I said. "Twenty-five bucks? For shoes that'll fit *how* long?"

Stu didn't answer. He stared at something—or nothing—in the distance. "Hey, just thought of a thing I need at CVS," he said. "Meet you in ten, out front? At the car?"

Why not ask me to come along? An innocent reason, surely. What nefarious business could be waiting at the drugstore? Maybe he thought I wanted to stay, that I wasn't finished browsing.

10

I almost said, "I'll just come with," but couldn't find the air, couldn't risk the cold and stifled Stu I might then see. The old feelings of shame and abandonment knocked me windless—just like when we'd partied at the Roxy, one last time.

That had been back in New York. A foolish final try to deal with Stu's immoderation.

I was not supposed to mind his sleeping with other men: Article 1 of the Gay Constitution. And truthfully, I'd always known, with Stu, what I was in for. After all, a *pilot?* Wasn't that half the draw? The glamour of the uniform, the randy Right Stuff strut. Sure enough, in his line of work, he'd gathered a pile of playmates. Shane in Miami; Owen in L.A.; a bunch more whose names I'd blocked out.

"You *let* him?" asked my editor, Steve, when I'd confessed this once. "Jesus Christ, if my wife ever caught me . . ."

Well, it wasn't like I hadn't had my own digressions, but Steve's amazement kept me from imparting this admission. (Educraft, the firm where we worked, produced texts for school kids, to prep them for state assessment tests. Because the books were sold in states like Georgia and Missouri, the office, despite its address, was more Mayberry than Gotham.)

I had lived so long within our orthodoxy of excess, I could forget how odd our customs must have seemed to Steve. For him and his faithful wife, sex was the wedding china: a spotless thing, saved for Sunday dinners. For us (so went the party line), the etiquette was less strict. Sure, we had the nice plates, the ones we used at home, but if sometimes, out of the house, we grabbed a snack on paper napkins, what earth-shaking calamity was that?

Actually, for me and Stu, it hadn't been calamitous. Not at first, especially not when we had strayed together.

We'd met in the early '90s, when AIDS was all we saw. Then came the new drugs, which nearly stopped the dying, and we were freed to take another sort of drugs, the *fun* ones. Weekends, we would pack the dance floors, licking strangers' lips, as if to spread our own subversive joyful epidemic. Stu or I would pick a guy, or two, or they'd choose us. Once, amid the dancing throng, Stu had nuzzled my armpit; a big-eyed boy observed and stepped right up: "I'm gonna *love* you." He did, right there in the strobe lights, on his knees, and then moved on.

It wasn't always easy, in that rush of restitution, to keep sight of each other, and of *us*. We'd do this thing on the dance floor sometimes, locking mouths and breathing as a unit: I'd take air in through my nose and blow it from my mouth to his; he would gulp, then puff the exhalation back through mine. A Möbius strip of breath. A promise, a profession: I'm your lungs, your heart; I'm your life.

Which made it all the harder, then, to lose our perfect sync.

We blinked and it was the 'oos: the "aughts," we awkwardly called them. I heard it as "oughts," but not from any outside, adult force, as in *Young man, you ought to mind your manners*. My mom had died the year before, six years after Dad, and being parentless totally derailed me, even if (or maybe because) they'd often braked my progress. Eventually, though, without them, my oughts welled up within me: ought to wipe the windshield and start searching for a turn ahead, ought to dream of what I'd do or make to leave a mark.

Meanwhile, Stu was letting himself get snared in the World Wide Web. Time was, if he overnighted in Phoenix or in Charlotte, and if he had some energy to spare, he'd head out to the bars and try his luck; the nights he scored were sweetened by the many when he hadn't. But now that he had Manhunt—and Gay.com, and Craigslist—Stu could scarcely take a trip without first making plans with some stranger he had ordered up like take-out. To satisfy his taste on any day he just clicked Search. A blond, green-eyed bottom between the ages of twenty and thirty, who lived within five miles of the airport Hilton? *Click.* A guy who favored dirty talk, or jockstraps? *Click, click.*

Soon he started surfing for tricks when he was in New York, disappearing for hours on every off day. The first few times I asked him where he'd been, he told the truth. After that, he lapsed into an adolescent vagueness: "Out," he'd say, or "You know, here and there."

How could I say this broke our rules? We'd chosen not to *have* rules. That was what we'd come to think constituted gay liberation.

In the past, my absence from the room when Stu was sleeping around had seemed to me mostly circumstantial: a matter of geography or timing. But now Stu's adventures seemed dependent on my absence; he wanted less to be with someone else than *not* to be with me—at least that was what I felt and feared. We had sex together, still, but that was disconnected from his drive to do things, to be things, on his own. A Stu I didn't know, a slippery, quenchless Stu, was coming to frightful life behind my back, but after years of seeing myself as part of Stu-and-Pat, I couldn't bear to break our hyphenation.

I had heard Stu's scorn when he talked about a friend of ours who made his boyfriend cancel his Manhunt profile: "You shitting me? What is he, a lesbian?" I wanted Stu back, I wanted *us* back, but didn't know how to get this, not without provoking similar salvos aimed at me.

Did that explain my mixed-up plan to go back to the Roxy, the site of our ecstatic early bonding, in hopes of finding someone for a three-way? I wanted to remind Stu of the glory days we'd shared, when we could turn the heads of any crowd we happened into—not because either of us was all that notable-looking, but because *as a unit* we gave off a fusive force: a couple so well crafted, so solidly adhered, that strangers hoped a touch of us might solder their own seams. (Maybe, like me, these strangers had grown weary of so much leeway.)

And so, with a week of off time coming up for Stu, I told him to get set for a blowout. He was spent—he'd flown through heavy weather up from Tampa—but rallied when I gave him two small pills with smiley faces. We bathed and flossed, donned our best show-off-your-pecs shirts, and sped to the club as if into our past.

(Stu had never—and wouldn't have ever—indulged in these activities without a good four days between flights. And no, not primarily due to fear of being tested; the Feds asked for his pee in a cup just once every two, three years. Stu played things safe because safety was his calling: sobriety as its own kind of high.)

13

The club was packed, though more than half the crowd was bridge-and-tunnel, dudes as squat as La-Z-Boys with soft slipcover girlfriends. We did spot some solo gays: punching the air, lock-jawed, wormholes where I'd hoped for smiling eyes. That was the difference crystal meth had made. I'd tried it once and hated it: it felt like someone hammered a Swiss army knife up my nose and opened all the blades inside my brain. Stu refused to touch the stuff at all.

We kept pushing ahead, to below the starry disco ball, where all the festive fags used to clump, and there was a group of old-time happy campers. Abracadabra: our pills kicked in. Everything went ribbony. The techno picked the lock of my impatience.

"Ahhh," said Stu. He reached around me, rubbed my sweaty neck. "It's great the way, when I rub yours, it feels like *mine* relaxes." He licked the honeysuckle of my ear.

"Yum," I said. "How long is your tongue? I love it."

Then Stu started to pollinate the group of guys around us. A peck to this one's cheek, a squeeze of that one's ass. "A pilot," I could hear him answer above the trippy beat. "No, really. And don't try any 'joystick' jokes, I've heard them!" An unconceited cockiness, a clean-state kind of glee, and under it all: boyish emancipation. My guess was, he'd looked the same in kosher days of Hebrew School, sneaking out to eat a BLT. Now, as then, what pleased him most was making people see the Stu he'd self-created, not the product of any faith or father.

He lingered by an acne-scarred Latino with smart blue eyes: jockey-small, dancing with an impish, clenched-hand focus. Stu quick-spun him, salsa style. They spoke with winking ease.

When I caught sight of his tramp stamp—Take It Easy, But Take It—I thought: *He's the one we're bringing home.*

"How 'bout him?" I asked when Stu returned. "You want to try? Work a little bit of our old magic?" In the old days, when we would take a third into our bedroom, it always seemed the granting of an honor. We were never haughty about it, or purposely exclusive. What we were was giddy with our own good luck in love; we longed to give someone else a glimpse.

14

"Nah," said Stu.

"Why not?"

"Don't know. Not really into it."

"You seemed into it a second ago. Have you met that guy before?"

Stu glanced at the man. "Define 'met.'"

I felt a twinge, but the music now was stoking up my stomach, boiling through me, turning me into vapor. Stu massaged my neck again. He sucked my Adam's apple. Then we kissed, the way we'd used to, figure-eighting air. We breathed and breathed: one big set of lungs.

A minute might have passed, or a hundred, or a half.

"Hey, I've got to pee," said Stu. "I'm heading to the bathroom."

Right—me, too; we were so in tune! "Yeah," I said. "Wait, I'll come with . . ."

Could eyes slump like shoulders? That was what Stu's did. He couldn't, or at least he didn't, hide his irritation. "I'll be quick, okay?" he said. "Stay right here. You're fine." He disappeared into the sweaty horde.

There I stood, abandoned, a hundred percent un-high. Had Stu and the Latino made a plan to go hook up? Was that why he was zipping off, without me? Or did he just want to be alone, away from me? I tried to keep dancing but my feet were like a leper's, decomposing with every little step. I didn't want Stu to catch me searching through the crowd for him, and so I bent my head and closed my eyes.

After fifteen minutes (time was sharp and strict again; I had checked and double-checked my watch), I went off to see if I could find him. He wasn't at the front bar or the back bar or the balcony. Not by the columns we had sometimes used as meeting points.

I did find the other guy, the acne-scarred Latino. Leaning against the wall outside the bathroom.

Brine on my tongue, acid up my throat. Everything burned. "Remember the guy," I said, "who you danced with? The pilot?"

He cocked his head, smiling, with a look of satiation. "Why?" he said. "You know him?"

A decent question.

15

What did I want to ask this fellow? If he had just had sex with Stu? And, if so, what the sex had been like? But no, what I wanted more to ask was what had *Stu* been like? The new Stu, who'd formed himself so pointedly apart.

How pathetic would that be? Asking a stranger to tell me what my lover was truly like.

What, then, could I ask? *Where is he?*

The guy's skin was shining, his sweaty nut-brown skin. Jealousy was a fuse alight within me. I battled a desperate urge to lift my hand and touch him, this creature whom my distant Stu had touched.

I didn't think I'd ever felt such shame. I said, "Forget it."

three

Could you *decide* to want kids?

Whether to have them: that was a choice. And when, and with whom. But *wanting* them? Wasn't that just an ore you had within? At least that's how it was for me: not chosen but discovered, uncovered. At first I saw just glimmers, gold flecks in the dross. Then, with every passing year, more glow, longer veins. The mother lode was everywhere inside me.

Was Stu's desire for kids like mine? Doubtful, but who could say? He was so good at willing himself and making it seem like wanting.

The first time I looked at him and thought what kind of dad he'd be was during one of our early trips, to Prague. We had spent a chastening afternoon touring Josefov, the remnants of the old Jewish ghetto. In borrowed yarmulkes we padded through the hushed, haunted sites: the cemetery, where graves were jammed in groups like panicked captives; a synagogue whose walls teemed with names of slaughtered Jews.

We'd planned next to find a shop mentioned in our *Rough Guide*, where Stu hoped to buy some old posters (he coveted a Czechoslovakia State Railway placard from the '30s that depicted Prague Castle), but now, as we walked down the hill to Old Town Square, our destination embarrassed me: too frivolous. And hell, if goyish *I* felt that way, how much more must Stu, who knew that but for God's good grace—or probably mindless luck—one of the corpses might have been his father's.

And yet, when you leave a place of doom and human cruelty, aren't you also sometimes pricked by weird, euphoric wildness? A sense of *Life is short, let your hair down.*

A Czech boy beckoned Stu just then, and Stu returned his flirt. I thought, *Oh, is* this *how Stu will cope?*

He wasn't like the hustlers we had seen at night, in New Town: slicksters with their polished porno come-ons. This boy was much younger—fifteen, sixteen, tops? Grubby at the neck, dressed in ratty castoffs, so skinny that his clothes resembled rags caught on barbed wire.

"Nice," he said. "Make feel nice, yes, yes? Okay?"—the words all diced up by his accent. He named a fee equal to the price I had seen at the airport for a carton of Camels.

Stu, without consulting me, said, "Come! Come with us." He hooked the boy's belt loop, pulled him close.

Telling the story later, in New York, I'd draw this moment out: my anger and confusion (*How could Stu not even ask* me?), my fear that the kid had hidden cronies who'd attack us. Plus, my sudden heartbreak at discovering this shady side to Stu—a man who'd exploit a teenage boy! More and more I'd lay it on, to heighten the coming twist: Stu just wanted to take the poor kid in.

His name was Mirek, and I had guessed too old: he was fourteen. After his parents died—a crash on the D5 highway—he'd lived on a beet farm with his uncle. (We pieced the tale together with a dictionary and pictograms; Mirek had already spent most of his English.) But then his uncle caught him with a boy—naked, rubbing—and kicked him out of the house, just like that. For six months he'd lived in Prague, begging, turning tricks, squatting in a vacant tool-and-die plant.

Stu let him move in with us, the three days we had left, and sleep on a rollaway in our room. He fed (and fed and fed) the kid, and bought him a winter coat, but nothing gladdened Mirek more than the Mets cap Stu gave him, which Mirek wore rapperishly raked.

I had never seen Stu be so trusting, so patient, so willing to revise all his plans. Mirek responded touchingly, softening by the hour. Walking through the sooty streets, he loved to mother-hen us, steering us from blocks he thought too dodgy. At night he would kiss us both, chastely, on the cheeks, then dive into zealous, boyish sleep.

A three-day-long threesome, but not of sex. Of sharing. (Part of me almost might have said *salvation*.)

Maybe Stu did more harm than good, by raising Mirek's hopes. Maybe he should have marched him to the Children's Welfare office, and sat there till they came up with a plan. But here was the thing: Stu was not behaving based on logic; his prudent, pilot's self was put on hold. Instead, he was guided by a fierce, blazing instinct to protect the boy—to *give*, and give *right now*.

I could remember thinking, *That's the part of parenthood you can't fake.*

Inevitably, though, we left Mirek and flew back to New York. Stu gave him some cash; what else could he do? For years, every Christmas, he sent more.

Occasionally, after Prague, he mused about *what ifs*. Going back and nabbing Mirek and flying him home to live with us, enrolling him in the Harvey Milk High School? Our place was already tiny enough—a coop—for just us two, especially since I'd left my in-house writing gig at Educraft and now did all my work for them from home. "But maybe," said Stu, "we'll build a Murphy bed inside the closet . . . or maybe we could find a bigger, cheaper place? In Brooklyn?"

He talked with great sincerity, but it was all just talk. Stu was still too married to his footloose, no-strings life, still too happy reaching for the low-hanging kind of happy.

He didn't get serious about having a kid until his sister's news.

Rina had bragged since toddlerhood of the huge brood she would rear, to rectify the family's rotten fate. Their father, Walter Nadler, said the clan had been tenacious—"needlers," as the family name suggested—but Walter's sister and brother, his four teenaged cousins, had all been turned to ash at Treblinka.

Stu could always taste that ash (that was how he talked of it), growing up in Walter Nadler's household: dense, smothering lungfuls of compulsion. The weight would have sunk him if it weren't for Rina's promise to their parents, after Stu came out as gay: *Shush, I'll give you grandkids till they're crawling out your ears!*

Things had looked good recently: she'd married Richard Feinberg, a man who absolutely wanted kids. Three, in fact: "A triangle is the strongest shape," he'd say. "Knock one side, the others hold it up."

They gave themselves a year of "just us" bliss (or so I guessed), then buckled down into baby-making mode. At Labor Day, when we all shared a house at Seaside Heights, the two of them conspicuously kept heading for the bedroom, at all hours, to—wink, wink—take naps. But at the next family klatch, at New Year's, in Manhattan, the news was that there wasn't any news. "Can't complain," said Richard bravely. "A few more rolls in the hay . . ."

Six more months of nothing, though, and Rina sought a doctor, who asked if sex was painful, if lately she'd been cranky. "Trying and getting nowhere? Of course it hurts," she told him. "Don't you think *you'd* be cranky, too?"

The doctor ran some tests and returned a diagnosis: premature ovarian failure. "A few women with POF—5 percent?—get pregnant. With your levels? I wouldn't hold my breath."

Rina asked if her eggs could be harvested, at least.

"Well, but see, there aren't really eggs left to be harvested. The point is that you started with too few."

"I wanted," she said later, "to shove the point right up his ass."

Stu doused his grief, as usual, with dark humor. Double whammy, he told me, for the dying-out Nadlers: one child has POF, the other is a poof.

But the humor, we both knew, was an overcompensation. And so was his ensuing bender, a flurry of online hook-ups that he plowed through with fatalistic haste—like someone in a high-speed chase who nears the cop-car barricade and wildly, for an instant, floors the gas.

This was the spree that led me to plan that awful Roxy night.

After the Roxy, I told Stu of my sickening beggar's shame: wanting to ask a stranger for some scrap of who Stu was. I told him that I couldn't afford to feel that way again, that if I did, I'd have to think of leaving.

"But Pat," he said. "You know me better than anyone in the world. Better than maybe I know myself, I honestly think. Believe me. So please: don't give up on me. I'm sorry."

I didn't want to give up. I wanted not to want to. But if I closed my eyes, the feelings all came back: alone in the club, that nausea of desertion.

Only a few weeks later, in bed, before sleep, Stu pressed close and cupped my naked shoulder. "What if," he said. "What if *we* had a baby?"

It caught me by surprise, as did my almost immediate inclination to say yes.

"Of course there's a million things to figure out," he said. "And most of the burden would fall on you, I know, since you're at home. But I'd be here as much as I could. And maybe my folks would, too. People do it. People work it out."

Whether to have a baby together was probably not the question that I should, at that moment, have been asking. More reasonable was whether to *stay* together. But Stu seemed convincingly to have come to the end of something: not just one particular binge, but the whole phase, the frantic, fruitless search. Rina's diagnosis seemed to change him almost physically, as if the capability that withered in his sister had somehow been transplanted into him. He looked . . . how could I say it? *More full.* His chest, his face.

Continuing the Nadler line was now, he felt, his duty. "Actually, more than a duty, though," he told me. "More like a privilege. Same as how I felt on my bar mitzvah."

"But Stu," I said. "You don't believe in Judaism. Did you ever?"

"Not the, you know . . . whatever, the stuff about God. But standing there, saying the words my father had said, and *his* father? It's almost like I hadn't learned the prayers: *they'd* learned *me*. Hard to describe. A bigness, you know? It's bigger than just *my* feelings."

He said he finally understood the word *reproduction*: he dreamed of seeing the family features reproduced again. The thick hair, the forceful Nadler nose.

Here, then, was our difference: keeping his family going was the gist, for Stu, of fatherhood; for me it meant inventing a family *separate* from my old one, showing myself (and everyone else) that I could be a parent—better at the job than my own folks.

Stu wanted to *father* a child, and I wanted to *raise* one. Couldn't our goals happily coincide?

My friend Joseph was less sanguine: "How about an *imaginary* baby, like *Who's Afraid of Virginia Woolf?* You could still fight about it, but no diapers."

I'd gone to see him at Educraft, where he was the managing editor. Joseph was making espresso for a red eye in the kitchen. Keyboards in the main room clacked like hamsters' wheeling feet.

"But I've been wanting kids," I said. "I've told you that already." I mentioned Zack and Glenn—my first gay-father friends—and Milo, their magnetic little son. Zack was white, Glenn was black, and they'd made Milo mixed: Glenn's sperm plus a Caucasian donor's egg. The boy had bewitching eyes, a sepia complexion like someone in an old family photo. "Every time I'm with him," I said, "I crave one of my own."

"Yes, but you and *Stu*? I wouldn't have thought."

Joseph and Stu, I'd had to accept, were not the best of pals. Stu complained (and not without a measure of justification) that Joseph's sense of humor was a trick birthday candle: amusing at first, but pretty soon you're desperate to put it out.

But Joseph had been my fairy godfather since I'd first hit New York. He'd landed me my job and my rent-controlled apartment, and took it upon himself to be my one-man homo Harvard: teaching subjects from literature (Isherwood, Capote) to geography (the city's cruisiest corners). Joseph, who'd outlived his lover, Luis, and two-thirds of the friends in their address book, had affection to spare, and I was glad to take it.

Lately I'd confided in him my growing spousal doubts. He knew all about Stu's extracurriculars.

"What if Stu continues with his wanton ways?" he said. "And you're barefoot and pregnant, as it were."

"I don't think he will," I said. "He's changing. This will help."

Joseph downed his red eye in a single shuddering gulp. "Having a baby to save the marriage? Yawn."

Fate then gave another little nudge. This time, *my* sisters.

Sally and Brenda, with whom I'd been sharing our parents' cottage, announced that they wanted to sell the place. They had never spent as much time there as I, and had less at stake in its upholding—maybe because they both had their own conventional families now (square holes in which they'd safely nestled their square selves), and didn't dread the judgment of our old-guard parents' ghosts.

The cottage was no longer worth the cost to them, they said, and, even if it were, neither could afford it. Sally, who had a son at Choate and another on the verge of applying, had recently given birth to twin girls (a shock to everyone, considering her complaints, last Thanksgiving, of the burn of an early menopause). And Brenda, the younger, had lost much of her savings when a pet-food business she'd bet on went bankrupt.

The house was admittedly a monster to maintain. Constructed in the pre–global warming, go-go '50s, it featured a convoluted system of copper pipes that could never quite successfully be drained, which meant we had to run the boiler all winter long. Practically the whole north-facing wall was picture windows, and heat leaked in torrents through the glass.

Now, after four grudging years of bill dividing—the mortgage, the insurance, the property taxes, the heat—my sisters both said they needed out. The only way to keep the cottage would be to buy their shares, which Stu and I could never swing, on top of our other expenses. We just couldn't. Not if we stayed in New York.

I took him to the cottage for Presidents' Day weekend. A storm had just tickled the Cape with snow.

The three days were empty in the healthiest of ways. We caught up on *Vanity Fair*s, played endless games of hearts; sometimes we just stared out at the bay. Hour by hour I watched as Stu shed his need for noise—the city's ceaseless peep show of distractions—and tuned in to the song of his own thoughts.

How I loved the cottage and its ambitious anachronisms, which brought me back to boyhood summers of big and careless dreams. My dad had only come down here as work allowed, on weekends; Sally and Brenda would canter off to horse camps in Maine; and so it was mostly me and Mom. We clammed and played badminton, puttered in the yard; she taught me names of hawks and oaks and blooms. Nights, we'd steam mussels we had plucked from a nearby jetty, or, if we were tuckered out from all our independence, drive to town for Baxter's fish and chips.

Once, on a foggy afternoon, we went to Plymouth, to see (for maybe the third time) the Rock. Circling for a parking spot, my mom suddenly braked. "Pat, look!" she said. "On that street sign: it's *you*!" The name of an alley we were passing was Faunce Place; I felt the satisfaction (and the onus) of entitlement. *Faunce Place.* The place where a Faunce belonged.

Nth-degreed, that was how I felt about the cottage—the place on earth where everything seemed unassailably mine, and more than that:

just plain unassailable. The sun rose exactly where a sun *should* in the windows; the air was the salty, ageless definition of air.

Stu must have had a hint or two of my intentions, because, when I proposed the plan, he didn't object in principle. He said, "I'd have to see about a transfer."

We were down at Sandy Neck, walking along the shore. The winter sky was paler than the sand.

"Logan's a busy base for us," he said. "I could commute—you know, take puddle-jumpers from Hyannis? Remember Chuck, my redhead friend from flight school? That's what he does now. Air-commutes to LGA from Montauk."

I knew he would have to deal with much more than logistics. Moving to the Cape, for me, would be a kind of homecoming; for him it would mean leaving the only place he'd lived. So maybe this was all just talk, like going back for Mirek.

But Stu wasn't spieling in the swollen tone he sometimes used; his voice now was flat and straight and small. "And you?" he said. "You'd keep your gig with Educraft? You could?"

Moving was no problem for me, work-wise, I assured him. All I needed? A laptop, an Internet connection, a road up which UPS could drive.

"All right, then," he said. "Fair enough."

He looked, as he scuffed along the surf, staid and doleful, squinting at the blankness of the sky. Far from draining my confidence, his look was what encouraged me: despite how much the move might sting, he was preparing to choose this. Choose us.

Life on the Cape wouldn't "solve" the problems we'd been having, or keep Stu from cruising on the Web, if he reverted. I knew he might still find men in various ports of call. But if we were to stay together, to have a kid together, I would need collateral—assurance of his commitment—and starting a new life out here could provide that.

This place was a calming force, an antidote to frenzy. I'd been struck, this weekend, sharing the empty hours with Stu: the cottage, more than anywhere else, left us *unadulterated*, by which I meant both closest to the essence of our union and farthest from our various infidelities.

"You know," said Stu, walking beside me, "it actually makes good sense. The condo's too small to raise a kid in. The city's too full of filth. Not to mention a hundred times more pricey." He ticked off the reasons on his fingers. "All of that would be different here. *Everything* would be, right?" He balled his fingers into a fist of conviction.

This was when he might have whooped or pulled me to his breast; a Stu in the movies might have done that. But my Stu, the one I loved—despite, still, regardless—my Stu only held my little finger. He spoke not a word but told me everything he needed to (*sorry, my sweet, so sorry; you're mine*; *I adore you*) with tiny, tender pulsings of his hand.

We listened to the landing waves, their message: *Kiss! Kiss!*

four

And now here we were, nearly at the Pancake King, to meet the woman who might bear our baby.

Here was the mall, where Mrs. Rita had etched our grains of rice; here was Filene's, where I'd faced my old fears. The nine months of Cape Cod life had given us some history, had cured the slurry beneath us into concrete.

I had never mentioned Joseph's "save the marriage" dig. But Stu was likely mindful—I knew for sure that *I* was—of building ourselves back up in advance of making a baby. I thought of us as sparrows, our happiness as tinsel we collected to adorn the natal nest. Every further episode we wove together spurred in me a silent *Take that, Joseph. See? See?*

Idling at a stop light, Stu returned to the topic, God help us, of settling on a restaurant for our meeting: "Honestly, the Yarmouth House? It would've been just fine," he said. "I mean, if this works out, it's not just *lunch* we'll pay for. Why pretend we can't afford some steak?"

I sensed he was pushing me to argue the other side. "Yeah, but we don't want to flaunt it, right? Or wield it over them. The Pancake King is . . . I think it's *inspired.*"

Instead of spinning our wheels like this, we could simply have asked Debora and Danny what they liked. Tellingly, perhaps, we hadn't thought to.

Was it nuts to be jazzed about this woman as a prospect, with only the flimsiest notion of who she was? We'd seen her photo (olive skin, richly dappled eyes, a bright, insurrectionary smile), we'd e-mailed maybe six or seven times (her syntax was a half-step off, which normally would have miffed me, but her particular oddness was alluring). We knew some pointed intimacies: her BMI, her bra size, her menstrual pattern (as regular as clockwork); we'd learned that she'd given birth vaginally to her daughter, without episiotomy or prolapse. But how this Debora Neuman thought, what made her tick or ticked her off—in short, who the hell she was—was guesswork. I could have told you more about the dame down at the Old Village Store who sold me cranberry muffins every Sunday.

So yes, this was nuts.

Which made it also thrilling. A dive into a lake of unknown depth.

Those of us afflicted with the malady of LOW Syndrome—the short-hand I'd devised for "Lack of Womb"—still had lots of ways of making babies. In fact, we'd been stymied by an overload of choice.

Adoption was off the table, as Stu was set on splicing himself into the Nadler family's fraying rope. To me it mattered less whose genes would tango with the mother's than who would feed and change the child, rock it through the night—and I, since I worked from home, would mostly take that role. As far as genes went, I was quite content that they be Stu's. Better for the baby to get his dark, hospitable looks than be saddled with my own WASPish features: nose and chin as sharp as little stingers.

Okay, then, that narrowed things: we'd have to find a surrogate. Even still, the range of choices was daunting. Neither of us ever seriously thought to try our sisters. Eggless Rina could have carried another woman's embryo for us, but asking her would only just rub salt into her wound. And my sisters? We'd never been that close. (Faunce family dealings were neither a burden nor a joy; they fell into that class of expected transactions that conscientious people made time for—like voting, or donating blood.)

I might have asked Marcie, my best lesbian pal. Ours was an un-encumbered homo–dyke dynamic, based on mutually assumed unattraction. My love for her had been sealed when, a few months into our friendship—a May Day party at her and her partner Erin's—Marcie learned that Stu had never seen a woman's privates; she hauled him into the bathroom, shimmied out of her jeans, spread her legs, and gave a guided tour. But Marcie, when she and Erin eventually wanted a family, had asked if I would be the sperm donor. No parental rights, no money for support, but I could be a "presence" for the child. In other words, a free ride: reward without the risk. Which proved to be the aspect of the deal that deeply tempted me but later, on reflection, put me off. Dadhood didn't strike me as a job to go partway on.

"Come on, man," said Marcie. "It's nothing. A five-minute wank. You've done that for *strangers*, I bet. You're gay!"

But I'd said no, and having declined to give her five quick minutes, I couldn't well ask her for nine months.

We thought of using an agency, to make things more official, to limit our list to pre-approved bidders, as it were. Our friends Zack and Glenn had gone that route when they'd made Milo, and that's what Glenn suggested we do, too.

It was the thick of summer now, four months since we'd moved out to the cottage. We made an appointment with the "intake coordinator" at Certain Surrogacy, a golden-voiced woman named Linda Po, who, to judge by the frequency and near-erotic delight with which she said, "Here at Certain Surrogacy . . . ," was enthralled by the name's triple sibilance. CS was in a refurbished Victorian in Jamaica Plain, a quaint, small-townish section of Boston where everyone had a scruffier-than-thou, aggressively placid appearance. The building, said a plaque, had once housed Maloney's Funeral Home. Maybe the ghosts of funeral directors past still haunted the place, because Linda's pitch reminded me of someone selling caskets—or, rather, someone trying to "up-sell" a posher model. Practically her every other word was *nontraditional*. If not that, then *nonjudgmental, alternative, accepting*. Christ, the way she slammed us with acceptance!

I knew, of course, we should have breathed relief to be so welcomed; mainstream clinics sometimes stopped queer couples at the door. But still, with Linda's steel-trap mantra ("Here at Certain Surrogacy . . ."), her inundation of über-PC buzzwords, Stu and I were starting to feel less like hopeful dads, and more like . . . well, a *niche market*.

"Can I ask something?" Stu said to Linda, who sat in an ergonomic chair on the far side of a wide walnut desk.

"By all means! That's why I'm here," she said. "Don't be squeamish. We're used to"—she winked—"sticky subjects."

"Okay, then. What's up with all the alliteration?"

Linda's grin glittered. "Alliteration?"

"Yeah," said Stu. "Every single agency we've looked into. Certain Surrogacy. Miracle Makers. Growing Generations."

"I guess it's just . . . well, no one's ever asked that." Linda laughed.

Stu laughed, too, but with an edge. "Wow," he said. "Why does that not surprise me?"

Oh, Stu. He had a rotten habit of letting his snideness show, especially when he felt pushed past comfort. Actually, though, despite the trouble he could get us into, I was mostly gladdened by his candor: frequently he said the things that I had lacked the guts to.

Linda Po was doing her very best to seem oblivious. She made a fuss of rolling her chair to our side of the desk ("There, that's better. I *hate* to talk with that big thing between us"), and unfurled a bullet-pointed pamphlet. She told us we could choose from one of six preset plans. "For example, a cost-conscious alternative is the Egg Bank Option. The donors are proven, and we use a new rapid-freeze vitrification process—you save almost twenty thousand bucks over going fresh. Or, though it's a little more expensive, we have Egg Sharing."

"Egg sharing?" I said. "I thought only twins could do that."

"Ha," she said. "That's good. Haven't heard that. No, egg sharing: you choose a variety of donors, as do other clients, and whichever has an egg ready when you are, that's your woman."

Linda was most stoked about their Certain Baby Plan, which guaranteed that couples not yet pregnant after four attempts would have their fees (but not expenses) refunded. "We have a cost calculator," she said, and swiveled her screen to let us see the spreadsheet.

Social worker support fees:	$3,000
Surrogate-related screening fee:	$4,860
Egg donor screening, legal fees, and compensation:	$9,640
Surrogate-related agency fees:	$18,400

Dizzied by the screen, its steepening heap of figures, I looked away and stared instead at Linda: her graceful neck, her autocratic chin. My hunch was, she'd had a child through surrogacy—she was barren—and working here was part of how she coped. Had life offered lemons? She'd squeeze and squeeze her lemonade, a way of doing well by doing good.

Her list went on: caseworker consults; psychological screenings (of the donor, the surrogate, the parents); a chaperone to be there when potential matches met . . .

"Back up," said Stu. "Screening of the parents? You mean *us*?"

"Absolutely!" she said, as though this were a bonus. "Intended parents meet with one of our licensed professionals, who—"

"Medical screening, fine," said Stu. "To look out for diseases. But *psychological*? We want to have a baby, is all. *Our* baby. I don't see what else you need to know." *Whap!* went his palm against the desk.

As Linda sputtered an answer (". . . responsibility to all parties . . ."), I pressed my shoe on Stu's, silently trying to tame him but hinting also at "Thanks, my sweet" and "You and me, together." Again: my love–hate romance with his temper.

But now that Stu was irked, we'd never get much further. I spun the monitor away. "How much, total?"

"As you know," Linda said, "we're committed to transparency, but it depends on which plan you select. In light of your situation? Ballpark figure, including all the medical and insurance costs? I'd say a hundred-ten, hundred-twenty thousand."

Transparency, indeed. I felt I had my nose pressed to inch-thick glass at Tiffany's, glimpsing jewels I never could afford.

Thing was, we'd never seen a clear-cut dollar figure. All our research sources seemed to tiptoe 'round the numbers—probably for the reason we'd avoided asking Zack and Glenn exactly what they'd spent to make Milo: Didn't it seem crude to put a price on someone's head?

But now we knew, and the number was a problem-solving slap. We'd have to find a surro on our own.

Also now resolved was a question that had vexed us: whether to go "traditional" or "gestational." A TS—traditional surro—would offer up her own egg, would be the baby's biological mother, as opposed to a GS, who'd incubate a fetus that would grow from a separate donor's egg. We'd known there were extra costs in using a separate donor, but not how many till seeing Linda's spreadsheet. A GS and donor would cost us fifty, maybe sixty grand above a TS who'd use her own egg.

There were other compelling reasons to take the TS option. For one thing, two women meant two tiers of complication. We'd obviously grow close—we'd *have* to—with the carrier, but we both also felt the need to know the genetic mom, beyond just some data on a checklist: to hear her laugh, to look into her eyes. Wouldn't it be simpler, less baffling to the child, to have those two mothers be the same? Another thing: I'd come across a medical-journal item. "Fatal Cancer in an Egg Donor: The Risks of Ovarian Stimulation." A donor and a GS both would go through hormone treatments; how could we justify risking their lives in order to make our new one, especially when a safer way existed?

But philosophy didn't pay the bills, and wasn't what decided us. Our choice, in the end, came down to cash.

Which is how we wound up at Surromoms, an online meeting point for all things surro.

The site was one of those twenty-first-century rabbit holes: type the name, hit Return, and *poof!*—a new dimension. Initially what you saw was a soothing pastel palette, the online equivalent of soft focus. Then, if you clicked the links (FAQ, Contracts), a fair bit of the now-expected alliterative annoyance—tiny treasures! blessed birth mothers!—but also tons of no-B.S. advice. How to get insurance. How to tell your family. How to deal with worried, jealous spouses.

Stu and I clicked "Classifieds," which featured ads from surros and from couples who intended to be parents (IPs, in Surrospeak, a patois we now practiced; Stu and I, more narrowly, were IFs: Intended Fathers). Some of the surros were pros, their postings full of stats: "I ovulate on day 12, meaning that if doing IUI, CD 11 is best." Others were almost lyrical in their folksy unrefinement: "I hope to hear from parents who want the bad as much as the good. I mean, who doesn't love it when their kid pukes down their shirt?!"

Stu, till I stopped him, actually started to draw a chart of all the various choices in the mix: surros who'd breastfeed and surros who'd pump; those who'd travel or wouldn't; and, most crucially, women who'd work with gay men or refused. (More than half the ads began with "Seeking a Christian family . . .")

But one thing, above all else, took me by surprise.

I'd supposed this would be a sellers' market, and that the surros, in charge of supply, would drive some hard bargains. The parents, I thought—the please-God-make-us-parents—would be desperate. And sure, they were (*we* were), but equally so were the surros: stricken, almost sickened, with a need.

"I'm not working with an agency because most of them won't take me for my age. But I promise, my body's not even close to being done . . ."

"I'm large, but now losing weight. I didn't have gestational diabetes when pregnant before, and if I'm blessed to carry your child, I'll only eat what's healthy . . ."

Their need wasn't money, at least not primarily: the fees went as low as fifteen thousand. But what if all these women had a kind of psychic poverty? How, then, would we *not* take advantage?

Maybe this uneasiness explained my twinging heart. For, despite my pleasure as our choices got more real—the ads like a magician's proffered deck: *Pick a card*—despite this, I'd battled a dark mood. (Because Stu had labored to be ready and un-nervous, to prove that he wouldn't get cold feet, I did not admit that I—the gung-ho one—was spooked. Besides, how would I talk about a gloom so sly and nameless?) Was I stung by the Christianist ads, the paucity of gay-friendly ones? Perhaps a little. But really, one good ad was all we needed. Still, my spine felt made of glass. Why?

It wasn't till the next night that I put my finger on it. Stu and I were searching again, hunched at the computer, scrolling through the multitude of ads. "No," he said. "Definitely not. Maybe. Maybe. Nope." His sheeps-from-goats assessments sounded cold, a little snobbish. Just as bad—worse?—his twitchy note of thrill when he flagged an ad that caught his full attention. "Ooh. *Yes!* She's—look. She's willing to do TS . . ." *Rat-tat-tat*, he ruled the mouse with the hoggish, quick adeptness of a coke addict razor-cutting lines.

I saw it, then. The face I'd never seen, his online hook-up face: this was how he'd looked when he surfed Manhunt.

How did I know? I knew. I just knew.

And even now—especially now—I felt a nervous pinch.

Lots of the surros seemed lovely, but none struck us as . . . ours. Of those willing to work with gay IPs, just one was Jewish. She lived on Bainbridge Island, near Seattle.

The obvious step? We had to place an ad.

This was tougher than it sounded. Should we be ultra-serious? Was drollness disallowed? Better to seem employer-like ("Seeking to fill position . . ."), or bid for buddy-buddyness ("Dear Surro!")? The challenge was what pulled me from the brink of my old doubts with Stu, not least because it launched him into flights of spousal praise: "Who else has an actual *writer* writing up his ad? Poet laureate of the Personals. My ringer!" The way to this writer's heart was through his ego.

Here was the ad I managed to come up with:

BEAUTIFUL VIEW!

Two gay men, recently relocated from NYC to Cape Cod, want to share their view—of Sandy Neck, and of life—with a child.

We need: a Jewish TS.

We prefer: someone within easy driving distance (MA or RI), who welcomes our involvement (not intrusion) in the pregnancy, who wants to stay in touch after the birth.

We dream: of someone who loves salt air, who sometimes laughs at naughty jokes, who asks as many questions as she answers.

We're eager to meet you. Please introduce yourself.

Women did, in droves. Almost all well-meaning. But no one even close to our requirements.

I'm not Jewish, but . . .

Although I live in Qatar, I . . .

Then there were the out-and-out kooks: one intended to surro as material for a memoir (would we object if she used our real names?); another wanted her fee to be paid in OJ futures.

Truthfully, though, I liked the loons. They let us let off steam. Think of all the tales, I said, we'd someday tell our kid. Stu said maybe *I* should write a memoir.

"*Two Flew Over the Cuckoo's Nest?*" I offered. "*Daddies Queerest?*"

I don't think we let ourselves admit how discomposed we were, till finally our first likely prospect surfaced. (Strange, how you could bear aloft your stacked-up load of hopelessness, but one small hope, on top, made it tumble.) This was maybe a couple of months before we found Debora. The woman was a postdoc in genetics, up at Harvard, and came from a storied old Jewish clan in Cleveland: synagogue founders, symphony benefactors. In photos she was preppily appealing. Her button nose, she warned us in a winningly humble e-mail, was Figure 19-B in *Rhinoplasty: The Art and the Science*—"No kidding, by Eugene Tardy; look it up!"—but vanity hadn't provoked the fix: she'd been in a scooter accident, and needed the nose rebuilt for proper breathing. Her point? That the nose we'd see on her was not hereditary. "My offspring can expect," she wrote, "a more Hebraic honker."

Stu and I, discussing her, never used her name; always it was Our Lady of the Womb. The promise of her practically unzipped us. We drove up to Cambridge for a meeting in her lab, and on the way we both could not stop crying. I would start, and Stu would say, "C'mon, now, this is a *good* day," but then his voice would crack, his eyes would water up—lord, what a couple of sobby queens! Twice I had to grab the wheel and ask, "Want me to drive?"

But that was nothing compared to how we were the whole way home.

Our Lady had integrity: she'd come clean pretty quickly—ten, fifteen minutes into the meeting. Completely under control, she swore. Took her meds religiously. But once, back in college: in-patient at McLean. Her mother, too, had once attempted to take her own life.

We both tried our best to smile. I said something along the lines of "Your candor speaks quite well of you," but I was sure Our Lady saw our instant airtight judgment.

"The jury's out on how much it's inheritable," she said, flushing. "Listen, it's the kind of thing I study, okay? Trust me?"

"Well," said Stu. "I hear you, yeah. We'll call."

And we were gone.

Driving back, I saw what looked like ambulances ahead, but it was only the taillights of the traffic in the distance, swirling through the prism of my tears. All the disappointment I'd been stuffing down and stuffing down now surged up like sickness in my throat. I was also sickened by our necessary ruthlessness. Angry, too, but mostly at myself. "Dumb," I said. "Ridiculous. I let myself believe that she might—"

"No," said Stu. "Me too. What were we thinking?"

Our ad expired, and we re-upped, and then re-upped again. Three long months of Surromoms, and not a single lead worth pursuing.

The Cape went into shedding mode—the summer folks had fled— cattails on the roadside gone to fluff for wrens to ravage, air as dry as the husks of Indian corn on neighbors' doors. Normally I loved this time: the clarity, the quiet, the spice of Concord grapes as they fermented on the vine. But now, as I walked the grape-strewn woods around our place, I smelled a world of sweet, spoiled potential.

Zack and Glenn kept clouting us with sympathetic e-mails. "Worthwhile things can *take* a while." "Keep trying." "Don't lose hope." Their faith made me think about the Democratic convention, a few months before, up in Boston: the crowd, hoisting Kerry signs, cried, "Hope is on the way!" But now had come the wet November night when we were kneecapped: Bush was reelected; he'd plague us four more years. Where was hope now? Bottom of the ocean.

Rina and Richard stayed with us, en route to a Deer Isle wedding.

Stu and I were happy that his sister was finally married, after what had been a trying search. (The furniture conservator at MoMA? No, too pouty. The underwriter? Nice but uninspired.) Finally, three years ago, she'd met Richard Feinberg, against whom she couldn't seem to make objections stick. Richard had worked briefly after college on a kibbutz, and still seemed to have a pilgrim's self-approving glow. He was observant—more so than Rina or her parents, but not to a lunatic extreme: ate at any restaurant, drove his car on the Sabbath. He was a manager at . . . I could never focus on the details. A firm that processed some sort of data? "Basically," he'd told us over dinner when we met, "what I do is make sure that the little guys, below me, don't p.o. the higher-ups, you know?"

"Isn't he a gas?" said Rina. "Oh, his funny talking! Too modest to tell the truth, aren't you?"

And though, to be honest, he often made my eyes ache, this visit, I decided, was successful: a Scrabble game, sans tantrums, out on the deck at dusk; a pot roast Richard praised as "magnifique"; and, over breakfast, a pleasant-enough chat that avoided talk of politics or God.

Even so, there wasn't any getting around the sadness.

"Half our savings, basically," said Richard, chewing his toast. "Because, you know, insurance only covered certain procedures."

Rina said, "You wouldn't believe the number of fucking lab tests. And hormone treatments. And third and fourth opinions. All of that, and never an inch closer."

"Sis," said Stu, "I'm sorry." He kissed the back of her hand.

I could see how painfully her pain entered into him. Not that he and she made a perfect sibling blend (more like oil and vinegar, whisked by fate together, that tended toward de-emulsification), but who else understood the weight of being Walter Nadler's child? Who else helped to cut that load in half?

Richard said, "I can't bear to watch her suffer through this. And so, no more. *Fini*. We give up."

Yes, I wanted to say. I know just how you feel.

But Stu gave me a look: *Don't you dare.*

The thing was, we hadn't told his family of our plans. In fact, we had told almost no one. Confiding in Joseph, of course, hadn't gone so well. Marcie, when I'd shared the news, had offered a hearty "Wow!"

that sounded supportive but wasn't necessarily. ("Will kids fit Stu's . . . lifestyle?" she asked later.) Zack and Glenn were really the only friends to fully back us, and so, for now, Stu had decreed that we should keep things quiet.

His family remained suspicious of our sudden decamping north, as Stu had told them only partial truths in explanation: the souring of Manhattan's mood in the years since 9/11, the solace of a cottage at the seashore. But nothing, naturally, about the strains his sexual sprees had caused us, and nothing of the baby we envisioned. I thought they would love to know: we'd save the Nadler line! But Stu said his reticence had good reason. "Think like my folks," he'd said to me. "A firstborn son to give them grandkids, but oops, cancel that, he's a homo. Then their daughter marries—good! Wants a family—good! But no, the doctors say she has no eggs. Up and down, up and down: emotional motion sickness." Wouldn't it be callous, he said, to lift his parents' hopes again, until those hopes had solid ground to stand on?

His parents were insisting that we visit for Thanksgiving. Stu had seen them half a dozen times since we had moved—bopping into the city when he flew through LGA—but Walter wanted "a *real* visit. Relaxed. Like civilized people." If only! I pictured his inevitable assault: *So, how's life in Nowheresville? You ready to strangle each other?* He still seemed convinced—and so did his wife, Ellie—that Stu's and my retreat was a fleeting, callow lapse: *Kiddo, are you sure it's not a phase?*

Stu argued for going, got pissy when I resisted. "What'll we prove by sitting out here, alone, knowing no one? Let's go home, chill out, see our friends."

That was my point, I told him. *This* was home now. Here. I wanted our eventual return to be in triumph.

Why were we getting nowhere? Why had our ad not worked?

Success, they say, has many fathers, while failure is an orphan, but Stu would not accept that old adage. Failures, he insisted, must be tested for paternity: Aha, look, it's *you*, you're the dad!

Fine, I'd be the fall guy. Someone had to do it.

"Must've been my text," I said. "Too strange. Too loosey-goosey."

Stu said yeah, he hadn't wanted to say, but . . . try again?

Good thing I was used to getting edits on my drafts, and knew that when my words were bad it didn't mean that *I* was. Writers never conflated those things, did we?

I kept the new ad basic: seeking a TS, Jewish, someone not too far from Cape Cod. For good measure I dropped in a couple of stock catchphrases ("Nonsmokers only," "Healthy BMI"). Off into the ether I dispatched it.

The very next morning, a message in my box:

I think you are maybe Beautiful View. Are you the same? If I'm right, for me it's sad you made your ad more normal. Before was perfect. Stay with who you are!

That was all. No name or identifying info. Only the return address, as lilting as the writer's zigzag syntax: Brazucamama@hotmail.com.

But oh, those lines were catnip to my hungry writer's ego: an audience, a positive review.

Yes, it's us, I wrote back in an instant. *Thanks for noticing! But maybe Surromoms isn't the place for washed-up poets? The first ad was a total bomb—we're still at square one. p.s. Tell me a little about yourself?*

All she said in answer was that her name was Debora Neuman; she lived with her husband in Hyannis.

Hyannis, wow, we're neighbors, I wrote. *Or almost. We're in West Barnstable. Are you looking for a surro too? Any more luck than us?*

A full three days passed. Had all my questions scared her? Or maybe she was worried I would try to steal her contacts. The competition— was that how Debora saw me?

Finally she replied, apologetic for having disappeared and ready to explain why she'd been nervous. She wanted to be a surro, had thought of it for years (*My husband and I, we have our own perfect little girl—she made all our dreams become true. And now I want to help somebody else make true* their *dream*), but she had planned to do a lot more research. She had read through Surromoms as something of a spectator, and hadn't yet composed her own ad. *Then I saw your ad, and I thought: too good. You know? Almost seemed like fate. A crazy thing! We live so near, I'm Jewish too—everything, it's a match.*

Debora said she'd told herself to wait and see what happened. If someone else came forward, the match was not to be. But then the ad was posted a second time, and then a third. *I thought: Okay. Maybe it is for me. Maybe it has to be. I wrote to you. But oh my God, it's scary.*

Scary for me, too, said my next note to Debora. *But awesome-scary. I'm pinching myself. It's like I made you up!* I wanted to inquire about her quirky way with words, but didn't for fear of scaring her off again.

When Stu asked, the next night, "Still no good responses?" why did I just shrug, duck my head? Why had I not breathed a word of Debora? First, he'd been flying: two nights away from home. Second, I was doing things according to *his* playbook: wait till we had solid ground to stand on. Those were reasons enough, but the deeper, clumsy truth? I liked having Debora to myself, just for now. I liked being the one in charge of wooing.

And so, working alone, I coaxed from her more details. Full name: Debora Cardozo Neuman. Age: twenty-six. Height and weight (just fine), surgical history (none), previous pregnancy (vaginal birth at thirty-six weeks, four days; no pre- or postpartum complications). Occasional drinker (never when pregnant), allergic to longhaired cats. Husband, Danny, successfully self-employed in home remodeling. Almost eight years happily married. No more children planned.

Down the checklist: check, check, check. I hardly believed it. Every time I read my mail I braced for an admission: *Oh, and did I mention my third eye, my hoary tusks?*

Then she sent her photo, which put the lie to that! Without a doubt, she was on the pretty side of normal. Her skin was clear and rustically tanned, a tan you couldn't buy; it looked fresh but not too untested.

The photo was what finally got me ready to talk with Stu. In the face of it—of Debora's face—he'd *have* to be convinced. I wanted him to not have any doubt.

I told him I had a surprise, and led him to the laptop.

"Nice," he said when I double-clicked, and I could tell he meant it. He studied the image, nose to screen, inspecting for booby traps. "Something intrepid about her," he said. "Tenacious. But also soft."

"So?" I said.

"So yeah, go ahead and ask some questions. Like, maybe, has she ever been on suicide watch before?" He gave a crisp, carbonized laugh.

"I have," I said. "Well, not *that*, specifically. But her history. Her health. So far, she gets straight As."

"When?" said Stu.

"When what?"

"Did you ask her all these questions?"

"Now," I said. "Today. We've e-mailed. Maybe twice."

Not sure why I lied, or why Stu didn't call me on it. I knew he could tell I was fudging.

"She's Jewish?" he asked.

"Yup."

"Okay. And where does she live?"

"That's my surprise. *Hyannis*. Like, seriously, less than ten miles!"

"Hyannis? Come on, Patrick. A little too good to be true? You're cruising for a fall, don't you think?"

"See? I knew you'd do this. That's why I didn't tell you yet. I wanted to check her out first. And I have."

Stu just sat there . . . stewing.

I said, "You don't trust me. You blamed my ad. Blamed *me*. But how're we going to do this thing without a little trust?"

That was cheeky, coming from the guy who'd just white-lied. But Stu, who had overdrawn his trust account so often, must have sensed I had more in the bank.

"Fine," he said, stripping the word of almost all its fineness. "Go ahead. What do her e-mails say?"

I pulled them up and read aloud the highlights: her happy, thriving husband; her easy-as-pie pregnancy; the daughter who had made her dreams come true.

"There," I said, "is that so terrible? Ask me, sort of great."

"Why'd they stop with one kid of their own, though? Think that's odd?"

"Maybe they can't . . . or maybe they don't—Jesus, how should *I* know? The point is that she wants to do this. Clearly they have *reasons*." I hadn't meant to, but I guess I was shouting.

Stu, looking chastened, said okay, okay, fine. Move ahead with . . . "what did you say her name was?"

"Debora Neuman. Maiden name: Cardozo."

"Cardozo?"

"Yeah. C-a-r—"

"No," he said. "I heard." Now he brightened, and stood erect, as if he might take wing. "Maybe she'll make a genius for us. A whiz kid in black robes!"

"Huh?" I said, baffled by the swiftness of his mood change, by whatever associative leap he had made.

"Benjamin Cardozo?" he said.

I smiled at him obtusely.

"Sorry, I know—you weren't weaned on *Heroes of American Jewry*. Supreme Court justice. The second-ever Jew, after Brandeis."

"Which means it's good if—?"

"Write her back. Find out when she's free."

five

I was unprepared for the accent Debora spoke with—"Patch" was the way she said my name—and even less prepared for the story she unspooled in response to my "Tell us about yourself."

She was from a village in Rio Grande do Norte, in Brazil. Her father was a cashew farmer, though *farmer* made him out to be more purposeful than he was, a man who let life's vagaries (mud, flat tires) guide his days. A halfhearted man to whom things happened. Eight children, for starters—that's how he made it seem: a happenstance. Debora was the fifth-oldest, the only girl.

Her mother was more driven, but toward what, exactly, Debora wasn't sure. Making her daughter feel useless? Like a mistake? She delegated chores to Debora that were predestined for failure: beating sweet butter from starting-to-sour cream, stitching pants her pudging father was bound to split again. Shouldn't a mother strive to expose her children's brilliance, the better to dispel her own shadows? Not *her* mother, who must have wanted company in the dark.

Debora understood she'd have to tend her own flame. Ignite a rocket beneath her feet and scream into the sky, nothing behind but ash and hush and envy.

When she was thirteen, a teacher, honoring her best-in-class marks, gave Debora a reward: a tiny wisp of clipping from an orchid. She taught Debora to mist it with rainwater at dawn; never to leave it wet overnight; to look for white-green roots, then repot it. If she was careful, it might live forever.

Debora nursed the plant, despite her family's scorn. (*A flower? Grow us something we can* eat.) For three years, four, devotedly she mothered it, taken with its moody flamboyance. The plant bore many flowers, uncanny and reassuring—like answers to a question she hadn't dared to ask.

The next spring, on All Souls' Day—the orchid was in rowdy bloom—her neighbor Dina's lover happened by. The man lived in Salvador (he kept a wife and children there) but owned a small salt refinery close to Debora's village, a pretext for his frequent trips north to see his mistress. He saw the orchid through the open door of Debora's house. This flower, he said—like holy angels' wings—he must have it! He offered fifty *reais*, on the spot.

This was back in '96, '97, when fifty *reais* was decent money. One of Debora's brothers—Waterston, her favorite—had just moved to Natal, the state capital; he said she should visit for the summer, for school vacation, now that she was such a wealthy girl. He offered a couch to sleep on and all the meat she wanted. (A waiter at a *churrascaria*, he carried scraps of *picanha* and filet home each night.) Their mother told her: Go! Go bug *him* for a while. Debora took the next day's early bus.

A month, that flower paid for. Just one orchid! A month of buggy rides and *cocos* on the beach, plus a pair of jeans—city jeans, was how she thought of them—stone-washed, with stars on the back pockets. Debora wore those jeans on the Friday when she met him, dancing in a nightclub called Gol: a big-limbed American named Danny. Americans were unheard of, back then, in Natal. Rio, maybe. São Paulo. But Natal? He said one of the workers at his home-construction business had grown up here and promised it was pretty as God's grin. And now, he said, he knew that this was true.

45

Danny knew no Portuguese, but between his high school Spanish and the English Debora knew from music videos, they quickly made their feelings' contours clear. The rest they fleshed out with . . . well, with *flesh*. She'd been with boys a few times—at night, beneath the mango tree—boys who stank of poverty and *cachaça*. But Danny! He had grand teeth and tender, sunburned skin that she wanted, by turns, to soothe and slap. He was twenty-eight but scarcely had to shave.

For a week they played at being honeymooners. She moved out of Waterston's room and into Danny's hotel, where the maids, abandoning their hopes of coming in, left clean towels stacked outside the door. Did they eat? Oh, they must have (room service trays gone cold), but their bodies felt unlimited, perpetual motion machines, drained and replenished by the very same exertions. Danny asked her how to say "one more time?" in Portuguese; she said no, he never had to *ask*.

At week's end he left, promising to write her ("I'll get my worker Nando to translate"), and Debora, having realized that summer's wave had sunk to shore, rode the jerky bus back to her parents'.

Now what? Her final year of school, and then a husband? A bullish, foul-breathed, local boy, a farmer like her father? She had always wanted more but not known how to want it, trying to climb a ladder with no rungs. Run away, like Waterston, to the city . . . okay, maybe. But then, though? A city job? A city man? And *then*?

Her new dream was Danny, his lordly, sun-stung arms, reaching down to hoist her past her worries.

He did write—he did!—his letters full of plans: the home he would build her in a place called Cape Cod, reached by a walkway made of flagstones shaped like hearts; the bedroom through whose windows she would hear the ocean's hum—the very same Atlantic she knew now but swept northward, just as he would sweep her, too, away.

He named the date when his flight would land; he told her to be ready.

Her mother called her crazy. A sex tourist, that's all he was; hadn't Debora heard the news reports? Her father, too, in his shrugging, hapless way, voiced disapproval. As did her brothers (all but Waterston, the seeker).

Debora didn't care. Or she *did*, but in reverse: their doubt made her all the more eager to prove them wrong, they with their adherence to their wilted little hopes, who hadn't seen the promise in her orchid. None of them could understand how fortunes might be made just from rainwater and sun and ambition.

When she met Danny's plane, she wore her city jeans. He grabbed her where the stars were sewn and lifted her off the ground.

Waterston was their witness when they signed the marriage license, after which he served them *casadinhos* in his kitchen, where the three of them danced *chachado* past midnight. If it wasn't the lavish *festa* she'd envisioned as a girl, with scores of friends and cousins making merry, it was better for being her invention.

Marrying Danny made everything move slaphappily fast. Before she knew it she was on an airplane, then another, then climbing into his tall green American pickup truck, which had a tailgate sticker saying "Carpenters Do It By Hand," another on the bumper reading "Measure Twice, Cut Once." Debora inhaled his woody, welcoming scent. She was eighteen.

That was what she told us as we tucked in to our lunches at the Pancake King, across from the Barnstable airport.

Brazil! Now her tan made sense, her zigzag sentence structures.

Stu and I had one side of the syrup-stained table, Debora and her husband the other. All the while she talked, I watched her shining eyes: brown flecks and green all dazzlingly jumbled, as if daring the world to sort them out. Even without her tale, I'd have pegged her as a dreamer. The single-minded way she looked at Danny, still. The fervor.

Danny, with his hooded gaze, was harder to decipher. He nodded as she talked, but also smirked impatiently, a champ hearing the legend of his biggest win again. Shyness might have prompted him to stare down at his hands—bulky, robust hands that crushed his napkin. Shyness, maybe, or shame (to be seen with two gay men?). Or maybe it was only nerves, like mine.

Above us, cardboard angels and Saint Nicks hung from strings, quivering in the heating duct's blast. I wanted to make a joke—*Santa's got the D.T.s*—but that might further alienate Danny.

Stu was also hard to read, as silent as the moon, running a hand along his crew cut's bristles. Christ, I wanted to swat him. Speak up! Charm their pants off!

Debora had finished; for just a second I thought about amusing her with Stu's and my first-acquaintance story. When people asked how we'd met, and we answered "Beating meat," they thought we were being euphemistic. But it was true: we'd both volunteered at Serve the World, cooking healthful meals for people with AIDS; we found ourselves stationed at a vast expanse of butcher block, tenderizing a thousand cuts of beef. With straight people I normally withheld further details: the rush to Stu's apartment, the other beaten meat. But even without those details, the story might seem flippant. And that was the very last thing we wanted her to think of us.

Fathers. We could be fathers. We were ready.

To fill the silence, I chose instead to ask her about cashews: Did they grow on vines? On trees? Underground? Already I was sketching out a reading lesson's draft. (More than a decade at Educraft had trained my nose for topics.) Also, now I'd get to hear her tuneful voice again, the way her accent breathed new life into the dullest words. *To* became *tchoo*—a blown kiss.

"You raised cashews?" I said. "Funny, but I've never even thought of where . . . I mean, for us, they just arrive in little cans! How do they—"

But Stu raised his hand to cut me off. "Sorry," he said. He looked at Debora, then Danny. "You seem like lovely people. You do. But clearly there's been a misunderstanding."

Debora's expression, still buoyant from the memory of her courtship, sank now to one of bemusement. She crossed her arms and stared at them—as if expecting, in place of her two elegant brown limbs, a defect (flippers?) that clearly would discredit her DNA.

48

"I mean," said Stu, "we weren't expecting someone . . . someone Brazilian."

Debora's face went rigid, persuasively panic-stricken. "Wait. What do you mean? You knew! You didn't know?"

"How?" said Stu.

"I thought I told. And, well, my name of e-mail."

"Brazucamama?"

"Brazuca means 'Brazilian in America.'"

"And anyway," said Danny, awakened from impassiveness. "So what if she is? What's the big problem?"

Good question. I was already a fan of her tropical force, her foreignness, which seemed nothing less than a free bonus. I wouldn't mind a mixed-race child: I thought of Milo's sweet sepia skin.

Benevolently, Stu laid a hand on Debora's wrist. "It's just—one of our things is for the mother to be Jewish. Jewish, you know, by *birth*. By blood. When you said, in your e-mail . . . we didn't know it was Jewish just by marriage."

Debora exchanged an inscrutable glance with Danny, who shook his head and loaded a link of sausage onto his fork. "Funny," he said, "'cause Debora's the one who cares about that stuff." He gulped down the link in one bite.

"What makes you think," she started, her tone not mad but curious. Then her eyes lit with a dawning recognition. "Oh! A brown Jew!" She laughed, pointing to the wrist that Stu had touched. "I'm Brazilian, so I can't be Jewish, yes? You think?"

"Well, no," Stu said. "No, it's just—" But his sheepish shrug conceded the point.

"Look," she said. The word came out as *looky*. "It's okay. In Brazil, even, many do not know. Many, many. The Inquisition—you've heard of this, no?"

Sure, we said. In Spain.

But remember, she said: Portugal was still then part of Spain. So Portugal, too, had its Inquisition. Jews fled to Portugal's new colony—to Brazil—so far away, so wild, they hoped they could live there with no problem. And where, in that far, wild New World, should they go? The wild northeast. Rio Grande do Norte.

"But even to here," she said, "Inquisitors, they arrived. The Jews had to hide, to convert to Catholicism. Converted but still Jewish in their hearts."

How strong is the heart, she asked? How long does it hold? A hundred years passed—two hundred—and in a few northeastern towns lived Brazilians who didn't know why they ate no pork, or why, at the start of April, bread was disallowed. They were Catholic but never knelt in church like their neighbors. On Fridays, every family lit two candles.

Gente da Nacão—the People of the Nation—that was what they called themselves, said Debora.

"Then a man, he came," she said. "A teacher. A rabbi. When he heard the way they lived, he told them who they were. Think of this!" She looked at Stu, then me—those eyes, with their complicated shine. "It's like for you, maybe, when you learned that you are gay. Except you knew *inside*, always, who you really are. These people, they didn't know. They had to be *explained*." She lifted her cup but couldn't seem to pause and take a sip; her words, blowing across the coffee's hot surface, churned up puffs of steam like an engine's. "Some of them didn't want to change, they wanted to stay converted. But others made a group for learning Jewish things, for prayer. My grandfather's home, this was where they met. My own *avô*! My mother didn't care so much, you know, but *Avô* taught me."

Now she drank her coffee—a long, contented draft—her smile a bit short of overproud. More or less the same goofy smile I'd worn in boyhood, when boasting of my great-times-something-grandfather John Faunce, who'd sailed to Massachusetts on the *Mayflower*. (Or so claimed Mom, booster of her family-by-marriage. The truth, as I'd learn in a high school history class: John Faunce had shown up three years after the *Mayflower*, his ship less stirringly named the *Anne*.)

I hoped Debora's pride wasn't misplaced. I could never tell what would pass muster with Stu: what would be Jewish enough, or too

Jewish. Take Richard, whose being a Jew was crucial, in Stu's eyes, to making him a suitable father for Rina's children, but whose tribalism sent Stu into fits. ("He writes checks to Lieberman—Senator fucking Lieberman!—just because he's, 'you know, one of ours'?") Or this: Why did Stu love my foreskin, and yet, when I'd cited the barbarity of circumcision, did he snap, "Any boy of mine is having a *bris*. Period"?

Now I stroked his thigh beneath the table like a rabbit's foot, trying to coax a positive response. But no coaxing was necessary: his face was bright with awe.

"Wow," he said to Debora. "Your story is just—wow. Talk about keeping the flame lit."

"We knew we were different," she said. "Special. But not why."

"Which almost makes it better. I mean, that's *faith*, right? Believing in something you don't understand?" His thigh, underneath my hand, was dancing.

Yes, I thought—*that's* the Stu to show them!

"Can I warm that up?" asked the suddenly looming waitress. Her nametag read: "Be gentle, I'm new!"

"Not for me, thanks," I said.

"You?" she said to Stu.

But he, still enthralled with Debora's story, didn't notice.

"Sir, coffee?"

"He's fine," I said, my hand atop Stu's mug.

I went back to my lunch, pleased that Stu was pleased—but what was this other proto-feeling, a pinching in my gut? I crushed the thought that it could be envy. I *wanted* Stu to click with Debora, of course I did. And yet. They shared this thing, this Jewishness, that I couldn't be a part of. I felt a tinge of adolescent angst.

The Pancake King's throwback vibe probably wasn't helping. Its Sputnik-era Formica, its cheap, sugary smells—I don't think it had changed by 2 percent since my first visits, as an achy-voiced, sexually flummoxed teen. This was where my summer pals and I had double-dated, paired off with whichever sunburned girls we liked that week.

And really, I did like the girls. They Benadryled my itch. But lord, the kilowatt hours I burned in trying to convince them—my bumbling way of trying to convince myself—that I wasn't *more* attracted to their boyfriends.

Flustered now, I fumbled a clump of hotcake in my lap. And then— crap!—a forkful of hash was capsized.

"Anxious?" Danny said. "Easy does it." He had clearly also noted Debora and Stu's bond; he angled his body to talk with me alone.

"No," I said, "it's just. Well, yeah. Anxious. Yes." I brushed bits of hash to the floor.

"Don't worry about it—I mean, when'd they start making these tables with seats, like, a hundred miles away?" He leaned forward conspiratorially, cutting his glance to one side then the next, at diners who were digging in to heaps of the trucker's special. "It must be 'cause everyone here is so f.a.t."

My laugh pulled the tension's thread and started its unsnarling.

"But seriously," he said. "Awful, isn't it? You look at what some of these people are eating—hell, what *we* are—and you realize it could feed, like, a dozen Ethiopians. Or"—he jerked his thumb at Debora— "Brazilians."

"But I *like* the seats like this." It was Debora, who'd swiveled toward us. "*Looky*—much more room for a woman to be pregnant."

Her closeness was disarming (I hadn't thought she'd heard us). Her closeness and her loaded word: *pregnant.*

It sent us skidding into a perilously intimate silence. There were griddle sounds from the kitchen, the cash register's ding. And then I remembered what I'd learned in driver's ed. Counterintuitive, but: *Steer into the skid.*

I sat up and wiped my lips, and said, "Debora. Tell us. Why would you have someone else's baby?"

"Yes," she said. "Thank you!"

She cried this with such ardor that I almost, honest to God, said, "You're welcome."

"It's good to talk direct," she clarified. She planted her elbows on the table. "So. Why a baby for someone else? 'For someone else' is the question, no? Not 'why a baby?' Because, well . . . babies," she said. "Children!" She sounded like a schoolgirl asked her favorite food (*Chocolate!*). "Our daughter, Paula, she is so wonderful. She changed everything." Debora gave the verb an extra syllable: *change-ed.* "For me she did. Like she came and washed"—*wash-ed*—"my eyes. Now I see everything so clear." She stared at me and Stu as if her sheer enthusiasm could make us, too, view life through her high-powered vision. She asked, "Would you like to see a picture?"

Of course we did!

From her purse she brought forth a laminated snapshot: a little pig-tailed girl, a shade paler than Debora, with squinty, gleaming, skeptical features. It wasn't hard to love Paula, even from just a picture. I wished the girl were here right now: I'd grab her by the wrists and—*whoosh*—turn us into a human helicopter.

"If you had a machine to make gold," Debora said, "and you'd already made some for yourself—nice house, nice car, everything—would you throw away this machine? Or would you make gold for other people?" She laid the photo on the tabletop. Her ace.

"Wow," said Stu, "is being pregnant really that much fun?"

"Oh, yes, I *love* this," she said. "I think it's why I'm made."

Stu picked up the photograph, turned it in his hands. Narrow-eyed, uncertain, he looked not unlike Paula. "Thing is," he said, "it's *not* gold. That's not what we're dealing with. A baby. Specifically, half your baby."

"What he's saying, I think?" I said. "We recognize how tough it is, for any surro, to give away a baby. Especially a TS, you know? It's almost . . . well, unfathomable. You're sure doing traditional's right for you?"

"I'll tell you serious, okay?" she said. "When I was thinking in doing this—the long time I was thinking?—I always planned that I will do gestational. It seemed just more simple, you know? For Danny's feelings, too."

Danny mugged a tell-me-something-I-don't-know expression.

"But then," she said, "your ad. *Never* I saw an ad like that. It's like I told to Pat: just too perfect. Except you wanted 'traditional'—so maybe, I thought, no. Maybe I was not the one for you. But everything else— everything!—was such a good connection. Maybe I would have to think again." She acted out *think*, her finger on her chin. "You know what I was doing when I changed my mind?" she asked. "Taking out a—well, in the bathroom, okay? Imagine. And look, I thought, I have these eggs, and every month I flush them. Flush, good-bye, *tchau*—but do I cry? The way I throw them out, just like that: what a waste! If someone wants to love a child the way we do with Paula, why not give them something that would only go to waste? It makes more sense, don't you think, to use it?"

Her logic sounded smart, but I had sensed already that surrogacy and logic rarely mixed. I said, "Trust me, the last thing I want to do is dissuade you . . . but actually being the mother? It takes a special woman. 'Cause then you've got to—*she* would have to—give the baby up."

"Because," Stu said, "we hope the mom will stay in touch, but—"

"Absolutely! And be an auntie. As long as you would want to."

"—but *we're* the parents," he finished. "Legally and otherwise. Any surro has to understand that."

"I understand, yes," she said. "But you also have to understand: I would do this for you, of course, but also, a lot, for me. I have this . . . well, this power, no? This gift that I can give? It's wrong—wrong for *me*—not to use it. And so, you see, you are giving me a gift, too. The gift of being who I'm supposed to."

I'd heard that claim before. Or, rather, I had read it—in other women's Surromoms ads. In writing, it could come across a little bit Hallmarky: not untrue but maybe sort of coached. But Debora spoke the words as though she didn't have a choice, spoke them with force of revelation.

Stu looked swayed, too, but still slightly quizzical. "Your spirit," he said, "is great. I mean, it's really gorgeous. But don't you—not to put, you know, too fine a point on it. Don't you want more children of your own?"

"Oh! Well," said Danny, butting forward. "You'll meet Paula, and when you do, you'll see she keeps us plenty busy! She's great, though. How would we ever top her?"

Pall-a, he'd pronounced it. As opposed to Debora's *Pow*-la.

"Excited to meet her," said Stu. "But still, it just seems logical that—"

"We've got Paula," said Danny, smiling. "Our own family's finished." He held out his hand for the snapshot.

Stu withheld the photo a moment longer. "We've been wanting to ask you, too, Danny. This must all be . . . I don't know. Isn't it sort of strange?"

"What, right now? To be here? I *have* to be, sort of, don't I? I mean, any freaks could've put that ad on Surromoms."

Beat.

Beat.

I waited for a wink. A signal of how little (or much) he meant this.

Then he said, "That's the vow I took, wasn't it, Deb? Sickness and health, defend you from all weirdos? Ha!" he laughed. "Ha!" He thumped an empty glass against the table.

"No, but really," said ever-persistent Stu. "You're okay? Is this what you want Debora to do?"

Here was Danny's laugh again, a series of sharp bursts. "Sorry," he said. "No. I forget you don't know her. You don't know: when she wants something, she *wants* it." He clinched her with a one-armed hug, and she, in turn, blinked at him: a Morse code of marital emotion. (Affectionate annoyance? Vice versa?) "But seriously," he went on. He let her go. "Weird at first? You bet. For starters, loving pregnancy? Fine, I'll just accept that. I mean, don't we have to, guys? What the hell do *we* know about it? But then doing it for *someone else* . . . well, no offense, but it's a little cuckoo, right? I mean, *right*? Just being honest."

I found myself nodding along—partly in agreement, partly just because he seemed so much to *need* agreement.

"But hey," he said, "one man's cuckoo's another man's . . . whatever. You don't think I've lived through that myself? I mean, okay, you heard Debora's version of how we met. *Once upon a time*, and all that. But now try to see the other side. Who am I? I'm just some local schmo from up in Brockton. No offense, Stu, but we weren't, you know, *New York* Jews. More bologna-on-Wonder-bread than bagels-and-lox, okay?

"But anyway, my parents run a used-equipment resale place. Washing machines, lawn mowers, pumps. Want to know the closest they would come to something foreign? Ordering a replacement valve from Honda! I mean, for me, growing up, *Boston* was exotic. Twenty miles, and could've been two million. Maybe twice a year we'd drive up to see a Sox game, and Dad, when we hit the city, always threatened to make us eat at one of the 'gook' restaurants we passed: 'What, don't you like roasted poodle?' All us kids would scream bloody murder.

"Got the picture? Okay, now, go from that to *this*: 'Mom, Dad, I want you to meet the girl I plan to marry. Actually, no, the girl I *already* married. She's ten years younger, and oh, by the way, can't speak English. I met her at some disco in Brazil.'

"They thought I was nuts. And, hell, I guess I *was*. I had no clue what I was getting into. I mean, as a kid, dreaming of my wedding, you think I ever imagined getting hitched to some Brazilian girl who couldn't even say 'Pass the salt'? So no, I didn't imagine her, all these years later, wanting to get pregnant with some other guy's baby. But *life* is nuts, right? Things don't always go the way you planned them. I mean, as kids, did you guys plan on being . . . well, on *this*?"

I was so unsettled—in a good way—by his candor (Hark, he speaks! The hunk of flesh has feelings!), that I forgot my vow to pose as solemnly parental, to keep my inner princess in her tower. "Haven't the foggiest concept what you mean," I said, lisping. "My high school yearbook photo says 'Most Likely to Borrow Eggs.'"

Stu shot me a look, but Danny seemed to like the joke; he heaved a load of laughter. "You're right. It *is* easier," he stage-whispered to Debora.

She warned him with a cocked, vaudeville elbow.

"Oh, come on," said Danny. "We're friends here, now, aren't we?"

"Fine," I said, "I'll take the bait. *What?*"

"Well, see, according to this book Debora gave me? Sometimes there's a problem for the husband of the surro: the thought of another guy's stuff inside her. Human nature, I guess, to be jealous." Danny had been toying with the leavings on his plate, forking through a residue of yolk. Now he stopped, as if it had just hit him what an egg was. Or what it could have been, if not food. "But Deb's theory?" he said. "She thought the whole thing through. She says, if the other guy is . . . well, if there are *two* guys. Know what I'm saying here? Guys like you? Then it's easier. What do I have to worry about, then, right?"

Stu had warned me, earlier, not to get political: "Remember, Pat, you can't assume the whole world thinks like us. We're not here to find out how they *vote*." But now he was saying how relieved he was to meet them—such kind, decent, open-minded people—"when the country has been hijacked by the wingnuts, don't you think?"

Danny jumped right in: "Oh, Christ, don't get me started. Know who they remind me of? The townies I grew up with. Shut their eyes and pray the world won't change."

"Right," said Stu. "Scared shitless. The bullies always are."

That led to a talk about Iraq and foreign wars, which then devolved to topics much less serious: Brazilians vs. Americans, the stiff-hipped way we gringos danced; Portuguese and its nasal tones, its word for knife, which sounded to us like *fuck*.

We didn't mention babies again—only just to say we'd think things over. We weren't skirting the topic so much as giving it room to breathe. That was definitely the mutually reached Rx: lots of breathing.

Eventually we arrived at a reassuring silence. Our third cups of coffee had been drained.

"So, I guess that does it," Danny said. "What do we owe?"

Stu said, "Please! Don't worry. Taken care of." Earlier, per our plan, he'd settled with the hostess, on the pretense of going to the men's room.

"You're sure?" said Danny, reaching for his wallet.

Stu took Danny's arm and returned it to his side, and both of them seemed startled by the contact, then relieved. "More than sure," said Stu. "It's our pleasure."

The parking lot was breezy with the front edge of a storm. A small jet, seconds away from landing at the airport, strafed us with its whole-hearted roar. We pledged again to mull things over ("Why don't we say a week?"), after which we'd talk some more, decide.

"Well," said Danny. "Back to work. And plus, the sitter's waiting." He shook his car keys: *ting-a-ling-a-ling.*

"Oh!" said Stu. "The sitter! We should reimburse you." Now he was the one reaching for his wallet.

Danny's expression hardened. He jabbed his keys at Stu. "This isn't just for the money, you know. That's not—we're not *desperate.*" He unlocked a midnight blue, late-model Explorer. (He must have traded up from his old pickup.) "The main thing," he said, "is to make Debora happy."

"I'm *already* hap," she said—her accent cut off the *y.* She spread her arms in what could have been a gesture of impatience, or an imitation of the plane that had roared past. She took my hand, and then took Stu's, and held us. "*This* is hap."

The way she said it made me think of "hap" as something tangible: a substance to hold on to or to lack. You could be full of hap (as I guessed I was, just then) or have the stuff withheld from you. *Hapless.*

Nothing more to say, really. Nothing short of everything. We lingered in the swirling wind, sweet with coming snow. Debora shivered and seemed totally tickled by the reflex.

I hope the baby gets her smile, I thought.

six

When Danny asked, "Did you plan on *this*?" he'd left *this* undefined: Being gay? Needing to hire a surro? I had parried by making my dumb joke. But late that night, when Stu had gone to bed, I sat alone—just me, in the quiet of the cottage—and tried to frame an answer to his question.

The truth was, through high school, and even more in college, I had held the expectation of having kids the usual way. My oversized attractions gummed things up.

I was always attracted to girls. Certain girls, sometimes: this girl over here, that one there. But boys I was drawn to categorically, essentially. Offer up a boy—almost any boy at all—and I could find something in him tempting. The ropy grace of one, the frailty of another; leg hair or its unexpected lack. A feature and its opposite could equally entice me because, in the end, it wasn't boys' particulars that moved me but their fundamental *maleness*.

When guys started pairing off with girls, I was pragmatic: I kept pure my love for boys, awaiting my ideal, meanwhile having fun with girls (why not, if they were willing?), to quell my most on-the-surface urges. Mary Beth O'Donnell, daughter of a fireman, who asked to slide along my arm, as if it were a fire pole. And then Rachel (what was her last name? Something-berg? Bloomberg?), who liked my blond hairs against her dark ones. A long string of Pancake King companions.

Meanwhile, boys were pulling away. Why? Had I done something wrong? Maybe I myself was the mistake.

I kept finding girls—or no, let them find *me*. My trick? The art of apparent indifference. Actually, though, the quality they saw was indecision. I wanted the girls, and clearly pictured someday tying the knot with one, so we could get to work on making babies; but also what I wanted was for *this* wanting to triumph, to nullify my less-accepted yearnings. Which wasn't possible: my love for boys was hard and imperishable, a hunger from a whole different stomach.

I was twenty, and prominently, stridently gay, before I found the woman I believed I'd settle down with.

I'd come out of the closet as soon as I hit college. I hadn't planned to, had expected to be fraught and frustrated, chalking this up as character-building and good for making Art: all those coded poems I would write. But college was another world entirely from home, a planet where the gravity was gone. The RA in my dorm was a dyke with spina bifida, her girlfriend a Haitian refugee. Everyone, it seemed, was *a something*. Pretty soon I tallied up a different calculation: sure, being gay would undoubtedly bring stigma, but maybe not as much (at least among my crowd) as being just a white-bread WASP.

The Homecoming Ball was Columbus Day weekend. "Bringing a date?" my roommate, Russ, asked. I told him no. Then I said, "I'm single." And then, in a torrent: "You know of any eligible bachelors?"

"Oh," said Russ.

"Oh!" I cried—surely, of us two, the more surprised.

One second to the next, I had a new identity. You had to stand on one side of the line; I'd picked mine.

Which wasn't to say being gay was easy. My gang was a small one at a small, rural school: a dozen other openly gay students, and none appealed. So far I was only gay in theory.

Like many *sayers* who haven't yet chanced to become *doers*, I often overcompensated with volume. I challenged any homophobic comments during class, led teach-ins, shouted from the rooftops (literally: the Dykes for Divestment staged a rally; I scaled the fire escape of College Hall). I also aimed my shrillness at my parents. My mom, when I came out to her, said, well, she'd always love me, but . . .

"But what?" I said.

"But don't you want kids?"

"Why? So I can tell them that I really love them, *but*?"

By the time I met Becky MacLeod, I was Big Fag on Campus, co-chair of the school's nascent chapter of Queer Nation, straight-A author of papers like "A Poetics of Promiscuity? Allen Ginsberg's Horny 'Howl.'" Since coming out, I hadn't had sex once.

Becky and I were named to the Ad Hoc Symbol Committee, saddled with proposing—and selling to alums—an inoffensive replacement for the school's Redskin mascot. In a room full of graybeards, we were the only students, and had to bond, if only by default. But there was nothing default about Becky. She came from Manitoba, the middle of the prairie, and had, like her homeland, a stark, windblown beauty. The latest in a long MacLeod lineage of bagpipers, she pitted her buffed-clean looks against a smutty wit. Her frank, focused gaze and her buck teeth intrigued me; she seemed to be hankering after something.

At every session, we sat together, a subcommittee of two, passing bitchy notes that often ended: "Eek! Burn this!" We dubbed our little private support group Obstreperous Anonymous.

The night before the final vote—our last chance at influence—I asked Becky over to my place so we could plan. "How about some pizza? Some Coke and Captain Morgan?"—my standard fare for pulling all-nighters. Sounded fun, she said, and she would bring the weed: *her* standard fare for any evening.

I was living off-campus in a tiny, stinky studio, big enough for a futon, not much else. Becky acted as if it were a marvel of less-is-more.

She praised my Frank O'Hara broadsheet, my framed ACT UP poster, my thick book of Mapplethorpe portraits. "May I?" she asked, making the book a bed tray on her lap, and emptied out her fragrant bag of pot. She did some expert sorting work—seeds from flaky leaves—then fashioned an impressive-looking joint.

When half the joint was history, passed and passed between us, Becky kissed its glowing end to stunt it. "Ah," she said. "That's better. Now we can do business."

The Symbol Committee's fogies favored lumbering clichés—their top choices were Trojans and Rams—and I was hoping to push them in the opposite direction, toward something less martial, less male.

"Less," said Becky, "like a brand name for rubbers?"

Other schools had already taken gender-neutral names, but none was especially inspiring. Dartmouth's was the Big Green ("Big green *what*?" asked Becky); the Crimson Tide sounded like a plague.

The two of us, stymied, smoked the joint's remainder. We freshened our drinks. The world's edges melted.

"Think big now," I said. "Really big. Sky's the limit."

"The Stars?" she tried. "Or . . . the Black Holes? Something astronomical."

"Something *gastronomical*? Maybe the Appetizers?"

"No," she said. "Better: Appe*teasers*."

The ring of it (or the rum, or the weed, or all three) knocked us down ditzily together. Crooning the word, we squeezed each other's thighs with galled delight. I found my thumb tickling her nipple.

Becky paused, the look in her eyes startled, surreptitious. "But Pat," she said.

"But what?"

"I thought you liked boys."

"I *do*," I said, and saying it—so surely, in this context—sent a zap of pure erotic lightning through my limbs. I pushed her to the floor; the rest seemed predetermined: fingers, lips, tongues, interlocking. Her mouth tasted smoky and alcoholic, like a party.

62

For weeks our sex was like that: fiery, free-falling. A renovation—letting ourselves be razed and then remade.

Liberated from my previous impossible expectations (that girls should set me right, should cure me), I could finally get and give a more complete enjoyment. I wasn't hiding anything from her, or from myself.

Together, though, we *did* hide, we kept our lust secret from the world—and oh, it was scrumptious! A freer kind of furtiveness than I had ever known before, without the guilt: *normalcy* as transgression. Some nights I would saunter home from chairing Queer Nation to find Becky waiting, buck-naked. "Careful," I'd say, laughing, my cock already hard. "If anyone found out, I'd be ruined."

Was this what love, unencumbered, felt like?

I tried to write a sonnet about it, which ended up as crap, but maybe the main simile was a keeper. Every year, at Christmas, my family went to Killington, and what I waxed poetic about, for fourteen lines, was skiing: not the pell-mell speed or the chairlift's lofty view but the time at day's end when you doffed your fat boots and your feet felt like helium balloons. Being with Becky was like that. A moonwalk.

The Symbol Committee wrapped things up—the vote went ten to two for Rams—but Becky and I were only just beginning. We spent a long weekend at a Poconos lodge. The soft-touch manager asked if we were newlyweds, and we said yes, which got us a room upgrade, on the house. It also got us talking about our plans: marriage, kids. "Adding a few more pipers to the band," Becky called it. "Yes," I said. "Absolutely!" My parents would be so happy, and so, I thought assuredly, would I. "I guess we should start 'rehearsing' right now, don't you think?"

Afterward I asked her if I'd have to wear a kilt. "You know, at the wedding. Please don't say you'll make me?" The MacLeod of Lewis tartan was a sickly mustard hue.

Becky said, "And so what if? What's so wrong with a kilt? Scared that folks'll think you're a *pansy*?"

How fine it was to have a girl and still to have *myself.*

One night I came home, abuzz, from Queer Nation, full of dizzy talk about a boy: a freshman from the hockey team (a freshman! from the hockey team!) who'd shown up, proclaiming he was gay. Ryan Harris: corn-blond hair, a wrinkled, nervous smile, forearms you could build a cabin out of. Ryan wanted to write a biting op-ed for the campus daily, on homophobia in the varsity sports system. I'd volunteered to help him with his draft.

Becky had been lying in wait, naked, on the futon; I undressed and lay down beside her. Then I boinged back up, my finger in the air, a mad doctor struck by inspiration. "Oh," I said. "Oh ho ho! What a smashing idea!" I spoke in the goofy private mode we'd developed. "Let's not have children of our own, let's *adopt*. In fact, let's adopt Ryan Harris! He's potty-trained already, and there's no blood relation, so fucking him wouldn't quite be incest. Can we, Beckles? Please? Pretty please?"

Becky rose—getting ready, I thought, for a dive. She did that when she felt extra-giddy with attraction: a flying leap, an all-body smother. But now she walked away, plodding toward the bathroom. Without looking back at me, she said, "It isn't nice. It's not nice and . . . actually, it's nasty."

"Whoa," I said. "Hey. What's happening here? C'mon."

Becky turned and faced me. Her features looked runny.

"Beck, I was kidding," I said. "That's what we do. We kid."

"You think it doesn't hurt? Hearing you go on and on? *Ooh, he's so hot, he's so hot.*"

I got up and went to her and held her in my arms. "But sweetie. You know I'm gay. You've known that since we met."

"What I've known—I've *thought* I've known," she said, "was that you're mine."

It took just a week, then, for everything to crumble. I promised I'd commit to her. Or, well, make *this* commitment: she would be the only woman, ever, I had sex with.

No, not enough, she said. *Person.* The only person.

Becky and I had clambered to the summit of Not Quite. Which seemed not an inch above nowhere.

She was a year ahead; she finished school and split. (A mutual friend reported she had moved to coastal Maine and was dating a Damariscotta oyster farmer.) As for me, in my senior year? I focused all my fantasies on grad school.

NYU took me for their semiotics program—all that work on the Symbol Committee had given me an interest. It wasn't my first choice but a bargain with my dad: not law school, thank God, but not "that touchy-feely stuff" (his judgment of an MFA in poetry) or, worse, being "some sort of professional homosexual" (the Human Rights Campaign Fund, knowing of my activism, had offered me a lobbying position). Semiotics: obscure enough to thumb my father's eye but rigorous, in-arguably weighty. My dad acquiesced to its complicated sound, the relative respectability it offered.

Respectability? If only he had known.

The first man I had—okay, who had *me*—was a transit cop who stopped me at the Bleecker Street station, asking if I needed any help. A ringer for my AP English teacher, Mr. Prior: monobrowed, kneelike jaw, tall, senatorial; the name patch on his pocket said Toomey. I was still considering what to say, when he said, "Good," and led me to a secret airless room that smelled of oil. He came up with a condom—an uncle with a magic coin—and shoved my fledgling self from the nest. Panic at first, my legs no good, my heart a skidding wheel. But then, *fup!*—my wings caught air, and everything went weightless.

After we wiped up, I wanted to trade numbers.

Toomey laughed. "You're cute, but that's not how it works. Don't worry, you won't need *me* again."

How could I have guessed how right he was?

It turned out that not being a "professional homosexual" didn't preclude a full-time occupation in gay sex. The textbooks I was studying said Derrida, Foucault, but what I crammed—in bodegas, on St. Mark's Place—was men. Each day was a course in *applied* semiotics, all the codes and signs (tilt of hips, shade of tie) that gave away who could be had, and almost never did I have the same man more than twice. New York: the cruise park that never sleeps.

Yes, there was the virus, which dangled all our "little deaths" high above the chasm of the big one. But we fucked at the frantic pace of soldiers weekend-furloughed, the taste of battle smoke still in our nostrils. Even ACT UP meetings were a carnival of flirting. After every die-in I got laid.

The Pat who had planned to don a kilt and marry Becky? I told myself that he was like our college's Redskin mascot, a relic from a quaint, plainer past.

This was just about the time that Joseph, as he'd say, "discovered" me—as though he were a mogul, and I a budding starlet, and gay life was the greatest show on earth. He took me home: not for sex—he'd never say he wanted that—but rather to show me his signed copy of *A Streetcar Named Desire* ("To J, a fellow passenger, with affection"), proof that he had once had "carnal knowledge" of its author. Passing me the book he let his hand alight on mine. "And now you've touched the hand," he said, "that jerked the cock of Tenn. And *that* is how we fags make family trees."

Having disclosed this story, he asked for one of mine. "Or more than one. Your whole erotic history. Don't hold back."

I told him of my catholic tastes, my years of sex with girls.

"Yuck," he said. "The thought."

"But no," I said, "I liked it. The sex and also something else: not feeling the pressure to be so 'other.'"

"Pat," he said, "don't kid yourself," his voice freezing over. "You *are* 'other.' That is what we are."

The world required categories, and I was now this thing: a man who picked up men for sex and rarely learned their names. That was what it meant to be gay, right? Why make a ruckus over the former version of me that hadn't flouted cultural conventions, even if I felt him still inside me? I heeded Joseph; I dropped the old Pat.

Soon enough, too, I dropped semiotics, which seemed more and more like an esoteric evasion of the new, no-pretensions world I lived in. *Clarify, clarify*, that was now my dogma. I withdrew from NYU, and sold back all my texts. "What are you going to do now?" my parents both demanded. "Don't expect us to support you." I didn't think to worry. Worrying was my old way. I was sure I'd find something good.

What I found, through Joseph? My schoolbook gig at Educraft, a calling that depended on forthrightness. Then, like a reward, a prize for having changed, I found the clearest thing of all: Stu.

Gorgeous Stu. Stand-up Stu. My life.

Being with Stu I didn't feel gay, straight, or elsewise, I felt only— wholly—like myself. Stu was my fruition, the *x* I'd been solving for. He roused again the Pat who would be happy to settle down.

But Stu's only rule, as I said earlier, was: no rules. That was the creed of all the guys—the gays—who surrounded us. We had all decided upon the same way to be different.

I never told Stu about Becky, the life I'd almost led, the truth that I *could* have led that life. At first, I stayed quiet to keep my gayness burnished—worried that Stu, like Joseph, would object. Then, before I knew it (or so went my excuse), *too soon to safely tell* had turned into *too late*. Stu would have bristled if I'd sprung it on him then: *Why didn't you say anything before?* Even years later, when we started talking kids, I chose not to tell him of my past. I wanted him to feel that we were breaking ground together—as truly, for the most part, we were.

The secret wasn't painful to keep; I would not have said I felt regret. I loved the life I'd chosen with Stu and all our outcast comrades: unremorsefully gay and apart. At least at first I'd loved it, when it meant liberation, before our brand of liberation became a kind of trap.

And now, on the Cape, with a baby in the offing, the path I had abandoned and the one I'd taken were merging. I might manage to make an end run around letdown.

Only now and then would I think of windblown Becky, and let myself feel the pinch of loss—as though I had moved to a more embracing neighborhood but kept my old house key and sometimes thumbed its ridges, longing for the place I once lived.

seven

At the Pancake King we had all agreed to wait a week, but the phone rang at eight the next morning.

"I'm listening to NPR," she said—no "Good morning" or "It's Debora"—"and the story, it's a man who finds a baby in the subway!"

"Debora," I mouthed to Stu, and switched to speakerphone.

"Just lying there," she went on, "in the station, in a blanket. He takes it to the cops, and when no one comes to get it, they ask him would he like to raise it. Not just him, but his boyfriend also—both. Can you believe? They say gays can't be parents, but now, when the heteros, they don't do what they should, the government asks the gays to help out."

Why was Debora saying this? To prove her lack of bias? To show us what a super match she'd make? I could see my own surprise mirrored in Stu's stare: we had thought that *we* might be the ones who'd have to plead. (The previous night, debriefing, we'd parsed Danny's reactions: the way he'd seemed, a couple of times at lunch, about to snap. We'd decided that we were actually glad to see his doubts, glad that his and Debora's stories weren't completely airtight. "If they were, that would be more worrisome," Stu had said. "The truth is, it *is* strange—it's craziness—to do this. No one's reasons are ever going to make perfect sense." "No," I said. "Not theirs . . . and probably not ours, either.")

". . . found it in the station," Debora was now repeating. "Just lying there. Isn't it amazing?"

At a loss, I looked to Stu, who motioned for me to answer. *Play along* seemed to be his meaning. "Wow," I said. "So, what you're saying is . . . we should troll the subways?"

"Troll?" she said.

I couldn't help but laugh. A tough translation!

Stu explained, "We hoped we wouldn't have to *find* a baby."

"Not if," I said—how close this was to flirting—"we have *you*."

"Of course," she said. "Of course you will. You do."

Stu was off that day, so the three of us decided we should meet again for lunch. Four, counting Paula. (Danny was up in Chatham, at a gut rehab of an old ship-captain's house.)

I chose Baxter's, for its chowder, its view of the chilly harbor. Maybe, too, because it was a favorite of my mom's. This time Stu had no neurotic doubts about our plan.

Debora was waiting with Paula at the food-ordering counter. The girl was even prettier and more mature than in her picture. Graver, in her four-year-old's way, than her own mother. She shared Debora's up-and-at-'em shine.

"I bet I know who *this* is," I said, crouching down.

Paula glared with show-me impatience.

"Snoopy, right?"

She shook her head.

"You *look* like a Snoopy. Let's see, then. Hmm. Cleopatra?"

Paula's impatience devolved to forbearing condescension.

I hated feeling, every time I met a new child, that all my personal worthiness depended entirely on whether I could make that child smile. But I myself was guilty of judging others thus. The first time I took Stu to my sister Sally's house—her kids were then three and almost six—I had watched him walk inside, then drop onto his belly and enter the boys' bed-sheet fortress. Squealing with delight, the nephews dubbed him Stooby-Doo. And not till my shoulders fell did I know I'd been cringing—a whole-body clench of apprehension—thinking, *What if they don't like him? How could I love someone* they *don't love?*

"Wait, I know," I said to Paula now. "A new idea." I held a palm before her face. "Here. Punch me."

Paula flinched and drew away, stepping close to Debora. Stu flinched too, and fixed me with a scowl.

"Really. Hit my hand. I'm testing something."

Paula looked to her mother—for permission? Protection? Debora shrugged: *Your guess is as good as mine.*

I thought I had bungled things, but *zam!* A snake-quick strike.

"Ouch," I said. "That's good. One more time."

Nimbly, determinedly, Paula punched again. A tiny, tight fist with outsize force.

"*That's* it. I should've guessed. Pow," I said. "Pow. Now I know your name for sure. *Pow*-la."

Paula grinned, her tongue poking out between her teeth; it pulsed like a small, happy heart.

Debora smiled, too, and then I saw her shoulders fall. Had she been asking of me what I'd asked of Stu at Sally's?

Our food came: fish and chips and chowder all around. We took it to a table by the water. But Debora didn't eat; she was busy talking. She wanted to know everything, she said, about our lives. "*Everything.* Tell me. Please tell!"

"Everything? Gosh," I said. "Who knows where to start?"

"Okay, then—how you got to here."

Stu said, "You mean to Cape Cod? From New York?"

I could see him getting ready to talk about his sister's diagnosis and the previous Nadler traumas, the duty he felt to procreate, the Cape as family-friendly. What would he say about our other reasons for starting fresh? Nothing, of course. (Not to Debora, no.) But I would have liked to know the way he thought about it. *I had to save my marriage with Pat? I had to save myself?*

71

Debora said, "To here in *life* is what I want to know. I have a teacher—sorry, *had*; I still confuse my tenses—in Brazil, when I was still small. She says to me: Debora, there's three kinds of people. Those who run away *from* something. Those who run *to* something. And those who never even think to run."

I feared Stu might bristle at this near-stranger's presumption, but Debora, with her undulating voice, pulled it off. Plus, if anyone deserved to be presumptuous, it was she. She who'd grow our baby in her womb.

"Sorry," she said. "Too fast? My problem, Danny says." She made a tumbling motion with her hands. "Something smaller, then, okay?" she ventured. "Maybe jobs?" She turned to Stu. "A pilot. How exciting! To have these people's lives all in your hands—this must be hard. Or maybe it's the best part, no? To have these people trust you?"

"Well, no. I mean, sure, I guess . . ." Stu chewed on his thumb.

"You flustered him," I told her. "A feat that few have managed! Prize goes to Debora. Gold medal."

"*Me*," said Paula. "I should get a prize. Prize for Paula!" She beat her small fist against the table.

"Oh, pardon me," I said. "Of course. Please forgive me." I offered her my soupspoon. "*Plastic* medal to Paula." Gleefully she popped it in her mouth.

Debora said, "And your work also, Pat: responsibility."

"For me? Ha. No. Nothing quite so lofty."

"But people trust you. With their children. To teach them, make them better. This is why, I think, you really like it."

Normally I pooh-poohed my work (*Shrug*. "Pays the bills . . ."); no one dreams of being a *textbook* writer. Certainly not the younger me, who'd fancied himself a wordsmith: someone who would remake the world, a couplet at a time. But really, once I'd purged myself of all those arty airs, I *did* like my work—I felt it as a calling—for just the reasons Debora had surmised.

"What you said?" Stu told her. "I tell Pat all the time. I'm still trying to get it through his skull."

I had to give Stu credit for handling my writer self. Back when we had met, before I'd sloughed my fantasies, I confessed I hoped to be a poet. With roiling gut and seized-up throat, I managed to ask The Question: Would Stu read a couple of my sonnets? "I don't think so, no," he said. "Not the best idea." "You're scared you won't like them," I said, "right? Is that the problem? And then you won't be able to like *me*." Immediately I pictured just exactly how I'd dump him: in public, maybe, in front of all his friends? "Wrong," he said. "A thousand percent wrong. Will you listen? What if I read them now and I tell you I adore them? You'll (a) think I'm only *saying* I do because I love you; or, worse, (b) think I hadn't truly loved you without them. But Pat, I love you by yourself. With or without your poems. And *not* reading them's the only way to prove that. So yeah, I want to read them. Can't wait to. Will be thrilled to. But not until I'm sure you understand that I don't *need* to."

Eventually he did read them, and forced me to accept his admiration.

Still, I wasn't good at getting praise—from him, or Debora, her presence like a sudden burst of sun that makes you swoon. "Well," I said, "fine. People trust the *work* I do, without knowing, you know, I'm *me*." I made a quick, deprecating flourish near my face. "I mean, people are weird about their children."

Debora turned instinctively—and so did I—toward Paula, who rollicked in her seat, immune to our attention, conducting a silent song with her new spoon.

I said, "Sorry, Sweetpea. We boring you to tears?"

Now she looked up at me perplexedly, self-doubting. "I'm not crying, am I? Am I, Mãe?"

"No, no," said Debora. "You almost never cry."

Paula regained her confidence. "I'm *building*."

Indeed she was. With her French fries. An enclosure of sorts: stacking walls, Lincoln Logs style.

"Paula, stop," said Debora, firmly but not sharply. "In restaurants we have to act like big girls."

"But look, it's a house. For the fly. He hurt his wing."

Sure enough, in the center of her structure stood a fly, tracing slow lopsided loops. It buzzed like a gadget miswired.

Debora said, "Now, Paula . . ." (I sensed her weighing different tones: Disgust? Reproof? Admiration?) "It's nice of you, *querida*. But sorry, it's no good. The fly with one wing, she can't live."

"No, Mãe, it can. It can. I'll be *its* mãe." Turning from her mother, she looked at me pleadingly, as if I might vouch for her powers.

But Debora rose, ending the discussion. "Eating with your fingers, and touching a fly also? Now it's time, I think, to wash up."

Together, hand in hand, they headed for the restroom. Ashamedly I caught myself vetting them—their traits—the way someone shopping for a pedigreed pup would scrutinize the mama dog's teeth. Of Paula I was thinking: creative, persistent. Of Debora: even-keeled, attentive.

"Isn't she great?" I said to Stu.

"Paula, you mean? Or Debora?"

I felt like a raving groupie. "Both!"

"The way Danny talked," said Stu, "I thought she'd be a handful. Paula. You know, a real hellion."

"She seems perfectly sweet to me. If I had a kid as good as her, I'd—"

"Right," said Stu. "Which makes me still . . . but hey. Not complaining. Happy to borrow those genes, if they're offering." He nicked a fry from Debora's plate and downed it.

"Debora seems so . . . open," I said. "So forward, but in a good way. Maybe it's a Brazilian thing? Ipanema, bikinis . . ."

"Not her part of Brazil," said Stu. "Up there, I think they're cowboys."

"But still, all that sunshine? I Googled it: purest air in the world. Or second-purest—and that's according to NASA."

"Funny thing?" said Stu. "I didn't plan to like her."

"Oh. Oh, that's lovely. You planned to—what? *Dis*like our baby's mother?"

"*Our baby's mother*. Exactly. That was how I thought of her: how healthy she'd be, how fertile, how Jewish. Never thought to care what she'd be like as just herself."

The restroom door marked Gulls (its counterpart said Buoys) swung open, and Debora and her daughter bounded out. Paula, as she neared the table, broke into a trot, and I got set to catch her if she leapt. But no, she barreled past me. "Look," she called. "A boat!"

I was turning to look when the ferry's horn blasted; I felt the sound churning in my chest.

Paula, unfazed, honked back to the boat. "Baaaa," she sang. "Baaaa. Where will they sail, Mãe? To Brazil?"

Debora laughed. "Much too far. No. Just Martha's Vineyard. Want to go and see? Should I take you?" She indicated the door out to the deck.

"No," said Paula. "Him." She pointed at me, grinning.

My kingdom for a little girl's grin!

"Delighted to," I said. I reached for Paula's hand. Then, catching the flare of a jealous glance from Stu, I tried to quash the joy of being chosen. I opened the door. "Find us in a few."

At first Paula clung to me, startled by the salt air's slap. "Hey," I said, sheltering her, "it's okay. See the people?" A few hardy passengers, despite the day's chill, clustered on the ferry's top deck. "See? They're saying hi to you. Wave back!"

Paula, emboldened, wriggled from my grip and twirled a small dance of salutation.

"There you go," I said. "That's a big brave girl."

"Watch," she called. "Watch me." Now she struck a model's pose, arms shaped to match the ferry's prow.

I did watch, but what I saw was overlaid with memory: my mom and me (at Paula's age? no, a few years older), one summer, riding the Vineyard boat.

Why were we, the two of us alone, on the ferry? I had heard her offering a reason to my dad: something about a species to be seen in

Chappaquiddick, a juvenile something-or-other. Mom had been a teacher—junior high biology—but stopped working after she got pregnant. Less because she could than because she couldn't not: what would all the other wives in Newtonville have said? Now, with the three of us kids safely out of diapers, she had found new outlets for her passion: secretary of the Sandy Neck Preservation League, organizer of weekend walks for birders down from Boston.

But where were her binoculars today, her battered field guide? She'd brought only her sunglasses. Her son.

"Oh," she said when I asked her. "Oh, Pat. I'm so sorry."

Sorry for what? What did I care? Birds were only birds.

"I told him," she said, and squeezed my hand. "I told him this was crazy, bringing you."

"*Dad* told you to bring me?"

"No, honey. Not him. You couldn't . . . you're too young to get it."

I didn't get it—not yet—but still, my backbone shrank.

At the Oak Bluffs terminal I stood to disembark, but Mom took my palm again. "No," she said. "No, let's just go home."

And so we sailed back, across the torpid sea.

Why on earth, if she had planned a lover's tryst, bring me? As cover, was the easy answer. To head off Dad's suspicion, making me a pawn in her deception.

Today, though, braced against the same stinging breeze, gearing up to have my own child, I could finally understand the opposite possibility: maybe she had brought me so she *wouldn't* take the risk—a grapnel that would keep her tied to home. Maybe that was part of why she'd had us kids, to start with.

Funny: all my life, I'd been bent on blazing a different path, but maybe, in the end, I followed in her footsteps. Did Debora's old teacher's scheme allow for this exception? Someone who ran away from things but also, in that running, turned back?

Debora herself had run—had *sprinted*—from her past, but now seemed to be her world's still point: the gravity that held Paula close.

Jesus Christ. *Paula.* Where was she?

I whipped around but didn't see her. Shit. My knees went soggy. Scanning left, then right—still nothing. And so I turned, with terrible cold logic, to the water, looking for some sign of aftermath.

That's when I heard, "Hey. *Hey!* Get away from me."

I traced the words to Paula, who crouched beneath a table, guarding something (crumbs?) from a seagull.

"Stop!" I yelled, and stomped, charging at the bird, happy to blame something but myself. The gull wryly flapped away, and I grabbed hold of Paula, not sure if I'd rather stroke or shake her.

"I thought," she said. "I thought . . . I wanted to feed him."

Her voice brimmed with fear and disillusion: why would any creature she'd been helping turn against her? I felt for her, for any child who sees its faith dethroned.

"Stupid, mean old bird," I said. "Let's go feed the ducks. They're nicer, 'kay? Not scary. I promise."

"Ducks?" she said, grasping at a lifeline.

"When I was little, my sisters and I would each choose ducks," I told her. "A contest: whose could catch the most crumbs."

Together, on our knees, we gathered up her bait, inching our way over to the railing. And there we sat, tossing fried batter to stubby birds (whose yips sounded much the same as Paula's), when Debora came bursting through the door.

"What are you two doing? You think I can't see?"

Quickly I cleared my fists, and stripped Paula's too, as if empty hands would acquit us. "Sorry," I said. "Don't worry, we'll wash up."

Debora ignored me. "I see," she said. "I see! You are *trolling.*" Now her voice was jovial. A smile snuck up her cheeks. "Well, not exactly—a fishing line, you need. But didn't I say? I said you wouldn't have to."

"Trolling?" I said. "But I thought . . . now, wait. You *know* that word?"

Debora knelt and hugged her beaming daughter from behind. She took a piece of batter from the handful I had dropped, and flung it to a happy, wagging duck.

"Look, Māinha—look!" Paula cheered. "It says thank you."

"Yes, *minha filha*. Like I say thanks for you." Then to me, playfully: "You think I'm dumb? My English? But Pat, *you* use the Internet. *I* can use it too. Dictionary.com—I looked it up."

I chuckled, basking in a coursing, clean relief. I was humming with Debora's words—*Internetchy, tchoo*—the weird, rousing cadence of her accent, thinking of a lucky child within her womb, who'd hear it. Life would seem a splendid lilt. A song.

eight

A doctor poked at Debora, her blood was drawn and tested, she suffered a psychologist's questions. A private investigator snooped through old records for signs of a criminal background.

Fine, everyone said. Full speed ahead.

Stu was also tested, his sperm count and motility. Nothing off the charts, but good enough.

Through it all, we took to phoning Debora every night, giddily gleaning knowledge of her life. She loathed milk but loved milk shakes; sunlight made her sneezy; *Cinderella*'s ending always left her partly sad ("Why nobody talks about the mice and rats and lizards, who have to be again the things they were?"). We spoke with Danny, too, when he was the one who answered, and sometimes he indulged our little quizzes: What's the thing you're proudest of? "Never raised a hand to anyone." Most ashamed of? "How often I still want to."

By the time we convened to endorse the legal papers, our friendship, we assured ourselves, didn't feel like business—which made it both less and more awkward when the lawyer reviewed each clause about what, precisely, Stu and I would pay for. Above the twenty thousand bucks for Debora's basic fee, we would foot for life insurance, medical visits, maternity clothes, maid service if she were put on bed rest. For pregnancy-related trips Debora made in her own car: forty-three and a half cents per mile. Lost wages for Danny if he missed work for the birth. If Debora's tubes got damaged? Five thousand.

Down the list the lawyer went—this, that, the other—adding to the sum we'd keep in escrow. The word sounded enough like *escargot* that I saw snails: nautili with endless extra chambers.

The lawyer wore a suit that sat queerly on her frame; her neck puffed soufflé-like from her collar. I sensed she would rather have been shagging outfield flies, chugging Bud, cheered on by her wife. (Well, not now, of course, not in January.) But here she was, all trussed up to fit in with her office, whose furniture was elegant but fussily unpretentious, every table expensively defaced with little dings. I liked her, though: the way she said, "Call me Kris—or, hell, K.C."; and how, when she thought we wouldn't notice, she kicked her pumps off.

Danny was the one who seemed unsure of how to take her. Walking in, he'd faltered when she rose to shake his hand, and then, on recovering, shook it overeagerly, clapping her arm, as though she were a frat boy. Since then he'd maybe said ten words.

My condescending, descended-from-Pilgrims mind read things this way: a simple tradesman humbled in the face of Mighty Law. Mustn't that explain, I thought, his self-protective hunch? He clicked and un-clicked a ballpoint pen.

"Relax," I whispered, recalling how he'd calmed me at the Pancake King. "Lawyers are just like us but overpaid. She won't bite."

K.C., who I hadn't thought could hear, said, "Yeah? Bite *this*," then let rip with a mischief-maker's laugh. Using the collective slack-jawed silence she had bought herself, she said, "So, then: mind if I continue with the contract? Next we come to all of Debora's can'ts."

Can't smoke, drink, take drugs.
Can't play unsafe sports.
Can't expose yourself to radiation.

"Wait," I said, taking inspiration from K.C.'s irreverence. "How about 'can't expose yourself'—full stop?"

"Patrick," said Stu. "For crying out—"

"Oh, now. Grow a funny bone."

His eyes, like two rifle bores, took aim.

I should have said "I'm sorry," or kept my big mouth shut, but I could have the tendency, when nervous, to entrench. "Doesn't this seem, to say the least, a little nuts?" I said.

Danny spun his pen, a compass in a storm. Debora looked demurely toward the ground.

"Didn't we say," I added, "—just now, earlier, didn't we?—how nice it was this didn't feel like business?"

"Oh," said K.C., "but it *is*, Pat. For everyone's sake, it has to be. You have to think of the worst—that's what *I'm* for."

Stu smiled a snappy little smile of vindication; the lawyer had just summarized his worldview.

"So," said K.C., "moving right along . . . I know the guys have told you of their hope you'll stay involved, as long as you want, after the baby's born. But I must point out, contractually, you'll have no *legal* claim . . ."

Debora nodded, and nodded again, as serious as a girl playing grownup. It dawned on me that she had said the least during this meeting—even less, I thought, than clammed-up Danny. Cold feet? Displeasure with the contract? Or maybe Danny's jitters had a dampening effect. Where was the jocular Debora who at Baxter's had so wowed us?

". . . and no rights of custody," K.C. added.

"Fine," said Danny, after which he left an edgy pause, his eyes like small skittery creatures, caged. "But what about financial responsibility?"

"I think we mostly addressed that, didn't we?" said K.C. "Any expense related to the pregnancy, they'll cover; plus we've got the what-if fees, for injury or for—"

"No," he said. "Us, is what I meant. Are we responsible? I mean, let's say—think of the worst, right?—let's say something awful happens to them, but the baby lives. We wouldn't be responsible, then, would we? You know, financially?"

"Oh, gosh, no. Pat and Stu will make their own contingencies. None of the rights or the responsibilities of parenting will be yours."

"Oh!" said Danny. "Okay, then"—and *flash*, his mood changed hue. "Truly sorry, guys," he said.

"Sorry?" said Stu. "For what?"

"Well, for, you know, picturing your doom."

"Ha!" I said. "Don't you think I'm used to that, from Stu?"

At last I got some laughs, even if just polite ones.

Danny promised, from here on out, his thoughts would all be sunny.

"Actually, Danny, to go back to your worries," said K.C., "*you* don't really have much of a legal role at all. The contract is between them and Debora."

"Obviously, though," Stu rushed to say, "we want you to approve of it. We can't do this unless you're both onboard."

"It's not as if it doesn't affect you," I said.

"Who, me?" said Danny.

"But seriously," I went on. "You've read the fine print?" I figured he would know the worst clause.

Danny laid his big hands, like offerings, on the contract. His hands that could rip the thing in two.

Mention surrogacy and most people said, "My God, why do they do it?"—the *they* being the women who got pregnant. The closer we came to the process, though, the *they* who vexed me even more were the husbands. After all, agree or not with the reasons surros gave, they did have reasons, clearly stated, that followed a certain logic. Like Debora, when she'd told us we were giving her a gift: *The gift of being who I'm supposed to.* The husbands, though—what did they get? Nothing, as far as I saw. Sure, there was the money, which might be viewed as gravy, since men did none of the procreative work. But Danny had said it wasn't that, and I didn't disbelieve him; he never got that *ka-ching* in his smile you see with greedy people.

And really, the money was paltry when you thought of the disruptions, most of which affected the husband, too. Say the surro had morning sickness. Who'd mop the puke? The husband. And who, when the surro was too tired to handle stairs, would have to haul the trash out and fold the loads of laundry? Who would bathe the child they had already?

On top of it all, the biggest hitch, the fine print I had cited: the mate's loss of rights to, well, *mate*. The contract said that Debora couldn't sleep with any man—including Danny—till after the surrogate pregnancy was confirmed. Nor could she "engage in any action" (went the legalese) that might "introduce semen into her body."

As I said, if Danny had to miss a day of work, we'd agreed to make up for his pay. But how would we ever compensate for weeks and months of what I'd come to think of as his "marital lost wages"?

Who was I to question why a man would let his sex life slump in deference to his spouse's separate yearnings? How many hours had I stayed home alone while Stu had fun?

Perhaps that comparison was a little bit Swiss cheesy. Still, I couldn't help but think that Danny and I were similar. Was that why I so badly wanted to *solve* him?

The week before, I'd e-mailed Zack and asked for his experience: had his and Glenn's surro's husband made *his* motives clear? *Shelly's husband was squeamish at first*, wrote Zack. *He's Special Forces. Thought it "unmanly" to let his wife have someone else's baby. But then he got called up, to go and get bin Laden, and, weirdly, that made everything go smoother. "Here I'm heading off," he said, "to do this risky job, asking Shelly to sacrifice without me. Least I can do, I guess, is support her." Maybe your surro's husband has a similar kind of reason. Learn to accept sincerity from strange sources!*

But Danny, if he felt obliged to sacrifice for Debora, didn't feel obliged to share the reason. Sitting there, in the lawyer's office, hands atop the contract, this was how he finally talked of forfeiting his sex life: "Hell," he said. "You guys have been together, what, ten years?"

"Twelve next fall," said Stu. "Knock on wood."

"Then you know how things are. Let's just say it's not as, well . . . as frequent an issue, these days."

Danny tried to leaven the jab by poking Debora's ribs—an affable little nudge, all in jest—but Debora bolted upright in her chair.

And here I went, entrenching myself again to fight off tension, spewing forth a hammy-humor smoke screen. "Hold on—whoa! You're saying that *straights* are prone to lesbian bed death? Oops—no offense," I added, addressing K.C. directly.

The lawyer rolled her eyes. "Forget it. None taken. How does that old saying go? We're all the same except for what we do *outside* the bedroom?"

"Well," said Danny, "that's a bit of . . . I don't know about *that*."

Debora grabbed the contract from beneath his splayed hands. She looked less hurt or angry than *resolved*. This was how she'd looked when she was eighteen, I supposed: boarding the bus, her mother calling "Crazy!" at her back.

"Here?" said Debora. "Or here?" She tapped two different blanks. "Show me where's the place to write my name."

I saw Debora a few more times, always during the day—just "us wives," plus Paula, since Danny and Stu were working. Mostly we did errands, whatever was on her list: Reebok outlet, Job Lot, Staples, Sears. For lunch we'd stop at Friendly's, for hot dogs on grilled buns. I wasn't sure I'd ever felt so wholesome.

Working as a freelancer, making my own hours, I could've mixed routinely with my fellow non-nine-to-fivers. Actually, though, I tended to take "work at home" quite literally, and almost never ventured into town ahead of dusk, when no one much seemed to be about. How strange, then, to see the place aswarm with moms and kids. (I thought of sixth-grade science, the shock of seeing a drop of water beneath a microscope: all those bubbly, zipping protozoa.)

I found this moms' world mesmerizing and wanted to decode it. Debora and the other women beamed at one another, trading grins that waterfalled with mutual understanding, but I could rarely tell if they were personally acquainted or simply bonding based on common lots. Occasionally a man, a one-line movie walk-on, would join the scene and, just as quickly, vanish. A stockroom clerk, a road-crew lackey sent to get the doughnuts. But mostly, in the guy department, I was the attraction: a family man (or so thought countless strangers) *doing my part*; I grew accustomed to looks of commendation. Debora also got her share of looks, bleary with envy, from solo moms attempting to corral their rowdy offspring, while also holding a pocketbook, a diaper bag, a basket . . .

"Isn't it sweet," said one lady, who stopped me at the Job Lot, when Debora had gone to browse the canned-goods aisle. "To see a family together. A husband who participates! I'd hug you, but . . ." She lifted her arms, laden with discount spices.

The old activist part of me was tempted to give a lecture: "Actually, I'm not the dad, I've got my own husband, and soon we're going to have our own baby." Technically speaking, though, Stu was not my husband; and now that, in Massachusetts, same-sex couples could marry, using the word was maybe insincere. Still and all, I could have simply—civilly—corrected her.

Was it a terrible thing that I loved the lady's mistake? I loved the little Pop Rocks burst of pride that it provoked.

"My, what a cutie pie. How old?" asked a checkout clerk at Sears, as I patty-caked with Paula. (Debora was in the fitting room, trying on crew-neck sweaters.)

"Four," I said.

"Oh! My grandson just turned four. Aren't they just a wonder at that age—such curiosity." The woman's rawhide face appeared to flush with camaraderie. Even her smoker's greasy eyes grew spirited and clear.

"Yes," I said. "You'd think she only knows two words: *How come?*"

That was true. Nothing at all untrue.

And so what if the clerk assumed my knowledge was a father's? I asked myself: Really, who gets harmed?

Stu, when I told him what had happened, made a squinchy face, something between amused and appalled. "Why do you get off," he said, "on being an impostor?"

"Hey, isn't that a little harsh? I mean, 'impostor'?"

"Well," he said, "pretending to be something that you're not."

"Something I'm not *yet*. But will be, right? Am meant to be? I guess I figured: couldn't hurt to practice."

Stu was changing light bulbs in the kitchen's recessed fixtures, swapping out the old electron-guzzlers for fluorescents. He stepped down from his stool, got a bulb, stepped back up. "It's good you're psyched, but aren't you, maybe, a little over the top?" he said. "At least for the stage of things we're at. You seem a little—what's the word?—hysterical."

"Careful," I said. I grabbed a bulb. "There's places I could shove this. 'Hysterical'?—that's misogynist, you know. You shouldn't say that."

"How can I be misogynist to *you*? You're a man."

"Doesn't *hyster*, or *hystera*, or something like that, mean *womb*? As in, you know, a doctor cuts it out: *hysterectomy*. So saying I'm 'hysterical' literally means I'm getting *womby*. Fine with me! A badge I'll wear with pride."

"Suit yourself," he said, and gestured for me to flip the switch, to see if the new light bulbs were working.

Nothing at first. But warily, then, withholdingly, they glowed.

Was Stu less excited than I? I didn't want to think so. I guessed he was focused on the *task* of having a baby, the technical steps to get from here to there. Save up cash, hire an expert, oversee the setup—an improvement, like adding on a deck. I, on the other hand, was woozy with emotion, thinking ahead to how I'd feel in various situations (what if there were a stillbirth? what if we had twins?), and how, then, would Stu feel, and Debora, how would we cope?

Okay, well, maybe I *was* hysterical.

But I had so many questions; I wanted to get things right. And every hour with Debora, I wondered if she judged me, waiting for a greenhorn's goof that proved I wasn't worthy.

The day after I talked to Stu I saw her again, with Paula. We were already at Toys"R"Us when Debora confessed our purpose: Paula's tiara had fallen into the bathtub and been wrecked, and now she needed a new one for her endless game of "princess," her ardent search for princely frogs to kiss.

I didn't mean to make an icky face when Debora said this, admitting she allowed the girl's obsession. I must have, though, given how quickly Debora got defensive.

"I try and try to get her wearing something else," she said. "A baseball cap, a sailor hat—something not so 'girl.'" Longingly, she touched a box of Aquaman apparel. "But girls, I think, sometimes they *are* girls. It's what they are."

"Wait," I said. "You don't think I . . . I wasn't criticizing."

"Come on, Pat. I saw the way you looked."

"But no, it's not *your* choices I'm worried about. It's mine."

This was true: I had no beef with Paula's girly conformity or with Debora for abiding the cliché. (Most of the real-life girls I knew were plenty princess-centric. The girls obsessed with quarterbacks, or big-game hunters, or pick-your-quirk were mostly just the ones in children's books.) No, what I was struggling with were questions about myself. How the hell would *I* teach gender roles?

"Listen, how can I win?" I said. "Let's say I have a daughter, and let's say she's just crazy for tiaras. My gay friends will laugh at me and say I'm only using her to live out all my secret faggy dreams. Or worse, they'll be mad at me—especially the lesbians—for reinforcing cultural expectations. But what if I refuse to buy tiaras for my daughter, and raise her as some kind of tomboy butch? Then I'll be accused of . . . of recruiting."

Debora inhaled. "I never thought of this. But yes, I see."

"Right?" I said. "Right? Okay, now, imagine me with a tiara-loving *son!*"

Oh, how Debora laughed. A sound like scattered beads. Laughed and laughed, then touched me on the cheek. "And I thought you were watching me with Paula," she revealed. "Watching to see if I would pass the test. A man from New York, you know. So stylish, so intelligent. Also your job: you write tests for a living!"

"Never crossed my mind," I said, "to fault you for your parenting. The way you are with Paula? It's a marvel. No, I thought you'd think that *I* was clueless."

Poof! Like a candle lit to cancel out a stink, honesty made our fears go up in smoke.

Later, riding home in my emphysemic Volvo, with Paula and her favorite frilly Barbie in the back, Debora turned and leaned to me and whispered: "Pat, I wonder. We get along so well now. What do you think of doing it ourselves?"

My breath caught. What did she mean by "it"? I said, "Ourselves?"

"This is a bad idea?" she said. "Maybe it is. I'm sorry."

"No, it's just"—my voice was thin—"I'm not sure what you're saying."

"Making the baby," she said. "Maybe it's better at home?"

"Oh! Oh, I see now. At home? Really? You'd want to?"

The thing was, she said, she'd started to imagine: lying in a doctor's room, on one of those awful tables, the cold, crinkly paper they rolled out (it made her feel like a flounder that the fish man would wrap up). Lying there, her feet up in the stirrups, with a stranger. "This is not the way to make a baby," she said. "Is it?"

"Mãe, what's a stirrups?" called Paula from her car seat.

How had she managed to hear us, above the rasping muffler? Debora nudged my thigh with incredulity.

"What is it, Mãinha? And how come you are whispering?"

"Stirrups is a grown-up word. It's something at the doctor's."

"Like lollipops? I like when Dr. Li gives me lollipops."

"No, *filha*. It's something doctors use to help them check you."

My hat was off to Debora for such head-on, honest answers— simplified but not at all deceitful. I wondered what she'd told Paula about me and Stu, and why we were spending time together. How would Debora explain when she got bigger- and bigger-bellied, and later, when we whisked the child away? Paula would be the baby's—what? Her half-surro-sister? How would we expect them to relate?

Debora turned and touched the tip of Paula's nose, anointing. "That's enough, now. Māinha needs to talk with Pat, okay? Play with Barbie. I think she seems alone."

Paula, looking pained—had she been called neglectful?—cuddled the doll and murmured near its mouth.

"I've been reading," said Debora to me, her voice now even lower. "And asking the women on Surromoms, you know? Everyone says it's more nice, if you have two good IPs, to do insems yourselves: more relaxed." She told me about a woman named Felicia ("Four times a surro"), who'd done both in-clinic and at-home. "The doctor, he took three tries, but at home? First time was charming."

Debora's English: talk about charming!

Cheaper, too, she said, if insems were done at home. IUI was four hundred dollars, easy, maybe five. Plus another hundred for the washing of the sperm, a hundred or two more for ultrasound. All of this for one in-clinic try that might still fail.

"The most important thing isn't the money," I insisted. "It's making you as comfortable as possible. You and Danny."

"I think he'll like this better, too. Like this, he can be part of it. And not so many strangers with their fingers on his wife."

"I can't argue with that," I said. "Just let me check with Stu."

Before that, though, I figured I had better check with Marcie, my go-to friend for all things gynecological.

"Took you long enough," she said. "I thought you'd never ask."

"Didn't want to impose," I said.

"Impose? Are you kidding? Asking a lesbian mom for tips on home insemination?"

89

How I'd missed her banging, mannish laugh!

The dykes had been DIYing for years, she assured me. Didn't I know that that's how she and Erin conceived Randall? Medically it was fine; politically it was preferable: "Not relying on the heteronormative system, yadda yadda. Just sit tight. I'll send you all you need."

Four days later her parcel arrived, its gifts flagged with Post-it annotations: bottles of zinc and vitamin E ("To make Stu's swimmers strong"); an ovulation predictor kit and needleless syringes ("Better than a turkey baster, trust me"); and then a strange device called an Instead Cup. "Sort of like a little plastic toque," said Marcie's note. "An alternative to tampons—at least that's what they're sold for. Fitted around the cervix as a way to catch the blood. The secret is, they work just as well to hold in *semen*. Watch the website video. You'll catch on."

Finally, at the bottom of the box, a spine-worn book: *No Penis? No Problem: The Compleat Guide to Home Insemination*. "Patriarchy is a towering wall," its cover blurb proclaimed, "but here's new light for readers—heterosexual and lesbian—who've had enough of living in its shadow."

Our problem wasn't a lack of penises; we probably had too many. But I supposed the book's advice would still provide some aid. It even had some old *Joy of Sex*–style pencil drawings, to help us picture Debora's undertaking. I planned to read it front to back, mustering all my data—the cost savings, the odds of successful fertilization—and then present the possibility to Stu.

But Stu came home early ("De-icer malfunction. Grounded"), and there I was in the living room, my nose buried in *No Penis? No Problem*.

"Um," said Stu. "Pat? Have you had some sort of accident?"

No, I assured him, I was still *all there*. Then, even though the case I'd make was unperfected, I began explaining our idea.

I figured he'd be skeptical, maybe even pissed. Why would I have talked to Marcie before I talked to him, and what was I doing, tinkering with our plan? But Stu said he'd wondered, too, about the at-home option. Given the way fertility docs had trampled over Rina, he wasn't eager to face the men in lab coats. So yeah, sure, if Debora herself preferred to do it that way . . .

"Really? You're not mad?" I said.

"Why would I be mad? You've been so good, doing all your homework."

If anything, he seemed almost impressed that I'd arranged this, as though, in the baby bazaar, I'd bargained for a discount. He seemed happy that Debora would be happy.

I guessed I should have emphasized that *she* had been the instigator. None of the credit fairly belonged to me. But Stu was so appreciative. He kissed me on the eyelids! I didn't see the upside of explaining.

nine

When the phone rang, a cold afternoon a few weeks later, I was watching the daily White House briefing on C-SPAN. *End the death tax. Enemy combatants.* A horror show, but soothing—in fact, the only soothing thing on days, like today, when I was steamed: a headbutt to a wall to cure a headache.

The thing that had me steamed was a spat with Steve, my editor, and his was the phone call I'd been dreading. I'd written a new lesson, on Marranos in Brazil, the ways they'd survived the Inquisition: their secret rites and prohibitions—no kneeling in church, no pork—the doggedness of Debora's brave forebears.

Steve's response? *Anti-Christian. Will never get through Texas.*

I hated his way, in e-mails, of leaving out the subjects of his sentences, as if he were too busy. *Baloney*, I shot back. How was it anti-*anything* to describe one group's strength in the face of unflagging persecution? Would it be "anti-white" to mention, say, the Underground Railroad? Should *those* facts be stricken from the books?

Not arguing facts, he typed. *Just warning you: won't fly. School board's very touchy about religion.*

I wrote back: *As touchy as they'll be if they discover that an open homosexual writes their books?*

92

My threat (an idle one; I needed to keep my job) provoked no return message from Steve. Which usually was the clue that he'd be calling.

I muted the White House fright show, and scuffled toward the phone. Steeled myself. Picked up the receiver.

"I searched," said Debora.

"Oh!" I said. "So happy that it's *you*." By now I was used to her zero-to-sixty style. Used to it but still, each time, enamored. "Searched?" I said. "Hold on. Searched for what?"

"No, no. Not searched," she said. "*Surged*."

"But wait, you weren't supposed to—"

"I know. But, well . . . I did."

According to the predictor kit, the daily temperatures charted, we'd thought *tomorrow* was the start of ovulation. We were supposed to have another day!

"Maybe I was making errors, using the kit," she said. "But now I looked another time: the second line, it's dark."

"Okay, then," I said. "Fine. I mean—great!" Blood pulsed on both sides of my throat. "Stu's not here. He's, I don't know, probably over Cleveland. He gets home at sevenish, I think." I felt dipsy, boundless, as though I'd guzzled gin straight from the jug. "I'll call the Saltwinds and see if they can bump us to tonight. Shouldn't be a problem, it's off-season."

The Saltwinds was the B&B where we held reservations, the result of a careful compromise. After we had all agreed to do insems at home— pleased for having hit upon this plan—only then did someone think to ask: At home, but *whose*? Ours, we had assumed. But they'd assumed theirs. Each side made a credible claim to reason: Shouldn't the baby, being ours, be made in our own house? Yes, but if one goal of DIY was Debora's comfort, shouldn't the deed be done in Debora's bed?

Before the tiff could escalate, Stu got all rabbinic and devised a way to thread the quarrel's needle. What we'd do was book adjacent rooms within a guesthouse. Neutral turf for all of us, a break from our routines. Comfy, yes, but special, too. A treat.

So now I had to phone the place and change our reservation. The thought of having a doable chore relaxed me.

"But Pat," said Debora. *Patch.* "Today it's Valentine's."

"Oh, good God, of course it is. And I didn't buy a gift. You think the B&B is . . . are we screwed?"

"That, but also: Danny was supposed to take me out. I think he has a table at Abbicci."

"Crap," I said. "Hold on. Call you back."

The Saltwinds had no vacancies, and nowhere else did, either. Not even the Days Inn in Hyannis. Lovers, I imagined, in every room.

I told Debora; we sat in foggy silence.

"Wait until tomorrow?" she said. "Maybe that's not too late. We don't want to wait another *month*, I don't think."

"A month?" I said. "Absolutely not."

I made an executive decision, which stemmed in part from guilt—I rued the thought of wrecking her and Danny's evening plans—but mostly just from sheer pragmatism. I would go to the airport and be waiting when Stu landed, and then we'd hustle straight to Debora's house. (Compromise be damned: we'd do this on her turf.) We'd be finished, with any luck, by nine, nine-thirty—in time for Debora and Danny to go out. By that hour, even tonight, they wouldn't need a booking.

"Sound okay to you?" I asked.

"Yes, if you are sure. Will Stu be angry?"

"No," I said. "Or, well, not at you."

At the airport I waited for Stu's plane to land, and waited. All the while I babied the dozen roses I had bought him. I paced and paced, left to right to left.

The monitor said nineteen minutes more.

Through the plate-glass windows I could see the runway traffic—a Cape Air flight to Nantucket; a pristine, private Lear—but couldn't make the clock speed up, or make the next plane his.

Watch and wait, was all. Watch and wait.

The screenlike separation, the idleness, the impotence . . . this was how I'd felt the time (I'd tried to kill the memory) when Stu almost couldn't land his plane.

We were still New Yorkers then. Mired in our old lives. Stu was in his bingeing phase, and I had started doubting: Was he the man with whom I'd someday hope to raise a kid? Should I go looking for someone else? And/or a different *self*?

I was at home, watching the news, and rose to crack a window: the first warm evening of the spring. When I sat down again, the screen now showed a jet. An anchorwoman's bossy, breathy voice was reassuring us: ". . . not, repeat *not*, an act of terrorism. Only an equipment malfunction." A relief to the public. But to the passengers? The pilot? If they died, would their deaths, due "only" to a failure of the landing gear, be any less deadly? If Stu were ever to crash, I thought—if Stu were on this flight—I would be more focused on the end than on the means. If Stu were . . .

I buried the question: *Is* he?

The anchorwoman appeared again, bearing further news: US Air flight 246, originating in D.C. It would attempt to land at LaGuardia.

I'd worked so hard learning to dismiss this possibility that all I could do, at first, was keep watching. I thought about the ethics of broadcasting disaster. The previous month, the Pentagon had tightened prohibitions on documenting servicemembers' coffins. (Generals spent the soldiers' lives like stacks of poker chips. But let us see their flag-draped caskets? No.) But this—a faulty plane, innocent folks at risk, a tragedy truly not fit for viewing—*this* would be shown on live TV.

I planned how I'd carp about it to Stu when he came home. But then, panic: What if Stu would never now come home? What if there were no Stu to carp to?

I bolted to the kitchen, where Stu, before leaving, posted each day's schedule on the fridge. He always used the same campy magnet— I ♥ Goyim—and sometimes scrawled a message in the margin. Today's read: *Don't worry about the garbage. I took care of it.*

There it was, his day's last flight, DCA to LGA. I zoomed in on the number: 246.

The next minutes passed in a hyperreal fever, my proxy life vivid on the screen (alarm lights, sirens), my life at home (couch, clicker) fraudulently calm. Rescue trucks and ambulances raced into position, commentators spoke of likely outcomes: *Fiery skid. Secondary blast.* At the terminal: an FAA spokesman, a priest. "A priest?" I could hear Stu say. "The ultimate indignity! Even in death, we Jews get short shrift."

Where would all Stu's outrage go, his melancholy humor? All his Stu-ness—where?

Fiery skid.

But then, in an instant, it was done: a gasp; applause.

Soon the doors broke open, emergency slides inflated, shoeless passengers sluiced out to safety. "Thank God," said the anchor, "for that pilot."

Yes, I thought. Thank God. Thank God.

As I said, those were the days when I had started doubting (maybe if I wanted kids, Stu was not the man for me; could someone so intemperate be a father?). But now, having watched him almost disappear for good, I saw beneath the rubble of my doubts. Maybe he wouldn't make the most assiduous father ever. But I didn't just want a child *with* Stu, I wanted a child *of* Stu's. I longed for this because a child of Stu's would spawn more Stu-ness. A further bit of him within the world.

Stu, who took care of all the garbage.

"Please," I said, when finally he came home and hugged me close. "Seriously, Stu. Don't ever scare me like that."

"Shh, okay? I'm here," he said. "I'm not going anywhere."

All that night: *I'm here I'm here I'm here.*

At *their* place?" said Stu. "But no. I don't want to!"

Striding through the gate just now, engrossed in his own thoughts, he had looked so handsome and august. His polished, brass-latched briefcase, his cap, his epaulets. Then, when he laid eyes on me and the dozen red roses, I saw his pleasure fighting with suspicion.

"What about the Saltwinds?" he said. He clonked his briefcase down. "Come on, Pat. I thought we'd worked this out."

I filled him in on Debora's early surge, the booked hotels. "Happy Valentine's!" I held out the bouquet.

"But Pat, it's not . . . I mean, I'm sorry, no. But this just isn't—"

I could see him struggling with the need to fling some blame. Probably he wasn't pissed so much about the switched locales as about the subversion of his plan. About his being bypassed, overruled.

I told him it was my fault. I should have had a backup plan. Should have booked *two* nights, just in case.

My mea culpa soothed him. He sighed at length. He nodded.

"Great," I said. "Now quick. They're waiting, as we speak. They're still trying to salvage a date tonight."

But Stu turned and walked the wrong way, deeper into the airport.

"Wait," I said. "Stu. Where are you going?"

"We can do the insem at their place. Fine," he said. "Okay. But not *my* part. Not in their house, with everybody there."

"But they won't be 'there.' I mean, not in the room when you—of course not! Anyway, where else are you going do it?"

Stu marched three more strides, to a sign above a doorway. He pointed. Men.

I followed him in, coughing at the fake-fruit scent of cleanser. We stood before a gray, graffitied stall door. Stu said I should hand him the specimen cup.

"Please," I said. "Not here. Could it be any less romantic? This is a moment we'll always want to remember. This is our kid."

"You think I don't know?" he said. "That's why I can't do it in *their* house."

I looked into his dutiful eyes, so earnest and, yes, *dadlike* (their gravity, their seriousness of purpose), and now the scene seemed less unromantic.

"Kiss me," he said, just as he had on the way to the Pancake King.

He tasted of airline peanuts, a perfect match of honeyed sweet and salt.

"Guess I'll leave you to it?" I said.

His gaze, for an instant, wavered.

"Or I could stay. Right outside the door, here, yeah? You want me to?"

"I do," he said, as though this were a wedding.

Stu's hands were busy, warming the cup against his armpit's skin, so I reached up, around him, to the doorbell. I held the insem kit and also the rose bouquet, which Stu said should go to Debora, a consolation prize ("Not much of a Valentine's Day, right?"). The roses hadn't fared well in the Volvo heater's blast—we'd tried to keep the car at body temp—and now the wind shook their petals loose.

Tick tick tick went Stu's tapping feet. How long did sperm stay viable—half an hour?

I rang again. Peered in through the saltbox Cape's curtains: lights but no human silhouettes. I felt at ease with Debora now, and mostly so with Danny, but certainly not enough to just walk in, unescorted. And so we stood there waiting, ready to hand off (literally) our future.

"Come on," said Stu. "Come *on*."

Finally, *clack*, the knob was turned, and Debora opened the door, a red-eyed Paula saddled on one hip. "Sorry," she said. "Somebody's having one of those nights, you know?" She gave the girl a peck on her skull, which only made her thrash.

"Hand her to me?" a voice from behind suggested.

"Yes, that would—" Debora started, but Paula thrashed again. "Not just yet. Hold on, okay? Maybe in a minute. And oh," she said, "Pat and Stu? Our babysitter, Libby."

The young woman—plump on top, twiggy beneath the hips; the build I'd always called "egg with legs"—leaned around Debora with a wave.

Our hands were full. We smiled at her uncertainly. Wind whipped past us.

Freeing the cup from under all his layers, Stu said, "Here."

"Ah," said Debora, and went to take it, but Paula started flailing again, drubbing her heels against her mother's leg.

"Wait, let me," said Libby, intercepting. But then, as Stu called, "Actually—" and tried to grab it back, the sitter seemed to recognize the liquid. She shrank, pushed the cup away, tipping it to the brink.

I could picture, frame by frame, a slow-mo tragicomedy: semen like a seagull's spattered droppings on her sweatshirt, which claimed "I'm a Cape Cod Chowdah-Head."

But here came Debora's superhero hand to save the day. She caught the cup; everything was righted.

Libby said, "I guess I'll just," and flapped her palms laxly. She backed down the hallway, out of sight.

The turmoil, for the moment, had seemed to sidetrack Paula. I tried to take advantage of the lull. "Well, well, my old duck-feeding pal, how's it going?"

Paula pulled a halfhearted grimace.

"Pow," I said, boxing at the air around her shoulders; the kid now indulged me with a chortle. "There!" I cheered. "There's my little sweetpea."

Stu said, "Hey, where's Danny? I hope he's not mad."

"Mad?" said Debora.

"Valentine's. Having to push back dinner."

"No," she said, then added, "I think this makes him timid. Timid? No, wait—in English: shy."

"Oh," I said belatedly, lifting the bouquet, "for you. Because . . . just because."

"*Que lindo!* You're so thoughtful. But—" She noted her taken hands: the cup in one, Paula in the other. A smart before-and-after advertisement.

Danny came downstairs. "Right," he said. "How thoughtful. Here, hand them over, I'll take them." His bearing was the last thing but shy. In shorts and a singlet, his burly arms exposed, he looked like a football coach, ready to dole out insults.

Maybe we'd upstaged him: had Danny forgotten roses, or brought Debora a not-as-nice bouquet?

"Sorry about the mix-up," I said. "No one was expecting this."

Danny loomed above me, two steps from the bottom. "Nothing to do about it. Shit happens."

Stu seemed to sense the same tension I was sensing. "You know," he said, "I have to tell you, doing my part felt . . . *weird.* Your part'll be weird, too. Even weirder, I bet. I mean, actually doing the—you're fine? You can do it?"

"Who the hell else would I let—obviously, not *you* guys. Ha!" said Danny. "Ha! Ha!"

I told myself: that's just how he laughs.

"I'll go put the flowers away," he said, and climbed the stairs.

"Nervous," said Debora softly.

"I heard!" he called. "Am not!"

She waited a beat, and then she whispered, "Is."

"Hell," I told her, "I am too, and *I'm* not even doing this." Indeed, I was starting to feel shaky, out of breath, as if jitters were solid things that cluttered up my lungs.

"Hate to be pushy," Stu interjected. "But sperm have a pretty short shelf life."

Debora nodded, then summoned Libby to put Paula to bed.

Paula didn't want to go; she clung to Debora, rigid. Libby had to peel her off, finger after finger. "How about your Dora doll?" she tried. "Sleep with dolly?"

Paula cut a glance at Debora, withering, aggrieved. "But Mãe, you said . . . you *promised . . .*" Her voice trailed off to nothing.

What was the promise? It didn't really matter. Only the primal promise from a parent truly counted, the one that went: *I'll always be here for you.* Didn't all parents, inherently—impossibly—make that pledge?

The girl, defeated at last, let herself be hauled away, ignoring all the kisses Debora blew her.

"She hates to be left out," said Debora. "A little like her mother."

"Just your luck," said Stu, "'cause this is yours to fly now. Pat, give her the kit. Get this rolling."

"Right, well, okay," I said, snapping into motion. "This here's the syringe; it's obvious how to use it. And here's that thing for later, the Instead Cup—you watched the video? More of a cartoon, I guess. They can't actually *show* the way you—"

"Patrick," said Stu. "Seriously."

"Relax," said Debora. "Everything will be fine." She did something twinkly with her eyes. "Have some drinks, maybe. Sit down in the living room. I'll send Danny to get you when we're done."

"Is he going to—" Stu paused. The tips of his ears colored. "Is Danny going to help you . . . to finish?"

"Sure," she said. "I'm clumsy. 'Only thumbs,' he tells me. But Danny—he's so good with his hands."

"But what I meant . . . the chance of getting pregnant, isn't it better? If the woman has—if her muscles, you know, contract?"

Now it was Debora's turn to blush. "I told you. He's very good with his hands."

She playacted a shiver—or wasn't she playacting?—and I shivered too, full of envy. (Envy of her? Of Danny? I wasn't sure.)

"So," she said. "All set? Good. Give me kisses."

We kissed her cheeks, right then left; she trotted up the stairs, showing us the back of her old jeans: a faded star sewn on each pocket.

The living room was strewn with Paula's projects: glue and glitter, a tiny loom strung with colored beads. Photos on the mantel depicted Debora and Danny's wedding, Paula's birth, not a whole lot since. A book was splayed on the couch: *O Alquimista.*

I bent to study a homemade-looking but cleverly built dollhouse, split into differently styled halves: on the left, a modern scene, as bright as the room we stood in; on the right, a more agrarian past (miniature straw baskets, hewn beams). The dolls on the right had coffee-tinted faces, the color of Debora's smooth skin.

Not just *a* past, it occurred to me. *Her* past. The cashew farm in Rio Grande do Norte.

My throat tightened—a swelling of esteem mixed with pity—to think of her so distant from the childhood she had known, forging her own singular, strange life. Then I turned this mournful admiration toward myself: spitting distance, map-wise, from where I'd thrived in boyhood (lounging on the beach at Sandy Neck beside my folks, sure that life was nothing more complex than sand and sun), but miles away from anything that boy could have foreseen—orphaned now, sitting beside my thorny, decent lover while, above us, our own child was being fashioned.

My parents had been, if anything, a negative example: a couple like a lock and its hasp fused by rust, who thought that, as parents, they were bound to cease being themselves. Proving them wrong was part of why I wanted to be a dad. But now I wished I had them here, to light the road they'd laid for me, even if that road was filled with potholes.

Stu placed his hand on my tight neck. "Are you okay?"

A second sooner, "okay" might have been an iffy answer. But Stu's hand had done the trick, his deep, steady voice. "Yeah," I said. "Overwhelmed, but fine. Here we go."

We would have kissed if Libby hadn't moped into the living room and perched on the sofa's very lip. She hovered there, consuming the space around her.

"Paula finally go down?" Stu asked.

"Yeah," she said, and sighed. She scratched at a blueberry-colored blemish on the sofa, studied it, scratched the spot again.

"So," I said. "Libby. You're Paula's babysitter." *The sky is blue! Two and two are four!* "What else do you do? You in school?"

She shrugged. "I go to the four Cs." Then she added, pedantically, "Cape Cod Community College." Her expression seemed served up from leftovers of niceness, now on the verge of going bad.

"Right," said Stu. "We know. We live just down the road." He drummed his hands on his knees. "What's your major?"

"Communications," she mumbled, missing her own punch line. She tugged her sweatshirt taut around her waist. Finally she added, "Really, you can take off. You don't have to stay. Paula's asleep and everything. I've got this."

My mood was still fragile, or I'd have let this pass. Probably she was only being thoughtful. But something about the way she said "I've got this" set me off. As if we were merely hangers-on. Was *that* how I'd be seen? A footnote, not a father: the boyfriend of the guy who shot his wad into a cup.

"You know, Libby," I said. "You know, I really have to say—"

A noise from above distracted me. A muffled call of revelry or anger.

Then a clunk—a bed? a body?—against the floor. Stu appeared to fight an urge to hurry up the stairs. Libby wrung her pale, pudgy hands.

Eventually, through the ceiling: the faint trill of laughter. We glanced at one another, glanced away. Now a new silent sinkhole opened up between us; no one bothered to fill it up with small talk.

A minute later Danny appeared, his singlet dark with sweat, looking like he'd just been pumping iron. "Herself would like to see you now," he said.

Libby strained to lever herself up and off the sofa, but Danny said, "The *guys*, I think, Libby. Just the guys."

I couldn't help but lift my chin in triumph.

Laid out on her bed, Debora was propped with pillows at her knees, her hips, her neck: something perishable packaged for an airlift. Scanning the room, I found no concrete signs of what they'd done. And yet, a loamy smell of sex faintly lingered. A little giggle welled up in my gut.

Danny put his pumped-up arms on Stu's and my shoulders. Vanished was his sulky threat, his territorial scowl. "So," he said. "As good for you as it was for me? Ha! Ha!"

"Danny, stop," said Debora. "Be serious, now. Okay?"

But he had earned the right, I thought, to act just as he pleased: the textbook definition of "good sport." Plus, I felt like goofing, too. Kicking up my heels. We had done it. We had really done it!

But Stu, ever himself, stuck to business. "You think you can stay in bed awhile—you know, to keep it in? I realize it's past nine o'clock."

Danny said, "No worries. We made a change of plans. Some pizza, some beer—beer for me, not her!—whatever corny movie's on cable."

"Shoot," said Stu. "I honestly feel so bad."

But I could see that Debora was content, or not displeased. Queen for a night, footman at her beck, a homey romance. A better gift than the flowers we had brought.

"Go," she said. "Celebrate. Go dancing. Drink champagne."

Danny seconded the motion: "Live it up."

The thought of taking off no longer made me feel tangential. The party would be wherever we would bring it.

We shook Danny's hand, and kissed Debora good-bye, then walked out, with Stu calling, "You guys are the best." I followed him downstairs, teetering with ecstasy—organic, little-e ecstasy, sweeter than the pills we used to swallow.

Libby stood awaiting us, propped against a wall, and now I saw, beneath her sullen bulk, the sweet and lonely girl. *Egg with legs!* I wanted to pinch her cheek.

"Bye," she said. "Good luck."

"You, too! Same to you."

Out we walked—we almost danced—to the car, and climbed inside. And only there, in the quiet of my parents' old Volvo, did all the fizzy queerness (what better word?) subside. We sat together, wordless, the engine still unstarted. The night was black. We could have been at sea, or in a cave.

Then Stu took my hand within his steady, skillful hands. Tethering me to . . . everything. To him.

Not at sea. Not in a cave. *Here*, beside Stu.

I leaned close, pressed his fevered cheek to mine, and clutched him, shivering in the still winter dark.

ten

The next evening we did it all again. This time we collected the sample (*collected?* the *sample?* as if all we hoped for was a science fair ribbon!) at home, in our very own bed. Then we swathed the cup in a microwave-warmed towel and hurried it across the Cape to Debora's. Again we sat downstairs (no Libby, now, looming); again Debora called us to her side: a routine of sorts, but one, like a jet lifting off, that still felt solemn and uncanny.

Then we waited.

Two weeks till we'd know: a find-religion fortnight, praying for the pregnancy test to pinken.

We tried to trundle on with life as normal: I was plugging away at the reading-comprehension quiz to go with my new textbook unit; Stu was shuttling in and out of Logan. I shopped for socks, a shower-curtain liner, a faster toaster. Took two months' bottles to the dump.

But I couldn't quit obsessing, my mind like a muddy greyhound track: thoughts in chase of the out-of-our-reach rabbit of what would happen. All I could do was to keep calling Debora, to ask how she felt—queasy, perhaps? (If only my own nausea were a sign that she was pregnant.)

"I'm perfect," she said. "Everything will be perfect now, believe me."

"But how does this compare to when you—"

"Pat," she said. "Come on. The Brazilians, we have a saying, okay? 'Between the beginning and the end is always a middle.' You understand? So please, now. Please try to relax."

Yeah, I wished.

I kept trying to picture what was going on inside her. If life was being formed—from infinitesimal to infinite—shouldn't we be able to hear the bang?

What do you think it's doing now?" I asked Stu over breakfast, talking to the back side of his *Times*.

"Assuming that she . . . ," he said. "That everything went—"

"Well, *don't* you?"

"Of course I want to. Hmm," he said. He folded shut the paper. Took a bite of his bagel, ruminated. "Week one? Swimming down the fallopian tube, I'd guess."

"But what's it *doing?* I mean, is it being . . . human yet? Does it have a, like—I wish there were a word besides *soul!*"

"I think it's sort of early to get quite so metaphysical. Remember, hon, right now, it'd only be as big as—"

"I know," I said. "A period." I tapped the *Times*. "I know." *Period* was the fallback word the op-ed writers used in their justifications of stem-cell research. When churchy types, against destroying embryos, preached of "human life," the columnists all scoffingly responded: *Human life? At that stage? It's barely the size of the period after this sentence.*

I'd tossed off that argument myself, on occasion, and I was still in favor of the research. (Sacrifice some embryos to save whole groups of people? A trade I was more than glad to make.) But not with glee or glibness now. Not lightly anymore. Now I felt what an embryo could contain, how *huge* it was.

Which scared me. And also honestly thrilled me.

If Stu felt the same, he wasn't letting on. "A period," he said. "A period. Can't those guys come up with something smarter?"

"What should they say? Isn't that just the size?"

"Fine, but do they all have to use the same comparison? Why not something . . . I don't know . . . ." He fiddled with his bagel. "Like poppy seed! It's perfect, right? 'Seed.' The double entendre?"

When I didn't respond, Stu flicked one such seed at me. "Well?" he said.

"Come on, Stu. Just stop. You're being silly."

"*You* come on." He took his *Times* and raised it again between us. The paper didn't muffle (and wasn't meant to) his next line: "Tell me you're not becoming one of those people."

Mostly, though, we got along. Joined in hopeful anxiousness, even if Stu rarely gave it voice.

The closest he came was something he said in Provincetown one day, riffing on a wholly different topic. We'd set aside the day for each other, and Stu suggested P-town—which might, in itself, have been a clue: the gayest spot this side of over the rainbow. Was Stu itching for queerness, a break from "family values"? Then again, the day-trip options from Sandy Neck were limited; it could have been that P-town was convenient.

We did the requisite beachfront brunch, a walk along the jetty, and then warmed up with Far Land Provisions coffee. Now we were gallery hopping, eastward on Commercial Street, and found ourselves admiring a handsome woodcut. The piece was huge—six feet wide, maybe, by four feet high—but filled with fine, fingerprint-like whorls. It showed a ship at wharf, in an old brickwork harbor: a placid scene that shouldn't have been foreboding, but it was. The sky was etched with furling gusts, like snickers of the gods.

"Isn't it just astounding?" said the husky gallery owner, himself a mix of handsomeness and menace: gruff gray beard but boyish sweet-tea eyes. "I had two, but the other was just nabbed by the Currier Museum. This is the tenth of ten, then they're gone."

"Gone?" said Stu impishly. "I bet he just prints more." He flashed a chummy grin that said he saw through all the huckstering, the fib of *Hurry! While supplies last!*

"Oh, no," said the owner, his eyes full of injury. "No no no, the artist destroys the block."

"The artist—" said Stu.

"Breaks the woodblock after he's made the run. Then burns it. An offering, if you will."

Stu's face changed. The grin was gone, and he gazed squarely at me. I sensed he had leapt from art to *us*. To having a kid.

At first I feared that he was thinking he was like the woodblock: create a precious copy of himself, be burned to ash. But his expression wasn't especially frightened or resentful; stunned-but-in-a-good-way was more like it. And later, in the car, he talked about his feelings: "I can't stop thinking about the guy who does those woodcuts. I guess I'd never thought how much the making of art *is* the art. The process as much as the product, you know. Commitment."

It hit me, then: he likened himself not to the burned-up wood but to the artist, the visionary shaper. Maybe he was feeling—for the first time, really *feeling*—that fatherhood required more than the siring of a child.

The whole hour's drive back he maintained his awestruck look, a *holy crap!* that didn't skimp on *holy*.

At home, in the driveway: an unfamiliar car. Smiley-face yellow, its hood all wax and wink, a child's fantasy notion of adulthood.

"Who the fuck?" said Stu.

"New York tags? Beats me," I said. My eyes went to the house, where the kitchen lights were on. "Okay, I'm officially creeped out."

"Me, too," said Stu. "You think we should call—"

But then the door swung open, and out strode his sister, hailing us coquettishly with . . . what was it? A piece of sandwich? "Boys, I could've walked away with everything," she called. "Try to be a little more careful."

Stu stepped from the car. "We locked," he said. "We always lock."

Rina popped the last of the sandwich into her mouth, tidied a bead of mayo with her tongue. "The deck, the sliding doors: open sesame!" Then, as if collecting a reward for her resourcefulness, she offered herself, on tiptoes, to be kissed.

I hadn't seen her in almost four months, since her and Richard's visit, and I was struck anew by her sharp, demanding beauty: her holographic skin (now ruddy, now translucent), her mouth (pretty, but always at risk of pouting). Her attractiveness was literal: you couldn't help but face her. The effect was bracing but also claustrophobic.

Was that why I was feeling so boxed-in—just her presence? No, I was remembering what had happened in November, after she and Richard had departed.

Their visit, as I said before, was sad but still successful. And so, when they were leaving, I'd been doubly glad: happy that the house would be restored to Stu and me, but happy, too, to realize that I could host my in-laws, could honestly say, "You're welcome any time." Hugs were traded. *Thanks for having. Thanks for being had.*

Then, three days later, a call came from Great Neck. Richard wanted to talk to me. (*Richard? To me?*) We were practically family, he said, right? So no B.S.? Okay, then: I should know how ill at ease he'd felt when I . . . well, he hated to use a loaded word like *groped* . . . when I had touched and squeezed him on the butt. Actually, no. More than ill at ease, he said. Invaded.

"What?" I said. "When?"

"Hugging 'bye, in the driveway. You reached around, and your hand . . . well, you groped."

Groped? Patted the small of his back. At most! The shock—the absurdity—of the charge was so hammering that I didn't think yet to be angry. Instead, I scrambled to the far ends of politeness. "Gee, if I—I mean, I certainly never meant . . . I feel bad that . . . that *you* felt bad."

"Not that I'm homophobic," he said. "I'm sure you know I'm not. But Pat, it wasn't appropriate. You're Rina's brother's . . . partner." He seemed to want bonus points for choosing that neutral term and also for the fact of having made this call himself, rather than leaving the dirty work to Rina.

How could I explain to him how off the mark he was? Even, I might say, if my sexual radar screen were as wide as the wide, wide world, Richard wouldn't make a blip upon it. (His clammy face; his toadish little eyes.)

"So, just to say it," he concluded, "not my thing. Plus, I'm faithful to Rina. A hundred and one percent. I thought it was important just to say that."

"No," I said. "No, of course. Sure."

We shot the breeze farcically for another thirty seconds (was it thundering as hard on the Cape as on Long Island?), and that was all. *Hi to Stu! Hi to Ree!* The end.

Stu and I, for days, tried to guess his motives. I put forth the "lady doth protest too much" theory, convinced Richard had *hoped* (even if unconsciously) for me to attempt a lewd pass. Stu said no, the guy was just Semitically conflicted. On the one hand, Jews preferred to side with the oppressed; on the other, they were trained to think in clear-cut categories: sea creatures, to be kosher, should swim and not crawl; flatware was for meat or milk, not both; and men should sleep with women, not with men. Gay men (gay *brothers-in-law*) must have melted his wires.

The rift had now nominally been mended, no hard feelings. Richard had even instigated, the last time we spoke, a "Hey, bud, I've missed you" rapprochement. But his voice, the thought of him, continued to make me qualmish—just the way, two decades past my first teenage bender, the word *Cointreau* could still turn my stomach.

I'd stayed mad at Rina, too—for not having prevented Richard from making that jackass call, for picking him as her husband in the first place—but now, in the driveway, I tried to set my anger aside. I grinned and bore her kiss's sandwich smell. "Wow," I said. "To what do we owe this pleasure?"

"Long story short," she said. "You know those things I'm selling?"

"Oh, you mean the candle chandeliers?" I almost added, *We love ours, it really does look good*, but Rina, having snooped around, would know we'd never hung it.

Wait. What else would she have seen in snooping around the house? Insem syringes . . . photographs of Debora . . . *No Penis, No Problem*? I elbowed Stu. Our secret might be blown.

But Rina seemed entirely caught up in her own business. "The chandeliers?" she said. "Nah, they never moved. Don't know why. But these are better. These are really good."

These, she explained, were aromatherapy pendants: hand-blown glass, filled with assorted essential oils. Whenever you needed a dose of, say, bergamot to becalm you, all you did was reach down for the pendant at your neck, uncork it, and take a long draft.

Lord, how the woman could hype a product. If only the stuff she peddled ever lived up to her pitch. Her master's in art history from CUNY notwithstanding, she seemed to be missing a sense of taste. Why she'd ever leapt from her sturdy career ladder (internship at the Jewish Museum, assistantship at Christie's) and plunged into the tchotchke-hawking business was a riddle.

"Aromatherapy?" said Stu. "Since when are you into that?"

"Wouldn't say I'm *into* it. But people are. It's hot."

She said the word so zestfully that I indeed felt heat: her breath, its sandwich smell, in my face. She'd led us into the house—backward, like a tour guide—and here we were, in the kitchen, a chaos of cans and jars: Starkist, Hellman's, Vlasic, Grey Poupon. A celery stalk rose from the Disposall like a drowned man's arm. Would Rina at least say "Sorry about the mess"?

What she said was, "The Christmas Tree Shops are *this close* to signing on. You know they're based practically down the road, in South Yarmouth? Their buyer said, 'Come on up'—our first face-to-face. The whole thing was sort of last-minute. I would've called, but . . ." She made a quick flutter with her hand, as if the reason were as obvious as air.

111

Her m.o.—"C'mon, you know me, I don't do trifling details"—was calculated to win free passes, even when the details weren't so trifling. Stu would often grouse about her chutzpah, her entitlement, but once, when I endorsed his jab, and twisted the knife a little, he stopped me: "Well, I'd rather she ask a lot than ask for nothing. *Your* sisters would be mortified to borrow a cup of flour. With them I feel like a perfect stranger."

Fair enough. Sally or Brenda would never "just drop by." But Stu couldn't fathom the way a family like ours related. Our adage: absence makes the WASP grow fonder.

"No worries," he told his sister now. "It's nice. A nice surprise. At first, to be honest, when we pulled up and we saw . . ."

"Oh," she said, "the Porsche. You'd have to ask Richard about that."

The roots of all my molars prickled. *Richard.*

"I'm sure he'll have to sell it back. No way can we afford it. But what can I really say, you know? That car"—she chuckled weakly—"is his baby."

Just like that, my malice was short-circuited. Free pass granted.

I couldn't help but think of Debora, propped in bed, inseminated. It wasn't as though we hadn't had to work to make that happen, but on some level, things for us were easier than for Rina. We could simply *choose* a fertile womb.

"You can't blame him," I said of Richard, meaning it sincerely, but feared I had sounded condescending. "Blame him for wanting," I tried again, "a little midlife fun. Are we there now, God forbid? Middle age?"

Rina smiled with what looked like charitable exhaustion: aware of my try, and grateful, but unmoved. By now she must be used to having pity cast her way, crumbs of consolation at her feet. "Middle age?" she said. "Is that the age when our middles grow? Or," she added—her hand approached her abdomen—"sometimes don't."

Stu, looking pained, retreated to the bedroom, leaving me to guide Rina—a VIP of grief—to the living room. I sat her on the couch.

"Nice what you did to the house," she said, sinking into the cushions. "It makes everything seem much less . . . manic."

"Oh? Oh, that's good. Thanks a lot!" I could think of nothing we had changed since she was here.

"But I don't know if I could live with all that *view*," she said.

The view, at present, was just the way I loved it. Frostinglike waves on the bay's broad expanse; beyond, creamy layers of cloud and sky—like a pastry, fattening just to look at.

"All that open space," she said. "On and on and on. Everything looks so relentlessly possible."

"Exactly. That's—"

"But, God!" she said. "Doesn't it get you down? How could real life ever live up?"

"Wow, you and Stu really are related, aren't you?"

"Well," she said, "you can take the Nadler out of New York . . ."

"But what?" said Stu, walking in. "You can't make me drink?"

Rina, like a Roman empress, stretched out on the couch. "Are you the only Nadler here? Who's to say we weren't describing *me*?"

"Were you?" he said.

"No."

"And so?"

"And so *what*?"

Stu shoved her legs away and flopped down beside her. Jesting with her, or jousting—who could ever tell? Their silences could snap me in two.

Time to get lost, I thought, so I said, "I'm remiss! Let me fix up something in the kitchen." (Something *more*, I could have said. Another tuna sandwich.)

"Nah, come on," said Rina. "Sit down with us. Relax. You're just back from—hold on. Have you said?"

"From Provincetown," said Stu.

"For work?"

"Just needed a break."

The elephant in the room: a break from what?

"Sweet," said Rina. "That must be nice—flitting off on a weekday. Dinks: that's what they call you, right? Dual income, no kids."

I clenched: *Did* she, after all, from snooping, know our secret? Now was she just fishing for a confession?

But who was she to call us Dinks? What were she and Richard? (Maybe you got exempted if you didn't *choose* your kidlessness. Dual income, a big chunk of it spent on *wanting* kids . . .)

"Speaking of which," she said. "The reason I dropped by . . ."

Stu said, "Ree, please. You never need a reason."

"*One* of the reasons." She smiled, stroked his knee. "I thought it'd be extra nice if . . . telling you in person. Richard and I. We're going to adopt."

"Adopt?" he said. "Wow," he said. "A baby?"

"No, a pet rock. What do you think?"

"Adopt," he said. "That's great. That's . . . so great!" He leaned over and kissed her on the brow.

Surely she could hear the complications in his voice. In case she did, to keep the scales tipped toward pure good wishes, I rushed to add my own "Congratulations!"

"I really want this now," she said. "We both do. We've decided. I mean, should we sit around forever feeling sorry? All that hoping and hoping—now it can get *used*. Aim that energy onto something real."

I could see—in her toughened jaw, her fluctuating color—the cost of having forced herself to feel no disappointment. But also I saw her readiness, her genuine relief. Saw the earnest mother she would be.

Fondness wicked up within me, a rising solidarity. "Yes, us too," I wanted to say. "We'll all of us be parents!"

But Stu shot me down with a let-me-do-this look. He asked his sister: Boy or girl? Where from? How soon?

"Richard wants a boy, of course; I'd be fine with either. But God, it's a pain in the ass to find a Jewish kid. Probably have to go to God-knows-where—deepest Russia? I'm sure we'll have to pay a modest fortune. But Dad always told us, right? You get—"

114

Stu finished with her: "—what you pay for. Speaking of Dad, you've told him? He and Mom must be thrilled."

"Don't say anything, please," she begged. "We'll spill the beans this weekend. They're coming to our place for Shabbos dinner."

Stu said he'd give an arm to see their kvelling faces.

"Come! We'd love to have you there. Both of you. Will you? Pat?" She sprang up and hurled her arms around me.

She must have sensed that I felt foiled, but she couldn't know the reason. When would Stu come clean about our news?

Stu demurred. "It's *your* surprise. It's yours, Ree. Enjoy it."

"Sure?" she said. "You're more than welcome."

"Enjoy it!" he commanded.

"I think this calls for a celebration," I said. "Let me make up the guest room, and then, what do you say, maybe up to Chillingsworth for dinner? I bet they would take us if I groveled."

Rina said, "No, no. I'm not staying."

"What?" said Stu. "All this way, then 'see ya'? That's ridiculous."

"Richard'll be expecting me. In fact, I'd better go. I hate to drive too much after dark."

Whenever they got together, a deadlock was inevitable: who could elicit the most favors, and who could most refuse? This time, though, I had hoped we might be spared. Not so.

We walked her to the driveway, Stu still urging "Stay," and Rina saying, "Stop, stop, I can't." The Porsche—its brightness, it blatancy—now looked poignant. I pictured Richard waxing it for hours.

Rina, with precise birdlike pecks, kissed us both. Promises were passed around to keep in better touch; Rina said she'd e-mail pics of their parents' gloating grins.

She got into the driver's seat and gunned the snarly engine, but then, just as quickly, popped out. "Wait, wait—forgot! Brought you something."

"Come on, Sis, you didn't have to."

"It's tiny. Just a token." She forced something into Stu's palm.

I had to smile. She wins! Round to Rina!

115

Stu let the pendant, on its leather thong, dangle. The glass vial was sea-colored, fashioned like a song note. Backlit by the sun, it looked liquid.

"You don't have to wear it around your neck," she assured us. "Hang it by the sliding doors. The light will look great through it."

"Sure," I said. "We will, absolutely. What's in it?"

"Holy Rose," she said. "The Queen of Flowers."

Stu squinted. "What's the claim for that one?"

"Love, of course. Healing emotional wounds, restoring trust."

"Wow, give me a gallon, then," I said.

Smiling wanly, Rina poked the vial and made it sway, spilling blue-green light along the drive. "Also, it works—or so they say, but who are *they*, you know?—for fertility. But heck, I just sell them."

Stu embraced her. "Another needler—the next in line," he bragged. "My little sis, Ree, will have a baby!"

Rina kissed him again and drove off.

After the Porsche was out of sight, I asked him, "Stu, how could you? How could you not tell her what we're planning?"

"Pat," he said. "Think. How would she have felt? 'Adopting, are you? Well, we're going to have our *own* baby.' It wouldn't have been right to steal her thunder."

Or maybe he'd kept silent, I thought, because his sister had already stolen *his*.

It's her!" he called, the next night, shielding the phone's mouthpiece. "It's Debora. Get the other cordless."

I dashed for it and back to him, the phone, like a hand-caught herring, silvery in my clutch. (My mom used to take me every April down to Mashpee, to watch the herring leaping so implausibly upstream, to touch their stubborn, coruscating luck.) Stu took my hand and we stood before the picture window, gazing at the open-ended view.

"Ready?" he whispered.

I nodded. I squeezed his sweaty palm.

"Not this time," said Debora. "Not yet. I'm so sorry."

Maybe she thought our silence meant she had to make things clearer. "My period," she said.

A period, a period.

eleven

I pelted Stu with pep talks. Normal, I said. Likely. Would have been sheer luck to hit the bull's eye right away. I pointed to the heading in our book that said "Don't Panic." "'Even the fittest couple,' I read, 'employing time-honored intercourse, is bound to fail four of five times.' So see?" I said. "We knew this. Or would've if we'd let ourselves. You were right: much better that we didn't tell your folks. Or Rina. Isn't that relieving?"

I was trying mostly to persuade myself, of course. I felt weak-kneed but not especially, or only, in the knees. All of me: a creaky, cranky joint.

I wished Stu might notice this and try to comfort me. But he was all pulled inward, the opposite of attentive—not quite glum, but sleepy-headed, stalled.

Zack advised reminding him of Debora's surro contract, which promised she would try for eight cycles. In other words, repeated attempts were not at all unusual. Focus on our seven cycles left.

Dutifully I gave the speech, one night as we undressed. I tried to give my voice the ring of reason.

Stu got stiff and stared at me, eyes like ripened blisters. "*Plan* to fail? Oh, right. That's perfect, Pat. Good thought." No, he said, he wouldn't think of seven tries, or six; he would do this *once* more, and succeed.

I wasn't hurt. I loved it! The rush of Stu's revival! A man who almost every day unclenched the grip of gravity, launching tons of steel into the sky, wasn't used to having his will bucked. What had seemed a lull had been the revving of his jets.

Now he grabbed his laptop and composed a Stu-ish chart: things that might have gone wrong, and remedies. "Time delay, for starters." He stroked a few more keys. "Some of the sperm dies, you know, with every passing second. Better to do it at their place, on the spot."

Wasn't that the plan I'd made, the one he had rebuffed?

"And build-up," he went on. "It's better to have build-up." Another flurry of typing on the laptop. "I promise, for a whole week before her ovulation . . ." Last time, he confessed, the tips of his ears blushing, Debora's surge had caught him unprepared: only about six hours before his services were called upon, he'd "wasted himself" in a men's room at O'Hare. "A week, okay?" he said now. "Work those counts up higher."

Hearing the way he coached himself—his gamer's fighting drive—I sensed Rina's visit had redoubled his competitiveness.

He put the laptop to sleep, and said he'd sleep now, too. I thought he'd nodded off—his breaths got thick as taffy—but then his hand reached out for me and cupped my hipbone's cliff. His voice, in the darkness, was a wraith: "You know what's a relief? That I didn't feel relief."

To *not* be let down, he said—that had been his worry. To have to sell himself on feeling sad.

Now he did drift off, but I stayed wide awake, wondering when I'd ever been so pleased with someone's sadness.

For two weeks, he nursed his lit candle of resolve, until, when he needed it, it guttered.

At Debora's. In the bathroom. *Doing it on the spot.*

Or, more likely, considering the time he'd spent in there: *not* doing it. How long, so far? Fifteen, twenty minutes?

Debora and I were trying not to hover, in the guest room, where

Paula played beside us with a doll. "Barbie has to pee," she said—the second time she'd told us.

"Barbie does, or you?" Debora asked.

"Maybe both?"

"Okay, well, you both will have to hold it."

Danny could be heard from down the hall, in the bedroom, barking at the ballgame on TV. "Grapefruit league, Sox against the Twins," he'd said when Stu and I arrived, not bothering to get up. Whether this showed his ease with us or the opposite, I couldn't tell.

Now I noticed Paula heading over to the bathroom. Her two little fists took the knob.

"No!" I shouted. "Paula. Don't go in there." I figured Stu had locked it, but just in case.

"Have to," Paula said. "Mãinha? I have to go."

"*Filha*, please have patience," Debora told her.

Paula stood there, scowling, despondent. I went to her and knelt, my eyes now at her level. "Sweetpea, he won't be long. We have to let him finish, though, okay?"

She gazed at me with moist, trusting eyes.

But two more minutes passed. Another two. Five.

"Swing, you dunce," called Danny. He banged or stomped on something. "Jesus Christ, you've got to swing the bat."

Oh, how I hoped Stu couldn't hear him.

I went to the door. I tapped. "Hon? You okay?"

Back came three crisp syllables: Go. A. Way.

Paula squirmed. "Mãinha?"

"Try, now. Be a big girl."

But after another endless minute, the poor thing couldn't contain herself. "I *have* to. It's my turn. Not fair!"

Here came Danny, thumping in, swooping her up, a strongman. "For Christ's sake, she's four years old. You can't ask her to hold it." He carried her downstairs, with Debora scrambling after.

I followed, too: to watch a father—a practiced one—in action.

In the kitchen, Danny hoisted Paula into the sink. "Here?" she said, humiliation pounding thin her voice. But there was no alternative: she squatted and let go, her pee tinkling brightly in the basin. Soon her anxious grimace was replaced by pure relief, and then by what looked like lawless glee.

Danny swooped her up again. "Don't get any ideas. This was just a one-time sort of deal." He was smiling; his pose of sternness wasn't fooling anyone. Paula's glee had turned him into putty.

The girl said, "Oh, Daddy, don't be silly."

I thought of my own father: a blustery man, especially when befuddled. He would not have dared to let me see his strictness crack, not have let me tease and flirt like Paula. Fatherhood, for him, had been a kind of hammer, and I could only ever be a nail.

Turning to head upstairs, we all laid eyes on Stu, who waited in the hallway, cup in hand. Oh-thank-God-he-did-it was replaced by creeping shame: must he hold the cup like that, a blind man selling pencils?

More shame, then: shame for feeling ashamed of my sweet Stu.

Debora took the cup and went, with Danny, to their bedroom, leaving me and Stu to mind Paula. We sat her in the living room, before the huge TV, where Snow White was biting a tainted apple.

"Hon," I said, "what happened?"

"It sucks," he hissed. "I hate this."

Paula jumped at the outburst, and I had to pet her neck, shushing her, telling her not to worry. Then, to Stu, I said, "Behave."

"Sorry. I know. Sorry." He damped his voice and spoke behind his hand: "I thought after a week I'd be ready to explode. But God, *you* try it—sitting there in someone else's bathroom, the whole universe knowing what you're doing. Plus, a girl banging on the door, wanting in. A four-year-old! I'm sorry. I just couldn't."

"It wasn't Paula," I said. "It was me. And I tapped."

"Bang, tap, whatever. Couldn't do it."

"But you did, didn't you?"

"Well, just barely." He stopped, swallowed sharply. "I could only think about my dad."

"It's no wonder! Next time think of, I don't know, Brad Pitt?"

Stu let my leaden joke go under. "The thought I had," he said. "Kept having, as I tried? Was how much I would love, when we're down there for the Seder . . ."

When Walter had phoned last week, from Rina and Richard's house, to share the news that he would be an *opa*, he'd demanded an all-family Passover celebration: next month, at their place, in New York. According to Stu, he'd sounded . . . Stu didn't know the word. His dad's native German, he guessed, contained some wacky noun: sadness to be thrilled by what previously would have saddened; fatigue from the toll of willful joy; submission to cheer.

". . . to tell them," Stu said now. "When we're down there, to be able—"

"But even if it works this time," I said, "I thought we wouldn't. Glenn said not to, till after the first trimester." (I'd called Glenn to say we'd be coming to the city—our first return, together, since the move— and hoped to see him and Zack and Milo.) "Imagine," I said, "we tell your folks too soon, and she miscarries."

"There you go again," said Stu. "Why do you plan for failure?"

Lest his voice spook Paula again, I simply tried to calm him. "Fine," I said. I whispered it. "You're right. It's fine, it's fine."

"What is fine?" asked Paula, escaping her TV trance. She left Snow White snoozing in her coma and clambered up to us, claiming a spot between us on the couch.

"*Everything's* fine," I said. "Aren't you fine?"

Paula considered the question, her dimpled brow making her look precociously philosophical. Grudgingly, it seemed, she said, "Guess so."

"Right! Perfectly fine," I said. "So go back to your movie?" I gave the slightest push in that direction.

But Stu said, "I bet you might be finer if I did *this*." Teasingly he tugged her frizzy pigtails.

"No!" she cried.

"Are you sure?" He tugged again. "Toot toot."

"No?" she said—this time as a question.

"Maybe this." He raised her shirt and razzed her egg-pale belly. "Wouldya?" he sang. "Wouldya, Paula, be finer in Carolina?" He kissed a sloppy trail toward her sternum.

She giggled—a smidgen, a scant burping leak—but that led to a shriek, and then full-bodied writhing, a conniption of spectacular amusement.

Stu dove down and kissed her again. "Mine mine mine," he said.

Up till now, I had really wanted a kid for *me*. I wanted Stu to want one, yes, but mostly so that my wish would come true. But watching him teasing Paula—so sweetly, so selflessly, setting aside his angst to keep her charmed—now I knew how much I also wanted a kid for *him*. Would go to whatever lengths to make it happen.

After the first round, our faith had been stubbornly naïve—we strove not to think of any outcome but the best—but this time, my certainty's source was trusty: Debora, who said she had a feeling.

"You know how cats, falling," she said, "always find their feet?" That was how she'd felt, she said, when Paula was conceived: balanced by a nimble feline sense of can't-do-wrong. "And now," she said, "it's how I'm feeling too. My feet. They stick."

At once I started to notice signs: five newborn fox kits—toothless, blind, gray—sleeping near an oak log in the yard; a tomato at the Stop & Shop with two distinctive halves (a valentine's twin lobes, a cell dividing). And then, when a last-of-winter ice storm brought its gleam—power lines and trees encased in spotless crystal sheaths—I was sure it prophesied our with-a-baby future: not unfamiliar but magnified, more clear; our lives *plus*.

As March's final week began, the mail brought more good news: a fat check for a textbook I'd written in 2000, which now, a letter said, had sold for French translation. I kept repeating "windfall," a word that matched my sudden sense of fluttering, airy luck. I told Stu we'd celebrate: a dinner splurge, on me. "The Cummaquid Inn." (I said the name by instinct.)

The Cummaquid was the grandest of the Cape's old-money main-stays: prime rib and popovers, waitresses in bonnets, men and boys required to dine in blazers. When I was a kid, we Faunces ate there once each end-of-summer—a family rite as sacred as the visit of the sandpipers (visible through the inn's bayfront windows), pausing on their hard homeward flight. The dress code pissed me off, and I fought it every year, showing up self-righteously in shirtsleeves. But every year, the maitre d' would notice—tut-tut!—and summon forth a loaner coat, raunchy with a lifetime's worth of mothballs. (Decades later, the thought of "dressing up" could still sicken me, filling me with camphorous chagrin.)

After a while it wasn't just the dress code that I shirked, but the whole enforced *we're-a-family* bonding—as flimsy and contrived as the popover girls' bonnets. "Why do we come?" I asked my dad, knifing a bloody steak. (I had ordered medium-well, but Dad had overruled me; "Blue," he told the waiter, "for us all.") "I mean, what's the big fucking occasion?"

"Patrick, dear! Language," Mom insisted.

"*This* is the occasion," said my father. "Just because. One small thing that makes us who we are."

I had thought: Who we are? Who *are* we?

My feeling of misfittedness—that awful loaner coat—only tightened after I announced that I was gay. The following summer I never even made it to the Cape, but lived above a bookstore in Northampton where I clerked, sharing a room with two flamboyant queens. My mom, at the end of August, asked if I would visit. "I thought you liked tradition, dear. Faunce Place—remember when we found it?"

I had liked that, yes. But hadn't I outgrown it? Or had I stayed the same and it had shrunk? "Does Dad want me to come?" I asked. "Maybe if *he* invites me."

But no, my dad refused to take the phone.

I shot back with some slick riff about my "chosen family"—even to my teenage ears it sounded awfully wooden.

Dad and I, by the next August, had somewhat patched things up, but Sally picked that month to get married; Cummaquid Inn dinner plans were canceled. And now that we had skipped the thing that once had been expected, skipping it became the expectation.

By now more summers had passed since I'd eaten at the Cummaquid than I had ever gone there with my folks. I'd driven by, occasionally, since Stu and I had moved, but hadn't paid much mind to what I saw. A snippet of the port-cochère, behind a pine-tree scrim. An old ship's anchor, holding fast to nothing.

But now I planned to take Stu there. Stu the earnest sperm-count booster, the rescuer of moody little girls.

The evening of our splurge I was nutty with nostalgia. I *yearned* to overpay for prime rib. For once, I took pleasure in picking out my duds: a springtimey olive linen blazer from Brooks Brothers; a tie, Italian silk, sleekly striped (one of the few of Dad's I had kept).

"You're not going to believe this place," I told Stu in the parking lot. "Prepare to take a step back in time."

But Stu, as we walked inside, said, "Back to when—last week?"

The inn was filled with polo-shirted, Levi'd, Nike'd patrons. Even the maitre d' (a crazy name to call him, this kid who looked fresh from glee club practice) was sloppy in his open-necked Oxford.

How could I explain my grief, my marrow-cooking grief?

"Lord, is nothing sacred?" My voice came as a shock, the sureness of my full-gale Faunce pretension. It might have made me mortified; I saw that path before me. Instead, I chose a brighter path and boldly marched ahead. I asked for the best table ("No, *there*, by the window"), my voice clogged with a chowdery Yankee accent. "Bottle of Veuve," I told the wide-eyed waiter.

Stu was wide-eyed, too. I hoped he was marveling, as I was, at my deftness. I could be as competent at reign as at rebellion.

"To windfalls" was my toast when we got our champagne flutes. "To agile cats who find their feet. To us."

"How would you like the beef?" asked the waiter when I ordered. I didn't have to think. I said, "Blue."

At home, a message on the machine, from Debora: "Call me." (Her accent made it—weirdly, cutely—"*cow* me.")

We each took a cordless. We held each other's hands, looking toward the lights beyond the bay. I wanted to be able to remember every detail, so I could someday tell this as a story: *The night we learned we'd have you I was silly with champagne—I guess we'd started celebrating early! All across the water were a million little sparkles, which looked just how the champagne made me feel . . .*

Stu had dialed. I heard him say, "It's us," then Debora's sigh.

"Sorry," she said. "So sorry. I was wrong."

Various other words were said, but what else really mattered?

Maybe this: I thought of how we'd used to breathe together, Stu and I, a unit, on the dance floor: mouth-to-mouth, making figure eights of *We're alive!* That was what I wanted now. Needed.

But Stu walked off and shut the bedroom door.

I set down the telephone and stepped out to the deck, the night's eerie, underworldish calm. Spring had come a week ago, but still it felt like winter, the air brittle, arduous, expunging.

I'd once had to research hypothermia for a textbook. I found out that its victims, in time, felt phantom heat. A trick of the mind that made them strip, despite the brutal cold. Search crews often discovered naked corpses.

I pulled off my jacket, my father's tie, my shirt. Bare-chested, I leaned against an icy uphill wind. The chill gave a baffling kind of comfort.

I watched the sparkly lights. My skin was goose-fleshed, shrinking. I stood there till I started burning up.

twelve

It couldn't be avoided: our trip back to New York.

Stu had flown down the day before, to help his folks prepare: making charoset, burning the leaven, all that Jewish oddness. I traced his path in the morning—Hyannis, Logan, LaGuardia—touching down with time to spare before my planned reunions: with Zack and Glenn and Milo, and (this one unnerved me) Joseph. I'd meet Stu at sundown, at the Seder.

My Bangladeshi cabbie was immediately on my case. I'd said that I wanted to be dropped at Sheridan Square, thinking I would maybe take a look at our old condo; I named all the shortcuts I preferred. His accent was so strong that I couldn't catch each word, but I could have no doubt about his meaning: "No, we go like *this*. I know better." And though I'd done this airport ride, oh, a trillion times, and won in similar fights with countless cabbies, now I just sat back and took my licks. Probably I was just a little stunned to watch Rafiq Rahman and to think: he's more a New Yorker now than I.

Strolling around the Village I felt out of practice, too. Living on the Cape I put a premium on *noticing*: pay attention, and maybe I'd be treated to rewards (fox kits near an oak log; waves upon the bay like swells of frosting). But back here in Manhattan it was all about indifference—

sometimes just pretended, often real. I tried to reclaim my air of blasé self-containment, but damn it all, I couldn't help but stop and smell the roses . . . or, at least, the belching subway, the hot-dog steam, the sweat. Gray's Papaya, Gristede's: I craned my neck like a tourist. Not a single person looked back.

Thank God, then, that I should see, leaving the West Fourth station, comrades from our joyful nightclub days, Hank and Darren. Stu and I, behind their backs, had dubbed them Hunky and Dory. Hunky had a salt-and-pepper, sheriffy sort of handsomeness: you wanted him to pull you over, frisk you, breathalyze you. Dory was more hayseed hot, with tractor-axle biceps, a 4-H Clubber's clean enthusiasm. Stu and I had almost had a four-way with them, once. Before . . . well, before that kind of thing had lost its shine.

I dashed across the street, and gave them hearty hugs. "Kismet!" I said. "Gosh. Great to see you."

Hank said, "Yeah. Nice to see you, too."

"I don't even want to think how long," I said. "How are you?"

"Oh, you know," said Darren. He shrugged. "Same old, same old."

"Right," I said. "Sure. But the city is just—wow! The *speed* of it all. I just can't believe it."

They stared at me like I was speaking Urdu.

"You know we moved away?" I said. "Stu and I? A year ago? Didn't you wonder why you never saw us?"

"Oh," said Hank.

"Really?" said Darren. "I guess we . . . I don't know . . ."

"The Cape," I blurted out. "Cape Cod. It's gorgeous."

"P-town?" Darren said. "We love it there, don't we, baby?" Rotely, he squeezed his lover's biceps.

I started to explain: not P-town, no; West Barnstable; a house above the dunes of Sandy Neck . . .

Hank said, "Sorry. Ten minutes late already. You'll forgive us?"

"Darn, he's right," said Darren, "but it's super nice to see you."

Air kiss, air kiss—*swish*, they were gone.

Downcast, I chose not to check on our old condo. What would be my gain from seeing someone else's drapes? Besides, it was almost time to meet with Zack and Glenn. Our date was at the Central Park Zoo.

I had sent a stuffed penguin to Milo for his birthday, and Glenn told me the boy was still gaga for the doll, refused to set it down to eat or sleep. "Penny" was now grey from drool and matted up with grunge, and lately Milo had begged to bring the bird to see her "cousins" at the zoo, so she would feel less lonely. "The kid insists you come along," said Glenn.

I was admittedly gratified—maybe a bit too much—to hear about the points I'd scored with Milo. The last time I'd seen the boy, he'd been one and a half. Puffy with growth, he'd seemed to enlarge before my very eyes, like canned biscuits popped from their container. I couldn't wait to see how much he'd changed.

He'd grown enough, as it turned out, to balk at what growth meant.

We'd timed our visit, at Milo's request, to watch the penguin feeding, but just when he should have been delighting in the birds—muscly little fussbudgets of hunger—Milo turned all inwardly idyllic.

"Are you doing what I think you're doing?" Glenn asked, accusing.

Milo tried to eat his smile but only spilled it wider.

"You are!" said Zack. "What's the rule? Milo? What's the rule?"

The boy hugged Penny, searching his toddler brain to find the words—or, more likely, for words that would exempt him.

"Quick," said Glenn, "let's go. There's a bathroom right there."

"But Papa Glenn—" Milo made an oddly complacent face.

"Now," said Glenn, and hauled his son away.

Zack explained that Milo was resisting potty training. The dads couldn't make him stop going in his diapers: "Wants to pee bad enough? He pees. But what we can do," added Zack, "is make sure *where* he goes. So what we've done, we've made him start standing in the bathroom. Stand there as he does it in his pants, or right after. Get him used to the whole bathroom process."

I laughed, thinking: *Good thing Stu declined to come along.* He would have rolled his eyes at their by-the-book solemnity, their rigid, almost governmental system. Glenn was a compliance officer who worked for Stu's airline—they'd met at a gay employees' social—and Stu complained that he and Zack were, well, too law abiding. (Zack was a ballet critic, hyper-attuned to deviations from form.) "They're just so fucking straitlaced," Stu would say.

Yes, but they were the only gay dads we knew enough to count on; they had offered so much good advice and, lately, sympathy. Most of the time, I found their utter squareness irresistible. In truth, I was more than a little jealous.

They had planned the zoo excursion, I guessed, to boost my ego, to make me feel believably parental. And I had fully expected my time with them to be inspiring. A happy surro family: *Yes, we can!*

But then, as we waited for Glenn and Milo to return, Zack said he had some news to share. They were trying to make a little sibling now for Milo; in fact, they'd been trying for a while. This time with Zack's sperm, and an African American surro—the goal being to have two kids, built from four genetic strands, who'd forge a kind of family resemblance.

"Wow," I said. My voice was thready. "I'm so happy for you."

"Let's not get ahead of ourselves," said Zack. "It's still an uphill climb. The surro lives in Pittsburgh; we've gone there three months running. So far, though, no go. It's not taking."

All of this was said, surely, by way of being supportive (*See? We're in the same boat. Even we have problems*). As such, it was worthy of my thanks. But something more like crankiness got jammed between my eyes. Sorry, but no: Stu and I were not in their same boat. They had a son already. They had Milo.

I didn't know what to say. I watched the feeding penguins, and now their gluttony didn't look as cute. I stood staring, out of focus, lonely.

Not the best condition for my next visit, with Joseph.

We had stayed on rotten terms since I had left the city. Shortly after the move I had e-mailed him a photo: the view out to the marsh from our deck. He had phoned me right away, and thanked me for the picture: "The kind of place," he said, "where people ask to have their ashes scattered." Actually, I'd thought of telling Stu that's what I wanted, and so at first I missed Joseph's tone. Then he added: "Ugh. Could you imagine? For all eternity?"

I'd hung up and hadn't called him since.

If I knew Joseph, he'd been stocking weaponry for months; to gird myself for this afternoon, I had been up-armoring, trying to envision his attacks.

So, sufficiently bored there yet? Never been less, I'd tell him. Honestly, his New Yorker's *pose* of boredom bored me more.

And Stu's a faithful husband now? The salt air has tempered his libido? I would chide Joseph for his poorly hidden jealousy, tinged with a touch of self-loathing: the implication that gay men were incapable of commitment. (So what if I'd wondered that myself?)

The question I feared most, for having no good answer yet: *The baby? Has it solved what you had hoped?*

I met him at the Monster (his idea), a kitschy piano bar: Broadway Playbills, movie stills, mythic faux-bronze figurines. At ten past four, the place was hushed; we were the only patrons.

Joseph was at the bar already, and just as I approached, the bartender set a highball glass before him. This was when I got a hint of trouble. I could clearly see a lime wedge floating in his cocktail, an oily film of Rose's on its surface. How many times had I heard Joseph call to task a server: "This here is a vodka gimlet. I asked for vodka *Gibson*." But Joseph simply thanked the man and took the drink and swigged. He turned to me. "Isn't it nice to see you."

He kissed me on the mouth—a cleansing ethyl sting—and held me in a meatless hug, as limp and bland as tofu. His calm was so unsettling, his lack of confrontation, that I was rendered impotently dumb.

Joseph freely filled the void with straight-up, friendly questions: How was work? The cottage? Were we settled?

Finally I'd had enough. I poked him. "Not still mad?"

"Mad?" he said. "After all these months? At you? Come on."

131

"Please! I know you, Joseph. Since when do you forgive?"

He ordered another gimlet, a Maker's Mark for me. Then he said, "It isn't really forgiveness. Not exactly." He drank, and his lips went tight, tart. "It's that when you're my age, nothing—and I mean nothing— ever stays hard too long."

It was a good line, and made me think of all his sharp and funny lines, over the dozen years of our acquaintance, the magic of his up-by-his-own-bootstraps, dauntless charm. Oddly enough, I realized, he put me in mind of Debora. Opposites stylistically but similarly magnetic. I longed to tell him about her, about our whole endeavor.

I thought of a segue: wasn't Luis, his late lover, Brazilian? "I ask," I said, "because our surrogate mom is from Brazil."

"Luis was only half," he said. "And half Japanese. Thankfully, the Brazilian half was the one, you know, that counted. Speaking of which, I have two phallic items, are you ready?"

Off he went on a ludicrous jag about men who'd been circumcised as infants, then sought to restore their foreskins: "I can't say I argue with the goal, but, well, the method! Basically what they do is tie a weight . . . but it gets worse. The name of the thing? The Penile Un-circumcising Device. Get it? PUD? People are so stupid."

Before I could respond, he teed up his next topic: "You heard about the Hasids spreading herpes?"

I told him no.

"Hasn't reached the Cape, I guess, but here, it's an uproar. So, you know, when Jews get snipped, the mohel then cleans the wound. Most just do it manually, but the Hasids use . . . wait for it . . . their *mouths*. 'Oral suction'—which doesn't sound half bad. But come to find out, they're spreading herpes to eight-day-old boys."

"Awful," I said. "That's totally child abuse."

"Abuse?" he said. "It's murder. At least three kids have died." Joseph took a dramatic gulp of his gimlet. "You'd think that the Hasids would back down a bit, PR-wise. But no, what do they do? They threaten to march on City Hall: the whole Holocausty bunch of them, decked out in yellow stars."

The thought of it appalled me. But *Holocausty*? Oh, Joseph.

"For Jews, this hits their guts," I said. "Especially for survivors. I asked Stu once, 'If ours is a little boy, will you insist?' and God, you should have heard the way he—"

"Really, now, enough," said Joseph. "Enough about foreskins."

As if *I'd* been the one-track-minded rambler!

"Surely we can find a more uplifting subject," he said, and then launched a filibuster of mind-numbing duration on interoffice politics at Educraft.

I'd wanted him to greet me as a just-back-home explorer, to ask about the new worlds I'd encountered. I would tell of Surromoms, and Linda Po, and Debora. But no, he only nattered on, through gimlets three and four, till finally it was time to say good-bye. Even factoring in my dread of all things Seder-related, I couldn't wait to get up to the Nadlers'.

Surprisingly, the first part of the evening was a breeze. The standoff didn't come till after dinner.

All of us were crowded around the table, stuffed with food: Walter and Ellie, and Rina and Richard, and, finally, Stu and me. Walter was demanding that we hide the Afikoman—"a special matzo," he translated for my benefit—without which he couldn't complete the Seder. Hiding it seemed to be a job for children.

I was lost: if he *needed* the matzo, why ask us to *hide* it? I had sat through Seders here a couple of times before, but hiding a matzo? It didn't ring a bell.

"Dad, we're not kids," said Stu.

"To me you are. You're mine."

"But why should we—"

"I'd like you to. Isn't that enough?" Walter scanned the table for support.

Rina shrugged and kittenishly snuggled close to Richard. (She used him this way commonly, playing at a helplessness that let her off the hook.) Richard, always mindful of a feud's emergency exits, made a grave but carefully neutral nod. Husband first, or son-in-law? He seemed to split the difference.

"Not enough?" pushed Walter. "A father saying 'please'?"

As the other son-in-law (son-*outlaw*, joked Walter), and as the only non-Jew at the table, I felt I should also keep mum. My policy with the Nadlers was generally to side with Stu, but now, I wondered, why not just accede to Walter's wish?

Stu could get so stony in his parents' presence sometimes. He yearned to please, but seemed to think that only he knew how. Lately, though—ever since the bad-news call from Debora—Stu had dug his heels in, not just with his parents but with me too, with the whole world, as though to concede defeat in *any* situation would show he'd given up on getting pregnant. At the movies, last Sunday, Stu had all but strangled the teenaged soda vendor, who rang up his medium as a large. "Stu, it's fifty cents," I'd said. "Come on. Doesn't matter." "Yes, it does," he snapped at me. "It *does*."

Even if I wanted now to enter this dispute, the thought of any action but submission was remote. This was the effect of the food I'd over-eaten (on top of all the Maker's Mark with Joseph): hard-boiled egg, matzo, gefilte fish, brisket, half a dozen chunky side dishes. Maybe, I thought, the CIA could try a new technique: subject evildoers to a Seder's endless courses, till finally, helpless, overwhelmed, they squealed.

Now Stu's mother brought another tray in from the kitchen, but, thank God, all it bore was coffee.

Walter humphed. "I bet if *she* asked—right? Ta-dah, you'd do it."

"Oh, my sweet martyr," Ellie said. "You finally learned? Children always love their mother best." She poured Walter a piping black cup.

Ellie was a slender woman, equable, unmade-up, with an air of elegance-in-reserve. She'd been a Barnard girl, fending off proposals right and left (a med student, a circuit court clerk), when Walter Nadler, installing new deadbolts in her dorm, had asked if he could treat her to a coffee. He was a decade older and the opposite of loaded—his locksmith shop was barely breaking even—but she liked his schussing accent (he'd squelched it less, back then), its suggestion of alpine adventure. *Whoosh!* She was avalanched away.

At least that was Ellie's version, the one she'd always told me. In Walter's account, she knew from the get-go who he was: not some mountain-breeze-in-his-hair, swashbuckling Teuton but a Yid from the ruins of Berlin. She knew, and she saw his lonely lostness, and took pity.

I could easily see Walter playing on her pity. But the landsliding brunt of him—that also rang true: all I had to do was think of Stu, and multiply. Walter, at seventy, wasn't appreciably taller than the gaunt boy he'd been when he arrived. (I had seen the photo on the Nadlers' bedroom wall: a stunned, stunted ten-year-old, standing at a ship's rail, Europe a dim, broken line behind him.) Neither was he much heavier, except for his high, proud paunch. The belly seemed less to be a part of Walter's body than a tactical accessory to it—a rucksack, ready-packed in case of a new disaster.

Leaning back possessively now, palming his stomach's dome, Walter said, "But really. Seriously, kids. Do it. When they were little," he told me in his Jew 101 voice, "I promise you, this was their favorite part. See, they go and hide it, and then I look and look. But *never* find— that's the father's rule. So: how to get it back? Offer a reward. A toy, maybe. For Stu? A model airplane kit. For Rina, a set of watercolors. The rewards, kids—right? How you loved!"

Stu and Rina leaked similar noises of annoyance.

"We're *not* little," said Rina. "It's late. Let's move on. I'm feeling"— she held her sides—"sort of queasy."

All night she'd been saying similar things, citing symptoms, bidding for the family's special treatment. (As if a woman planning to *adopt* got morning sickness.)

"Indulge him," Ellie told her. "You'll be glad. Especially you."

Stu said, "Please just drop it. This is silly."

But *he* was being silly. I wasn't in the mood. Not after the kind of day I'd had. "C'mon, hon." I stood; I tugged at Stu's elbow. "Let's go hide the whatsit, right now."

Stu could have his superstitions, fine. But I had mine. Here was one: The way to build your be-a-parent karma? Honor your own parents. Do their bidding.

"C'mon," I said again. "Stu, get up."

Richard said, "You know what, Stu? He's right. Pat is right." (Trying still to make up for his shittiness last November? Maybe, but so what? I would take it.) "Up," he said. "Up! We'll have fun."

Stu could see the writing on the wall; he gave in. His frown, as he stood up, was laden with indignity but also (I was guessing) with relief: the soothing pain of yielding to a parent.

His look was not dissimilar from Milo's, at the zoo, just before Glenn had hauled him off: agreeable abjection, miserable coziness, the quintessential face of *I'm a son.*

Oh, I wanted a Milo of my own.

Glenn, when he'd brought the boy back from the bathroom, had given us a recap of the lesson: "Babies pee in their diapers, we decided—remember, Milo? And big boys pee where? In the bathroom."

"Well, then," I'd chimed in, "your choice is pretty easy. I mean, you don't want to be a *baby.*"

Milo firmly shook his head no.

"You want to be a big boy, now, right? Dontcha, Milo?"

But once again Milo shook his head.

"No? Not a baby *or* a big boy? But then . . . what?"

Milo squeezed his penguin to his chest. "Stay the same."

If only I could have bottled his charm and sold it!

"That's how I feel sometimes, too," said Zack, "but it's impossible. Everybody has to grow up sometime."

Milo's eyes narrowed to a disbelieving squint. Then he asked, wonderingly, "*Him* go in the bathroom?"

"Who do you mean—Pat?"

He nodded. "Him go too? Papa Pat? Him go in the bathroom?"

"*Uncle* Pat," corrected Glenn. "You know he's not your papa."

"No one's," I said, "yet. But soon. Fingers crossed. And yes, bud. I do go in the bathroom."

Milo's eyes went wide as he scanned me up and down: another bizarre creature at the zoo.

Back at the Seder table I was feeling a bit like Milo, watching these strange specimens, the Nadlers.

Walter, having failed, by design, to find his matzo, had finally asked his children to relent. Now he clutched the Afikoman with beady-eyed relief, as if its fate had ever been in doubt. "Boys," he said, addressing me and Stu. "You won't mind? This year's ransom will go to Richard and Rina."

"What?" said Richard. "No—we'll share it, four ways 'round. Heck, the hiding place was *their* idea."

But Walter, with a brick-wall grin, shook his head. "Trust me."

The hiding place, in point of fact, had been Richard's idea (a teetering stack of last year's *Security Systems News*, the matzo safely tucked between two issues). Why would he be lying now, on Stu's and my behalf?

Although I'd built him up, with good cause, as a bogeyman, tonight Richard was earning his redemption. A minute ago, when Rina and Stu had bickered about the matzo ("Put it somewhere blatant, Stu—he's still not going to 'find' it"; "Slap Dad in the face? What's the point?"), Richard had stepped between them and distracted them with a joke. I ignored the details, but noted instead his style: his broad put-on accent, a parody of Borscht Belt comics. It made me see the possibility that Richard's whole persona was a shtick, a highly skilled choice. His narcissism, his oiliness: perhaps they were a master craftsman's tools.

And now, too, with Walter, Richard was trying—wasn't he?—to wield his tools to fix a confrontation: "The only reward we need," he said, "is being here, as a family. Ree and I—we don't want more than that."

"Can it, Rich," said Walter. "Not buying what you're selling."

"Walter," Ellie warned him.

"Don't 'Walter' me, my dear. It's both of our idea. Am I wrong?"

"Yes, *my dear*, but the point . . . the point is to be generous. You don't have to be antagonistic."

Walter offered his wife a chilly smile. "Geez," he said, turning to his son-in-law and daughter, "who'd have thought that it would be so hard to give a gift? But anyway, here we go. Drumroll, please."

All there was was sticky nervous silence.

From somewhere in the heirloom Seder plate, he pulled an envelope, its flap inked in smudgy, old-man scrawl: "R&R."

I coughed to hide a laugh at the thought that this was *restful*. But maybe Walter had missed his own pun.

"By now you kids know that your mom and I are planners, always trying to think ahead, for you." Walter beamed; he relished this performance. "The days you kids were born, we set aside some money—as much as we could manage—and invested."

"They know this," Ellie said. "You've told them this before. They know it's what paid for their tuition."

"Right, but what they don't know: we set aside *more* money. Only a thousand bucks for each—'only,' but believe me, even that was hard enough, back then. The good thing, though—that money? Today it's . . . guess how much."

"Walter, it's unseemly," Ellie said. "Please just tell."

"What, unseemly?" He raised his arm so quickly that I flinched. "Okay, see, the notion?" he said. "The money wasn't for you. For your *kids*. Saved up for the day your first was born. But now, you know, since . . . now that you . . ."

"Lord!" said Ellie. "Just take it already." She thrust the gift at Rina.

Rina opened the envelope. She saw the check. She gasped.

Richard took it next, and echoed his wife's noise. "Walter, Ellie—no! It's too much."

Walter wiped his eyes. "On this—" Again, he faltered. "On your *future*, you think that we would skimp?"

Stu leaned across the table, trying to see the numbers, but Richard held the check beyond his view. "Walter," Richard said. His voice was hushed, clubby. "The appreciation. How? Is your broker a magician? A measly thousand bucks into *thirty*!"

Walter chuckled wishfully. "He's good but not that good. It wasn't just one thousand, it was two. It's both. See?"

I did see, immediately. That chauvinistic prick! But Stu, for another beat, didn't seem to get it; he looked puzzled (stumped by the *puzzle* of the math) but not yet enraged by the unfairness.

"We realized," said Walter, his arm on Stu's shoulder. "What's the point of holding on to the grandkid fund for *you* when you're . . . well, when the two of *them*" — he winked at Richard and Rina— "when adoption is such a costly thing?"

Now Stu understood. His lips went thin, bloodless.

But gosh, no, not both of the funds—we couldn't take Stu's away! That was what I kept expecting Richard to cut in with. That or something grand and Solomonic: *Bring me a sword. Half goes to the one, half to the other.* Where was the craftsman of family harmony now?

Pumping Walter's hand, that was where. "So generous," Richard said. "We're just . . . we're flabbergasted."

"Oh, Daddy!" Rina cried. "This just means the world to us." She came around and hugged him, bouncing on her toes. Her queasiness had seemed to find its cure.

"Now are you happy," said Ellie, "that you hid the Afikoman?"

"I'd happily hide a hundred more," said Richard.

Walter slugged his coffee down, then tipped his cup toward Stu. "What do you say, brother Stu? Proud of your little sis, the mom-to-be?"

"*Uncle* Stu," said Ellie (like Glenn correcting Milo). "Of course he's proud. Proud as can be. Look!"

Tell them, I thought. *For fuck's sake, Stu.* But Stu just palely smiled.

All but choke a soda jerk for fifty measly cents, but fifteen grand robbed, and not a peep? Worse than the money lost: the absolute erasure.

A bloat made of emptiness was rising in my chest. It boiled up and burst within my mouth. "Stu and I," I said, "we've got our own surprise."

Now he met my glance: a look of fearful scolding.

Walter said, "A better surprise than mine? Good luck with that."

Oh, Stu's eyes: so very small, so smallened.

Why? Shouldn't his parents be elated by our plan? *Another* grandchild. This one from their son, their stalwart son, whom they had wrongly thought a full stop.

"I have a guess," said Ellie. "You're moving back to New York." She clapped her hands. "The family close again?"

"No," I said, "sorry. We're staying on the Cape. But *family*, yeah—you're on the right track."

In one long liberating rush, I told them everything: Stu would be the father, the mother would be Jewish, the Cape was ideal for raising kids. Well, not everything; nothing about our streak of disappointments. I worked to keep my voice full of nerve. "And so," I finished, "if all goes well, by next year—next Seder—we'll have *two* new Nadlers at the table!"

I raised both my hands in a *how-about-that?* gesture, and held them there, as if to lead a chorus of good tidings.

The Nadlers' mouths were open, but no glad song emerged. Stu was dumbstruck, too; he looked smacked.

"I know it's out of the blue," I said. "It takes some getting used to." For me, too, I told them, at first it had seemed odd. "But where a baby starts its life isn't what's important. Where it ends up, that's what counts—same as with adoption. So," I added, "mazel tov to Rina and to Richard. And mazel tov to me and Stu, also. Or, wait—can you 'mazel tov' yourself? I don't remember. I need some remedial Jewish lessons." I laughed, but the sound only boomeranged around.

Come on, Stu, I thought. Don't just let me *hang* . . .

Walter finally turned to me, his mouth no longer slackened but screwed into a pout of distaste. "A woman who would have a child for cash, she must be crazy—and *that* would be the mother of your baby?" He held his gut, a bomb that he might toss.

"No," I said, "she's not like that at all. Wait and see! Debora's . . . you'll just love her. Especially you, Walter. An immigrant, too, like you—so much gumption."

"Hold on, now. *Debora?* You've hired someone already? It's more than just . . . you're telling me it's *happening?*" He wheeled to Stu, fiery-eyed, righteous.

"Yeah," said Stu. (The meekness of his voice. A gutless grunt.) "A couple of months," he said, "we've been trying."

Ellie said, "Who knows this yet? Rina, dear, did *you* know?" To Stu again: "You tell your parents last?"

"News to me," said Rina. "News to me! Even when I went up there and told you what we're doing . . . even *then* you didn't say a thing?"

"But Rina," I said, "Stu was only trying to be thoughtful. Trying not to steal the stage from you, from your good news."

"And," said Stu, "we wanted to keep this private, just in case."

"In case *what?*" said Ellie. "In case you find a different mom and dad? Someone else to tell about your lives?"

Stu crushed a matzo crumb into the holiday tablecloth. "In case," he said, "something went wrong."

"Something?" shouted Walter. "The whole damn thing is wrong. Ask me, it's nothing else but wrong."

A fog of quiet socked us in. A New York sort of quiet: car alarms, the screech of someone's bumper being hit.

Richard was the only one who hadn't spoken yet. Richard, with the check still in hand. "So much hate is out there," he said. "It hurts you guys. It must. But you both know—I hope you do—that that's not how I feel." He touched my wrist. He furrowed his brow humanely. "And so," he said, "you know it's not from prejudice when I tell you: this thing you're attempting is misguided." He and Rina had also considered the option, he confessed: egg donors, surrogacy, a seeming miracle cure. But here was what his rabbi, thank Hashem, had helped

141

them see: To turn a person—a woman—into a *paid incubator,* to make the gift of life into a chit? This was an affront to God. A slap to human dignity. "The woman signs her life away. Can't do *x* and *y*. Can't—get this!—make love with her husband. Slavery," he said. "It's nothing less than slavery."

"No," said Walter, "you know what it's like? The Nazis, is what. Mengele! Engineering babies in a dish."

"It isn't, Dad," said Stu.

"Oh, no? Please enlighten me."

"We don't, well . . . there isn't any dish."

That was the extent of Stu's defense? There's not a *dish?*

"*I'll* enlighten you," I said. "You want a clearer picture?"

Ellie thrust her napkin at me, as if to stuff my throat. Too little, too late: she couldn't halt my outburst.

"Stu whacks off and cums into a cup—okay, you picture that? And Debora's husband shoots it up inside her."

"Stop," said Ellie. "Not at this table. Stop!"

"Well," I said, "I'm not . . . I mean"—my tongue's senseless motions, twitching like a beast after slaughter.

"Grace," she said. "The Grace after Meals. Please. Let's skip to that."

A flash in the pan. That was all my courage.

"No!" said Walter. "The Afikoman. First we have to eat it. I won't let this . . . this filth wreck our Seder."

"Okay, then, fine," Ellie said. "The Afikoman."

Afikoman, Afikoman—a crunch of nonsense syllables.

When Stu handed a piece to me he kept our skin from touching. The matzo turned to mortar in my mouth.

thirteen

Our next try with Debora also failed. This despite her conscientious diet of Robitussin (two teaspoons, three times a day, eight days straight), designed to thin her vaginal secretions. Despite, too, our method's fine-tuning: Stu did his business now straight into the Instead Cup, not a drop lost in the specimen cup or syringe; Debora stayed in bed, hips high, for two hours, then kept the Instead Cup, for two further hours, deep inside, snug against her cervix.

So diligent, so loyal to the cause, our surro was. I was glad I'd thought to bring her something from New York: a T-shirt from the zoo, emblazoned with a two-toed sloth, upside-down, smiling. Hang Tight! I'd bought the same, in kids' size, for Paula. "I know they're dumb," I'd said, handing Debora the gifts. (I did this while Stu was in the bathroom, getting busy; Danny, in a heads-up bid to avert a scene like last time's, had whisked Paula out to the back yard.) "But hey," I said, "they're *Brazilian*. The guy in the zoo shop told me. The sloths, not the shirt—that's from China."

"A sloth . . . well. Why not bring me something *nice*? A toucan?"

"I asked for a toucan. No, I did! They—"

Feigning indignation, she hurled the shirt aside. But later, when she summoned me and Stu back to the bedroom (smells of sweat and cough syrup muggy in the air), she wore it like a winning team's colors. "I love this. I *love*," she said. "Danny, find the camera."

"What?" he said. "Seriously?"

"Paula should wear hers, too. Go and get her changed. Make it quick."

I'd worried, when Stu and I agreed to use a surro, about how we'd honor such a debt. The moral, not financial, obligation. But Debora's outsize joy, now, for just a silly shirt, made me think the most valuable thing we were giving her was treating her as someone worthy of value.

Debora, from her perch in bed, caught us up on news, the most important piece of which was: she had hosted a Seder! The very first she'd hosted for the Neumans. "You see, Stu?" she said. "See how you inspire me?" Danny's entire clan had come from Brockton for the evening, and everyone assured her she had done a lovely job. "Next year in Hyannis," they all joked. The funniest part: Paula had actually *liked* to eat the horseradish, the way it made her eyes swell with tears. "A Jew, no? Even at her age. It's in the genes!"

And how, she asked, was our Seder? A nice trip to New York?

Shit, I thought. Here we go again. I was already up to my chin with telling Stu I was sorry: *Sorry I spoke too soon. I should have let you tell your folks. I know I should have chosen different words.*

"Go ahead, explain," he said. "Tell her about what happened. You're the one who's so good at divulging."

"I don't know, Stu. Maybe it's better if—"

"No," he said. "Go on."

Fine, I did. Described the Nadlers' protest of our plan (omitting mention of grandkid funds, and also Dr. Mengele), trying my best to show its comic aspects. "They're sure you're being used," I said. "A woman enslaved, they think."

"Ai," said Debora, "look at how I'm chained in bed. Help!"

Paula, from downstairs, called, "Mãinha? You okay?"

"Yes, yes, *filhinha*." Debora laughed. "I am perfect."

"But listen," I said, seriously, "I understand their fears. They're older, and old-fashioned. Surrogacy is new. We knew they might need a little coaching."

"Oh, 'we' did? We knew?" said Stu. "Is that why 'we' just ambushed them?"

Debora scooched up higher on the bed, inch by inch, as though trying to keep intact a house of cards atop her. "I told you about my parents, no? The way they thought of Danny? A sex tourist, they called him. A loser, full of lies. And me they called a stupid fool, to love him. After I left I wrote to them. For years I wrote them letters. Nobody would even send an answer." She brushed her hands briskly: *that's that!* "But then, when I have Paula, and send to them some photos? Then my mother mails to me a dress she made for Paula, a dress cut from one I used to wear: yellow flowers all around, and little shining suns. My mother, she had kept that small old dress for all those years."

I was about to thank her for that shot-in-the-arm story, but Danny bustled in, camera around his neck, holding up a peevish, bucking Paula.

"Please," he said, "don't say now you want her in that dress. I just barely got her into the T-shirt."

"The dress was just a story," Debora said. "About parents. About, you know, giving them some time."

"Giving them some time?" said Stu. "That's what I was trying to do, but—"

"Stu," I said.

"Forget it, Pat. Just drop it."

At least he had the sense not to keep fighting in front of them. We made our excuses and went home.

Stu hadn't spoken to his father since the Seder, but finally, after a couple of weeks, Walter Nadler phoned. According to Stu, the talk boiled down to this:

"Money's always the issue, Stu. People just lose their heads."

"Dad, it isn't about the money. Truly. It's way beyond that. What it's about is treating us as equal."

"Not the money—you sure? Okay, then, forget it. Rina will get the full amount, as planned. And as for what *you're* planning to do . . ."

"Giving you guys a grandkid?"

"Your private life is your business, Stu. But please, keep it private. Spare your mother and me the details, yeah?"

Stu tried to spin this as a minor sign of progress, but afterward he lapsed again to sulking—a state that only worsened, later that same day, when Debora called to tell us that the Robitussin, the hours in bed . . . none of it had done a bit of good.

Square one. I wanted to punch the ground.

But dealing with Stu, who crawled farther into his bunker of brooding, kept me from unraveling my own sadness.

I knew he blamed himself. He couldn't well blame Debora (Paula was such pushy, gleaming proof that *she* was fertile). Months ago, when he was tested, his numbers had looked fine. But maybe we should run some tests again, I was thinking. Take another look, to ease his mind.

"I know this must be hard for you," I said to him one night, conscious of avoiding words like *sterile*.

"Isn't it hard for all of us?"

"No, but what I mean," I said. "I'm sure you must be doubting if—"

"Let me deal with my own doubts," he said.

Who could I talk to? Not our New York friends, not after my fruitless trip. My sisters? No, we never dug that deep.

The person I kept thinking of was Debora. Only Debora. But Stu was already bugging her (cut way back on coffee? try a fresh-garlic suppository?), and I didn't want to amplify her stress.

The message board on Surromoms was where I finally turned. After all, the site was what had hooked us up with Debora. Maybe it would work its magic twice.

At first I was put off by the cutesy tropes of Surrospeak: DW, for "darling wife"; FT, for "fertile thoughts." A strange form of baby talk. Craving-a-baby talk. Eventually, though, the members' lack of irony drew me in. I thought of how deliciously unironic children were. Milo, for example, or Paula, or my nephews. They never smirked, they *smiled*; they did nothing "in quotes." Maybe, then, to have a kid I needed to be more kidlike—earnest and unguarded. It felt good.

Implausibly, I grew close—if pixels brought you "close"—to Pentecostal Texans, to housewives in Duluth. Like LuvToShare, who couldn't carry her own child (hysterectomy) but offered up her frozen eggs so others could be fruitful. And Pray4Life, who hoped to carry her brother-in-law's baby, to give her paraplegic sister a child. Eight long months she'd tried and failed, but still her spirits soared.

All the moms who wrote to me said: Calm way down, be patient. I was told of someone who for *twenty months* had struggled, cycle after cycle after cycle, and then, on the brink of quitting: bull's-eye. No one could explain it—not rationally, at least—and so they spoke of answered prayers, God's will.

This talk of divine intervention made me nervous. "God's will" rarely favored guys like us.

But then one night I logged on, and there was a post from Pray4Life: *Thrilled to let you know, two pink stripes!* The story was so providential, I hoped it might cheer Stu. When he came home, I handed him the laptop.

He scanned the screen. "Pray4Life? Seriously? You're kidding."

"Read it, Stu. The point here is, good things can still happen."

"And you need *them*, with their precious little acronyms, to know that? Jesus, Pat—oops, I mean, SandyNeckDad—is this really the best you can do?"

If Stu didn't want the help, no matter: I would take it. He could have a belly laugh at all the silly acronyms, while I enjoyed my network of new friends. And I alone, not he, would know the secret thrill of the question often posed to me online: *What's your role? Are you the IF?* I loved the sharp rise of those two capital letters, their dignified boldness on the screen. Typing my response— *That's me, the IF*—what I meant, beyond the basic code (*intended father*), was the *if*: the incalculable chance.

In May we tried (a word I now despised) a fourth time. Then, of course, we had to wait again.

The weather, I was figuring, would match my fragile mood—partly because I'd always been a fan of the pathetic fallacy, and partly just because of how a Cape spring usually went: fickle warmth, a sky that longed to crack. Weirdly, though, every day dawned clearer than the last. Daffodils, exploding from the ends of their thin stalks, looked like gaudy cartoon bursts of cheer.

The fallacy wasn't called *pathetic* for nothing, I reminded myself: don't be dumb and take these things as signs.

The day arrived. We'd told Debora we'd call her in the evening. Stu wanted to pose ourselves, for luck, like the last time (even though that time had been unlucky): hand in hand before our sweeping view. Maybe he was looking for a way to tell me sorry. Maybe he was tossing me a bone.

The greening marsh, the dunes beyond, whitecaps on the bay, and sunset basting all of it with soft, refined light that fired through Rina's Holy Rose pendant. (Weeks ago we'd hung it at the pane, as she'd advised.)

Stu squeezed my hand, and squeezed again. He dialed.

Much of the time, Debora's nasal vowels could still confuse me: her sounds for *no* and *now* seemed the same. And oh, how I would have liked, just then, to misconstrue her. But there was no mistaking the word *negative*.

A week later we met again at the Pancake King, both couples. Paula had been handed off to Libby at the multiplex, to see a film that starred a singing fish—which sounded much more fun than what we faced.

We'd waited twenty minutes for a table, tempers spiking (a busload of Japanese tourists swamped the place, enjoying their Memorial Day trip), and now, finally seated, having ordered, we were silent. A doctor's-office silence—anxiety and shame—but sharper edged, layered through with anger.

Or maybe it was this: the high-G-force queasiness of having sped to intimacy too fast.

A neighbor in New York, who hustled to pay for med school, had once explained the job's biggest drawback: "The sex isn't terrible. It's even good, occasionally. The terrible thing is lying there, afterward, and talking. *Talking* is the thing I make them pay for." Was this how Debora and Danny saw us: the payers and the paid? No, I couldn't believe that. But why was no one talking?

Past us whooshed the rapids of the restaurant's commotion; I felt like a river rock, eroding. All around, the hatchet chops of chats in Japanese. (Did our English, to them, sound as violent?)

A dainty-boned man with a credit card–sized camera cradled in his chic, stemlike fingers, hovered over a golden stack of hotcakes. He snapped a shot and showed it to the woman at his table, who frowned and gestured: *You can do better.*

I thought I saw a chance to break our gridlock. "If I'm ever lucky enough to visit Japan," I said, talking in a forced, roguish whisper, "I hope I eat better than, whatever, Sushi King. If all they want is shitty food, you'd think they'd stay at home."

"I wish they'd stay home, period," said Danny.

I braced for a possible racist rant.

But Danny added, "Not just them. Everyone. All the tourists. Every year it's worse, I swear. Did you guys see the traffic? More and more, I just—I'm sick of everyone."

"But not us, though," said Debora coyly. She touched her heart. "Not me?"

"Ha! Sick of *you?* Ha! Ha!"

Danny's tone, the muscle of it, shoved us back to silence.

Stu was locked in something like an autism of anxiety, moving his fork left of his spoon, then right, then left, then right. He had been the one who'd made arrangements for this check-in ("See where we all stand," he'd suggested), but now he looked as though he'd been dragooned.

The waitress brought our drinks and was greeting her next table, when Danny reached back and tapped her shoulder. "Miss? Hey, excuse me. I asked was the iced tea sweetened. You said it wasn't, but here—here, taste this."

"Hold on just a sec, sir, okay? I'm with this table."

"No!" he snarled. "Come on. It's like syrup."

Debora, looking mortified, said, "Here, take my soda. Danny, please. Dan. Turn around."

"Don't want soda. The point is, I asked for unsweetened. But the waitress"—he jabbed his hand; it seemed he might swat her—"the waitress doesn't know her own menu."

Diners at the tables all around us now stared. The man with the camera turned; I feared he'd snap our picture: *Trip to America. View of vulgar natives.*

The waitress came and knelt beside Danny, eyes reddened. "I'll get you another, sir—of whatever, on the house. But please, would you—" Her voice cracked. "Would you please not yell?"

Her tears, or her splintered voice, finally got to Danny. He broke out of his trance of self-pity. "Sorry," he said. "Sorry. It's—forget it, this is fine."

"I'd be happy to—"

"Really, no. It's fine." Then he faced us. "Sorry, guys. Really, really sorry. It's work," he explained. "I'm letting it get me down. A couple of my lots failed their perc tests last week. And the INS—my crew is almost all, you know, Brazilians—the INS is breathing down my neck."

Debora cringed. At the notion of her countrymen being hounded? No, I thought: at the not-quite-glance Danny had just given her. He looked limp and thwarted, could scarcely meet her eyes.

Watching this exchange, this *lack* of one, I got it: Danny's problem must not be his work, or not just that. The real problem? His marriage—the way that we had crimped it: four months-plus since he had been allowed in Debora's bed. Wouldn't any husband's nerves have frayed?

No intercourse until the surrogate pregnancy is confirmed . . .
No action that could introduce semen into her body . . .

Standard clauses. Boilerplate. The lawyer had insisted. But did we really have to be so strict? Maybe we could grant a one-time variance, for morale: using a condom, and spermicide, the day after her period . . .

How to raise the subject, though, without seeming even more intrusive? Plus, I had to ask Stu first. No more surprise announcements.

Danny was now looking at his tea, not at Debora. Flexing his bite with tension. Poor guy.

"Hey," I said. "Don't worry. We've all been under stress." I went to pat his hand, but he jerked it out of reach.

"Yeah, well, for you," he said, "for you the stress is worth it." He gripped his glass. Tea sloshed to the rim.

Stu jolted forward, his face suddenly focused: a cloud about to dump a spate of rain. "What are you really trying to say?" he challenged.

Danny shrugged. "If all this works? Bang, you've got a family. For us, it's . . . the thing of it is, we've already got a family. Maybe for us this does more harm than good."

Stu said, "We didn't come to talk about quitting."

"Hold on," Debora said. "Does anyone say we're quitting?"

"It sounded like your husband did. Sounded like that to me."

Debora grinned: an appliqué of poise.

"Remember the contract," Stu went on. "The contract says you'll try for eight cycles."

"Don't sit there and boss her," Danny said. "Don't talk like that."

Stu said, "Don't talk to *me* like that."

"Hey hey hey. Please!" I said. "Can't we please stay decent? Everyone please just calm down for a sec." I won an instant's lull, but I guessed it wouldn't last. "We knew this would be tricky," I said. "Didn't we, going in? I mean, hell, it's tricky enough just trying to get pregnant."

"Appreciate your expert view, there, Pat," said Danny tightly. "Actually, though, it wasn't all that 'tricky' making Paula. Pretty easy, in fact, and—correct me if I'm wrong—a hell of a lot more fun to do, right, Deb?"

151

Stu bared his teeth. "What's that supposed to mean?"

"Not *supposed* to mean anything. Means just what it means: Maybe you're having trouble because this isn't something natural. Maybe this just isn't meant to be."

"Christ, don't start me with *natural*. What is it with you people? Strut around like God's gift, just because when *you* have sex, ta-dah!—your wife gets pregnant. As if that's some major moral achievement."

I put my arm around him, hoping to rein him in. "Stu," I said. "Stu, please."

"Please what? Please swallow this crap again? And not from my family but from *them*?"

"Stop!" said Debora. "I hate to hear this. Danny didn't mean it how you think."

"Right," said Danny. "All I meant—"

But here was the waitress, doling out our plates with practiced flicks. "There," she said. "All set for now? And sir, I'm going to bring a brand-new tea."

The tourists stared, awaiting another brawl.

Danny only nodded. I did, too. We all did.

"Okay, great," the waitress said. "Holler if you need me."

The food was steaming sweetly. It softened the air between us. The smell of bacon acted like a balm.

"Look," I said. "We've waited for this food so long. We're cranky. Let's just say we're sorry, and dig in."

"Yes," said Debora. "What we need is food."

But Stu said, "I am sorry. I've actually lost my appetite. Pat, do you mind? Let's just pay the bill and go on home."

I wanted to kick his shins. And maybe Danny's, too.

Stu got up, and as I followed, Debora caught my eye. When Danny wasn't looking, I mouthed, "Call me."

fourteen

It felt sneaky: our men still crouched behind barricades of sancti-mony, licking their wounds, nixing any truce, and here we were, Debora and I, meeting on the sly, at the cool, sweeping shore of Sandy Neck. My alibi was simple but sufficient: "Off to the library," I'd said to Stu, a stack of books as proof, and he had scarcely looked up from his *Times*.

The furtive mood was heightened by the afternoon's conditions: the sun like a secret agent, stealing from cloud to cloud; a shifty wind that disarranged the dunes. Debora and I had the beach almost to ourselves. Two lovebirds, khaki cuffs rolled up to their knees, held hands and hurdled low breakers. A smoky-haired woman and her not-so-golden retriever hobbled with the same arthritic gait.

We headed east, skirting between sand and sea-buffed stones. Debora looked undaunted as she walked across the scree. She wore a crimson windbreaker, buttoned at the bottom, which kept catching gusts of breeze and puffing on both sides, calling to mind the bulging cheeks of someone about to blow out birthday candles.

"Wow," she said. "So beautiful." Her arms stretched up, outward; her cheeklike jacket caught another gust.

"My folks chose well," I said. "We're lucky to live so close."

"And me, I am dumb," she said. "Living on the Cape so long, and never have I come here. We go always to Seagull Beach. Or Craigville."

"Better sand on that side, I guess. But aren't they pretty crowded?"

"Yes, too crowded. And there, it's just the beach, you know. Not these." She pointed to the field of dunes, rising on our right, dignified behind their fence of No Trespassing placards.

When I was a kid, the dunes weren't cordoned off for conservation, and so I had free rein to rove among them. Nothing much but sand out there, endless sun-baked piles, but I had found affinity with the scattered clumps of dune grass, improbable little tufts of green that somehow stayed alive. I was perched unstably, too: within my arid family. An alien life form, a boy who liked boys. No wonder I admired those blades of grass.

"Where I live," said Debora. "Where I come from. Near Natal. The dunes, oh my God, they're so high."

"Bigger than these?"

"Oh! Like sugar mountains, miles and miles. Genipabu, it's called. You can even ride a camel. Also, if you want, do *esquibunda*. It means to ski the hills of sand, sitting on your *bumbum*." To translate, she smacked me on the butt. "And the men there, the *bugeiros*—the ones who have the boogies?"

"The boogies?" I said.

"The open cars . . . no roof on top . . . like jeeps."

"Dune buggies?"

"You know them!" she cried, as if this proved a bond. "The *bugeiros* drive you out, way way up to the very top, then they ask, 'Would you like it with emotion, or without?' 'Without' is only normal driving, slow, down the dune. But 'with emotion'—it's *so fast*, no brake, almost crashing. Wonderful, just wonderful, it's perfect!" She beamed with the memory, her features going burnished. "Danny, when we met? He loved so much to go. Hugging to each other when the buggy it went flying. That's what it was like, you know. Exactly like that: flying."

Here she paused, and seemed to find something by her feet. She bent down and scooped a bunch of sand.

"He wanted to go again," she said. "No matter what the price. One more time. One more, with emotion." She let the sand drop between her fingers.

"How is Danny now?" I asked. "I mean, you know, with this." I tried making a gesture to encompass the scope of *this*, but what could stand for all the strain and oddness of our efforts? What could stand for borrowing someone's wife?

"He took Paula to Brockton. To visit with her grandmother." She said this as though it were an answer to my question, and then veered off, closer to the water.

"To Brockton?" I asked, following. "For a day trip, or . . . how long?"

"Not for long. But still, it's too long." She took a phone from her jacket pocket, and held it like an amulet. "Four times I have called today, thinking of new excuses. 'Don't forget her cream for rash!' 'Nothing to eat with walnuts!' Just so I can ask to hear her voice." Her eyes went big, quivery with tears. "All her life, and we have been apart three nights only."

"Three nights? In all of Paula's life? Are you serious?"

"Three. Or maybe two, I think. Maybe only two. But Pat," she said. "Don't worry." She stroked my tensing arm. "You will be the same with yours. You'll see."

She must have thought I panicked at a future so kid-tethered, but truly I looked forward to that, to feeling that utmost tug. No, what made me tense was a vision of Stu, of *our* future, the way a child would bind us even tighter. Given the way he'd acted lately, it wasn't an easy thought.

"I'm sure you're right. I hope so," I said. "My only comparison's Stu. And with him, well . . ."

"But no," she said. "To love a child, it's much more simple, I think, than with a husband." She knuckled a tear from one eye, then the other. "To be the parent is not a choice: you are, you always will be. And so you don't waste time wondering 'Should I?'"

I smiled. "Yeah, I sometimes ask that question."

"And," she said, "Stu? How is Stu?"

"Stu? Well, he's . . . hard to say. Mostly 'without emotion.'" I waited for a laugh, but none came. "Except, of course, the other day, with Danny and you, at lunch. 'With emotion' then, for sure. A glut."

"Glut?" she said. "I don't know this word."

"Um . . . more than needed? Too much."

Now she laughed, with no apparent pleasure. "Glut," she said. "It sounds maybe dirty."

"Honestly, though?" I said. I picked a stone up, skipped it over the surf. "I can't say I really disagreed with what Stu said."

I'd expressed the same to him, driving home from lunch: he'd been right, Danny had been a prick. Stu's response? "Not especially useful to say that *now*." "As if it's useful," I'd countered, "to totally piss off Danny? Not if you still hope to work things out."

Stalemate: a word more apt than I had ever noticed. Same old mate, same old stale maneuvers.

And now, when I turned to Debora, it wasn't to defend Stu—not entirely. More like to interpret. "The things he said to Danny," I said, "were pretty much on target. The *way* he said them: that was what was off. You don't catch flies with vinegar, right? Stu has got a big chip on his shoulder."

Cliché, cliché. What was I avoiding? Maybe I just couldn't say exactly what I meant till I figured out exactly how I felt.

Okay, then: I tried to sketch an image of Stu's childhood. Living in the shadow of his aunt's and uncle's deaths, of Walter's lucky dodge from destruction. *Don't get used to anything*, was Walter's constant mantra. *Let yourself be beaten once, the next time's not so bad—and that's the kind of "better" you don't need.* "Because of this, Stu's fantastic as someone on your side," I said. "Never lets an insult go unchallenged. A loyal boyfriend—and father, too, I hope. But God forbid you do something that makes him side *against* you . . ."

Debora wore a look now of private, feline pleasure, her brow lined with filigrees of wrinkle.

"What?" I asked.

She shook her head.

"*What?*"

"It's just—sorry. What you said, it sounds so much like *Danny.*" Doubting, always doubting, she said: that was his way with everything—a hand-me-down, like Stu's, from his parents. Running their shop in Brockton? A used-equipment business? How could they make money if they *trusted*?

Danny had been the first of the Neumans to try college. Emphasis on *try*. Never finished. "This is why he's nervous to be with you guys," she said. "You talk so smooth, you have your education. I think he thinks, *What will they sneak past me?*"

"Sneak? Not a thing," I said. "Nothing."

"And jealous," she said, her grin now gone. "I think. Mostly that."

I wanted to say he had things backward: Stu and I were jealous. Jealous of him and Debora, of their family.

Debora took my forearm in her hand with great care. "I'm sorry," she said. "The fighting, it was . . . really, I'm so sorry."

"No," I said, "*I* am." I put my hand on hers. I felt a pleasant tremor of contrition.

She nodded sympathetically, and on we walked, linked, hand over hand over arm. The lovebirds we had seen before, hopping over the breakers, reappeared, their shins splashed with surf. What would they assume of me and Debora? I didn't care. The *push, push* of waves was compelling.

"Wait," said Debora, stopping short. "Why should we be—what did *we* do wrong?"

A wave crashed, a perfectly timed gag, and sprayed us both.

"You and I? That's a decent question. I don't know."

The joke of it—our penitence, when we had done no sin; our arrogance, in taking on the blame—sent us into purging fits of laughter. Soon we were galloping arm in arm along the shore, mocking ourselves, a game of verbal Ping-Pong: *I'm* sorry . . . no, *I* am . . . no *I* . . .

Finally, we both flopped down, winded, at the tide line. Sand was in my shoes and socks, maybe in my lungs. Tiny trails of salt along my cheeks.

Suddenly Debora froze again. "Oh my God. What *is* that?"

"What?" I said. I tried to glance beyond her. A shiv of tail was what I glimpsed, a spiny dome of armor. "Haven't you ever seen a horseshoe crab?"

"Yes, but it's . . . it's *two* of them, fighting. It scared me."

I rose to my knees till I saw what she referred to, a reckless-looking rear-end crab collision. The crabs had the long-enduring, humbling look of artifacts: coppery and patinated, priceless. "They're not fighting. They're mating," I said. "This is when they spawn. The full moon and the new moon, in May and June. Spring tide."

"Ah," she said. "Spring fever." Her sprightly tone was back. "Everything in the world feels so sex."

"No," I said, flustered by her charming dropped *y*. "Or yes, maybe, but that's not what 'spring' means, why it's called that. 'Spring' as in 'spring up.' As in 'leap.' The spring tides are higher, right? The moon's effect, I guess. So horseshoe crabs can make it onto shore, farther than normal. The females lay eggs, and then the males go after them. They do it in the nighttime, then swim back with the tide, but some are too worn out—like these two, right here. They burrow in the sand, and wait for the next tide. They have to stay moist to survive."

Debora put her hand near the crabs but not quite touching. "How do you know so much?" she said. "You've written a book about it?"

"No," I said. "My mother. She took me to see. She taught me."

"Oh, then, a memory. This is nice."

Actually, no, the memory was more mixed. I shared it with her.

I had been thirteen. Memorial Day weekend. My mom woke me up in the hours after midnight, saying she had a special treat to show me. We drove down 6A—silver-plated with moonlight—then parked and went wading through a sloping nook of marsh.

"Here," she said, her smile also silvered. "Here, Pat. Look."

The grass was shivering. But how? The night was still, windless.

Then I saw a horseshoe crab, a second . . . no, *heaps*. A huge crab ringed by a frantic scrum of smaller ones, each trying to scrabble to the top. Beyond that, another clot of crabs, then another, the whole quaking chaos of them bright with tiny clackings, as if the moonlight flashing on their shells produced a noise.

Mom explained the rite, the same as every other spring since long before the dinosaurs had roamed. "Tough to think of creatures like this mating, no?" she whispered. "They look too weird—like stones. But what choice do they have?"

Now the clacking called to mind a Geiger counter's tick, gauging the intensity of awesome, hidden forces—the same ones that I had lately felt the first ignition of and sensed would lead to shaming and exclusion.

"Your father brought me here," she said. "He wasn't your father yet. Loony, I thought—the middle of the night, middle of nowhere! But I was nuts about him. I would've followed him anywhere. And then," she said. "Then I saw"—she swept her arms wide—"this."

The pile was growing ever wilder, closer, more ecstatic, the chains of the crabs getting longer. A large crab had latched on to my boot.

"I wanted," I told Debora, "to kick the damn thing off. Kick it as far as I could, into the ocean."

"Why?" she said. "Scared?"

"Yeah, but not of the crab. More about me, my own life. Would I ever bring a girl out here, the way my father had? Or would I turn out to be, you know, a disappointment? Not just to my parents—to myself."

Tenderly, she brushed away a misplaced hair from my brow. "Your parents, I think, they must have been so proud of you. So proud."

I knew the truth to be a good deal more complicated. My parents had loved me, I was sure, but pride, in my family, was frugally disbursed, as though it were the interest on an untouchable nest egg of emotion. (If and when I got the chance, I had vowed never to stint on fatherly admiration.)

159

For now, though, with Debora, I chose not to explain. Instead, I told her, "Thanks. It's sweet of you to say that, especially knowing how proud you are of Paula." I smiled, and gazed out at the simmer of the bay, trying to shake off my web of sadness, to shake it so it wouldn't snare her, too. But looking at her eyes—their scrambled, sullen light—I saw she had already been tainted by my mood, mournfulness as catching as a yawn.

The horseshoe crabs remained locked together, hardly moving. Debora dug some moist sand and patted it around them, as if tucking children into bed. "Paula," she said. "She loves the beach. The sand. Always making things. 'This is where the princess lives. This is for her ostriches.' Ostriches! She plays so *big*, you know?"

"You want to call her? You can," I said.

"Yes?" she said. "I should?" She opened up her phone, and showed me its start-up picture: Paula in a strawberry patch, her smile a big red smear. "Maybe just . . . or no," she said. "Maybe I should wait. For her it can be hard, I think. Confusing. I will wait."

Out on the water, stripers jumped like little tricks of light. A laughing gull—immature, its feathers mostly brown—drifted above, loosing its manic call.

"Don't you ever wish," I said, "that you could turn back time, and go back, you know, to your childhood? Back to when you hadn't closed off any possibilities?"

Debora's face was tipped up to the clouds, her eyes shut. "Back to my childhood? No," she said. "So poor we were. And my mother! But somehow going back? Oh yes, I'd like to do this. Back to when I had Paula inside me."

Her eyes were now open again but lost-looking, glassy. She buried both her fists in the sand.

"When I came to this country, I could not do anything. Shopping, even: how is *this* thing called, and *this* and *this*? Or winter here, the snow—even *to walk* was hard! The people, they were nice, but a sad kind of nice, like, 'Oh, she's not so smart, we should help her.'"

She buried herself further, right up to the elbows. She looked disconcertingly dismembered.

"Also, for a long time, what did I do? Nothing. No job—only watching television. Danny was in charge: his country, his house. Everything I had comes from him. We don't have much money, but still he says no, I can't leave the house to go working. What I can do, anyway, but maybe, you know, McDonald's, and *'No wife of mine is flipping burgers!'* Three years of a life like this, or four—can you believe? *This* is why I came to America, I am thinking? To sit around and sit around and . . . nothing?

"But then," she said, her shoulders slackening, "then we saved enough, and Danny says it's time to have a baby." She spoke the word precisely, as if she had rehearsed. "Just like this, I'm pregnant, and everything—pa!—it's different. My belly gets so big, and I am like an *expert*. People ask me, 'Boy or girl?' they ask, 'How far along?'—and now I know exactly what to say. I'm good at something!

"Other women—I met them at the doctor's, pregnant also—they don't like the way so many strangers look and touch: 'Just because we're having babies, what gives them a right?' But me, oh, I liked it—I adored! Walk into a room and the people turn to stare, maybe like they think my dress is pretty. But no, it's not the dress, you see? It's *me*. *I'm* the thing. I'm what all the people want to look at."

Now she pulled her arms up, her fists full of sand. Wetter than the surface sand, finer grained, darker.

"And Danny," she said.

"Danny what?"

"Danny also . . . looked." She dumped the sand. "And touched, too. He liked it."

"Of course he did. Women are so glowing when they're pregnant." Another cliché, but I was too late to catch it.

"Yes, but you don't know," she said. "I think you maybe don't. Hair on the . . . down there, grows longer, very big. And the skin here"—she traced a path southward from her belly—"makes a strange, dark kind of

161

line. Darker nipples, also. So dark! But Danny, well, he liked this, he played with all this hair. He liked *everything*, more than in a very long time. It's okay to tell you this? Yes?"

"Yes, of course. Tell me all you want."

Debora looked both bolder and more bashful. "Even after seven, eight months pregnant, we made sex. With fingers, tongue—for *me*, not just him."

"But don't you, well, do that now? I mean, didn't you tell me? Danny is 'so good with his hands'?"

"Yes," said Debora, "but that doesn't mean . . . not *these days*, you know?"

"Wait, then. He doesn't really, after the insems—"

"No, no. I wanted you to think so."

The tide was creeping higher, matching my distress. Exactly at the line dividing dry beach from moist, the crabs sat, awaiting inundation.

"What I still don't get," I said, "if pregnancy was *all that*? Why don't you just have another kid? Don't you want one?"

Debora made a sound that wasn't laughing, quite, or sighing. "Don't you see? I *do* want, Pat. I do."

"So why don't you?"

"It's Danny. He won't. He'll never let me."

"Why, because Paula 'keeps you busy'? Didn't he say that? Or no, wait. 'How would we ever top her?'"

"Pat, you didn't—you couldn't really believe that."

No, I guessed I hadn't. But doubting wouldn't have gotten us as far along as faith; therefore, I'd chosen to believe, or not to disbelieve.

"So," I said, "you lied about that, too. Anything else?"

"No," she said. "No, no. Please don't call this lying. Please, can I explain the situation?"

I shrugged. I looked out at the water.

"Remember how it was," she said, "when I came first to here: Danny was the only thing I have. But then Danny, he says, he has to tell a secret. What he tells? When he was a new student in the college, he made some

162

girl, by accident, pregnant. She wasn't even his girlfriend. Only some girl who visited sometimes to see her cousin."

He'd offered, Debora explained, to pay for the girl's abortion. At least, to pay her *back* for one, as soon as he had money. But the girl wouldn't do it; her parents wouldn't let her.

"The father was police," Debora said. "A Catholic cop. He made Danny sign, I don't know, some piece of paper, to make Danny pay, every month, to help the girl. Every month until her child would have twenty-one years old."

Danny himself was only nineteen, a first-year college student. He couldn't pay for child support and tuition all at once.

"Did you know what he wanted?" Debora said. "To be a lawyer. A lawyer for the public. What's the name?"

"A public defender?"

"Yes," she said. "To help the poor. But now he had to stop. This is when he started building houses."

I thought of how he'd faltered when he met K.C., the lawyer. At the time, I'd figured his discomfort was mundane—nothing more than unfamiliarity—but now I saw what must have been his anger and his envy. K.C. had achieved what he'd abandoned.

"But wait," I said. "What happened with the girl? She had the baby?"

"A son," said Debora. "Nine years old already when Danny told me. Oh my God, I cried, Pat. I *cried*. But what I was supposed to do? Here I was, married, living in a country where I almost couldn't talk. No money for a ticket home, and even if I had it, how I could go back there, to my mother? *Mother, you were right: I'm so dumb.*"

Danny had said she'd never have to meet the son, the woman; in fact, the boy's mother would forbid it. He promised there were no further secrets.

"So," said Debora, "I stayed. I tried to trust. I had to."

Soon, she told me, Paula was born. Things were looking better. But Danny had been burned. Kids, for him, meant sacrifice; kids meant you had to kill your hopes.

163

"He loved Paula—he did—but two kids was enough, he said. What I said, I told to him, 'We don't have two kids. *You* do. But us, together, we have only one.' I ask him shouldn't Paula have a little brother or sister? Do it for her, I say, not for me. But no, Danny says. He has no more to give. And after this," said Debora, "he touched me less and less. Now there's sex together almost never."

Danny's jerked-tight voice, the day we'd met, came back to me: *Our own family's finished*, he had said.

"I'm sorry," she went on. "To tell this, I have shame. But that's why Danny said okay, I think, for me to surro. Or didn't try, not so hard, to stop me. Guilt, I think. He must feel very guilt."

"Boy, you had me fooled," I said. "That first lunch? When we met? The way you were looking at him, all starry-eyed and . . . *wifely*. Wow, I thought: this husband must be something."

Debora groaned. "The truth? We fought so bad, driving there, Danny almost wouldn't come inside. But then I put a smile on. I made him do it, also. Because, you know, if we weren't perfect, you would never want me."

"Right," I said, "of course." The logic snapped in place. "And, well, you *had* to have us want you. Because, you thought, if you could make the surro plan seem real, Danny'd get so jealous that he'd change his mind, is that it? And you could have another kid with him?"

What, I wondered, would Joseph think of this twist on the hackneyed trope? *Making a threat to have a stranger's baby to save the marriage.*

"No," said Debora. "No, that's not why." She scraped her sandy palms together punishingly. "Or maybe very early, yes"—scrape, scrape, scrape—"maybe this was something in my mind. But this was just a stupid thought, *much* before I met you. By the time I wrote to you, I wanted to have your baby. Really, please believe, Pat. Please believe. You have to." She reached out her thin, shaking arms.

I looked at her—the wet flecks of sand along her arms, her body but a fleck on the planet's sandy skin—and felt, to my surprise, less indignation than kinship. Confusion, too, and some annoyance, to learn of all

164

her secrets, but most of all, a soft commiseration. Here we humans are, I thought, grotesquely on our own, smidgens that will wash out to sea; we build connections and cling to them at any cost—we *must*. Wasn't that what Stu and I were trying?

Maybe she'd been using us, more than she admitted, hoping we'd provoke a change in Danny. Or maybe she had truly quashed that thought a long time back. In any case, of course she had her own private motives. So did we. Everyone always did.

Debora's eyes were bloated with the threat of backed-up tears. She would understand, she said, if now we didn't want her, if we couldn't look at her the same . . .

Well, we'd have to see. I'd have to talk with Stu. Tell him and decide if we could trust her.

That was what I should have said, and what I should have planned. Instead I told her, "No, you're still . . . you're the one we want."

We, I said. Even though I only thought of *I*.

I took her hand and held it—her smooth, nimble hand—and felt her anguish start to wick away. "But what if *you* don't want this," I said. "What if what you really want is still for you and Danny . . ."

Debora pulled her arm away and shook it, shedding sand. She stared over the welted-looking water. From our deck, on cloudless days, you could see to P-town, all the way across Cape Cod Bay. From here, though, the view was blocked; the earth's curve obscured the far shore.

Debora said, "We have a word in Portuguese. *Saudade*."

I tried to say it after her, but couldn't get it right.

"You taught *glut*. I will teach you this," she said. "Okay?" Slowly, then, she stood, tugging me up beside her. She paused like a schoolgirl solving sums. "Maybe I can't explain it good. It's hard. But I will try. *Saudade*—it's a longing. A sadness for what is gone. You had a thing and dream of it to come back maybe sometime—oh, you want, you *want* it to come back—even though you know the chance, it isn't very good." She nodded once, sharply, as if in self-rebuke. "For Danny I feel *saudade*. For how we used to be. But I don't think I'll get it back. I don't."

Her eyes were moist—all those backed-up tears had broken through—but I might not have said that she was crying. The tears had the look of a vital lubrication, fluid that would keep her systems sharp.

"We love Paula together," she said. "I know that Danny does. And when I see him loving her, I only love him more. But for him, I think, it's different: his love for her, it takes away from what he feels for me. And maybe another baby—I wonder, you know, sometimes—maybe it would make him then have even less for me. And so," she said, "not another. No. Not our own."

"But Deb," I said—the nickname Danny used, my first time using it. "The baby *will* be yours. The one we're going to make. How will you—how *could* you—give it up?"

Debora turned and started heading back the way we'd come. For a long time—too long—she didn't speak.

The woman we had seen before, walking her retriever, passed us now, calling for the dog: "Molly, where the—come back down, right now! Molly? Come?"

"*Making* life," said Debora at last. "This is what I want. Making it, not holding on, you see? Giving up the baby is the way that I can give."

Now the wind was at our backs, whisking us along. The dunes towered, stately, on our left. From this angle, sunlight made the hills appear harder: less like sand than monumental marble.

"I don't think I could," I said.

"What?"

"Let go a baby."

Debora smiled. "Of course not. That's not what your job is. You're the one who's going to be the keeper."

fifteen

Horseshoe crabs are among the oldest species on earth. Ironically, the very trait that led to their survival—a uniquely adapted immune system—now threatens their further existence. An element in the crabs' blood reacts to all contaminants, which makes the blood useful as a test for pharmaceuticals: if the blood reacts, the batch of drugs is tainted. To fill industrial needs for this naturally helpful substance, thousands of crabs are gathered every year. The crabs, after being bled, are brought back to the sea, but many of them die in the process.

Many? Some? Find stats to support this.

Some die in the process, and this, along with fishermen's overuse of crabs as bait, and so on and so forth.

Classic case of natural order being disturbed by humans, and too: the thing that saves you also may doom you.

E-mail Steve. Any conceivable objections?

I sat on the deck, in sudsy morning brightness, vigorously scrawling on my notepad: every cell and synapse tuned to working. Blue jays pecked coyly at birdseed on the feeder; squirrels leapt from tree to tree above— all God's creatures, doing what we should.

The phone rang inside, and I thought: *Let Stu get it.* Just because I worked from home—barefoot, in the sun—didn't mean I didn't need to work; but Stu, at the cottage, was simply, freely *home.* (He'd called in some chits again with Cynthia, his scheduler, and traded for today and tomorrow off, to be on hand for Debora's ovulation.) Plus, the phone—*Get it, already!*—was always for Stu, lately. His mother would call, then Rina, then Walter, Rina again . . . all the Nadlers mobilized in crisis.

The trouble's source was Richard: a change of heart, a waffling. Not about *whether* to adopt, but *from whom.* Rina had assumed they would find a Jewish child, a child whose birth mother was Jewish. Harder, of course. More costly. But continuity was priceless: the chain back to Abraham, unbroken. Richard had agreed, at first; it seemed a no-brainer. "What else would we do?" he said. "Get some Chinese baby? Sorry, folks, but Ling-Ling Feinberg? Doesn't quite sound right."

But now Richard's rabbi—his parents' rabbi, really—was warning they would make a big mistake. The logic was obtuse to me, but Stu tried to help me understand.

Say a Jewish woman got pregnant in adultery, or even, God forbid, in incest. Her baby, in official Jewish terms, was a *bastard*, which meant it wouldn't be eligible, ever, for Jewish marriage—and, for the Orthodox, that was like a death. Okay, so: what did that mean for Jews who were adopting? A Jewish birth mother could insist things were proper—her baby really, really wasn't a bastard—but how was there a way to *truly* know? Safer to adopt a little gentile, then convert him, in which case the danger would be skirted, for conversion, if done properly, was foolproof.

Fine, then, said Rina: "convert" the *Jewish* baby! Just in case, better safe than sorry . . .

But the rabbi explained that a Jewish mother's standing at the birth was what classified her child; no *mamzer*, no bastard born of someone who was Jewish, could ever change its status as a bastard.

"Wait," I said, when Stu conveyed this. "Let me get this straight. Something that you *know* is fake is better than a thing with an infinitesimal *chance* of being fake?"

"According to the black hats, yeah. It's driving my father nuts."

At first it had seemed Richard's parents were the sticklers, and Richard, for his own part, might be swayed. But then Walter phoned them—his counterparts, the Feinbergs—to offer them an earful of his anger, and Richard, the protective son, cemented his position: the child must be gentile, then made Jewish. ("What?" said Walter. "More Jewish than *Jewish*?")

All this was relayed to Stu in growingly frantic phone calls, the Nadlers in a welter of ambivalence. Should Rina hold her ground, or cave in to the Feinbergs? Was *any* child better than *no* child? And what about the household such a baby would grow up in? If Richard was unbending now, when else might he be so? At heart was he a black hat himself?

Stu listened, consoled, devised counterarguments. He searched on the Web for rabbinical authorities with points of view to controvert the Feinbergs'. (The Yahoo Talmud listserv—from what I read, peeking—seemed a lot like Surromoms, as loony and as lovely, but I decided not to bring this up.)

How could Stu be helping his family—and so goddamn agreeably!—when they had all turned their backs on us?

"Asking for my help," he'd said, "is how they're saying sorry. Saying yes is how I'll find forgiveness."

So, then, get the phone, I thought, returning to my notepad. *Take the call. Solve your sister's problems.* I lay down on the sun-pummeled deck.

A squirrel made a flying leap from one tree to another, and pounced onto the bird feeder's platform, sending a jay anxiously aflutter. The squirrel, with what looked like pubescent bravado, stuffed his small greedy mouth with seeds.

Birds, I scribbled. *Interconnections? Lesson in globalization?*

Seabirds, flying to the Arctic from Brazil—Brazil, Brazil, everywhere I turn!—stopping off on Cape coast, just at spring spawning, eating horseshoe crab eggs by the millions. If crabs disappear, then birds disappear. If birds disappear . . .

Sidebar on extinction?

If I recalled correctly, scientists had already measured losses in population. I made a note to check my book on crabs.

I'd found the book last week, when I visited the library, after my walk at Sandy Neck with Debora. (I still hadn't been sure what I'd say to Stu, if anything, about the walk, the secrets Debora'd shared, and so I planned at least to have this token truth to hold to: I'd said I'd go to the library, and I did.) The case by the checkout desk displayed a new exhibit: a diorama of seasonal Cape ecology. Beach peas and sea tomatoes—fashioned out of silk?—"grew" from the top of a low sandy pile on which a stuffed sanderling was poised. Behind that, where blue crepe simulated water: a horseshoe crab, its spiny dome shellacked. Then I saw the book, propped up on the desk: a whole volume devoted to horseshoe crabs. Debora had asked if I had written a textbook on the subject. No, but now I could, or at least one lesson's essay. I checked out the book and headed home.

Finding such an object, just then, had felt ordained: the cloak of fate snug, a perfect fit. And so, driving back, I'd vowed I *would* tell Stu—I'd describe the day in all its details—honoring this omen I'd been shown. It wasn't guilt inspiring me but something like guilt's opposite, a sense that in my sneaking off I'd done a worthy thing.

At home, as I'd reached out for the door, it swung open. I fell onto the gritty front-hall rug.

"Shit, I didn't mean—" said Stu. "I mean, I *meant* to greet you. Didn't mean to make you go flying." He bent down and offered me a hand, hauled me up. "Hey, you smell . . . does *windblown* have a smell? Where've you been?"

"Stu," I said, "I told you I was going to the library, but really—"

"Really what? You met your secret lover?"

"No! Jesus, no . . ."

"I'm kidding, Pat. Just kidding." He wagged a finger, teasing at my windpipe. "Truth be told, I'm the one who had a secret meeting."

A dirty thread of rug had somehow wound up on my tongue. "A secret—" I said. "What do you mean? With who?"

"Well, not a 'meeting' . . . but I bucked up, and talked to Danny. While you were out. I called, smoothed things over."

"Seriously? You did?"

"We had a pleasant talk, actually. I think we'll be fine from here on out."

"But what did you say?" Relief was edged with rivalrous surprise: it hadn't crossed my mind that while I was off with Debora, Stu might be contriving his own moves.

"We didn't get all kissy-weepy. That's not quite his style. More like: *Pretend it never happened.* He's up at his parents', I guess. Asked me to a Brockton Rox game."

I was thrilled, mostly. Really, how could I not be? Still, though, a little pucker of anger persisted—why? Maybe because he'd once again made peace with someone else but me. Or maybe because I knew that if *I'd* placed the call to Danny, Stu would have asked me why I'd felt I had the right.

I hoped anger wasn't what provoked my change of heart; I hoped I was acting in good faith. Either way, it seemed to me that telling Stu what Debora had said—telling him of our walk—was now needless. If Danny was back onboard, if all of us were happy, why do something that might again derail us?

"The Brockton *Rox*?" I asked.

"Baseball," Stu explained. "Which interests me, to be honest, not at all."

"But Danny asked."

"He did."

"Generously. So you'll go?"

He groped my crotch. "I'd rather play our own game, here at home."

This was his first overture in three weeks, maybe four. I leaned into his hand, let him cup me. But could it be that simple, really, forgiving and forgetting? *All is well, and now let's go make love . . .*

I pulled away. "But Danny," I said. "And Debora. You're really fine with them? I mean, you're not having second thoughts?"

"Second thoughts—you're joking? *Second* thoughts were forever ago. Now I'm on to twentieth thoughts. Two hundredth. The point is, though, I *had* those doubts, and yes, I still want this." He blew a quick, frisky puff of air against my lips, dousing the last flicker of my worry.

Which was why, when Stu now emerged onto the deck and said it wasn't Rina on the phone, it was Debora—she'd surged, she was ready for Round Five—I enjoyed my own surge: of certainty restored. I grabbed my pen and notepad, threw some seed to the blue jays, and dashed into the house after Stu.

Debora asked if we wanted anything. Oreos? Grape Fanta?

"Oh, poor thing," I said. "You must be missing Paula. Are you feeling *saudade* for snack time?"

"Sow-*whatchy*?" asked Stu.

"Forget it," I said. "Later."

Of course Debora missed Paula—I saw it in her face, her mouth, its stung little smile. Still, there was a feeling of vacation in the house, a sense that Debora was making the most of being on her own. In the kitchen: a *People* magazine, a Burger King wrapper, a garlic press with pimply garlic mush left in its pores. A blackened iron pot of stew chuckled on the stove, sending out a fruity, foreign scent.

Stu declined the snacks and beelined to the bathroom, focused on the job he had to do. I said yes to the Fanta, and swallowed a bright gulp, but Debora, for herself, selected another brand: something in a lurid green can.

"What is *that*?" I asked.

"You wouldn't like. It's Brazilian."

"But that's not what I asked."

"It's guaraná. It tastes . . . different."

"Different from what?"

"From what I think you like."

She grinned in a sharper way than I had ever seen from her. Impudence? Intimacy? Both?

"But why?" I asked.

Before she could respond, I snatched the can. She chased me around the table, around a second time, as breathless as we'd been at Sandy Neck.

At last, I let her catch me, surrendering the can, but Debora pushed it back: "Okay. Try."

I sipped. The taste was part vile, part electric: if neon had a taste, it would be this.

"Like?" she said.

"Hmm. Not sure 'like' is the right word." I took another sip. "Compelled, maybe?"

Stu emerged from the bathroom. Already? Had he finished?

"Geez," I said. "Wow, speedy delivery!"

Debora laughed, but Stu scoffed. "She probably doesn't get it."

"Huh? What's not to get?"

"Your joke. 'Speedy delivery.' She didn't grow up on Mr. Rogers, like us."

What had happened? Where was the new, even-tempered Stu?

"I watch," she said sharply. "With Paula. They have reruns."

Quick, cut this off, I thought. I pointed to the Instead Cup, which Stu held, balanced in his hands. "Good job, hon," I said, tinny with false cheer. "Shouldn't we give those guys a good home?"

"Yes," said Debora. "Let's start."

"You're set?" I asked. "Do you need help?"

"No," she said. "I'll call you when I'm finished."

The kitchen, in her absence, should have seemed more spacious, but actually it felt even smaller: Stu's gloom was filling every inch.

"Try this drink," I said, in my pep-squad captain voice.

"No," he said.

"But really. It's guaraná. It's crazy."

"I said no thanks."

"Party pooper. Why?"

From Debora's plate of snacks, Stu picked up an Oreo (to eat it or to crush it into dust?). "You don't know what it's like," he said.

"What *what's* like?"

"In that bathroom. I hear you guys having a blast down here, you know, relaxing. And I'm up there, beating off for the billionth fucking time."

"I don't know. That doesn't sound so lousy."

"It is, Pat. It sucks. It absolutely sucks. I feel like a . . . a teenager or something." He split apart his cookie, exposing its white filling, the sudden, bared whiteness somehow lewd. "And anyway," he said darkly, "it isn't going to work."

"What? Why on earth would you say that?"

"Well, it hasn't worked yet. How many times? Four? What do we think is going to be different now?" His eyes looked like little linty filters.

"With *that* attitude? No," I said. "Nothing will be different. Jesus, Stu! She's up there, doing all she can, and you're already . . . Talk about bad vibes."

"'Bad vibes'? Is that how all your online yentas talk?" He dropped the split cookie halves, uneaten. "I'm not sure what's worse, Pat, this touchy-feely stuff or the rah-rah business from before: 'Shouldn't we give those guys a good home?'"

Stu had always been adept at finding my armor's cracks, and then: insert chisel, *tap tap.*

"Aw, is it so hard?" I said. "So *hard* to be Stu! Everyone always persecutes Stu! But try being the one who has to *listen* to it all, to stroke you and stroke you, but oops—not too much, 'cause pitying is the worst. Can't stand to be pitied! By anyone, that is, but yourself." I paused to breathe the keen, clanging air. "I'm sorry you're discouraged, Stu. You think I'm not, too? But hearing you go on, like it's some kind of torture, when you're the one who—"

"*You* should try it."

"Ha!" I said.

"Exactly."

"Wait, what is *that* supposed to—"

"You? Since when do—*you*? I thought you aspired to be the mommy."

I should have said: As if a mom is somehow something lesser?

And: Which of us has wanted all along to be a parent, has pushed us here, pushed you past your doubts? Which of us sees *parent* as a verb, not just a noun?

Most of all, though, what I should have said was: Fine, let's talk. Maybe it *is* my time to take a turn.

Instead, I let his challenge hang, an apple of temptation. There it stayed, within my reach, so ripe.

When Debora beckoned, I carried her a fresh, cold guaraná. "Thanks," she said. "But go home now, okay? I am fine." Stu and I, she obviously sensed, were not.

We drove away enveloped in a carapace of silence, which, at home, was cracked by a crude, atonal melody: *whang* (the screen door), *stomp* (hallway), *chank* (a key ring, flung), the phone machine's unforgiving *eee!*

The phone machine, at least, provided a joint activity—a small goal the two of us could share: we stood together, waiting for our messages. A couple of quick hang-ups, a debt consolidation pitch, and then the voice of Cynthia, Stu's scheduler. An unforeseen problem with the roster for tomorrow: Acuff's line assigned him to the Logan–Hartsfield route, but a death in the family, a funeral in Texas . . . any chance Stu could sub in?

Stu looked stoic. "I guess I'd better."

All I said was, "Stu."

"She needs me, Pat. Never would've called me if she didn't."

The thing that irked me most was that Stu sounded relieved. I darted him with reason after reason not to go: the chances of conception were who-knew-how-much greater with two back-to-back inseminations; how could we expect Debora to honor her commitments if *we*, at the last sec, reneged?

"*Her* commitments?" said Stu. "What about *my* commitments?"

"Hello?" I said. "Seniority! You're not still some junior on reserve."

He thrust his chin, throbbing with impatience. "How many goddamn duty days have I already bagged so I could jerk off into a cup? I took those days off—you know this, Pat, I know you do—by trading them for other times on call. And now *I'm* being asked to trade. I have to."

The phone rang.

I pinned him with my sharpest spousal stare—daring him, just daring him, to answer.

A message started recording: not Cynthia but Rina. "Are you there? If you're there, Stu, pick up."

He touched the phone, but stopped. Stopped and turned and looked at me. He dropped his hand, and he and I just listened.

"Crap," she said. "Well, anyway, we just came from the rabbi's—a 'counseling session,' if you could call it that. I asked the schmuck, tell me how you actually *do* conversions. Send the kid to a Hebrew school with other adopted kids? Kind of like a bar mitzvah, but sooner? And he says, 'Oh, no. You don't understand. We do the conversion right away, when they're babies. As soon as the baby is in hand.' *In hand*, he says. As if the baby's, I don't know, a check! 'As soon as it's in hand, we perform the conversion. A bris, for boys. Immerse it in the mikvah.'

"Again I'm like, hold on. You take a baby—a newborn!—and dunk it in some holy water, and *presto*, now it's Jewish? Doesn't that sound a tad bit *less* than Jewish? I was under the impression that converting should be hard, that Jews purposely put up all these hoops for folks to jump through. *Why do you want to be Jewish? You're really sure you want to?* But no, Mr. Rabbi has his little Talmud handy, and *flip flip*, here's the page he wants: 'We can act to someone's advantage even without his permission.' It's sick, how they've got an answer for everything.

"Richard and I, on the way home, we had a *massive* fight. He kept saying, 'But the rabbi said, the rabbi said, the rabbi . . .' Any time I tried to talk, his face just went on screen saver.

"What am I going to do, Stu? I mean, if things go on like this, I don't even *want* to have a baby! I don't know right now. I—"

176

The answering machine beeped and cut her off.

Rina must have known, of course, that I would likely hear her; she had freely chosen to leave a message; but standing there, in real time, listening to her heartache, standing there and never picking up . . . God, it made me feel like such a creep.

Or maybe what disturbed me was the way she spoke of Richard, which matched the way I felt right now about my own companion.

Stu hadn't said a thing. (Why had he not answered? Rina was his sister, after all.) Now he ran some water into a glass, gulped it down. "I *have* to fly tomorrow," he said. "Seriously. I do." Opening the tap again, he switched on the Disposall, even though there was no trash to grind. The gadget made a dry, grating crunch. "But," he said. "You're right."

"I'm right?"

"About Debora. Have to do it. Can't just leave her hanging." Maybe he, too, had recognized himself in wretched Richard, and shriveled at the thought of their alikeness. "I have an idea," he said. "A way we might do both."

Just before he headed for the airport in the morning, he would do his mortifying duty in our bathroom; and then, as he hurried off to make his early flight, I would speed the sample, on the double, to Hyannis, where Debora would be ready for her role.

"Does that sound like a plan? Can you live with that?" he asked.

"Well, I guess if . . . sure, I guess. Yeah. That sounds fine."

Actually, sort of brilliant, but I didn't want to say that. Neither did I admit to him, and hardly to myself, my snapped-rope jolt of disappointment: for one second, I had thought that he was going to say—for maybe a nanosecond I had guessed this—that I should just go and take his place.

What I said was, "Rina's call? You really could have answered."

"I know," he said.

"I know you know. I just wanted to say it. You could've. I would've understood."

"I wanted to focus on *us*," he said. "Isn't that what—"

Yes, I told him. Yes.

sixteen

A bullion-bright day, two weeks before the year's longest. All the world in crisp, flawless focus—and me, too. The air was cool, but here inside my Volvo, who would know? Windows closed, heater cranked to high. Tucked away, snug within the crotch of my fleece sweatpants (trying to maintain 98.6): the specimen cup filled with Stu's semen.

Such focus, such flawlessness: Did carrying a piece of Stu enable me to feel like this—the fact that he had found a way, though gone, still to be here? Or did his *absence* free me for the feeling?

At Debora's, I moved the cup to underneath my armpit, and quick-stepped my way up the walk. She met me at the door in a vivid yellow robe, which seemed to luminesce in fireflyish winks with each of her tiniest movements.

"I hope you don't mind," she said, pointing to the robe and then to her off-kilter hair. "Why try to make myself together so early, only to make myself apart again?"

"Make yourself apart? That doesn't sound too pleasant."

"Stop," she said. She glared at me with chummy irritation. "It's not nice to tease about my English."

"No, you're right. I'm sorry. Accept this in apology?" I brought the cup out into view.

"Ah, *here* you are," she said, and took the cup and cradled it, as if it were already an infant.

A breakfast smell of butter and burnt crumbs suffused the house. I wished we could loiter in the kitchen, just to chat, to lessen the sense of doing a *transaction*.

"It's quiet," I said, stalling.

"Yes, and I don't like. Danny says a day or two more and he returns." Debora's facial expression was full of twists and turns. "But oh! Paula called. She left the most sweet message. Come, do you want? You *must* hear."

And so we did linger in the kitchen, while she played it.

"Mãinha? Guess who. Did you guess *me*? You're right!" Paula's voice swung from too loud to barely audible, as Danny fought (I pictured it) to keep her near the phone. "Mãe, we're in Friendly's, and I just got some onion rings, but they're so big, they're not rings, they're *bracelets*. I would like to bring you one to wear, but Daddy says I can't, these rings are for eating not for keeping, and now . . . now . . . I love you, Mãinha. Come back soon!"

Danny could be heard chiming, "Wow! Good job, sweetie," and then, in a private voice, "Love you, too, Deb. Bye."

"Cute," I said. "Especially how she tells you to 'come back'—as if you're the one who went away."

"To her, I am," said Debora. "Away from *her*. You see?"

The topic of maternal duty returned us to our mission.

"Well," she said, raising the cup. "It's time to start. You'll wait?"

"Waiting's really all I do these days."

"Yes, but later—later you will *dream* of all this free time."

"Oh, you're right. Of course you're right. When have you ever not been?"

Debora turned and made her way efficiently to the staircase, and up she marched, into her hall of mysteries.

Footsteps through the ceiling . . .

The sound of no more footsteps . . .

179

Debora had been reading a glossy rag. I picked it up. "Tom's Crazy Love. Will Katie Say 'I Do'?"

I walked from the kitchen to the living room, the den, mapping out the bounds of my irrelevance. The rooms were tight, narrowed by their clutter, like clogged valves: Paula's clothes and dolls, a blueprint tube, a plumb bob—nothing with the glow of being Debora's.

Up in bed, what was she now doing?

Aimlessly I circled back to the kitchen. A saucepot in the sink held expressionist eggy froth. I sniffed a hint of vinegar, the gourmet's trick to poaching. Debora clearly knew this trick; now I knew she knew. Why did this small intimacy stir me?

The urge to snoop, to open doors, was bodily, erotic. Refrigerator (Coors Light cans, graying cuts of beef), broom closet (piles and piles of grocery bags, no brooms). The cupboard by the fridge brimmed with unfamiliar dry goods: *farofa, goiaba roladinho*. Finally, a place that was just hers! An image came: Debora, a newly minted immigrant, knowing no one other than her husband; and then being walloped by that same husband's news, that he had fathered someone else's baby. And yet she had found a way—ways—to make life work. Like this, here: a cupboard full of home.

The next cupboard held dinner plates, salad plates, bowls. Well ordered—the neatest spot, so far, in the house. I thought of a night with Stu, many years ago, a week or two after we'd shacked up. I had cooked us supper: meatloaf, mashed potatoes; our place, for the first time, smelled homey. Later, cleaning up, I saw that when he stored a plate, instead of simply placing it atop the cupboard's stacked ones, he lifted them and laid the new plate under.

"What're you doing?" I'd asked.

"Sorry—is that a problem?"

Of course not. I only wanted to know.

Blushing a bit, Stu explained his theory of "equal time": place clean plates on top, the same ones would get used too much; place them under, they would always rotate.

"Exactly," I said. I did this, too, but hadn't told a soul. "For me, though, it isn't about giving equal wear, it's—"

"Emotional, sort of, right?" he said. "Like, what if they have *feelings*? You wouldn't want some plates to feel left out."

Adorable! I kissed him robustly on the mouth, thankful for the luck—the fate—of having found him. From out of all the five-plus billion plate-misstacking humans, I had been assigned a task to share with him at Serve the World, and now we shared a love, a home, a life.

Where had that feeling gone?

Where had *we*?

I was admiring one of Debora's neatly stacked plates— cobalt-rimmed, sturdy-looking, plain—when something above me thunked. The lights in the kitchen wavered.

The ceiling didn't do a lot to muffle Debora's voice. "Ai, no! *Porra! Caralho!*"

I whipped shut the cupboard, and raced up to her room. "Hey, you okay in there?"

"Wait," she said. "Hold on."

Another thunk. Rustling. Then a high-pitched yelp.

"Okay, now I'm coming in!" I warned her.

She sat on the tall bed's edge, naked legs dangling. The yellow robe was draped over her shoulders but not tied. A patch of brown belly could be seen, a fist of hair. The specimen cup, the syringe, in her hands.

"I tried," she said. "Was trying. But I lost my balance. I fell."

"Fell? From the—how? From the bed onto the *floor*?"

She nodded. She looked like a child who'd wet the sheets. "Danny usually helps," she said, "and I just lie and wait. But *this*. This stupid thing!" She throttled the syringe.

We'd used it for the first couple of goes but not since; Stu had lately aimed his spurts straight into the Instead Cup, which Debora could insert right away, no sperm lost. But not today. Not with Stu at thirty thousand feet.

181

It wasn't Debora's fault, it was Stu's—should I say that?

"To put it in myself," she said, "is hard. Now it's ruined."

"No. No, I'm sure it's not. Give."

At first glance, it was true, things looked less than great. All around the outside of the tube was wet and gummy. But some semen—a few cc's—had stayed in the syringe, and that was what I chose to home in on. "It's fine," I said. "Don't worry, now. Everything is just fine." I caught myself talking like a cop at some big tragedy: self-important, sternly reassuring. But then it struck me: Tragedy? Is that what this scene was? A woman tumbling half-nude out of bed, a sticky gizmo . . . no, what we were dealing with was slapstick.

"What," she said, "you laugh?"

I tried to stop but couldn't.

"What?" she said again, sounding tight.

In lieu of words, I wiggled all my glistening, gummy fingers. Waved their gross absurdness in her eyes.

Something in her face gave way, a kind of unchaining. A gorgeous thing to witness, like water becoming steam, molecule by liberated molecule.

"*Caralho*," she said merrily. "Look at me! So dumb."

Look? All right, I did, through her still-unfastened robe: hairless thighs, a single glossy smear of what she'd spilled. But maybe she hadn't meant for me to . . . of course not. I dropped my gaze.

"Now what do we do?" she said. "You'll tell Stu? No. You won't."

This was not instruction but appraisal.

I had not yet thought that far but knew that she was savvy. "No," I said, smiling. "No, I won't."

Now we had another truth to hide.

Debora nodded, considering. She tapped her front teeth. "How much is left? Enough?"

"Maybe, I think. Sure."

"Okay. What we do—we try again. You think?" She scooched herself back, to the center of the bed. Her robe threw off tiny darts of light.

182

Had she meant "look" literally? She hadn't tied the robe. Could have, during all this time, but hadn't.

By swiveling her hips, she rearranged some pillows. Tossed her hair to clear it from her face. I didn't ask if I should stay; she didn't say to leave. The quickest of glances passed between us: fear and its dismissal.

"Lean back, now," I said. "Spread your legs."

A classic nightmare put the dreamer standing on a stage, unable to recall any lines. This, now, for me, was curiously the opposite: a play I didn't know but whose lines, somehow, splendidly, I did. I knew that whatever I might say right now would be okay. Whatever I might ask, she'd say yes.

"Aim like this and push?" I asked.

"Yes."

"Just right here?"

"Yes. Just right there. It goes in."

I wasn't seeing *her*, exactly, but entrances and angles, a problem of geometry and physics.

Debora laid her hand on mine and smiled a depthless smile. One, two . . . I eased the tube inside her.

"All okay? Still good?"

"Yes," she said. "Perfect."

"All right, then. Ready? In they go."

I pushed the plastic plunger, and held it for a five count, waiting for the onset of unease, or more slapstick: shouldn't something leak or slip back out? But no, what had started with the makings of a farce now was all balletic style and balance. The syringe, a magic pen, inscribing our new life.

Debora inserted the Instead Cup, to keep the sperm inside. Just as fast, her hand was out; she dried it on the sheet. She settled back, tilting her pelvis upward. Once again I wondered if she'd pull her bathrobe closed, but now that I had . . . well, now why bother?

And so we then . . .

And so . . .

Could that be all there was?

Shouldn't we be able to know when Stu's cells met hers? When would life spark? Now, already? Or *now*?

"Pat," she said.

"Yes?"

"Thank you."

"No, thank *you*. It's just so amazing, you know? Amazing it's so simple. Except it's not. I know it's not. But—"

"Stop." She took my wrist. "Relax, Pat, okay? You did good."

"Really?" I said. My fingers thrummed, authoritative, strong. I looked into the jumble of her eyes, their green-brown dare.

"Yes. You were good." She gripped me tighter. "Very."

I looked again, and Debora's eyes were greener now, more true, as if the flecks were magnetized, aligned.

Did my hand start? Did hers? (She still controlled my wrist.) Either way, the outcome was the same: hands together hovering on her Ouija board of skin, tracing up her goose-bumped thigh till—

There.

If she had flinched at all—the slightest hint of hesitancy—I would have stopped.

But she didn't. I didn't.

My thumb crossed the line from her outer self to inner, taking in the difference, the custardy damp give: the same stuff on either side (skin!) but so changed, as a loaf's doughy center is from crust.

Out again, my thumb rubbing smaller and smaller circles. She pushed it back in. We said nothing.

We had an easy excuse: *Only to help the odds . . .*

But whom would we be trying to convince?

This time I was seeing her—all of her, unabashed. Her softness, her raw pink skin, her faded razor burn. She squeezed from somewhere far inside and made my thumb feel small. I hadn't been with a woman since my college days: Becky. Debora, I saw, possessed her same disarming pushy bluntness. How had I resisted that connection?

184

With a woman. A euphemism, an empty shuck of speech. And yet, as I moved my hand—as I let Debora move it—*with her* was exactly how I felt. I huffed with her, sweating, vicariously hard, spellbound by her deep ferocious clenching. Her hips arched; her fingers pressed on mine to do their work. She shut her eyes—*pressing*—and arched— *pressing, pressing*—and shuddered like a sleeping dog that's hunted down its dreams.

There had been no awkwardness, but now Debora frowned at me— the startled frown you'd give a Peeping Tom who caught you naked: exasperation interlocked with shame. I just hovered, heedful, hoping she would speak, waiting for something. Approval? Rebuke?

Eventually she did speak, but not of what we'd done. "Now I'll lie and wait," she said, "and listen to some music."

Back to friendly business, the black hole of politeness, and so I followed her lead, and asked her what she needed: An extra pillow? Some water? The remote?

No, she was fine, she said. Everything was just fine. (Wasn't that what I had said before?)

"Really?" I asked. "Nothing?"

"Nothing, no. I'm tired." She did look tired. Depleted of her poise.

"Okay, then I'll . . ."

What? What came after *this*?

". . . I'll go now," was all I could come up with.

seventeen

They say that what you see depends on where you stand, and Stu and I were bolted to the viewpoints we'd grown used to.

He was profligate, out of control, the breaker of our trust; self-destructive and *us*-destructive; the problem.

I was restrained, long-suffering, the martyr to our cause; self-aware and selfless; the solution.

I couldn't necessarily have defended those assessments, but they were now essential to the system we'd created, the way we both made sense of our dynamic. Once the rules were set in place, we had to play accordingly: the batter couldn't start to pitch at the pitcher. And so the same behavior that from Stu we'd score as "bad," from myself I might account as "good."

That was what happened, more or less, when he came home that night.

All day I had paced the house, edgy and uncertain, tasting the sweet-tart flavor of transgression. Guilty, yes, but invigorated. Tipsy with *Why not?* It seemed I had access to the thinking of a creature who'd stepped to a cliff's edge of change; I was curious to see what move this creature—I—would make.

Debora had said I wouldn't tell, and I had thought her right. Still, I'd have to say something—a snippet of the truth—when Stu asked for details from the morning. Maybe I would simply say his plan had worked (true). Or tell him I had thought about him (also very true: my memory of his stacking of the plates).

But what did he ask, when he came home? Nothing. Not a thing.

I was half-asleep in front of CNN, on the couch, and Stu flopped down next to me, sending pillows flying.

"Hey," he said.

"Hey."

"Watching something good?"

I shrugged. "Is the news ever good?"

"I know, right?" His skin had a sharp, chemical smell, from hours in a plane's reprocessed air. "So maybe I shouldn't . . . forget it, no. Maybe I'll tell you later?"

What could it be? Another concession at work, to fly more routes? Or Rina and Richard, another looming roadblock?

"It's just," he said, "I figured I would get it off my chest. I don't want to have to dwell about it."

I couldn't tell if he was really remorseful or sort of gloating. "Okay, now you've *got* to," I said. "What?"

"Well, the weirdest thing," he said. "In the crew lounge, in Atlanta. Usually it's, you know, some sandwiches, stale coffee. Otherwise you're on your own, good luck. But here comes this guy, in a double-breasted suit, like a boy all dolled up for *The Nutcracker*. Has to be a dancer. You know that walk they have?"

"Walk?" I said.

"You know, like their ass is a nose, sniffing? So anyway, this guy goes, 'Hello, Captain . . . ,' and leans in close, closer than he needs to read my nametag. 'Captain *Nadler*. Can I offer you a soda? Or something sweet?' I ask him what he is, a concierge or something? 'Sure, concierge,' he says, 'if that's what you want to call me. My name is Kip. I'm here for *all* your needs.' And then—"

But Stu stopped. He must have read the anguish on my face.

"Nothing like this has happened in . . . I promise you, it's been ages," he said. "And all we did was kiss. He wanted more, but I stopped him. I thought you'd want to hear that. To hear that I, you know, could resist."

No, I didn't want to hear. I didn't want to think about him doing, or resisting doing, anything with a stranger—even the barest details made me queasy. But that wasn't the main source of my torment. The problem that had hit me as he launched into his story was how badly I was yearning to share *mine*, of me and Debora. To tell Stu, the last man I should tell.

On CNN, a correspondent leaned into a gale; she joggled her earpiece, trying to hear the anchor. My hand, in an aping reflex, drifted to my ear. The skin was dry and cool, distant-feeling. I thought of Debora's skin, the line my thumb had crossed. How could I explain that change to Stu?

"You want to know the rest?" he said, nestling up against me.

"Stu, come on," I said. "I mean, aren't you even going to *ask?*"

"Ask?" he said, clueless.

"Today," I said. "With Debora? Don't you even care how it all went?"

What was I doing, taunting him? Challenging him to catch me? What would I now say when he *did* ask?

But no: Stu was the cheater, and I was the repairer. Neither of us would question that alignment.

"Sorry! Oh, God—sorry," he said. "I just . . . I wasn't thinking. Tell me, okay? I want to hear it all."

How readily he played the bad guy; how easily I got off.

What a relief.

What a peculiar letdown.

I felt I'd broken someone's faith, but wasn't certain whose. Stu's, I guessed, although I could have argued he deserved it; Debora's, too, although she'd been as eager as I, or more. Maybe the faith I'd broken the most was mine. Wasn't I the one who'd said (against our gay men's dogma) that "casual sex" was necessarily a contradiction in terms? But here I'd gone and let myself get sexual with Debora—without so much as pausing to feel doubt—as if I didn't know the repercussions would be profound.

Now my doubts were potent. More so by the hour.

Which was why, at dawn, after a night of fidgeting, I left Stu and went into my workroom. I couldn't talk to Debora, of course. Not at this crazy hour, and not till I could think of what to say. Instead, I turned my laptop on, and signed in to Surromoms.

I worded my questions carefully, couched in hypotheticals:

Would it be really weird if . . .

Has anyone ever heard of . . .

Do IF's ever get these kinds of feelings?

Barely a minute passed before the first response appeared. (Baby-lovers were an early-rising bunch.) Mom2AngelSarah wrote, *Relax. You're talking transference—at least I think that's what the shrinks call it. Happens to almost everyone, probably, no? I wouldn't sweat it. I mean: your sperm is *penetrating* her. *Of course* you think of her sexually. You'd hardly be a man if you didn't. LOL.*

Totally normal, GiftOfKids concurred. *No big deal.*

Well, typed WannaBeMom, *as long as you don't *act* on it!*—which prompted another burst of virtual laughter.

I hung back, declining to correct their misconceptions, wanting to retract what I had posted.

Then my old correspondent, Pray4Life, weighed in. *Wait*, she wrote. *Stop. SandyNeckDad . . . it's you? Pardon me, and sorry if I'm getting this all wrong, but aren't you *gay*? Isn't that why you need to use a surro? I'm confused. If you like women, why not do it *that* way?*

I was confused, too, but not about liking women; I'd known that capacity always lay within me, dormant. The trouble was my liking of this one woman, of Debora. I was worried my feelings might extend beyond mere "liking," beyond curiosity or lust. I feared Debora offered something—what?—that I'd been missing.

I could put a positive spin on my deep bond with her: an unexpected outgrowth of my loyalty to Stu-and-me, of how much I aspired to build our family. But was it? Or was it something born of self-allegiance (a fancy way of saying it was selfish)?

Hey, still there? wrote Pray4Life. *I'm serious. What's the deal?* ☹

I started typing, beginning at the beginning, or somewhere near, recounting all my bedrock contradictions: my craving for belonging, my hatred of that craving; my want to break away from family, my want to make my own.

My fingers were so flubby I kept knocking the Caps Lock key, and had to go back and retype. I told of coming out but then falling in love with Becky, with all the possibilities she could offer; of breaking up, because I couldn't limit myself to her, and then the seemingly limitless world of gay men in Manhattan; of feeling a misfit, no matter what identity I bought into.

At last I came to Stu, my oxymoronic lover: my Jewish pilot, my high-flyer who sometimes zoomed in close. I had feared so terribly the thought that I might lose him, but now I sometimes also feared the thought of staying together. What if we were trying to catch a slipstream in our hands?

That's what I was writing when my fingers flubbed again. The ever-vigilant laptop asked: *Are you sure you want to delete?* And though I could have rescued the whole saga with one stroke, I hit Return and watched it disappear.

eighteen

What did I really want when I placed the call to Debora? To hear her laugh things off and say, "We won't being doing *that* again"? To hear her say she *burned* to do it again?

But no, when she answered with her lyrical "Alô?" I knew what I'd wanted the most was only this: her voice.

"Oh," she said. "It's you."

"Yup. Your favorite delivery man." I heard my phony nonchalance, as stiff as old chewed gum. "I'm just calling to find out how you're feeling."

"Normal, I think. It's very early—too early, still—to tell."

No, I said, not that; I knew she wouldn't feel pregnant yet. How did she feel about . . . about us?

"Pat, I can't—" she started, and let the sentence snap.

"Wait, sorry. Did Danny come back? He's there? You can't talk?"

"He's here, yes, but sleeping. Tired from being with Paula."

"Good—so, then, you *can* talk."

But Debora still said nothing.

The silence was a whirlpool. Swirl, swirl.

Softly she said, "I don't think that we should talk about it."

"But Deb," I pleaded (pleading, too, with my own inner watchdog), "don't you think you're making a bigger deal than maybe we have to? Don't you think that—"

"No," she said. "Let's not."

I knew she must be right: we should just move on. We had many months ahead—years, I hoped—of partnership, and couldn't afford to mess things up now. A fluke, we'd felt. We'd kill it while we could. Starve the fire.

That was what I told myself. I promised to believe it.

The fire I should foster was the one I felt for Stu, should use its heat to cauterize our leaks.

The good news was, Stu seemed even readier than I was. From penitence, partly, I guessed, about his recent slip-up, even if it hadn't gone past kissing. Maybe, too, that incident had jump-started his confidence. Was all he'd needed, really, that bit of reinforcement? Whatever it was, it worked. Gone was his gloomy self-defeat, replaced by a sudden carnal zeal.

We made love in bed, in the shower, on the deck, and even, for the first time in forever, engaged in dream sex: coming to in the dead hours, already locked together, voracious (if not a hundred percent conscious). It seemed, in those moments, we dreamt the same dream, or separate dreams with a common set of props. Afterward, we lay together, muscles all unsprung, blissfully—almost Buddhistly—erased.

But our revival encompassed more than sex. We also went on dates, of the new-romance variety: mini-golf, an evening bike along the Cape Cod Rail Trail. Drinks at Aqua Grille, above the bright marina. A passable *West Side Story* at Sandwich High.

At the Cape Cinema we saw a film—exquisitely, gallingly French. Stu's review? "Great, except the bad parts." Afterward we bought each other cones at Cap'n Frosty's, and how could I not smile as Stu attacked his melting ice cream—as if any drip he missed might set off Armageddon, as if his licks alone could save the world. Yes, I thought. Yes, of course: I love him.

A busboy hurtled past, a tray atop his arm.

"Didn't you tell me, once," said Stu, "you had a crush that worked here?"

"Yeah, Liam Mehegan. *Crush* is right: he flattened me."

"Why? Because he didn't want you back?"

I paused to watch the busboy—nervous little nose, minor-league mustache damp with sweat—probably the age I'd been when I fell hard for Liam. "No," I said. "Because I think he *did* but wouldn't admit it."

"Ah," said Stu. "And that's why you picked me. I'm *demonstrative*."

"When you are, you are," I said.

Great, except the bad parts.

Driving home we talked about getting away together. Of course we already lived "away," according to most people's yardstick. Maybe we needed to go still farther—Nantucket? Prince Edward Island?

In any case, as soon as possible: July Fourth would be perfect. It felt good to look ahead, even if uncertainly. To reach a brink and see how we might find a way across.

At first it seemed our new détente would reap extra dividends, would spark a chain reaction of reconciliations.

Out of the blue, Ellie called, wanting to clear her conscience. She and Walter regretted how they'd acted since the Seder, ashamed at having treated us so coldly. She wouldn't lie: they weren't exactly *comfortable*, not quite yet. But family was family, and they would do their best to keep adjusting.

Even more amazing? She said this all to *me*. (She'd known when she called that I'd be home and Stu would not.)

"And so," she said, "this woman"—she forced her voice box clear—"the one you've hired. Maybe we should meet her?"

"My mom said that?" Stu gushed, that evening, when I briefed him. "Yes! I just knew she'd come around."

Now he got ahead of himself, plotting possibilities. The Nadlers would fly up for a week of seaside leisure (early-morning beachcombing, sunning on the deck), after which, fully relaxed, they'd meet Debora and Danny. Dinner at the Pancake King? No, somewhere nicer. And maybe not a dinner, at all; meals were always risky: no escape if anything went wrong. Maybe just a walk along the harbor—and Paula could come! Ellie and Walter loved to be with kids . . .

I was doing my best to keep up with Stu's pace, even though a *crunch, crunch* of worry dogged my strides. For one thing, he would want us working overtime—the two of us, and also Danny and Debora—to show his folks how wholesome we all were. But what if Debora and I, tripped up by our secret, couldn't keep from acting self-conscious? Also, there was no news yet to cheer (had Stu forgotten?) and still might not be, when his parents came. Presenting a pregnant Debora or a Debora five times failed—that could make a universe's difference.

Luckily, the Nadlers' visit remained merely a promise. The impulse itself was progress enough to start with.

Now, if we could only make another peace agreement, one between Stu's sister and her husband.

In call after call to Stu, Rina revealed her woes: Richard said he didn't trust her judgment anymore . . . he balked when she asked to see a non-rabbinic counselor . . . now he'd started sleeping in the guest room . . .

She needed a break, she said. Some time apart, to breathe.

"Time apart is the *last* thing you need," I heard him telling her. "What you need's to force yourselves together."

Stu was giving Rina the same prescription we'd been taking: our date nights continued, and I was eager to plan our holiday trip. Things were going so well, in fact, that I'd decided to try this new approach with others, too: to keep my hackles lowered, to offer plenty of leeway, to make clear my yearning for accord.

This was my approach, days later, when Richard phoned. I figured he was calling for Stu, to argue about Rina, but first I would try to cool him down. "This is a tough time," I said, "for everyone involved. I hope you know we're pulling for you. We hope you work this out."

"Thanks, Pat," he said. "That means a lot. Really. I would understand if you were taking Rina's side."

"We're on the side of happiness," I said. "For both of you."

"Well, I hope that we can be as close as you and Stu," he said. "You have a lot more years together than we do."

This was the awful black hat? The marriage-wrecking tyrant? Maybe all he'd needed was some friendship.

Now my spine went tingly with a sure-thing premonition: that his and Rina's marriage would heal, and Debora's too, and mine. All our bonds restored, as in a Shakespeare comedy: a stage full of broadly smiling couples.

I gave Richard my best, and said I'd go find Stu, but he said no, please, stay on the phone.

"I'm glad I got *you*," he said, "'cause Stu's been just stonewalling. Every time I ask what we can bring, he tells me 'nothing.' Nothing, nothing—the guy just won't budge!"

"Bring?" I said.

"For the party. Or something for the house. Isn't there anything you guys want, or need?"

Bit by bit I ascertained the plan he took for granted: that he and Rina were coming here, to the cottage, July Fourth weekend. I tried to make it seem as if I'd known.

"Nothing at all? Really?" he said. "Well, we'll think of something. Hopefully, Stu is right, it'll be a healthy getaway. You guys are awfully generous to invite us."

I would not have described myself as generous when I found Stu.

He was mowing the lawn, barefoot and bare-chested, lost within the music from his iPod (its cords like two IV tubes, mainlining his brain). I had to step into his path to stop him.

He cut the engine. "Careful, hon. I could've run you over."

The mower released a sharp, explosive smell. I wanted to punt it. "Without even asking me, Stu? After all our progress?" I told him about the phone call; how dumb I'd felt, not knowing, faking my excitement for the visit . . .

195

"Shit. Didn't we talk about it? I meant to, Pat. Honest."

"But wait, do you not remember? Really? You really don't?"

He searched the air for revelation. He rubbed his buzz-cut hair.

"The holiday, Stu? July Fourth? *We* were going away."

"Were we?" he said. "I mean, was it . . . we really made it definite? Wasn't it just a notion you had floated?"

"We hadn't decided where," I said. "But yes, we had decided."

"Sorry if you'd been counting on it, but Rina's really struggling now. Honestly, she's hanging by a thread. The chance to give some help to her just seemed a lot more pressing than—" He looked at me with hooded, sheepish eyes.

I looked back: his pale, sweaty chest, smudged with engine oil, the oil flecked with stuck-on bits of grass. How I would have liked a more traditional tar-and-feathering.

"But no," he said. "Hold on. Am I the only screw-up here? Aren't *you* forgetting something, too?"

I was stumped. I tried to think of promises made and broken—ones, at least, of which Stu was aware.

"Debora," he said.

Forgetting Debora? Not even if I tried.

"Her cycle," he went on. "Haven't you checked the calendar? The fourth is when she ovulates. The fourth, maybe the fifth. I mean, of course, I hope we won't be needing another cycle. But just in case, we can't go out of town."

Wait. This wasn't right. *Stu* was the selfish scoundrel, and *I* was the one . . . the good one . . .

I felt my pedestal crumbling.

I saw Debora's Caller ID but kept myself from answering. Stu was out of town—an overnight in Phoenix—and I wasn't sure I trusted myself to speak with her, alone. We hadn't talked in more than a week, not since my bungled try. Better, I thought, to stick with *Don't pick up*.

I went back to my work, an eighth-grade language unit for Missouri, about the distinction between facts and opinions.

Statement: The Earth is round.

Fact or Opinion? Fact.

Test: Can be proven true or false.

Statement: Children shouldn't speak unless they're spoken to.

Fact or Opinion? Opinion.

But then: Debora's voice, scarcely like a voice, more like a structure being flattened. "Sorry, I . . . I'm so sorry . . . it came again. My period."

Test, I typed, and sat there feeling feeble.

"Maybe I'm no good," she said. "No good for this. Not right. Maybe I am just a bad person."

I grabbed the phone. "You're *not*, Debora. Okay? You are not."

"Pat?" she said. "It doesn't work. Why?"

"It will. It will!"

"But I thought just this little thing, this *one thing*, I can do. I thought"—and her voice slid away.

Her anguish cut right through me. I felt accountable for it, since I had put her—Stu and I had put her—in this bind. Was this what drove me forward? My sense of culpability? Or was I, again, just being selfish?

"Is Paula there?" I asked.

"At preschool. I'm alone."

"Okay, then. Meet me at the beach in half an hour."

nineteen

The parking lot was chockablock—out-of-staters, mostly; I had to circle four or five times. At last I found a spot by the small lookout platform, where Debora, I realized as I climbed out of the car, was standing, arms crossed, facing the water. I'd seen her as I scouted, but not known whom I saw. From the back, she'd looked so insubstantial.

I called to her and waved both hands, a dumb, redundant greeting. Debora turned and strode to me, spreading wide her arms, a gesture I now saw I had invited. I dropped my hands. "The beach is packed," I said. "Hike the marsh?"

Debora's arms froze in her own aborted gesture. "Whatever you think, it's good," she said. "I'll follow."

We walked down the road single-file, skirting traffic. I went first, and couldn't see her, but pictured her shaken gait. I wanted to start over, to give her a kindly hug. Surely she could tell between condolence and a come-on.

We turned at the ranger hut from asphalt onto sand. To our left, the dunes; our right, the Great Marsh, whose sedge shone a fierce, chafing green. The sky was bright, pungent, stunning in a literal sense: looking at it put me in a daze.

The trail followed an old road, a pair of sunken ruts, which Debora and I took, side by side. With every step she winced; maybe the hot

sand hurt? Watching her face—her flinching, even if caused by pain—
sent me back inevitably to our last time together: the way, pressed
against me, she had shuddered.

Fast, I had to ball that thought up, hurl it to the marsh . . .

"Things okay at home?" I asked. "You know, with Danny back?"

"Yes," she said. "Fine. All is normal." Her flip-flops were smacking
hard against her striding soles. Sand sprayed, and clung against her
calves.

In the sedge, a shadow landed. I shielded my eyes to watch. Something big and sharp, slashing down.

"And?" I said. "You told him?"

"Told him? No!" She stopped.

"Today," I said. "Your period."

"Oh," she said. "*That.*"

The shadow flapped up again, gorgeously ungainly. The sun caught
its wings: a great blue heron.

"No," she said. "Danny's working. Tonight we'll talk, at home. And
you? You talked with Stu already?"

"Stu is on his way home from Phoenix. Couldn't reach him." In
truth, I hadn't tried; I couldn't bear the thought, knowing what a toll
the news would take. Also maybe—selfish again—I wanted, for a little
while, to keep the grief as mine. Mine and Debora's.

Now she started off again, scuffing through the sand, a freer look
about her, no wincing. The mended verbal mix-up seemed to settle
things between us: her pregnancy, her lack of it, was fair game for
discussion, but not the other thing. What we'd done.

I gazed over the marsh again, its taunting green lushness (as if to be
so fertile was a cinch). "The sun," I said. "It's—God, I feel clobbered."

"The start of summer," she said. "The longest day in the year."

"Really?" I said. "Guess you're right. Forgot."

Debora plucked some dune grass and tossed it to the wind. "In
Brazil, it's the shortest day. It's winter, now, that starts." She said this
like a proverb, a puzzle's introduction: for every start, a matching end;
for every end, a start.

Around a bend, we saw another couple coming near. Man and woman, both gray-haired, she a half-foot taller but hunched as if from years of leaning toward her mate; their hands, held together, loosely swung. The couple appeared to hesitate, ready to drop their grasp, but Debora and I both stepped off to our respective sides. The woman smiled gratefully, pulling her partner closer as they passed. She looked like a little girl who'd just unwrapped a box to discover the exact gift she'd wished for.

I asked Debora, "If you were still at home, in Brazil—I mean, if you'd never met Danny—what do you think you'd be doing now?"

That didn't seem to sit well. She shuffled heavily forward, her calves—their sandy skin—rasping. I was on the brink of saying, *No, no, forget it*, when Debora answered, "Married. To one of the boys my brothers knew. Nilson or Henrique or Thiago"—she spat their names. "They were all the same: grabbing always, looking. Their looking, it was like a *smell* in the air. A bad smell. But what choice did I have, you know? What choice?"

Well, the choice you made, I thought. You left. Don't forget.

"And wait," I said. "Remind me. How many brothers were there?"

"Seven."

"And they all stayed? All of them stayed and married?"

"Yes, of course. As soon as they had eighteen, nineteen years. Two of them, they even married sisters—stupid cows." She looked up to the cutting sun, her eyes clear, unsquinting. "Well, all but Waterston. Who I told you. That summer."

"The one who lives in the city, in . . . what's it called?"

"Natal."

"—who lives in Natal. Never married?"

Debora shook her head. She said, "Lived."

"Why? Did he move back to your village?"

"No. He died."

The bluntness of it caught me at the knees.

I should have asked what happened, or told her I was sorry, but sorrow didn't come as fast as self-indulgent anger: why the hell was *loss* our only topic?

I looked up uncomfortably, worried she'd seen my thoughts, but Debora wore a crisp, vivid smile. "I told about my summer in Natal?" she said. "With Waterston? The orchid from my teacher, that I sold?"

"Yes," I said. "The summer you met Danny."

"Fifty *reais* I earned," she said. "For you, this would mean nothing. A dinner, maybe. A few beers in a bar. But for me!" She clenched her hands then burst them brightly open. "For Waterston and me—our best time."

I was even more ashamed now of my reaction—my nonreaction—to hearing about her brother. I wanted to redeem myself. How?

"Maybe we could find an orchid now," I said. "You want to?"

"Where?" she said.

"Here. There's wild ones, if you're lucky."

Debora tucked her chin. She looked doubtful.

"Trust me," I said. "I know the perfect spot." A swale in the dunes by an old duck-hunting shack, another mile or so down the trail. Years ago, my mom had led me there, and we'd hit pay dirt: a grass-pink, according to our guidebook. "Well?" I said.

"Okay, I guess."

"Great, come on. Let's go!"

Why was I injected with the urge to hurry so? If orchids were there, they'd be there for a while. But I could feel my spirits being whipped to stiff peaks. Debora was in the left rut, and I the grassy middle, and we both started picking up our pace.

Now was the time, I knew—when we were feeling hardy—to talk about the subject we'd been dodging. The crater we kept landing in: our failure to conceive.

I brought it up, but hastened to say, "Not that we think *you've* failed. I hope you know, we never think like that. And actually, if someone is . . . Stu's the one. He must be."

"He's not failing, either," she said. "Maybe his sperm. Not *him*."

"No, you're right, you're right. It doesn't help to blame."

It didn't help, but that didn't seem to stop me. And blame or not, the doubts about Stu's sperm, its health, remained. (So far he'd resisted further testing.) Weren't we, then, banging up against a brick wall? Wouldn't we keep banging it, and banging?

"Yes," she said, "and I'm not sure, you know, how much longer . . ."

At least three more months, I pictured Stu insisting. *Take a look at the contract you agreed to.*

Debora worried for Paula, she said, and Danny too—their moods; they suffered when they saw her get so sad. Danny had said the right things when he came back home from Brockton, had promised he'd support her, if she wanted. "But I don't know, the way he's being nice to me," she said, "the way he is giving his support—all this almost makes me want to make things better for *us*. Almost makes me think that I should stop."

Everything she said—its content—was depressing. But her voice, her being together with me, here and now: within my husk of hopelessness, these little seeds of hope . . .

"Please," I said. "Please don't quit. Not yet."

Soon we saw the hunting shack, worse than I'd remembered: siding scabbed with tarpaper, stovepipe pocked by rust. Off behind the shack, though, the dunes were uncorrupted. Scattered clumps of poverty grass, in brilliant yellow bloom, looked like little campfires in the sand.

"It's off-limits, of course," I said. "All the dunes here are."

"And so, if they catch us?" she asked.

"Cite us, I guess? Fine us?"

"Yes, but—" She raised her wrists, as if to say, *Arrest me.* "By then, it's too late. We are here."

Up and down a slope we climbed, and up a second, higher one, and then, there it was, below: the swale. Just as I'd recalled, a thriving bit of bog. Not quite dune and not quite marsh: a curious in-betweenness.

Skidding together down the slope, we carved a sandy wake. Debora slipped and stumbled, but leapt right back to balance, sunlit face aflash with satisfaction. "So?" she said. "Where are all these orchids that you promised?"

The ground here was damp. The air felt somehow softer. Maybe the plants, I postulated, filtered something sharp from it, socking away sunlight in their stalks. I tried to call to mind, from four or five years back, a piece I'd done on interdunal flora. "See this, here?" I said to her. "Below those weeds? That's cranberry." It looked about a blink away from flowering. Farther on: a sundew with reddish hairy leaves, a devious liquid drop on each hair. "That one is a carnivore. Those drops? Bugs get stuck."

"Ai!" she said. "Thank you. I'll be careful."

I would have to concentrate, if I would find an orchid. Squatted down, I duck-walked, scanning along the ground. Scanning, scanning, every inch of sand. I'd spot something, but no: an optical illusion. Amazing what desire could make you see.

My thighs were killing, but still I waddled onward (scanning, scanning). More cranberry . . . another scrubby plant I couldn't name . . . plenty of budding life, but no orchid.

Debora was strolling, brushing shrubs, barely even looking. *Focus!* I wanted to shout at her. *Don't you even care?* But she must have seen the truth, sooner than I did now: our search had very little to do with flowers.

I was sweating, my throat was dry, my body needed a break. I sank onto the swale's sandy edge. "Fuck," I said. "Forget it. There's nothing. It's no use." I felt like crying, like laughing at my foolish sobby self. The colors of my mood ran together.

Debora plopped down next to me and kicked her flip-flops off. Her brown, beat-up feet had a rough sort of dignity; they looked like a long-surviving heirloom.

I started to say how sorry I was; she cut me off with "Don't be."

She had plucked a flower, a pink one I didn't know, and planted it now, buried to its bloom, in gathered sand. "My brother," she said. "He was so much like you: the way he searched." She smiled the crisp smile she'd shown before. "Our mother, she was baking, once, and Waterston had such questions: how much this, how much that, Mãinha, how do you make? She was getting bored, so she tells him that it's *butterflies*. A nice cake like hers, to be sweet: fifteen butterflies."

"And he believed her?"

"Of course! Just a boy, you know? A child. The next day he goes out. All day, until it's dark. Time for the dinner, time for the bed—still he isn't home. My mother says to my brothers: 'Go, go and see.' And so, all around the farm they're looking. The barn? No. The ditch? No. He's gone! And then, finally, the most old brother, Uílliam, he discovers him: sitting in a far, far field, crying. 'Waterston! What happened? Why are you out here crying?' 'The butterfly,' he tells him. 'I chased it, but I lost it. A butterfly to make our cake sweet.'" Debora's smile looked aimless now: indulgence with no object. "After this they always called him butterfly. *Borboleta*. Even then, I guess, they maybe knew."

"Knew?" I said, but as soon as I had asked, I understood.

"Moving away, to Natal?" she said. "That was still a searching. He went there to look for others like him. But that was also, you know, how he died."

To keep Debora from having to say the word, I did it: "AIDS?"

"Yes," she said. "And that is why, when I first saw your ad, I thought: this is extra good, to help two men like him. Not that I was thinking I can—how should I say?—*replace* him. But help some men like him to . . . to continue."

Her phrase was an imprecise translation, I imagined. A grope at expressing something tricky. Nonetheless, she'd found the perfect wording: *to continue*. A heartbeat, a heartbeat, another, then the next (the ones within my chest were growing harder), and then, when our hearts gave out, what would still survive? All the bloody effort of our lives, the love and bother: would any of what made us *us* go on?

"It's bad," she said, "to tell you all these things about my brother?"

"Bad?" I said. "You kidding me? Of course it's not. I'm glad."

Glad that she had told me, and glad she'd felt she could.

Glad to be right next to her, so close.

A breeze eddied, bringing hints of moisture from the marsh. I felt my pulse poking at my throat.

I told myself my touch would be a simple one, of solace. I rubbed her knee, its smooth, hard-boiled knob. But then we both . . . what happened? A sudden sluice of craving. We fell together, grappling in the sand.

Why else had I asked her here? Why else had she come? We had both tied blinders on but left the knots too loose, and now here we were, eye to eye.

I worked her shirt, stripped it. Debora ditched her bra. And though I'd seen her private parts—the last time, I'd had to—her chest now seemed to me a million times more private: not her breasts, *between* them, the caviar of freckles.

Debora glanced behind her. "The shack?" she said. "It's better?"

"No," I said. I muzzled her mouth. "Here."

After that we didn't talk till we were both undressed, I on my back, Debora above, astride me. The previous time, her nakedness had had a worthy purpose, a context that blunted its effect. Now, the only purpose was . . . well, *this.*

I edged up, but stalled, caught by the thought of birth control. I hadn't faced that issue in so long.

Debora seemed to spot my fear. "Pat," she said. "Think. Today came my period—we're safe."

Yes, of course. What day could be safer?

But this, too, presented its own problem. "What if there's—" I faltered; I didn't want to say *a mess.* Finally what I managed was, "The blood?"

"How you worry!" She laughed. "It's nice, but you don't need. Look, you know the cup we use, for doing the insems?"

"The Instead Cup?"

"Yes. Why they make this, do you know?"

Hadn't she just said why? For insems.

"No, not to keep *your* stuff inside. To keep *mine*. To hold the blood in. That is what it's made for."

A menstrual cup, right. *Instead* of using tampons. When Marcie sent her care package, she had made this clear. It hadn't seemed germane. I'd forgotten.

"You have it?" I said.

She nodded.

"Now? It's in already?"

"Yes," she said. "So stop this worrying. Yes? Okay? Good!"

She raised up, slammed back down, and oh! I was in.

"Easy, now," I started to say, but this time I was muzzled. Jesus, how she pounded me, and with such concentration, as though she were digging a hole to bury stolen loot.

The sand scraped and scraped my back, a pleasant stinging pain. An exclamation point, painted along my spine.

Afterward we scurried for the shack, to tidy up: naked, still; clothing in our fists. The door was locked, but shiplap boards beside it were coming loose. Prying them back, we made an easy passage.

The overheated air had an unnutritious taste. Smoke-darkened, fly-stained windows scarcely let in light. My eyes adjusted: a sprung mattress, a woodstove strewn with mouse crap. Had no one used the place since hunting season?

Debora was looking jelly-eyed: a boxer after a blow. She found some paper towels, only slightly mouse-gnawed, tore a bunch, and handed them to me. I sat down at a card table, stacked with Bud Light empties, one of which was now a homemade bong. A soggy soft-core magazine lay opened to its middle, ripped so that the centerfold—a blonde with smug eyes—looked like a double amputee.

As soon as we'd de-sanded ourselves and swabbed our skin, we dressed, then faced each other, in hair-trigger silence. Gazes lowered. Bared, despite our clothes.

"Sorry," she said, "I hate to . . . but I need to ask. Forgive me." Still, she couldn't force herself. She couldn't meet my eyes.

"Ask," I said. "I mean, by now, what've we got to hide?"

"Okay, well . . . you have taken the test? I can ask this?"

"Oh!" I said. "Oh God, no, don't worry. Yes, of course."

"Ah, okay. Thanks God. I should have asked before. I knew Stu must take the test, of course, for our insems. But you, well, maybe I never saw you in this way." Finally, she looked up at me. Into me. Appraising. "Pat, you have been with women?"

"Yes, but not in ages," I said.

"And you liked?"

"I certainly liked *this*."

She took one of the beer cans and shook it, shook it, shook it; the broken-off tab inside jangled. "At home, the gays are *gay*, you know? Like Waterston. Only gay. Yes, there are some hetero men who sometimes sleep with men, but only . . . I think you call it 'active'?"

"We might say 'tops.'"

"Yes, but they are hetero, really. The other is just for pleasure. But gays who *live* as gays and sleep with *women*? I've never heard."

"Well, it's not so common here, either, I guess. Not really. Like Stu," I said. "He's never, I don't think. Not even once."

Debora shut the magazine, as if to shield its model, as if we might offend her sensibilities. "And you and Stu. You're still . . . you are satisfied?"

"Our sex life? It's good," I said. "Especially lately. Yes."

"Then why?" she said. "You still want more? I don't understand."

Did I want more? I guessed I must. I wasn't sure why, either. "For gay guys, it's different," I said, slinging the old excuse. "We don't necessarily expect one partner to give us everything. Know what I mean?"

Her face was like fogged glass.

"Okay, well, with two men there's . . . without a woman's taming—or, no, that's not, not *taming* . . ." My tongue was in a twist. I hadn't spouted the party line in eons. "When sex isn't ever about babies, it sort of frees you. It doesn't have the same sense of consequence. And that means you can sleep around—this is how the theory goes—without threatening the basis of your marriage. Improving it, even, maybe, because, you know, you're more contented."

Debora pinched her chin. Her eyes got small and frosty. "*This* is like that? *I* am?" she said. "I am less of 'consequence'?" She picked up the magazine and tossed it.

"Jesus, no. Of course not, Deb. Come on," I said. "Come on."

The space where the magazine had lain was darker, dustless—its cleanness like a haughty accusation.

"No, the truth," I said. I owed it to her, finally. "The truth is that, with Stu and me, things weren't all that easy. The theory I just told you? That was what *he* argued. But it caused lots of problems between us. Back in New York, you know?" I wanted to stop, but knew I had to abrade another layer. "Stu was hooking up with strangers, more and more—too many. It didn't have to do with me, he said, but how could it not? I mean, he was setting our life aside, that's what it felt like. I felt those strangers knew him more than I did. That was part of why we moved up here, you know, to work on 'us.' And now, ironically . . . look at *me*." I tried to make my most forgivable face.

Debora said, "I've never."

"What—had sex with a stranger?"

She shrank. "Someone other than Danny. Not since we were married."

I couldn't tell how much of her disquiet came from guilt, and how much from her shock at guilt's weakness to have stopped us. Plus, I guessed, she must have felt upended by my confession, as I had been when she'd made hers, about her life with Danny. Was I supposed to follow her lead, and say I'd understand, now, if she no longer wanted to be our surro?

I reached across and cupped her hands. "Maybe this wasn't right," I said. "Maybe nobody else would comprehend it. I mean, do *we*?"

She took her hands back, blew into her palms. She didn't answer.

Perhaps she expected me to make a solemn pledge. Never to sleep together again? To do it again, and soon? How could I abide by either vow?

The jab of such uncertainty had left me feeling charley-horsed. The longer we stayed, the stiffer I was getting.

"We should talk. We have to," I said. "About what we are doing. But maybe this is enough for now. You think? Is this enough?"

She looked down at the table, as if to study something: a crystal ball, a map to safer ground.

"We *will*," I said. "We'll talk."

"Okay," she said. "Okay."

We sat, then, silent, in the smoky, virile haze. The marsh made muffled grassy tickings.

At last I rose and paced the shack, gathering up our trash. Next I fetched the magazine, returned it to its spot. This felt like a kind of restoration.

"Should we?" I said.

"Yes," said Debora. "I am ready now."

We squeezed through the secret shiplap door.

The sun and sand: *too much*. After the shack, they stung. The air provided an antidote—its pure, consoling smell. A primary smell, as basic as red or blue.

The shack was quickly lost, and all we saw was wildness: sedge and sky and shadow-stippled dunes. We didn't talk, but walking was its own conversation: one of us would drift toward the road's unrutted center; the other would respond, stepping closer. In and out, but never quite together. I saw a scratch at her neckline (mine? could I have made it?); I didn't know if I should point it out.

I hit a soft patch, wavered, and Debora grabbed my waist, propping me till I could gain my balance. Then she joined her hand with mine and set our arms to swinging. Recalling the couple from earlier—the woman's struck-rich look—I wished they were here to witness us.

Soon we reached the parking lot. At Debora's car, we lingered—technically not quite hugging, but close enough that I could smell her hair, which smelled familiar. It smelled just like . . . no, I couldn't place it.

She leaned away. Tapped my chest. "You," she said. "*You.*" Still she couldn't seem to drop my hand.

Not that I'd have wanted her to. I wanted to hold and hold her. To stand here as the tide came up, receded, rose again.

At last, though, we had to part. She stepped into her car, and backed it out, and left without a wave.

Then I knew. *Herself*: that's what her hair smelled of. Nothing more or less than her own scent.

twenty

Well?" Stu asked as soon as he came home.

I felt stupid. I stared at him and thickly said, "Well what?"

"What do you mean, 'Well what'? Did she call? Any news?"

"Oh. Oh, right. Yeah. Called this morning." As if Debora's news had been nothing but a sidelight. Was that what she and I had turned it into?

"I guess she didn't . . ."

"No," I said.

"No. You would've told me." He headed for the liquor shelf and poured a double Dewar's. His feet looked like wheels in need of tightening. "Great," he said. "Fantastic, then. This is just ideal." He held the Scotch underneath his nose, like smelling salts. "My folks are finally ready—starting to be ready—to think about accepting what we're doing. They even want to come and meet Debora. And sure, I can picture it now: 'Mom, Dad, meet the woman who still hasn't—'"

"But Stu, come on. It's not as if it's *Debora's*—"

Damn. Too late.

Stu's humiliation pitched its black tent above us. "Oh, I see," he said. "It's me? Not man enough?" He chuckled but it sounded more like someone being sick. He toasted with his Scotch, tossed it back.

What had I been thinking? I had to stop. I had to. No more seeing Debora now. Not us two, alone. No more playing dumb with my own conscience.

But even in berating myself, I had to picture Debora. *Never do* x *or* y *again* brought *x* and *y* alive. Her soft mouth. The freckles on her chest.

Fantasies rose; I gouged them with the chisel of remorse. It worked . . . at least, till the next time.

She didn't make things easy. She called. Whispered, "Can we?"

No, I told her. We shouldn't.

No, she said. You're right.

But three days later, she called again: "One more time? We can't?"

The miracle was that I managed to resist. Not from being certain that to see her would be bad but from being less certain than I should have. I wanted my resistance to provide some reward—a feeling of proficiency or honor. So far, all I'd felt was more at sea.

That, and more mortifyingly lustful.

I dealt with this by masturbating, often twice a day: rushed, expunging sessions in my workroom. I understood the term *self-abuse*.

I surfed the Web, to sites I had condemned when Stu used them. On Craigslist, it wasn't the raunchy sex dates that compelled me but the melancholic "Missed Connections" postings:

Saw you at Marshalls—m4m—19 (Cape Cod Mall)

You were at the register when I bought a blue hoodie. Wanted to flirt but have no idea how. I keep imagining . . .

I knew I'd act on no one's ad. Why, then, was I looking? I was appalled and comforted by all that lonely hunger.

I felt, strangely, closer to Stu. Was I now feeling what he had felt? Longing for something not much more specific than longing itself? Well, that wasn't wholly true; I longed for Debora, specifically. But also for the pleasures she provoked in me, apart from her: the sense that I could do and be my own thing, undefined.

I thought of Becky, my old flame, and Googled for her picture. (Was Debora just a substitute for her?) Her name was way too common: almost a million hits. I added *Manitoba*, then *bagpipes*, and there she was, her hair shorter, tinselly with gray. On either side, her sons (I presumed), in mustard plaid: toothy boys with mild blue eyes and frizzy ginger curls, inherited from a redhead dad, no doubt. Instinctively I tried to subtract his genes and add my own. Maybe then the boys would have my blonder, straighter hair; maybe they would boast my Faunce cheekbones . . .

But no, I didn't pine for what I might have had with Becky. I didn't want Debora as a rerun. As much as I craved a justification for what I felt for her, a grand theory to make it all make sense, maybe the truth— so commonplace, so rattlingly mundane—was simply that I wanted her, and wanted her to want me.

How could wants so simple cause such awful complications?

Meanwhile Stu, upstandingly, was facing his disappointment head-on. Instead of moping, he was giving voice to his emotions. "I know I've been a pain to get along with," he admitted. "I hope you know it's my own sadness, and nothing to do with you."

He even called his parents for a forthright conversation. "I explained," he told me later, "that Debora hasn't—or, well, that *we* . . ."

"Good," I said. "It's good to let them in. Let them help."

"Know what my father told me then?" he said. "That this is *his* fault."

"What, that we can't—"

"Me and Rina both. 'The Nadler curse.' Dad's just sure it's all because of him."

We were in bed. Midnight. An underwater darkness.

"He thinks it's God's punishment," said Stu. "For surviving."

"But Stu, come on, that's absolutely crazy."

"I said that! I said why would God have spared my dad, just to make his kids a dead end?"

The wind made a sound like someone sandpapering the night. The blackness of the sky through the window screen's web was lighter than the blackness of our room.

"You're not, Stu," I said. "You're not a dead end."

He coughed up a throaty, mirthless "Ha."

"Seriously, hon. You don't know. Not for sure, at least. The doc said your counts were normal, right?"

He didn't answer.

A distant car tore past: the sound of someone hurried. Rushing away, before his sudden absence would be noted? Rushing home, to someone's loving arms?

July third, driving back from errands in Hyannis (bags of ice, Uncle Sam napkins), I suffered another spasm of temptation. I pictured myself veering from the smoggy line of cars—a left here, another left, a right, and there I'd be—and pulling up stealthily at Debora's. Check for Danny's truck (gone!), call her to the door. Paula at home? (Oh please, be at preschool.)

Now would be the perfect time, my alibi impeccable: Stu himself had drafted me to head off into town, to shop for tomorrow's holiday bash, while he would stay at home, awaiting his sister and Richard, due up from Long Island any minute.

I'd see Debora tomorrow: her surge, the next insem. Tomorrow or the fifth was what we figured. But wouldn't it be better if I saw her now, alone? Inoculated with pleasure, I would then come home, immunized against my in-laws' onslaught.

I could do it. *A left, another left, a right . . .*

I'd passed the turn, but pulled off now and idled on the shoulder. A flag-draped Hummer's driver—partying a day early—hurtled by, giving me thumbs up. I didn't lift my fingers from the wheel.

I was recalling the sound of Stu, the other night: *dead end*. Recalling

214

how that conversation had finished. I had said, "You want to get another sperm count done? Or see another specialist? Or . . . something?" Stu had slowed his breathing, *in* and two and *out* and two: someone who didn't know him well would think he was asleep. But I had still felt him there, his straining brain, awake, telling me yes by not telling me no.

That was what I thought of now, idling on the shoulder, weighing whether to make the turn for Debora's. Late-day sun was burning down; the ice I'd bought would melt. Another car of early revelers hollered.

A trooper stopped behind me, approached with hand on holster. "Sir, is there a problem here? Anything I can help with?"

No, I told him.

"All right, then, get moving."

Richard's Porsche was angled across our driveway, wasting space, its yellow sheen, in full-on sun, redundant. Someone had keyed a scratch into the hood.

I loaded my arms with grocery bags, and ambled toward the house, giving myself time to practice niceness: Ask him how his work is going. Beg to hear a joke.

"Hey, sorry I'm late," I called jauntily, going in. "A certain someone gave me twenty zillion things to do. How was your drive? Traffic is a killer."

But here was Stu, rushing at me, panic in his eyes. "Shh, shh! Give me the—just wait, okay? Keep quiet." He took the bags, set them on the counter.

"Why? What's going on? I saw the car. They're here?"

"Yes, they're here, but—" He pantomimed an incoherent message. "The guest room. They went in, won't come out."

"Maybe they're just, you know. Kissing and making up." I thought of them at Seaside Heights, at Labor Day some years ago, stealing away incessantly to "nap."

"No," said Stu. "She was crying."

"When?"

"When they got here. Her eyes were just these red, puffy *nothings*."

"And they didn't say . . ."

"No. Just 'Hi,' and 'Please excuse us.' And now they've been in there half an hour."

Which turned into forty minutes, forty-five, fifty.

Long silent gaps would pass, and then a burst of voices: smothered shouts, like someone buried alive. Stu, after one such burst, knocked. "You guys okay?" The question was absurd—of course they weren't okay. I could hear Stu's hopes hissing out.

At last they came lurching—Richard first, then Rina—like land-lubbers searching for their sea legs.

"Hi," I said, too loudly.

They both bleakly nodded.

"Sit?" said Stu, pointing to the couch's free cushions.

"Thanks, Stu," said Richard, but didn't change position. He stood there, self-contained, steeled.

Rina took a seat, or let it take her. Stu was right: her eyes were all but zeroes.

"I hope you don't mind," he said. "But honestly, I feel that I . . . that Pat and I deserve an explanation."

"Of course you do," said Richard. "You do. We're so sorry."

"We?" said Rina. "*Now* we're 'we'? Give me a goddamn break."

"Easy, please. I thought we agreed to—"

"*You* agreed to. You."

Richard cracked a mannered smile. "Okay, fine. Sure. But please, Ree. Can't we not shout?"

"Yeah," she said. "Let's *whisper* about it. Tell it to them *real soft*."

Richard clasped his hands before his chest ministerially. "The thing is—it's a hard thing, obviously, for both of us—Rina and I, we're getting a separation."

"What? What are you talking about?" Stu leapt from his chair. It seemed he might go for Richard's throat.

"Sorry," said Richard, making a vague gesture of defense. "Didn't mean for it to happen this way, but at this point, you're right, you deserve to hear the truth."

"But wait," I said. "All because she wants a Jewish baby? A baby who is *actually* Jewish? Maybe it's hard for a non-Jew to understand, I guess, but . . . seriously?"

"Not just that," said Richard. "Irreconcilable differences."

"Oh, please," I said. "What are you now, a lawyer?"

"I'm sorry," he said. "Really. I know you've gone to a lot of trouble, planning this whole weekend, and—"

"Don't you be polite," said Stu. "Don't you dare be polite."

"I told him I would do it how he wanted," Rina said. "Born Jewish, converted—whatever. But it doesn't matter. He's already made up his mind."

"Then why," I said, pointing at him, "why'd you bother coming? I mean, what, you *just* made up your mind? Something about the drive up here just made you think: dump her?"

"No," he said. "It's just that . . . I guess I was confused. Or scared, I guess. Don't know. Hard to explain."

"Hard?" said Rina. "Hard? There's only one reason, and it's—"

"Ree, I've told you it's not—"

"—because I'm infertile."

"It's not, Rina, it's—"

"Of course it is! What else would it be?" Tears began to boil out from her eyes.

Stu thrust his face about an inch away from Richard's. "You're a schmuck, do you know that? From the moment I laid eyes on you, I didn't like you. I tried to, for my sister's sake. But my God! All your ridiculous 'humor'? And your *Look at me, I worked on a kibbutz, I'm so holy*? To say nothing of when you came here, as our guest, and accused Pat of making a pass at you." He laughed thinly. "A pass? At you? As if, if there were an Uzi at his head, he'd so much as want to touch you. I don't know why I never laid you out for that one. Or why, God, I ever invited you back."

217

With that, he ordered Richard out.

"What do you mean, 'out'?"

"I mean leave. Now!"

"But I can't. We just got here, and Rina—"

"Shut the fuck up. *We'll* take care of Rina," Stu declared. He turned to her for confirmation, but Rina wouldn't look up from her feet.

Richard was still standing there. I grabbed him with a bouncer's grip and rammed him through the hallway, to the door. "Here," I said, and clapped my free palm against his ass. "Here's your grope, okay? Now get out."

A man's voice was jimmying the vacuum seal of sleep. Stu's voice. Had he been speaking long?

"Hon?" he said. "I've been thinking. Maybe *you* should do it."

I was still bobbing on the surface of my dreams. I knew, from the window, that day was coming close (the dark was graining, giving forth the shapes of trees and clouds). I had slept a couple of hours, I guessed.

We had stayed awake past two, Stu and I and Rina, shaky with the high of what we'd done. Rina did most of the talking: "I can't fucking believe it. I mean, sure, we'd spoken before of maybe splitting up, but not unless . . . unless . . . I can't fucking believe it." Finally we had all given up, taken pills. Rina refused to sleep where she would have slept with Richard; instead she chose the couch, in the TV's mottled glow. Stu and I had holed up in our room.

"Was I too harsh?" he'd asked. "Did I do the right thing?"

"The *only* thing," I said. "I'm really proud."

Then my pill had softened me; I rode a chute to sleep.

But now Stu had woken me with "Maybe *you* should do it."

I cleared my throat of morning crust. "Do what?"

"Go to see the doctor and get your counts done. Or no, skip the stupid test. Just do it."

"Stu, come on, it's—I don't think you mean that. Not really." The last time he had said this, he was bluffing.

218

"No," he said. "I'm serious. The *goal* is what's important. Now that we're the only hope for grandkids . . ."

(He had phoned his parents after Richard left, to tell them. Walter's response: "Don't get used to anything—didn't I always say? And here I did, I went and did: the thought of being an *opa*.")

"The baby'd still be Jewish," Stu went on. "It's matrilineal. Don't you think it's time for you to try?"

"You know I would—I'd love to—if you want me to," I said. Immediately the possibility started to build beneath me: a brick, another brick, a solid mortared block. "But still, how do *I* solve . . . you know, I'm not *your* family. Your dad could still call himself cursed."

"Maybe he wouldn't know," said Stu. "Maybe he wouldn't have to. And hey, what're you talking about? You are so my family." He turned to me and gently traced my jaw. "Think of how fucked-up it's been, this pressure from my dad, all the ways it's messed with me and Rina. And Richard, that little shit, I swear I won't be like that! So hung up on 'Jewish family'—his fantasy of family—he ends up wrecking the one he *has*."

Should I have been surprised? Had Stu forsworn his Stu-ness?

The opposite: he'd found himself again.

Dawn had buffed the window to a dazzling pinkish shine. The light put an ember in Stu's eyes. "Maybe I'll try one more time?" he said. "Not sure why—it's not like I'm holding out much hope. And then, if it still doesn't work, *you* should do it. Wouldn't that make sense? Don't you think?"

twenty-one

And so it was that when Danny called, shortly before noon ("I know you've got your in-laws there, but Deb just double-checked. Today's a go. What time can you get here?"), I was feeling oddly optimistic.

Being in Debora's presence would still test me, I was sure. But Stu's altered outlook, his new flexibility, offered me a kind of dispensation. Not that I felt pardoned for the things I'd done with Debora, or felt released to let us lapse again. But now that Stu had raised the chance that I might make a child with her—now that she and I might form a kind of sanctioned union—I suspected our outlaw lust might ebb.

Suspected it would? Convinced myself it should?

Stu explained to Danny about yesterday's debacle: Richard's ouster, our holiday party scuttled. Screw that, Danny told him; the party would be at *their* house. "Bring whatever goodies you bought, but we've got more than plenty—hamburgers, hot dogs, the works. Bring your sister, too. Take her mind off."

Rina was appreciative, but no, she wouldn't go. What could be more miserable, today of all days, than standing by while somebody else tried to have a baby? "All I really want?" she said. "I want to be at home."

"But Ree," said Stu. "Really? Richard'll be there, won't he?"

"No," she said. "*Home.* Mom and Dad's."

We dropped her at the airport, on the way to Debora's. Stu used up a buddy pass to buy her a discount seat.

"Thanks," she said. She kissed him.

"For what? I feel awful."

"The ticket," she said. "And for standing up. For being my big brother."

"I don't know. I just wish—"

"Let me do the wishing. What I wish is for everything today to go perfect. I can't wait to hear the good news."

A hug to Stu, another to me, and Rina headed off—unself-consciously wiping away her tears. Just before the X-ray machine, she turned to wave good-bye. "Prepare yourself," she called, her voice pinched but steady. "Auntie Rina will spoil that baby rotten!"

No gamesmanship, no strings attached, just unreserved endorsement. I wished I could hug her again, harder.

Back in the glary car, I asked Stu, "How do you feel?"

"Like I told her: absolutely awful." Watery-eyed, he flipped down the sunshade. "But also, you know, probably more than anything? *Relieved.* For you and me. The plan we made this morning."

I rolled down my window. Muggy air sloshed in, the stoked scent of not-quite-mustered rain. The only right word for it was *pregnant.*

Debora greeted us equally, with quick pecks to our cheeks—cordial but with hostessy reserve—and I knew I could trust her, and therefore trust myself.

Still, I couldn't help a little stirring. She wore a baggy T-shirt, a pair of Danny's gym trunks: clothes that, in their over-obvious body-masking purpose, only brought my focus to her body. Her hair was down, which made her look young, luxuriant, nervous. I wouldn't have pegged her as anybody's mother.

Danny seemed intent on making up for her low-keyness. Immediately he filled our hands with smoking burgers, with beers, then opened beach chairs, commanding us to sit. Despite the soupy heat, he sported a hooded sweatshirt, like someone trying to shed his gut by sweating. But why? Danny had no gut to shed. Before I could remark on it, he did a coy striptease, peeling the hoodie off to show his T-shirt. Snug and pink: Nobody Knows I'm a Lesbian. "Awesome, right?" he said. "How could you not love it?" His newest clients, he told us, a dyke couple in P-town ("No—they said to call them that, they gave me their permission"), owned a pair of shirts exactly like it, and seeing how he'd laughed at theirs, they'd bought him this, a gift. "Such great ladies, I'm telling you. I'm working on their carriage house, turning it into a bedroom for their daughter. Did I explain that? They had a kid together, one of them using sperm from the other's brother. I know you guys would love them. You should meet!"

This was my first time with Danny since Debora had told his secrets; I had thought my skin would crawl, for her sake. And yes, he was making me cringe a little with his overkill, the way he slathered words on top of words like too much frosting, but part of what repelled me was a twinge of recognition: I knew my own weakness for ingratiating blather. Mostly I was thankful: for how he strove to please, for throwing us this party of diversion. The glowing grill, the frigid beer, samba at full blast . . . not too bad a way to spend the Fourth.

We settled in, sun-doped, reveling in our summertime amusements. The clank-and-shout of someone's nearby horseshoes game was soothing.

Paula was like her dad today, manically convivial. She dashed through the yard in a Stars-and-Stripes bikini, a frantic spider, weaving her web of cheer. She made us watch her soak herself, tumbling over the lawn sprinkler: cartwheel after cartwheel through its steady pulsing spray.

The day, like that dot-dot-dot of water, would drift on, I guessed: an afternoon of sentences elided. Left between the lines was the reason we had come. And: the reason I might mess things up.

Paula's glee had given me a kind of contact high. Or maybe I was just a little drunk. Danny had been presenting me with one beer after another, as though each were a brilliant new invention. Stu was also drinking more, and faster, than was normal. (Debora couldn't; she guzzled guaraná.)

Paula stripped her bathing suit and flounced about us, naked, squirming to the samba's saucy beat. Debora said, "Behave," but her heart wasn't in it, and Paula took off streaking through the sprinkler. "It tickles," she said. She did it again. "A hundred little pokies!" Then she called, "Okay, now *you*," and ran to take Stu's hand.

Stu said, "Nope! No way. No no no."

"But why, Stu? Why not? I'll do it with you, 'kay?"

"Because . . ." He braced himself against her munchkin tugging. "My birthday suit isn't as nice as yours."

The girl paused, perplexed, scanning her bare skin, and Stu took the chance to wriggle free.

"Mãe," she complained. "Make him do it, Mãe."

"I can't, *minha filha*. Not if he doesn't want to."

"And what am *I*," I said to Paula, stepping in, "chopped liver?"

Paula appeared spellbound by the kooky phrase; she stared.

"Why are you only bugging him," I added. "Can't I do it?"

"You!" she screamed, and galloped up, trilling a bright song: "Sprinkler sprinkler sprinkler sprinkler sprinkler." Her smile showed me every tiny tooth.

My sneakers: off. Socks: off. T-shirt: doffed and twirled.

"Nice," called Danny. "Show us a little skin."

"Danny," chided Debora, cutting her glance to Paula.

"Oh, she doesn't understand. Do you, sweetie? Nah."

True enough, Paula didn't catch the dirty talk. She was busy laying down the rules for me to follow. "A hop on this foot, a hop on this, and then . . . and then, *jump*."

"Hmm," I said gravely. "You'd better show me first."

She did, then she bolted back—glistening, newly birthed. "See? Just like that. Like me."

"Okey-doke," I told her. "Here goes nothing." A hop and a hop, a lumbering jeté. The water was so cold it almost burned.

"Now again," she said. "Now together."

We breasted through, holding hands, buoyed by the spray. We made a kind of clumsy, footloose sense.

The music got more drummy, and Paula started dancing. She still gripped my hand, so I was forced to join her. "Faster," she said, her feet like popping corn. I didn't think it possible (the beer had slowed my limbs), but somehow I kept up with her explosions.

Danny raised his grilling tongs and danced them down the lawn. Then Stu joined us, getting his sludgy legs to find the groove.

"Mãinha, too," said Paula, as if she'd always planned this: push the grownups into a four-way fit of self-forgetting.

Debora took a half-step back. From me, in particular? Worried she might give away our secret? I wished I could let her know that Stu had had a turnaround, that she and I might find a safer way to be connected. Plus, I'd have told her: Your *hesitancy* is the giveaway. Play things cool, or they'll all be suspicious . . .

"Okay, then, we'll *get* you," Danny said. "Come on. Let's go!"

The gang of us, a monstrous pod, quickly overtook her. Debora started shrieking; she sounded truly scared. But then Paula writhed her little sinewy naked self, and Debora's voice slackened, and slipped till it was laughter. She fell into our arms. She was dancing.

The music was a coiling rope; to match it, we all whirled. A blur of limbs and faces, with Paula as our center point, our goad, our grinning inspiration. Over the backyard fence, I saw the horseshoes-playing neighbors, caught up in their own celebration. What would they be seeing if they turned and looked at us? Tighter and tighter we clamped together, faster, intertwining, a beast with no right to be so balanced.

Suddenly I was thrust against Debora. Had someone pushed? Maybe just the speed of our rotation. I glanced at Stu, at Danny, at Paula's blissed-out face, waiting for a sign that they objected . . .

Debora hugged me closer. I smelled her sandy smell; I felt her heaving weight and heat against me. Her shirt soaked up water from my sprinkler-wettened chest; her nipples, tight and bossy, prodded mine.

Why did no one notice us, and stop her? (Just too drunk?)

Why did I not stop myself? (Ditto?)

I loved getting away with this, but also felt the strain of it; maybe, then, subconsciously, I wanted to get us caught. But none of that psychologizing mattered as we hugged. All that mattered? Our wanting trumped our wanting not to want.

I knew I had to find a way to be alone with Debora, but also knew I'd have to wait a while. First, we had to do the insem.

Stu was more relaxed than he had been the times before, due to the drinks and dancing, I guessed, but also to our new plan. Before trooping off to the bathroom with his cup, he told Debora this was his last try.

"What?" she said. "Why? And after that, we quit?"

"No," he said. "If I don't do it, Pat will take my place."

I watched for her reaction. Was she as eager as I?

Debora calmly nodded. She said she understood. "But," she added, "right now your job is still to think you *can*. So go in there"—she nudged Stu on the back, toward the bathroom—"go in there and do your best. Believe."

This was even better than the fervor I had hoped for: heartfelt, unfailingly humane. The screws of my attraction turned tighter.

When Stu was done, he and I took Paula to the yard again, while Danny, behind the bedroom door, worked with Debora. Paula wanted to dance some more, to boogie through the sprinkler, but I was past that mood, anxious to go back in; I withstood her poking attempts to roust me from my chair.

Paula found the volume control on Danny's CD player, and cranked the music to stomach-churning strength. I told her to turn it down, and she did, for just a second, before annoyingly twisting the knob, high to low to high. Finally, I had to get up, to confiscate the disc, but I sat down again and wouldn't budge.

"Grownups are so boring," Paula announced. (If only she knew . . .)

"No," said Stu. "We just get tired a lot more quick than you do."

In truth, he looked, just now, the opposite of tired; he looked like a rusty hinge unstuck. It was so good to see him finally loosened.

Paula crossed her arms. "Do you need to take a nap? I think someone maybe needs a nap."

Her words, clearly cribbed from a parent's speech to her, made me laugh, and I forgave her brattiness. "Thanks, but we'll be fine," I said. "Don't worry."

"Well," she said officiously, "you have to rest up good. Have to stay awake tonight, for fireworks!"

"Oh, we're going, are we?" I said. "I don't know about that."

"Of course we are, silly," she said. "My daddy made a promise."

Stu said, "Well, now, honey. Today's a little different."

"No," she said. "I know what day it is. Fourth of July."

Stu must have seen a meltdown coming, and hoped to stall it. "We'd just better wait," he said, "and talk to your dad, okay?"

"But—" she said.

"Just wait, okay? I love fireworks, too. I honestly do, but we'll just have to see."

And I started to formulate a plan . . .

Back in the house, we gathered around Debora, who lay in bed. "All went good," she told us. "Much more easy now, you know, with Danny here again."

"Really got the hang, I think," he said, "if I do say so. Maybe I should open up a business?"

We were laughing, when Paula started in about the fireworks, whining about Danny's vow to bring her. The girl sat atop the bed but banished to its foot, worrying a blanket's fringed edge.

Danny explained that they couldn't go, they had to stay with Mommy, and Mommy had to stay right here, in bed.

"But you said. You said I'd see the flowery ones!" cried Paula.

Next year, Danny told her. Next year she would see them. Tonight they were doing something special and important: helping Pat and Stu to make a baby.

"But the flag," Paula said. "The flag that's made of fire."

"Go," I said, trying to sound casual, uninvested. "I can keep Deb company. We'll be fine."

Danny appeared enticed, but said no, he should stay. "A husband's job is never done, ha ha."

"But look at her," I said. I tapped Paula's chin. "Look at her! She wants to go so badly." Once again, it seemed Paula was offering instigation. I had started to think that she was secretly in cahoots.

"Please?" she said. "Oh please, Daddy, can we?"

"Not if you—be careful," Danny said. "Don't shake Mommy."

Paula froze, a statue of high hopes.

Danny bent toward Debora. "What do *you* want, Deb?"

"You did promise," she said. "And Paula's been a good girl. If Pat really doesn't seem to mind . . ."

I couldn't read her smile. Did she see what I was aiming for? "Really," I said. "Happy to stay. Honest."

A gleam came into Danny's eyes, and I could guess his logic: he saw how he'd bank the points from having pledged to stay, while also still getting to escape. "All right, then, I'll take her," he said. "And Pat and Stu can stay."

"No," I said. "That's silly: Stu can go along."

"Me?" said Stu, high-voiced with surprise.

"Yes," I said. "You need a break, after all you've been through. This stuff and the business with your sister, too—you've earned it."

"Well . . . ," he said.

"But Stu, you just said how you love fireworks! Live a little. Give yourself a treat."

"Treats!" Paula chimed in. "A treat for me and you." She clasped Stu's hand, just as she had done out in the yard, trying to persuade him to get wet.

This time he didn't squirm; he kissed her clutching hand. *"You're the treat,"* he said. "You. My little sweetmeat!"

Danny said, "We'll take that as a yes?"

In a rush they gathered what they needed for the outing. A cute cardigan for Paula, in case the night got chilly. Bug dope. An old navy blanket. Stu borrowed a Brockton: City of Champions sweatshirt from Danny.

"Oh, you'll have a ball," I said. "I'm glad we worked this out." I tried not to let my voice get yolky with too much pleasure, and also not to berate myself for being so persuasive.

"You're sure you're okay?" said Stu. "I don't have to go."

"Yes," said Debora. "No more questions. Go."

Kiss, kiss, kiss good-bye, and Stu and Danny and Paula left, footsteps fading quickly down the stairs. The front door creaked, clattered shut, and just like that, there we were, Debora and I, alone.

Alone. What I'd feared. What I'd dreamed of.

I felt I should have a speech prepared . . . but saying what? I had thought of getting to this point but not beyond it. Tell her about my talk with Stu? But this was not about him; whatever this was, whatever we'd do, above all else, was *ours*.

We were arranged like actors in a deathbed vigil scene: Debora lying, patient-like, and I standing beside her, close enough to mop her beading brow.

The silence sharpened—thinner, thinner. Brittle.

Debora made a jagged sound. Did something hurt her? Where? Then I saw her curled-up lips, and heard the sound correctly: a cackle of relief, of disclaimer.

Oh, I thought. Is *this* how we'll clomp across these eggshells?

I tickled her, the scoop behind her knee; she giggled harder. I pinched her side. I climbed up on the bed.

Like peeing in the ocean—a furtive liberation—that's how sweet it felt to laugh, and laugh and laugh and laugh. I wrapped myself like gift wrap around her body.

Music, Debora suggested. Shouldn't we have some music?

She couldn't leave the bed, and I . . . I didn't want to. All right, then: the dinky old clock radio on the nightstand, which only seemed to get a single station. The station beamed a clunker from my youth (angel, centerfold). Together again we laughed our high-test laugh. The only thing that stopped it was her kiss, deep and greedy. Trying to dig to China with her tongue.

I pulled away. "But aren't you supposed to stay in bed and rest?"

"Bed, yes. But rest?" she said. "Rest is not the question. Lie on my back, is all—it's for *gravity*."

"I see. On your back? I think I can work with that."

And so I did, hovering, hands along her neck, painting down her smooth, freckled chest. The oldie's chorus came around (". . . my memory has just been sold . . ."); Debora's breathing rose and fell in time.

A noise, then.

A car door? Footsteps in the hall?

"Wait," I said. "Listen." My muscles turned to wire.

But it was just the song, I guessed. My humming skull. My pulse. "Sorry," I said, and killed the tune. "You mind? I think it's safer."

Safety, not morality. That was my concern.

I thought about the AC, too. So loud. Turn it down? But no, the heat up here would get oppressive.

More important than safety, even: comfort.

Where had I left off? Her chest; her bone-smooth chest; all those gourmet freckles to consume. I zoomed down and licked her there, and let my hands keep moving. Down, down . . . another inch . . . another.

"Did Danny already . . . finish you off?"

"No," she said.

"Okay, then." My fingers did a rain dance on her skin.

"It's not your *hands* I need," she said. "I need—"

And that was it.

My clothes came off. I tossed the sheet and blanket to the floor. Clambered atop her. Knees between her thighs.

229

All of this crazy-quick. Crazy-crazy.

My hands pinned her hands against the mattress, near her hips, but I could push inside of her without the help of hands. Squirm and grind: an inch would give a mile.

Protection was the only thing that gave me pause, like last time. The Instead Cup—she had it up inside her still, now, right? The thing was leakproof, holding in Stu's sperm. And clearly, if it kept Stu's *in*, wouldn't it keep mine *out*? The risk that mine would somehow get inside was awfully small . . .

I was in the middle of saying that, when something struck me. "Wait," I said. "Think about it. Wouldn't it only help? I mean, if by some wacky chance . . . we'd never know *whose*, would we?"

"Well, if it is blond," she said. "Then it must be yours." She smiled. Did she figure I was kidding?

"Seriously, Deb. Stu's all but given up—you heard him, right? You heard. He's ready for me to try."

Debora seemed too deep in thought—or thoughtlessness—to talk.

"To tell the truth," I added, "I'd want it to be his. Or anyway, you know, for him to think so. Isn't there a precept? From Jesus, or . . . from someone. But anyway, the point is that, according to the precept, to help someone who doesn't know you're helping: that's okay. It's good, actually. You don't need permission."

"Pat," she said.

I still loved the way she said it: *Patch*. Maybe, though, I should have thought of what that word could mean: something makeshift, something temporary.

"You *need* something to happen," she said. "Something soon, for you and Stu. So, I think, whatever works, it's good."

"Yes?" I said. "You really think so, too? I mean, if—"

"Yes."

Our faces were an inch apart; her breath was wet against me. All of her, against me: wet, wet.

This time there was no mistaking the sounds: a car, a creaking door.

"Oh my God, they're back," I said. "Shit. Shit shit shit."

"How?" said Debora. "Finish, Pat. Come on."

She was in her nightie again, covered up in bed. I had showered, dressed . . . or almost finished dressing. Shirt and shorts but not yet socks and shoes.

Lucky I had gotten this far, and lucky I had heard. Given the noisy AC, I might not have. Why had I left it blowing? Inviting my comeuppance?

I fought with one sock, two, my fingers dull and flimsy. I checked my hair: Was it still damp? Would that incriminate me?

"Why would they be back so soon?" I said. "This is crazy."

"Fast," said Debora, just as we heard someone bounding up.

"Mãe and Pat, Mãe and Pat, we're home!" came Paula's singsong.

I had tied one shoe but not managed to reach the other, when Paula landed just beyond the threshold: windblown hair, cardigan with its topmost button fastened, flowing like a superhero's cape.

"The fireworks broke," she said. "But guess what we did then. Lookit, Mãe. Look. We got ice cream." With twiggish, suntanned arms, she offered forth two Fudgsicles. "One for you and one for Pat. Quick," she said. "They're melting."

Then she saw me fumbling with my socked-but-shoeless foot.

"Hey—where's your shoe, silly? Why are you wearing *one*?"

A simple question that could have had a very simple answer. *Oh, I had to scratch an itchy toe.* Paula wouldn't ever guess that I had just been naked.

But I went mute. How could I account for all I'd done?

"Mãe," said Paula, "why's he wearing just one shoe? How come?"

I heard Danny's booming voice: "Surprise, surprise, we're back."

Behind him, Stu: "Ice-cream crew to the rescue. Are you hungry?"

My heart blasted buckshot at my chest; my brain was tattered. Paula stood there, staring at me. Staring.

231

She'd seemed, all day long, a kind of covert helper: pushing me and Debora together, clearing our path to closeness. But now I faced a crazy dread that she had just been teasing. Fooling us both into walking the plank.

Mindlessly, I grabbed at her. I almost knocked the ice cream from her hand.

"Shh!" I said, squeezing her wrist. "Okay? You hear me? Shh!"

What did I want her not to tell? About my missing shoe? About my having grabbed her, now, too hard?

What if she started to cry? Why had I made things worse?

Paula's eyes went wide, the pupils polished, dancing. "Shh," she mimicked, and puckered up, and sputtered against her index finger. She tip-tapped a happy little jig. "A secret," she sang, "a secret, someone's got a secret . . ."

Covert helper? Trickster? Of course not. I felt sick.

Just a girl she was. A little girl.

twenty-two

Fourth Fireworks Fizzle; None Hurt."

That was the banner headline in the next day's *Cape Cod Times*. Why did I suspect it was untrue?

The paper said that less than five minutes into the gala, one of the mortars misfired, its shell exploding low, and scattered ash and panic through the crowd. With memories still too raw of the Station night-club blaze (a botched pyrotechnics display during a band's performance, a hundred dead, more than twice that injured), the fire department wasn't taking chances. They stopped the show, and sent the throng packing.

And sent Danny, Stu, and Paula home, to not-quite-catch us.

I read the story sitting in the Cape Cod Mall food court, sipping a ginger ale I'd nursed all morning. In front of Sarku Japan, an old runtish counterwoman was stabbing scraps of chicken onto toothpicks. She had the hounded look of a former child laborer, empty-faced, listlessly suspicious. "Come," she called to passersby, thrusting toothpicked pieces. "Take flee samples! Taste some chicken. Flee!"

Flee indeed.

Debora and I had escaped, if only by a hair. No one knew what we had done; no one ever had to. But I had woken up today full of the need to run from Stu. I couldn't bear the brunt of his *not* knowing.

We were supposed to head right back to Debora's again this evening, to do the second, extra-insurance insem. I didn't know how I was going to face it; I needed time and space away, to think. Flailing about, I'd said to Stu—inventing an excuse—that I was working on a research project. A piece on, um, Pilgrims. I'd have to drive to Plymouth. Would have to be there almost all day long. (How easily a little lie could snowball.)

"Fine," said Stu, "but make sure you get back by five. I love you."

"Love you, too." (Which wasn't a lie, but felt like one just then.)

Loitering at the mall, I thought: *Today*. Get through today. Tomorrow will be a smaller hill to climb.

I sipped my flattened ginger ale, but it couldn't ease my symptoms. The only cure? Keep my distance from Debora.

Soon enough, this all would fade: the lust, the laceration . . .

Paula's memory of yesterday's encounter would also fade. Besides, what was the worst the girl could say? That she had seen me with one shoe off? That I had yanked her wrist? Even if she spoke of all she knew, I'd be safe.

Still, the thought of guileless Paula soured my soda's taste. The way she'd danced so joyfully, believing we were playing. Her face: so suggestible and pure.

I stood, tossed the soda in the trash.

I did drive to Plymouth, with no good reason why. Maybe to chip away at my deceit?

This was my first visit since the '70s, I was sure. I walked along the sullen Main Street, past the dingy one-room stores (a shop that sold used Harlequins, a British-foods boutique): hardly the cute town of my remembrance. I even saw a homeless man, leaning against a lamppost, collecting change in a greasy pizza box.

The waterfront was likely to have kept more of its charm. Tracking the scent of frying clams, I strolled down to the harbor. Bring some back for Stu, I thought, to sate his ex-kosher hungers. But no, by the time he got the clams they'd all be soggy. I hoped my good intentions weren't as perishable.

In the pursuit of solidness, I walked to Plymouth Rock. I stepped into the grotto, peered down. But wait: *this* was all, this grimy little stone? How had my mother, bringing me here, made it seem so lofty? A memory, then: the time she'd seen a street sign with our name on it. Her hearty yelp: "Pat, look . . . it's *you!*"

Now I knew the purpose of my trip: to find that street. I'd come here to stand upon Faunce Place.

A block or two away, if memory served correctly. Maybe up the hill and to the left? Off I went, checking out each alleyway and lane, squinting at the signs. I didn't see it.

Retreating toward the water, then back again, I searched. Winslow, Brewster, Howland, Brewster, Winslow. Still no Faunce.

Ten, fifteen minutes, I searched that goddamn town. I asked a passing family, but they were tourists, clueless. I tripped on crooked cobblestones. Got lost.

Then I saw the homeless man, against a different lamppost. Even from a yard away, I smelled his rummy breath.

"Excuse me, sir," I said. "You know where Faunce Place is?"

"Faunce Place? No such thing," he told me.

But no, I said. I'd *been* there. I knew it was nearby. Maybe he could think a little harder?

"Lived here all my life," he said. "Know it like my hand." He seemed to stare into his box of change.

Christ, was there a cost, now, for every human contact? I dug into my pocket for some quarters, tossed two in. "There," I said. "Now do you remember?"

The man trained his faded-denim eyes up at mine. "Told you," he said. "No such thing. Don't you think I'd know it?"

I made a fist. "You don't know shit. You're fucking drunk, is all. What was I thinking, talking to a bum?"

I found my car and headed quickly home, full of shame.

On the road, I started owning up to what I'd done. Maybe not quite consciously, I had been succumbing to a poetry major's grandiose dramatics. Seeing myself as playing out some great Homeric epic: of loss and love and faithfulness, of origins and kin. And I, the hero—flawed, perhaps, but weren't the best ones always? In Plymouth, though, railing against that helpless homeless man, I had seen how minuscule and base I had become. No one's hero, but only a regular asshole, and a fool.

Now I knew what I would do—what I must do—at home: start to make amends by telling Stu the whole long truth. Yes, that was it; I'd confess, before I wavered. I would do so, not because I thought it was heroic but because it was all I could come up with: the way a worthy man—a would-be father—might behave.

Coming clean, I hoped, would be better than getting caught, better than always fearing I soon might be. Maybe if I started acting more honorable, I'd become so.

I sped home, racing my resolve.

"What are you doing back?" said Stu. "Said you'd be gone till late."

"I know," I said. "Things changed. Sit with me for a minute?"

I led him to the couch. My skin was hot, alive. Behind us, noise: squirrels and blue jays, bickering at the feeder. Before us, sets of footprints in the carpet, his and mine—from just now, from walking to the couch.

"Stu," I said. I touched his thigh. "There's something you need to know." Clichés were fine, I told myself. Clichés were maybe good. Maybe if I hadn't been so bent on being "original," I'd have caught my run-of-the-mill selfishness much sooner.

"What?" he said. "*What*, Pat? You're sort of freaking me out."

"Something happened," I said. "With Debora. Me and Debora." I stared at one of his travel posters: "Come to Ulster . . . for a Real Change and Happy Days." "I swear it wouldn't have happened if"—*if you hadn't gone away?*—"if I hadn't had to help with the insem. Remember that day? The morning when I had to bring your sample?"

Stu looked straight ahead. He said, "'It'?"

"Debora and I. We slept together. Or, well, not even really, you know? The first time? The first time it was just—" Just what? *My fingers?* "You weren't there," I said, "and Danny wasn't, either. Someone had to help her out. The guidebook said—remember? Remember how the chances of conception are increased?"

Stu removed my hand from on his thigh. His arm was shaking. "Pat," he said.

"No, listen, Stu. Please! Hear me out. It happened just a couple times, I swear to you. That's all. And now it's done. It's over. I could've just not told you. But I *am* telling, because it's done. To make sure that it's done. I didn't want to have this thing between us."

All the time I talked at him, my thoughts were in a cage. Pacing, pacing, rattling at the bars. I wished he would throttle me or punch me in the face. But Stu was just . . . just sitting there. A lump of meat, deboned.

"It's hard," I said, "because we've never had, exactly, rules, and—"

"Rules?" he all but whispered. "You need a fucking *rule*? To let you know it's wrong to screw our surro?"

A puny voice. So awfully, awfully hushed.

Sunlight through his earlobe, a glowing coal of flesh; one small puff, his skull might catch on fire.

He said, "If I weren't so mad, I think I'd be amazed. You fucked up in so many ways at once. Cheating on your boyfriend with your baby's surrogate mother? It's like some kind of degenerate trifecta."

This was maybe a couple of hours later, back on the couch. After a lot of slamming doors and silence.

He said, "Did you *plan* to be so dumb? You must have planned it. Dumbness like that isn't just a fluke."

And: "Really? You? The one who said that fucking around was fucking us up? Who moved us to the boonies so we'd leave all that behind? Mr. Restraint? Mr. Picket Fences?"

I wasn't sure exactly how I'd thought he would react. Shocked, at first, and puzzled, perhaps. Stung. But given his many years of scoffing at convention, of arguing that spouses should not be sexual possessions, I had thought he'd take this more in stride. Plus, after all the times I'd looked the other way for him, maybe he could try to be forgiving. Shouldn't my confession count for something?

"Stu," I said. "I'm sorry. You know I'm really sorry. But I'm not sure it helps to get so . . . well, so hysterical."

"'Hysterical'? Oh, that's good," he said. He shook with soundless laughter. "You know you shouldn't say that, right?" he mocked, namby-pamby. "'Hysterical.' That's misogynist. It means I'm getting womby."

Cringing, I recognized my own barbs aimed at me. And also, now, I recognized the extra threat that Stu must feel: the fact that I had cheated with a *woman*. He had worked so hard to get past his sissy boyhood, to forge the Stu whose dread of girls would never be a hindrance as he barnstormed through our gay-men-only world. But now, at a moment when his manhood was in doubt, when he was failing, metaphorically, to get it up with Debora, I had gone beyond our realm, to her: I'd outmanned him.

"Is it—" I said. "Is the issue that I had sex with a woman?"

Stu was toeing his shoe into the carpet's dusty shag. The carpet showed our footprints, still, from when I'd first come home today and led him here, before I spilled my secret. Where were the men who'd made those tracks? Ghosts.

"You think," he said, "because she is 'a' woman, that's the problem? Pat, get real. The problem is that she's *this* one."

"But Stu, you've been seeing all along how close we've gotten. Does this, now—does sex—have to make such a difference? How many times have I heard you say that sex can be just sex?"

"*Can* be—that's what I said. Not that it always is. The guys I used to trick with, I hardly knew their names. Certainly wasn't planning *babies* with them. Please, please don't try to pretend that Debora was just some hook-up."

No, I couldn't. I'd heard my own hypocrisy. I wouldn't.

238

"The crazy thing?" he added. "I'd come around to your way. I mean, just the other day, that guy I met? In Atlanta? He was nothing. *Would've* been nothing. I'll never see him again. But still, I didn't let it go past kissing—do you know why? Because I gave up everything for *this*, Pat. For you. Moved up here, away from everyone, to show you how I feel, to prove that all those other guys meant zero. And now," he said. "Now . . . I'm a chump."

Danny's voice through the phone machine: "Guys? Aren't you coming? Deb's all set to go. We've been waiting."

We were an hour late, it seemed. We'd lost track of time, our least concern.

"Leave it," I said. "Don't answer." We'd make excuses later. Engine breakdown. Medical trauma. Something.

But Stu reached right past me. He picked up.

Only then, with a jolt of grief—seeing his fist around the phone, watching him lift it stiffly to his face—only then did I think of what I might have done to Debora.

Even in my need to make amends, so purely selfish.

". . . no," I heard Stu saying. "Tell her to just forget it."

"Please," I mouthed.

Stu to Danny: "I told you, no. Not coming."

"*Please*, Stu." I tried to take his elbow.

He shook me off. "You want to know, Danny? You really do? Go and ask your cheating wife what she did with Pat, why don't you."

Please, Stu," I begged. "Please don't punish *her*. This is for us, for you and me, to work out, okay? Please? There are things you couldn't know—"

"Oh, really? Wonder why. Maybe because my boyfriend has been sneaking—"

"About Deb's life, I meant. Complications with Danny. Things from way before we ever met them."

"And that's an excuse? Why the hell should I care?"

"Right, that's what I'm saying, hon, that—"

"No. You said I *should*. And give your 'hon' a rest. It's not helping."

I didn't know if I should try again, or just keep quiet. What did I owe him more: Answers? Silence?

"Know what you said before?" I said. "That this wasn't just a hook-up? You were right, okay? This wasn't just routine."

"Spare me, Pat. No one thinks their own affair's routine."

"No, but what I'm saying . . . it wasn't just the sex. The sex was part of something more, okay? It had a point."

"What, to mess up everything we've worked for?"

"The opposite, I swear! I know this must sound mental, but . . . maybe we were trying to work things out, you know? For everyone."

Stu asked what the fuck that meant. What in the fucking hell?

So far I'd withheld most of the details of my cheating. Stu didn't know, for instance, that I'd slept with Deb just yesterday. Didn't know we'd done it without a condom. I should have seen (how could I not?) how damaging those specifics were. But I was desperate to prove to him that we'd been more than rash and ruttish, that we had acted partly in good faith. That was the crumbling handhold I still clung to.

Panicked, I set off on a babbling explanation, deeper and deeper into the muck, but I couldn't seem to quit. I hoped—I prayed—that if I kept on talking, I'd buy time to clamber back to safety. The odds of any of my sperm getting through, I said, were tiny; the cup should have acted as a barrier. But if they did get through, I said, wouldn't that be a good thing? Hadn't Stu said that I should try, that it should be my turn now? The *goal* was what we cared about. The outcome, not the means. Wasn't that what he himself had told me?

I was so caught up in my rush of explanation, trying to skim across its quicksand surface, I hadn't yet assessed his reaction. His face was pale, his neck gone limp, his gaze loose and blunted. I had never seen him look so small.

"I know this sucks. I know," I said. "Again, I'm so, so sorry. But practically speaking, looking ahead, where are we now, okay? Either she's still *not* pregnant, which means things stay the same, or she *is*, in which case . . . well, in which amazing case we'll have a baby—right, hon? A baby."

He sat trembling, hand at his own throat.

"Ninety percent—ninety-nine—the baby would be yours," I said. "And if it isn't, who the hell would know? Not even us! *You're* the dad, no matter what, you see? It's what we've wanted." That was what I'd meant, I said, by "working things out for everyone." Just like what the ancient precept taught—he knew it, right? To act for someone's benefit, even without his say-so, is good to do. Maybe it's even better.

So quickly, so capably, he flensed my flabby logic: "But what about the first time? The time you fucked before?"

Earlier, in my baby-stepping start at the confession, I had said my first "real" sex with Debora had grown from solace: the day she got her period and learned she wasn't pregnant.

"Fucking her then," said Stu, "the day she was *least* fertile? Was *that* about 'working things out for everyone'?"

I loved him too much, and loathed myself too much, to say a word.

"You're full of shit," he said. "Trying to rewrite history just to make yourself less wretched." He glared at me as though I were ablaze, as though he wished I were. "And worse, that you thought it maybe *would* make you less wretched. Don't you see? Are you really so fucked-up that you can't see it? To not care if . . . no, to actually *try* to get her pregnant? A hundred times more wretched, Pat. More wretched."

"And," he finished, spinning away, speaking over his shoulder, "your precious little 'precept'—you know where that crap came from? From *Richard*. From his asshole of a rabbi."

twenty-three

I got the same shove-off Richard had gotten, without the grope. "Out," said Stu. "Get out of my house. Now."

At least, I thought, he finally saw the cottage as being his—a rueful joke I wanted to share but couldn't. I left without arguing (I would have lost, and should have). I didn't bargain about how long he wanted me away.

I went to New York, to Joseph. Who else could I face? Zack and Glenn, the Good Gays? No, I didn't think so. And not Marcie and Erin, either, the ardent lesbian moms. I would have to tell them all, if not my trip's cause, the fact that we had still not conceived. Their sympathy would smother me: *No baby yet? It's hard.*

Hard? They didn't know our kind of hard. The hard part, for them, had only been logistical, finding an egg or sperm to commandeer. To make a baby, yes, that had been hard for them. But not, as it was for Stu, for me, to make a *parent.*

I tried to call Debora from the bus, on my way down. Tried when we were leaving the Cape, and then again near Providence, a third time when we hit the New York line. She didn't answer: angry at my betrayal, I was sure (assuming Danny had grilled her, compelled her to confess), angry at the collateral damage my dumbness had inflicted.

242

I deserved the silent treatment and any other penalty. But what if something worse was going on, to force her silence? What if Danny . . .

I didn't even know what to envision. Please, Danny, I pleaded as the bus crossed Manhattan. Prove that you're a better man than I.

All I'd said to Joseph was that Stu and I had fought, that I could really use a couch to crash on. "Oh, poor thing. Come," he'd said. "As long as you want. Of course."

I still planned to tell him just the outline, or not even. Tough enough to face him when he knew that Stu had kicked me out, but if he knew the details—that I had slept with someone else, and that the someone else had been our surro—Joseph would be withering, I could bet. The more I told, the more he'd turn it into *told you so*.

But something happened when I walked in and smelled his old apartment, where I had not set foot for two full years. A sharpness like the air above an ice-cold glass of vodka, a scent of *Pay attention! Don't miss out!* This was the smell of my twenties: my great gay education. The smell of staying up till dawn—high on booze and coke—while Joseph showed me who I was and who I someday might be.

And now, here I was again, amid the old fraught totems. The first-edition *Streetcar* on the shelf, signed by "Tenn." The water-buckled placard from the Continental Baths. The poster saying IGNORANCE = FEAR. On the mantel, a row of photos of Joseph and Luis: bow-tied at a Met premiere, shirtless in Southampton. Also one of the younger me: my would-be poet's shag, my wide-pupiled, idealistic eyes.

Suddenly I was pouring forth my whole dark tale to Joseph. All the stupid, reckless things I'd done behind Stu's back, the kinks of self-delusion that allowed me to excuse them, the wanting and the wanting and the wanting. I'd wanted Stu and more than Stu; loyalty and leeway. Now each want might cancel out another.

"What a fucking mess," I said. "Why'd I tell Stu? Why? I thought I owed him honesty, and that would be enough. Or maybe, I don't know, did part of me want to *punish* him? For all those times he slept with other guys?"

By now we had stretched out on the couch and lay there, spooning. I felt childish, wobbly. All my strings were snapped.

Joseph stroked me. "Hey, calm down, okay? Just relax."

His touch felt so good: a chaste, paternal warmth. But I didn't want to feel good; that's not why I'd come. I had come to Joseph for the comfort of discomfort, the antidote to sentimental bullshit. "You were right," I said. "All along. I should have listened."

He held me tighter. "Right about what part?"

"We were never cut out for this. Not Stu and I, not any of us. Maybe it's genetic, you know? If gayness is? You think? Maybe there's a gene for settling down, being responsible, and gay men just . . . we just aren't *equipped*."

"Oh?" he said. "So what about the ones who are, like Zack and Glenn? Aren't there hundreds—thousands—of guys like them?"

"Exceptions that prove the rule?" I tried, confused by his response. Hardly the gloating smugness I'd expected.

"The rule?" he said. "The rule that, by your lights, makes gay men 'less than'?"

"No, not that. It's not that we're not good enough. Just different. We have our own culture," I said. I gestured toward his bookshelves. His placard from the baths. His whole life. "Once we've lived more freely, you know—once we've seen we can—how are we supposed to ever go back to conformity? It's like a kind of virus or something, that gets inside your cells. Changes the way your system works. You change."

Joseph pulled his arm away, and stood up from the couch. Glanced at all his pictures of Luis. "It's nothing like a virus," he said. "A virus doesn't *choose*. A virus doesn't have a moral choice."

"Shit, Joseph, I didn't mean . . . you know I didn't mean that."

"Stop," he said, "before you make a bigger ass of yourself."

He strode into the kitchen and returned with a vodka rocks. He didn't offer me one; I didn't ask. The couch cushions threatened to close around me.

Joseph sat cross-legged on the floor, unguarded, humble. The cocktail might have been a cup of cocoa. "I've told you the story of how we met?" he asked. "Luis and I?"

Of course he had. A dozen times. I always liked to hear it. "Tell me again. You managed to steal him away from . . . was it Gielgud?"

"Well, that's the quippy version, the one I tell at parties. Stole him away from being Gielgud's *dresser*, is the truth. The night before the tour of *No Man's Land* was leaving town. I was backstage, because I had a friend who worked the lights. I saw Luis, and we made eyes; I asked him back to mine; and we both knew, just knew, that this was it. In the morning, he called Sir John and told him he was quitting." Joseph swirled his drink and sipped. The ice cubes smartly chimed. "But he had only *worked* for Gielgud—they'd never been romantic. That was one of the first things I had asked. Because, you know, I may have been a slut, but not a home wrecker. And also not—never once—a cheater."

Joseph was staring hard at me now. I sat up, knowing I had to. Knowing a man should take his lashes upright.

"Sure, I slept around," he said. "Hundreds of guys. Who knows? But after Luis, how many others? Zero, Pat. Not one. You think I didn't sometimes want to? Or didn't have my chances? Yes, I know you look at me and only see 'old maid,' but believe me I was not. I was not. No, I stayed faithful because I'd told Luis I would. One of the many, many promises we made—and kept—together. And how do I know he kept them, too? I *trust* him."

Almost twenty years since he had laid Luis to rest—but *trust*, Joseph had said. Not trust*ed*.

"'Oh, we gays are different,'" he mocked. "'We get too used to freedom.' Baloney, Pat! We're just as free to stick by our commitments. Gayness doesn't exempt you from being *decent*."

"Then why," I said, "have you been so against what Stu and I've been trying? Every time I brought it up, you changed the goddamn topic. You hate the thought of gay men having kids."

"Gay men having kids," he said, "is fine. It can be gorgeous. But not just automatically. Not just any men. You and Stu, you can't just press some magic 'family' button." Joseph set his vodka tumbler down with great precision. "'Gay men' aren't the ones," he said, "who fucked this up, Pat. *You* did."

twenty-four

The bus back to Hyannis was sold-out with summer travelers; by the time I boarded only one seat was available: in the last row, up against the bathroom. If the bus had air-conditioning, it didn't reach this far, or not enough to counteract the steamy bodily odors that escaped every time the bathroom opened. For six overheated hours, I was wedged between the wall and a slumped, dozing woman—my metaphorical sweatbox of self-blame brought to life.

From Joseph's I had called Stu and said again how sorry I was. Told him I was ready to make things right.

"Oh?" he'd said. "Make things right? Uh-huh."

As he spoke, I'd heard him doing something—chopping vegetables? I envisioned him cooking dinner for one.

Wouldn't we hear from Debora soon, I asked, with test results? Shouldn't I be home for that? Shouldn't we be together? I hoped he was hearing something new in my voice, more honest. In Joseph's heat, I had tried to burn off the impurities. "Stu, I want to be with you," I said.

Thunk thunk thunk, his knife kept coming down. A deadened sound, hard but also hollow.

At last there was a pause. Stu exhaled deliberately. "If you want, fine," he said. "Come back."

The bus now approached the bridge to bring us to the Cape, passing a big blue-lettered sign: "Desperate? Call the Samaritans." As a boy, I had found this sign—its location—baffling. Why here, of all places, would anyone feel distressed? For me, the bridge to the Cape was an all-but-holy passage, the entry point to a fun, unfettered world. (My parents had instructions that if I had fallen asleep on the drive, I was to be woken when we crossed it.) Today, though, I better understood a jumper's impulse. To stare from on high toward the dark, unjudging water; to leap into an endless end of guilt . . .

Soon we reached Hyannis. I was the last one off: clammy, bleary, mouth and muscles stale. I stumbled from the station, looking for a taxi, praying there might still be one unclaimed.

Then I heard, "You're going the wrong direction. Over here."

There was Stu, leaning back against the Volvo's hood. Looking a little rumpled—unshaven, in shorts and tank top—but still, to me, as striking as he would have been in uniform. His deep, commanding eyes. His crew cut, with its recent stars of gray around the sideburns.

I was used to being the one who waited for his return. All those years of fighting off the loneliness and jealousy, trying not to fret about his absence. But now, here he was, after everything, fetching me. *Collecting me at the station* was the phrase that came to mind. As if I had been scattered into pieces, then gathered up.

"Thanks," I said. "I didn't expect . . ."

He shrugged. "Why waste money on a cab?"

He offered nothing more effusive than that as we drove off. He steered us silently home with one stiff arm.

The cottage smelled of vacuuming, of dusty agitation. The living room chairs looked repositioned by two or three degrees. We both stood there, seemingly in fear of impoliteness but not knowing what politeness called for.

I had long admired Stu's pose of calm, his airman's training: *Buckle up your seat belts, folks; stormy skies ahead; heading for a safer altitude.* But now I was wishing he would strip the seat belts off, for once, and fling us into the turbulence, and *feel* this.

I fell back on a stranger's questions: How had the weather been up here? What was his take on the latest news, terror attacks in London?

The weather: "Nothing much." The terror attacks: "Awful."

If I had to, this was what I'd settle for, I thought. This was a start. At least I had him talking.

Stu said he was going to bed. A flight tomorrow, early.

I was longing to lie with him, to press against his warmth. But I stayed up, watching the late-night comics, drinking beer. I drank one can too many, and left the empties around me, to give us both a ready excuse for why I crashed on the couch. I hadn't wanted to make Stu say he'd rather sleep alone.

The next day, when Stu was gone, I tried Debora again. Nothing sneaky or sexy now—an overdue apology. To tell her why I'd leveled with Stu. To ask about the fallout on her end.

I called at ten: no answer. Again at noon: nothing.

I thought to try e-mail, and started to type a note, but what if Danny had her password? What if he would read this? I had no idea what, if anything, she had told him. I couldn't take the risk. I hit Delete.

When, at last, she called us, Stu and I weren't ready. We hadn't talked of how we'd face this moment.

We took the call the way we'd taken the one, five months back, when Debora first had test results to share: Stu and I were standing in the living room, on separate phones, staring past the deck, toward the dunes. This time, though, we didn't take each other's hands. Or touch at all. We hadn't touched since I'd returned from Joseph's.

Why had we not spoken of our hopes for Debora's news, of how we'd now navigate this crossroads? Stu, I figured, maybe didn't want to jinx the outcome. The thing was, I didn't know what outcome he desired, and I was scared of what he might be feeling. All these months, we'd hoped and hoped to spark the start of life, but might he now be thinking that the best result was failure? Or, if not the best, the least hurtful? Maybe he thought another "no" would let us end things cleanly here: dismiss Debora, bury our mistakes. And then what? Mourn, forgive? Try with a different surro? (How could we? I couldn't picture anyone else but her.) Or maybe, worse: *not* forgive, *not* try someone new. Maybe dismiss not just her but me.

Too late, now, to ask him: the phones were in our hands; Stu and I stared out at Sandy Neck. In February the view had been brown and bare and calm. Now the marsh was stuffed with light, belligerently sunny; the steep, glaring dunes looked like icebergs.

"It's me," she said. "It's Debora."

"Yes," I said. "We know."

"I did the test. I checked two times. Pregnant."

An "oh" rose from my throat. Another, louder: "Oh!" I had planned to wait for Stu, to hear how he reacted, but I could not contain my welling joy. "Deb," I said, "thank you! I don't know what to say."

Neither did she, apparently. Quiet on the line.

I turned to Stu, to hug him, and saw his blurry eyes, the lines of complication in his face. "Stu, we did it. We did it," I said. "Finally! Let's be happy."

He was crying, accepting my hug but not reciprocating. I could feel the trembling in his core.

Through the phone I heard that Debora, too, had started crying. What was she saying? "I" something? Or no, not even a word at all. An exclamation, pure emotion: *Ai!*

"Guys," I said, "we're here. I know I fucked up, *getting* us here. I know I have to answer for a lot. But now, right now, listen to me: we're here."

I tried to hold Stu tighter but he turned and slid away, hanging up the phone as he escaped; I only grazed his elbow as he rushed out to the deck. Rina's pendant, the Holy Rose, was knocked against the sliding glass. A shrapnel of light. A sound like snapped bone.

"Pat?" said Debora.

"Yes."

"I thought that you hung up."

"No," I said. "That was Stu. I'm here."

The phone's empty-seashell hum. Debora's broken breath.

"You should go?" she said. "Go after him. To talk."

"Yes, I should. I will," I said. "But quickly: what's the deal? Called you a dozen times, you know. Guess I can't blame you for not answering."

Debora made the *psh* of a tire being punctured. "I didn't have my phone," she said. "He took it from me. Danny."

"Oh my God. Really, Deb? It's that bad between you?"

"More bad than you think," she said. "I'm calling from a pay phone. How did Danny know, Pat? How did he discover? He made me tell him everything. I had to."

My blood banged in every throbbing vein: guilt, guilt. "Deb, it's all my fault," I said. "I told Stu, and he told Danny. I didn't mean to—Jesus, I'm so sorry."

Silence for the longest time. I yearned to scream, to crack it. But I did not deserve to say a thing.

Finally she said, "You?" Again, more softly: "You?" A mewling. A tiny, abandoned sound.

"What about Danny now?" I said. "Deb, are you okay? What does he say? He knows the test was positive?"

"No," she said. "I called you first. How I am going to tell him?"

I thought of the Samaritans sign, of all the tempting cop-outs. But no, I was finished, now, with cowardly evasions. "We just have to tell," I said. "Like I said: *we're here.*"

"Yes, but Pat—"

"We'll work it out together, okay? We will. But listen, I really have to go; I have talk with Stu. I'll call you back. I'm sorry, Deb. For everything."

"No," she said decisively. "No, I think you're not."

"I am, I swear. It kills me. I never meant to screw your life up, too."

"But not sorry for what's inside me. Don't be, Pat. We can't be. This is not a thing to make us sad."

"Oh!" I said. "Oh, Deb. You know I'm not. I'm thrilled." Despite myself, I told her what I'd never said: "I love you."

Stu stood at the deck's far end, holding to the rail, as if on a blizzard-tossed ship. His eyes were shut against the slashing sun, or with emotion. I called his name, trying not to spook him.

"Hi," he said, eyes still shut.

"Hi," I said. "Just me."

His shoulders rose. He took a deep and careful breath. "You smell that?"

"What?" I said. "The marsh? Or no, I guess, the water." What I smelled was salty, unadulterated, boundless.

"I love these days," he said, "when the wind pattern turns around and we get all that open-ocean air. It smells like—I know this will sound stupid, but who cares—it smells like we can smell our own future." He opened his eyes. He set his hand lightly on my elbow. "Sorry about just now," he said. "It *hit* me. I needed a minute."

"No," I said. "Me, too. It's—God, you can't prepare."

He hadn't moved his hand. His touch was soft, surprising, a butterfly that I might scare away.

"And so?" I said. "How do you feel now? Are you okay?"

He turned to me, fixed me with his close, imposing gaze. "Okay? What do you mean, 'okay'? Isn't this what we wanted?"

"Yes! Oh, yes, yes. But I was worried that you might . . . that you might not, anymore."

Now his touch got harder. He gripped me, pulled me close. "Really, Pat? Still?" he said. "After all we've been through? You still have so little faith in me?"

The rest of the day, we were at a loss for what to do. Nothing was required of us logistically, not yet. Our lives in every aspect stood to change, but nothing had changed. Plus, we were out of practice being glad together.

Any flashy celebration would have felt improper—our pleasure still provisional, perhaps two separate pleasures. We hadn't talked of how we'd handle Debora now, for nine more months, or Danny, who I feared would sulk and snipe. We still had some delicate work to do.

Finally Stu proposed a walk in the woods. I agreed. We headed for a lane I remembered from my boyhood, supposedly an old stagecoach route. Now the lane was overgrown with puckerbrush and prickers. We took turns clearing a path through. We passed a caved-in woodshed, a tumbledown stone fence. The ground beneath our feet was damp and giving. Stu seemed not to want to talk; that was fine by me. I was mute with wonder at the thought of Debora pregnant. Something of Stu's or mine inside her—must it matter whose? Something of *us* was how I hoped we'd see it.

Across the Cape Cod Railway tracks, over a little knoll, and down to the surprise of a leafy cranberry bog. (Was it new? I had not recalled it.) A row of beehives along one side, a pile of surplus sand, and then the placid Christmassy sweep of berry-studded shrubs.

Stu leapt over the ditch. He knelt to pick some berries.

"Don't," I said. "Too tart."

"I like them tart," he said. Chomping one, he winced with satisfaction. Then he turned a circle, scanning the scrubby lowland. "It looks so different, doesn't it, when you're standing here?" he said. "I mean, as opposed to from the air, flying over."

Our flight in the rented Skylane, my special birthday treat, shortly after we had made the move: swooping above the fallow bogs, like purple square-cut gems. Stu's confession: *I see what I was missing.*

"That was another season, though," I said. "The end of March?"

"I know," he said, "but that's not why it's different. Not all of why. It's not as grand, up close; it's uglier, in a way. But then, it's also prettier, too: you see every little shining berry."

He bent down and plucked another one, and gave it to me. I bit it in two, and swallowed half, spat the other out. I saw what Stu liked: the acid woke my tongue.

"What a crazy thing," he said. "What we did? Moving up here?"

What was he saying—did he regret it? Did he plan now to say he'd had his fill?

Then he added, "*You* were crazy. To give me another chance." He shook his head, surrendering to what might have been a smile.

I could only hope I understood his point correctly: against his judgment, he would try to stand by me now, too.

Stu looked quickly around the bog, as if we might get caught here. "Hey, should we collect a bunch of cranberries?" he said. "For pie?"

"No," I said. "Not ripe enough. Not for two, three months."

Stu made a pout of disappointment.

"Blueberries, though—is that okay?" I said. "We should have plenty." The bushes I'd de-brambled when we first moved to the cottage had responded well, thriving in their new light. A bumper crop had ripened in the time I'd been at Joseph's.

"Sure," said Stu. "You want, I'll help you pick."

"Maybe we'll make *two* pies," I said. "An extra one. For them." Danny and Debora, I meant. A peace offering.

We walked home quickly through the sunlight-marbled woods. The way was freer, cleared by all the work of our approach.

We were picking berries together, around the biggest bush, each with a cleaned-out yogurt tub to hold our yield, when something cracked: a gunshot? I flinched, dropped the tub. Berries tumbled all around my feet.

Then I heard an engine; another, softer crack: gravel on the driveway, that was all. Danny's blue Explorer, gleaming and imperial, skidded to a stop beside our car.

At first I was relieved. Just Danny, only Danny. "Shoot," I said, trying to save the fruit I hadn't stepped on. "I lost almost everything I'd picked."

"Leave it," said Stu. "Just leave it now. Come on, Pat. Get ready."

Then it started to hit me: Oh. *Danny.*

He was in the driver's seat, a pale Debora beside him. Stepping out, she staggered slightly. (Morning sickness, already? Or maybe it was emotional: a vertigo of chagrin.) Danny stepped out, too, with seemingly willful calm, and said, "We have to talk about this. Now."

"Yes, we do. Of course," said Stu. "Why don't you come on in?"

Danny paused, as though he'd envisioned something different: A shouting match in the driveway? A fistfight?

The four of us, in sleepwalk steps, filed into the house—as far as the living room, where we stalled. *Wheel of Fortune* tinkled from the TV (had I left it on?). I muted it, then thought again, clicked Off.

Danny and Debora, it suddenly struck me, had never seen our home. All our meetings had taken place at their house or in public. I would have liked to think this was an inadvertent omission. But surely they had noticed; probably they were hurt. Why had we not thought to have them over, or they not asked to come? Had they—or had we—felt unworthy?

Weeks ago, I'd feared the prospect of Danny bursting in on me—on me and Debora, catching us in the act. Why did I feel now as I had dreaded feeling then? I saw my piles of magazines, my laptop, empty beer cans: not immaculate, but not especially messy. On the wall: Stu's travel posters, a photo of us in Prague, possessions neither damning nor salacious. What was Danny seeing that he shouldn't, that was private? Nothing but my life with Stu. Our life.

Stu asked, "Can I get you something? Drinks? Fresh-picked berries?"

"No," said Danny. "Sit down"—as if this were his house.

Compliance was hardly conscious; his voice's gravity moved me. We all sat in various rigid poses.

I stole a glance at Debora, who seemed dazed, deflated; even her hair, in cluttered strands, looked thin. She was in a halter top that showed a sunburned shoulder. At least I thought the roughed-up swath was sunburn.

She saw me staring. "From cooking," she said lowly, not meeting my eyes. "The pressure cooker. Making some beans. I opened it too soon."

But how would it have burned her only there, on one shoulder? And what about the Band-Aid on her palm?

Danny said, "We're here to get this settled, now, for good. Better to do it in person, I thought. I thought we owed you that." He was sweating, veiny. The clenching at the corners of his jaw made little bolts. "But honestly, no," he added. "I don't owe you guys shit. I wanted you to look me in the eye."

Debora seemed to shrivel further, staring at her hands. She picked at her Band-Aid's peeling edge.

Help her, I thought. Shield her.

I feared I was too late.

"Let me talk, please," I said. "Before you say a thing. I don't know what Deb has said, but *I* was the one to blame, okay? I was the one who—"

"Seriously, Pat?" Danny thrust his palms at me. "Give me a break. You think I want the *details*?" The only thing that mattered now, he said, was how to deal with it.

It, he said, as if the word were held with bloody forceps.

Or no, not *how* to deal, he said. *When* was what he meant: "We have an appointment, the day after tomorrow, at a clinic."

"Wait," I said. "You can't be saying . . . no! No way, come on. Deb," I pleaded, and reached for her, but Stu stayed my hand.

"Danny," he said, "it's not your plan to make alone, okay? It's ours. We're all in this together." He spoke firmly but evenly, using his return-to-your-seats voice. "No matter what was going on between these two," he said, "the thing is that—"

"Of *course* it matters. Jesus Christ!" said Danny. "Don't you guys have any sense at all of right and wrong?"

"Yes," said Stu. "I do. I'm just as pissed as you." He shot a hardened glance in my direction. "But listen to me. Danny. We can't overreact. Really, there's no reason to be so rash. We've got time."

"How would time change anything?" Danny asked. "What's done is done. And *I'm* done. I'm finished. I never agreed to this. This was not the bargain I signed off on."

I appealed again to Debora, who still avoided my eyes. "He makes it sound like, I don't know, a business deal," I said.

Danny snorted. "What do you think it is? That's all it's ever been. But now it's through. We're ending it. It's over."

Stu got up and took a step; his hands were stiffened blades. "You think you can intimidate us? You think you can? You can't." Now he started to drub Danny with *breach of contract, lawsuit,* hacking at the air with every phrase.

Danny stood up, too. "The contract? Ha! Ha!" He took from his back pocket a folded piece of paper, opened it, and read in acid tones: "'The Surrogate promises that she will not have sexual intercourse with any man from the time of the signing of the contract until pregnancy has been confirmed by a physician. The Surrogate further promises that she will not engage in any action in which the possibility of semen other than that utilized in inseminations from the Natural Father could be introduced into her body, such that the possibility—'"

"Stop," said Debora. "Stop, stop, stop!" The word was like a stone within a sling; she whirled and whirled it, keeping us all away from striking distance.

"Deb, do you feel safe?" I said. "You need a place to stay? I swear, I'll call the cops if you—"

"Just stop," she said. "You, too."

The air between us quaked. My breath felt made of shards.

"The deal is void," said Danny, and tossed the contract down. "Because of Pat. What *he* did." He jerked his meaty thumb at me. "That contract doesn't mean fuck-all now."

"You're wrong," said Stu. "You're wrong! That stuff is there for us—to let *us* void the contract if we want to. And plus, keep reading: No abortions, except for the surro's health."

"As if that would stand up in a court," Danny said. "But we won't have the time to find out, will we?"

I was on the floor now. I knelt in front of Debora. "You're just going to *let* him, Deb? Don't you have some say? I mean, it's your . . . your body, right? Your baby, Deb. Come on!"

"Danny says that—"

"No," I said. "What *you* say. What do *you* say?"

Debora clasped her hands together, locking something in. "Danny says we have to put our family first," she said. "And I," she said. "I can't," she said. She squeezed her fingers tighter; interlaced, they looked like a grenade.

"What about the woman you're 'supposed to be'?" I asked. "The woman 'made for having babies.' How could you even *consider*?"

Her eyes, now, her green-brown eyes, chilled me with their nullness. "Pat," she said. "Please."

Please leave me be? Please save me?

Danny helped her up and walked her swiftly to the door, hugging her so hard she lost her balance. He was saying softly, "Don't look back."

Stu was calling after them—"You can't" and "You won't"—promising to stop them, to sue them, make them pay. Shouting that they'd hear from us tomorrow.

Neither of them answered. I heard their crackling footsteps, the engine as it roared and then retreated.

Where was I? Still kneeling on the floor.

twenty-five

Sorry to say, Danny's probably right," K.C. told us, setting down the contract on her desk. "The case law really isn't in your favor."

The last time we'd seen K.C., I'd liked her homely frankness, the way she hadn't tried too hard to buff her ragged edges. Now I looked at her puffy neck, her wrinkled, too-tight suit, and wondered if we'd hired the wrong attorney.

"But *read* the thing," I said. "'The Surrogate agrees that she will not abort the Child, except if, in the opinion of her physician,' etcetera, etcetera."

"Yes, but did you see this subclause, here?" she pointed out. "'A court may determine that a woman has the right to abort, or not abort, any fetus she is carrying, and any promise to the contrary may be unenforceable.' The truth," she added, "is that a contract's only just a contract. Without a judge's enforcement, it means nothing. And surro contracts, at least so far, have not fared well in court."

"What the hell?" said Stu. "Why did we even bother, then? Just so we could pay you for the honor?"

K.C. shrugged. "What was your other option? Better than nothing."

But wasn't she saying our contract was exactly the same as nothing? Or worse than nothing, because it had allowed us to rest easy.

Stu and I had waited almost two hours to be seen. The paralegal had warned us K.C. might be gone till noon—something about a long divorce proceeding. But where else should we go? What else could we do? (Stu had called in sick the night before.) And so we'd sat in the anteroom, numbed by the smell of potpourri, staring at a brass sailor's clock. Stu had not said much beyond a periodic "Son of a bitch." The words did not seem aimed at me, despite how well I'd earned them, for Stu had turned his blame almost wholly, now, to Danny; maybe he had only so much blame to hurl at once. Every time the clock's bells chimed, I cringed: a cold and brittle sound that made me think of Debora's deadened eyes.

At last K.C. had bustled in, sweaty in her pants suit, and looked at us with weary recognition; she must have seen the turmoil in our faces. "Call my twelve o'clock," she'd told the paralegal. "Reschedule."

Now, in her office, she tipped back in her chair. "Start again," she said. "I still don't get the basics. Why did Danny and Debora change their minds, you think? What happened?"

Stu and I had agreed we would say as little as possible. How could K.C., or anyone else, hear the sordid details and not doubt our fitness to be fathers? But now I saw that our dilemma made no sense without them. We had to tell K.C. the whole truth.

Or no: *I* had to.

I couldn't gauge, when I was done, how she was reacting. She looked as though she couldn't, or didn't want to, hide aversion: a turned-up chin, a tensing of her lips. But what repelled her: Debora's and my affair, or Danny's response?

"Listen," I said. "I know I made mistakes. I know I did." I looked at Stu, but he was staring down at K.C.'s desk, the wood deliberately scarred (*distressed*, they called it). "But that shouldn't mean," I said, "that Danny and Debora can just . . . just decide."

"What you call 'mistakes,'" said K.C., "are for you and your spouses to reckon with. Legally, I'm not sure they're material." She squared a piece of paper on her desk. "As I said, a judge might well discard the 'no abortion' clause, regardless of any breach or lack of breach by the signing parties. Judges aren't in the business of compelling the birth of children."

Breach went banging around my skull. I kept getting stuck on the phrase *breech birth*: a hazard, backwards.

Stu said, "You're telling us there's nothing we can do? This is not some legalese at stake. This is a *life*."

"Trust me, I'm aware of that. I am," K.C. said.

"Okay, wait. Wait," I said. I flipped the contract's pages. "What about the clause where she agrees to a paternity test? Here it is: '. . . agrees to submit . . . establish the paternity.' Doesn't it also state that if a test *excludes* the Intended Father, that if he's *not* the father, that's a breach? But if Deb takes a test, and it shows Stu *is* the father, then they have no grounds to say that—damn, does that make sense? Maybe a judge would weigh that in our favor?"

"No," said K.C. "I'm sorry. I just don't see it working." She leaned forward. Her neck bulged against her buttoned collar. "And plus," she said, "I have to say—speaking as a woman, now, and not just as a lawyer—that any woman's reproductive choices should be sacrosanct. If Debora wants to terminate her pregnancy for any reason, I'm not ready to help you block her path."

"But no! That's the thing," I said. I pounded on the desk. "She doesn't want to. I can't believe she does. It's *Danny's* choice."

K.C. squinted, as if her own emotions were in the distance. "But still, that's between them, no? A marital decision. I'm not sure how I should be involved."

I wanted to say what Debora had told me, privately, on the phone: that she could not be sorry for the life (*our* life?) inside her. *This is not a thing*, she had said, *to make us sad*. Telling this, though, would rub our bond in Stu's face again. I had already caused him so much pain.

But Stu himself pressed further, coming to Debora's defense: "He's hurting her," he told K.C. "Danny is. I think."

261

"Hurting her how?" she said. "What makes you believe that?"

"A burn mark," said Stu. "She claimed it was an accident— something in the kitchen. Sounded fishy."

"Plus, she had a Band-Aid on her hand," I said. "A fresh one. She could barely look me in the eye."

K.C. swiveled. She unbuttoned her collar and wiped her neck. Undid her cuffs, too, and turned them up. The clock out in the anteroom rang with four sharp chimes.

"Okay, listen," she said at last. "We can try your plan. Legally, to be honest, I have to think it's useless. If Danny lawyers up, he'll find that out. But maybe, just to buy a little time, it's worth a shot."

She would write a letter, she said, full of fancy language: cease and desist, interdict, enjoinder. Threatening legal action if the pregnancy were terminated before a paternity test could be conducted.

"Ten weeks is the soonest you can do a test," she said. "Ten weeks at the least, for safe sampling. And so, if Danny's cowed by this, it gives you two-plus months. Or, if not, you'll slow things down at least by days or weeks—however long it takes for him to find a decent lawyer."

Go have lunch, she told us; by the time we finished our meal, the letter would be waiting.

We thanked her and thanked her. I shook her small, firm hand.

"I hope it all works out for you," she said.

We had called to give fair warning that we were coming over—the home phone and also Debora's cell—but no one answered.

"Well," said Stu, "why *would* they? Whatever we'll say, Danny knows he doesn't want to hear it."

"And Debora doesn't have her phone. He took it," I said. "She told me."

"Who is he, the Taliban?" said Stu. "What a dick."

And so here we were, driving across Hyannis, about to show up unannounced, unwelcome, at their house. Or, perhaps, in Debora's eyes, more welcome than we knew. I had crazy thoughts about abducting her and cutting her off from all the world, till she could have the baby. Would that make me the good guy, or only just as domineering as Danny?

"Maybe he's not home," said Stu, slowing for a stoplight. "Middle of a workday. Probably not."

No, I thought. Just Debora. And maybe Paula, too. I pictured the girl: her twiggish arms, her uncorrupted smile. I wasn't sure if I could see her face and not break down.

"But if he *is* there," Stu went on, "let me do the talking. I know how to handle a guy like him." He clutched the wheel, his trigger fingers tight.

I was happy to let Stu play the heavy, if need be. Eventually, though, I was hoping to soften our approach. That had been Stu's way with me, it seemed, these past few days. By holding back, he had sped the pace of my atonement.

I clutched the lawyer's letter: a crisp ivory envelope with K.C.'s name embossed in dark blue letters. Ten weeks it could earn us, in which to talk down Danny. A short span, but long enough to shift a life's foundations. (Ten weeks back, I'd never slept with Debora.) Danny was at his angriest now, understandably so, ruled by his need to gain command. But time could change that; time could help me help him to save face.

Two and a half months, I thought. Beginning of October. Debora might be showing by then; the baby would seem more real. Danny might have had the chance to feel its beating heart.

Danny was in his driveway, hugging a clutch of grocery bags, stumbling toward the back of his Explorer. The bags bulged with dirty laundry, rumpled shirts and briefs. Blindly Danny groped to lift the hatch. He hadn't seen us.

"Here, let me," I said.

He startled. "What the fuck?"

"We tried to call," said Stu. "Couldn't get an answer."

"Yeah, well," said Danny. "No, you couldn't."

The air above the sun-baked driveway warped with heat mirages. The asphalt's smell was tarry and inflammable.

Danny set his bags of laundry down inside the hatch. A ball of socks came tumbling out and rolled off, disappearing. "Anyway, I'm sure you know you missed her by now," he said. "You win, okay? So leave me alone, why don't you."

Stu said, "Missed her? What do you mean we missed her?"

"Seriously?" Danny said. "I figured she'd have told you. Or at least"—he whipped around to bark at me—"told *you*."

Stu gave me a questioning look, full of trepidation—preparing himself, it seemed, for more betrayal. I shook my head.

"She really didn't?" said Danny.

"I'm in the dark," I said.

Now the storm within his eyes was stalled. He stepped back and leaned his full weight on the Explorer, trembling like the heat above the asphalt. "She left," he said. "She's gone. She went back to Brazil."

My spine crackled. "Brazil? But how?" I asked. "Today?"

Stu, searching wildly, said, "Where's Paula?"

Danny winced. "Her, too. Took her with." He shut the hatch, whose window's rubber stripping had come loose. With thick thumbs he tried to tuck it back. "They packed up and took off after I'd gone to work," he said. "Debora called from Logan, switching planes."

"But wait," I said. "How long? How long will she be gone?" The number *ten* was in my head. *Ten weeks at the least.* Somehow I still thought that was important.

"She doesn't know," said Danny. "Or, no, that isn't what she said. 'I *can't* know.' That's what she kept saying."

At first I thought to cheer. She'd saved herself! The baby, too! But just as fast, I felt myself filling up with jiltedness. Saved the baby for whom? Without having told us? I stared at Danny. I wanted to shout: *How could you let her go?*

"What are you going to do?" asked Stu. He looked around, calculating, as if to find an instrument panel to captain, a control stick. "Won't you go? Won't you go down after them?"

"I don't know," said Danny. "She warned me not to. Maybe." He poked an end of stripping in; the other end popped out. "For now, I'm headed up to Brockton. A couple days," he said. "Comforts of home." He pointed at the bags of dirty laundry.

He looked like a little boy whose kite the wind has robbed, feeling the chafe of string yanked through his hands. Why was he not raging, not rushing for the airport? Coldcocked by the loss, I guessed, or trying to hide his torment. I didn't know how much longer I could mask my own.

"You'll tell us when you hear from her?" I asked. "When you know more?"

Danny grimaced. "I'm heading off, okay?" he said. "Excuse me."

He walked around and climbed into the driver's seat and turned the key. He backed out without checking his mirrors.

Stu and I were left alone, there on the burning blacktop. I still had the envelope from K.C. in my hands: its flap sealed, its folded edges sharp.

twenty-six

The next days passed in a furor of mixed feelings. Proud of Debora, pissed at her. Relieved, apprehensive. Altogether sick with incompletion.

Stu and I, in crisis mode, made a decent team, assessing our options, propping up each other's frames of mind. About the central issues, we agreed: we had to get in touch with Debora, to see what she was planning, to work out ways we'd help her with the pregnancy, the birth. Now that she was safely away from Danny, we'd take charge. We would give her everything she needed.

But e-mails to Brazucamama at Hotmail all bounced back: *This address has permanent, fatal errors.*

I kept thinking every day would be the one she'd call. Of course she'd call; I couldn't believe she wouldn't. But doubt was a dislodged clot, floating through my bloodstream, ready to make my flimsy heart seize up.

Stu, at first, was also swinging wildly among emotions: overwrought one moment, technocratic the next, plotting steps to solve the situation. Maybe now the legal system would work for us, he said. Or, if not for us, then for Danny: he would have a strong case for seeking Paula's custody, since Debora, strictly speaking, was guilty of kidnapping. Couldn't we, then, ask K.C. to get involved again, and find Debora by helping Danny file a suit against her?

But no, I couldn't stomach helping Danny to track her down, I said. Not when she had finally fled his grasp.

"It's not Debora I'm worried about," said Stu. "It's the baby."

In any case, we knew this line of thought was likely moot: Danny wanted nothing to do with us.

"Forget Danny," I said. "If he won't chase her, *we* should. Fly down there and find her in Brazil."

Debora's descriptions of where she had grown up had been so vivid, I felt sure I'd recognize her town, her family's farm: the field where her brother had lost his way, seeking butterflies; the mango tree under which she'd first been touched by boys; the house where she'd grown her lucky orchid. But now it struck me: she had never told me the town's name.

The shock of Debora's disappearance had ripped us from our moorings. In the immediate breakneck flail, it helped for us to cling together, keeping each other's heads above water. Eventually, though, the rapids of our panic petered out, and we emerged, alone and sore, to tend to our own bruises.

I was hurt that Debora had not trusted me to aid her, ashamed that she was arguably wise not to. I waited for an e-mail from an unfamiliar name, thinking she might start a new account. Any time we came back to the house from doing errands, I could not disguise my hopeful rush to check the phone machine. Breathlessly, I'd stab its buttons, hungry for her voice.

"Please, Pat," said Stu, one night after grocery shopping, when I had left the frozen foods melting on the counter, had gone straight to check for a new message. "Please," he said, "can't you try to pretend you're not obsessing?"

"But why?" I said. "Aren't you, too? I mean, shouldn't we both be?"

"Depends," he said, "on what you're obsessing over."

I focused on the baby, imagining its development: bigger than the proverbial period now but not by much, a C-shaped curl of cells with little buds where limbs would grow. My image of it should have been a purely joyous thing, but now, of course, now that Debora had stolen off, it couldn't be: what if the image was all I'd ever have? I found myself blaming the baby as much as I blamed her, angry that something barely formed—a concept more than a being, still—could wring me with such handicapping force.

I attempted to talk to Stu about my misplaced anger, about the way a parent's hard emotions toward a child could gather, long before the child was ever born. I brought this up on a Sunday, part of the way through August, when Stu had just finished a flight from Denver. He'd removed his epauletted shirt and donned an apron, to help me do the dishes after dinner.

"Maybe we could talk of something different tonight," he said. "Can't we do that? Remember how to do that?"

"But Stu," I said, envisioning the baby's budding limbs. "Somewhere Debora's sitting there, a baby growing inside her. A baby that, the chances are, you made—that has you in it."

"Or maybe," he said, "*you* made it. You and Debora together." He went back to scrubbing out a saucepan.

Stu started taking as many duty days as possible, signing on for longer flights, sleeping in hotels. Two years back, I would have suspected he was up to something, but these days it was clear to me he wanted no one's company, wanted only to be away, alone, to rinse his thoughts.

It was now high season, and everywhere I went—the Old Village Store, the Lobster Mart, the beach—I was thrust into the midst of seemingly carefree families, the patter of their flip-flops like the sound of self-applause. More and more I stayed at home, but the cottage gave no comfort, swollen with new silences, its endless view a taunt. I sought, as I hadn't done in years, the balm of poetry, but found myself with shards of Auden catching in my throat: *Blow the cobwebs from the mirror / See yourself at last.*

Stu had warned me—ordered me—not to contact Danny, at least not without his okay: "Trust me: all you'll do is make things worse."

But on the one-month anniversary of Debora having left, when Stu was in . . . I'd forgotten, the cities blurred together . . . I could bear to be cut off no longer. I called Danny, to learn if he had gotten any word from her, and also to attempt to ask forgiveness. Maybe, I thought, I had to do a little karmic cleansing, to earn a forward step for me and Stu.

"If I had," said Danny, when I asked if he'd heard from her. "If I had, do you think I would tell you?"

"But Danny," I said. "Listen. We've got a common interest here. Don't you think it might make sense if—"

"No," he said, "*you* listen. Keep the fuck away from me. Don't call; don't come over. Swear to God, I'll get a restraining order."

I didn't plan to mention this miscarried call to Stu, but then one day, when we were fighting, it came slipping out.

We were on our way to see a movie at the mall. Sometimes it was simpler for us to sit in the dark with strangers than to stay alone together at the cottage. It was Labor Day weekend; the roads were crushed with traffic. A hurricane supposedly was creeping up the coast, somewhere off Long Island's tip by now, but here you wouldn't have known it yet: the sky was bland and passive, the blue of a newborn's blind eyes.

Between our car and the Honda ahead, Stu kept a civil gap, as though this were a funeral procession. Balloons tied to its bumper (a honeymoon? a birthday?) had swollen in the heat; most had popped.

Stu had cranked the AC up to high; I was shivering. "Cold," I said, and showed him all my goose bumps. "Kill the air?"

"I want it cold," he said. "Just roll your window down."

Our convoy of the disconnected stuttered, stopped, resumed. Someone cut in front of us, an SUV like Danny's: the same model but slightly lighter blue.

"Wonder what he's up to now," said Stu. No need to name him. "Wonder if he's crawled down there and begged to win her back. What an asshole. Got what he had coming."

"Well, not to defend," I said. "But he's a lot less black-and-white, maybe, than you think."

"Oh?" said Stu. "Oh, really? Somehow I'm not seeing the gray areas."

I had never expected to be making excuses for Danny, but now I told Stu the story Debora had divulged: Danny's attempt at college, his dream of public defending, and then the pregnant co-ed, the baby when he was just nineteen, all the years of paying child support . . .

"People, you know, have histories," I said. "People's histories matter."

Stu upped the AC even higher: a scolding hiss.

"I called him," I said. I blurted it out, without having meant to.

"Oh, and let me guess," said Stu. "He was just as sweet as he could be?"

"He threatened he would get a restraining order."

Stu slammed the steering wheel. "Jesus, what did I tell you? Fuck you, Pat. Don't you *ever* listen?"

I hated the way he looked at me. Hated the thought of how I looked to him.

"Why?" he said. "Why can't you just keep your big mouth shut?"

"*My* big mouth? Mine?" I said. "Stu, without what *you* said, none of all this fuck-up would have happened."

Stu's jaw hung open. He huffed disbelievingly.

"I mean," I said, "if you had never snitched on us to Danny. Yes, I messed up—fine. But if you'd maybe thought for just a single goddamn second before deciding to mouth off the way you did . . ." I hadn't known till the words came out that they'd been building in me. I hadn't let the truth of them—what felt like truth—arise.

Stu said, "Fine. But let's just try a different 'if and then.'" His voice was square, tidy, algebraic. "If you'd never slept with her, *that's* what would have stopped this. *You*, Pat. If you were more the saint you claim to be." He stared ahead. The spastic traffic lurched. "Every bad thing that happens to us, you pin on me," he said. "Just because of things I used to do. How long will you think that, Pat? Tell me how long. Forever?"

Smog was seeping in through the AC vents, the window. I could taste its blackness on my tongue.

"You think people's histories matter? Sorry," said Stu, "but no. How they get *beyond* their histories—that's what really matters. Not what people did but what they do. What they do next."

What we did, for the moment, was park at the mall and walk inside, heading for the movie that we needed all the more now, to let us spend two hours together safely.

The mall was more crowded than I'd ever remembered seeing it: showboat teens, retirees in casual, untucked shirts, parents toting babies strapped in Scandinavian slings. Maybe they were stocking up ahead of the looming storm, or maybe they were blissfully oblivious of its approach.

We barged through the throng together, close but saying nothing, our argument still smoking from its coals. I was so intent on pushing forth through all the shoppers that I didn't notice the booth we'd neared till someone beside me brayed, "Write your name on a piece of rice. Five dollars!"

I tried to shrink away but the crowd had hemmed me in, and here came Mrs. Rita, waving a pink-nailed hand. Her smile was so big it crowded out her other features. "Get over here. That's right, you two. Come on."

Dread came crashing down on me: she knew us; she remembered. "The newlyweds," she'd say. "More than a year later, and still glowing!" She would ask if we had kept our matching grains: Till Death.

I looked at Stu. I couldn't tell if he knew what was happening. How embarrassing to have to grin and nod, to lie for both of us, but what choice would I have? I got ready.

"Good to see you," said Mrs. Rita, her voice, like shaken soda, over-fizzed. "Now, don't tell me. Let me guess." She looked us up and

271

down. "That's my expertise, you know: guessing who people are to each other. You two, hmm, I'd say . . . definitely some kind of family. But not too closely related, right? Not brothers. Maybe brothers-in-law? Yes, that's right. That's what I'll guess: you're in-laws."

I let no one block me as I tore away from her.

I made it through the crowd to a clear space by the wall, a small nook in front of a janitor's closet. I squatted down, facing the door, my forehead on its steel, not sure if I'd vomit or just cry. Tears turned my vision of the scene into a drowned man's. How could I have had so much with Stu, and thought so little of it? How could I have squandered it so fast?

He was there beside me now, also squatting down. He didn't talk, but laid his hand squarely on my back. He left it there, making tiny pulsings.

We skipped the movie. We drove straight back home.

Stu took me out onto the deck and sat me down. The scent of pine was in the air, and also the first hints of churned-up moisture from the tropics. The hair along my forearms felt alive. Stu said he would ask me something—ask something *of* me—only once, and I should give an answer, yes or no. Not right now; I could take my time to think it through.

"Give this up," he said. "Debora, the baby—all of it. Let it go now. Let's go back to us."

I stared out, past the dunes—the water glinted sharply—thinking of a sailor's proverb: *The farther the sight, the nearer the rain.* I remembered walking along the shore, all those months ago, the day we'd agreed to move up here. The way Stu had squinted at the pale winter sky. The way his fingers balled up with conviction.

twenty-seven

We live now in Washington, a transfer that made sense for Stu: all those shuttle flights from DCA. Not in Dupont Circle—the gay "Fruit Loop" ghetto—but out here at the city line, a place called Friendship Heights. D.C. is a rootless town, where people's ships arrive and leave on fickle political winds. It suits us fine, for the time being. No one really knows us.

Our place is in a complex overlooking the GEICO building, a two-bedroom, tenth-floor condominium. Sometimes I still miss having a yard to be in charge of; I wake up fretting, worried the berry bushes might need water. A crew of Salvadorans—our building's management hires them—takes care of the hostas by the sidewalk. The condo has a balcony, onto which we've squeezed two lawn chairs, plus a little hibachi (in violation of the bylaws), about as big as an Easy-Bake Oven. The summers can be ghastly, though, and we have central air; only rarely do we sit outside.

Inside, we've left the condo mostly as it came, the walls bare, painted an inoffensive not-quite-white; I don't think we've hung a single item. We haven't talked about this, but I trace it to what happened when we ran into trouble selling the cottage. Plenty of buyers came to look, but no one placed a bid, and so, finally, the Realtor said we'd better hire a "stager": someone to strip the cottage of what made it seem too "ours," to let would-be buyers picture their own possessions in it. The stager took down all Stu's travel posters, and Rina's pendant, and stashed our subway-token-inlaid table in the basement. Also removed: our bamboo shades, our campy fisherman whirligig, the framed photo of Stu and me in Prague. It took two more months before we got a reasonable offer, and maybe, in that time, we adjusted to the emptiness. Maybe that's why, here in D.C., we've kept our place so bare.

I don't know how long we'll stay. Almost three years we've lived here. We keep saying we should meet our neighbors, but we haven't. The guy next door invited us once, when he was having a party, but Stu was flying, and I didn't feel like showing up alone. D.C. makes a convenient base for traveling, which we do more now. New Year's, for example, we went to Quebec City. We stayed in the Ice Hotel: an ice bed.

Recounting all this, I can use a storyteller's tricks. Skip a space and then, with a phrase ("Almost three years . . ."), crush the rock of time into dust. In truth, when we first moved here—and even now, too often—hours and days could stymie us, immovable as boulders. The lull times were the worst—lying in bed, or breakfast—when nothing could distract us from the shame. Stu was ashamed of me, I knew, but also, I think, more pointedly, ashamed of *himself*, for still staying with me. I was lonely, and not just from the distance Stu was keeping. I had also lost another long-time, staunch companion: the vision of the father I had always hoped to be.

We did our best to isolate ourselves from our old life. We changed our phones, and left without giving the numbers to Danny; we switched our e-mail addresses and providers.

Still, of course, if Debora wanted to track us down, she could. (There are not too many Patrick Faunces.) I've dreamt she will, then fought that dream; its jab always leaves me feeling battered.

A dozen times I've Googled her name, and searched for her on Orkut, a social-networking site Brazilians use: never have I found the slightest trace. And last year—just once—I placed a call to Danny's, standing in a phone booth behind an Exxon station. I was wanting just to hear her voice, if she was there, just to hear the way she said "Alô."

A different woman answered. She had a Boston accent.

I said, "May I speak with Debora, please?" My voice quavered.

"There's no Debora living here," she said, and cut the line.

I walked around, all that day and the next, feeling wretched. I hope I don't try to call again.

Stu has not been perfect, either, in letting go what happened. One morning, we went together to mail things at the post office; I was sending a contract off to Educraft, for a Georgia textbook, and Stu was shipping a Marimekko scarf for Rina's birthday. A little dimpled boy—raven-haired, ravishing—was standing on the steps when we came out, slurping at an ice-cream treat as big as both his fists. I smiled at him provisionally, and he became excited, licking so hard he almost knocked the scoop right off the cone; his small, standstill eyes filled with panic. "Here," I said, and knelt to grab the cone, and set it right. "Hold on, now—I got it. That was close!" His smile came back, impossibly wide; I stroked his sun-warmed cheek. That was when a woman (she'd been in line behind us) gusted through the door, shouting, "Sir! Just leave my son—sir, please!" and sucked the boy up into her arms. Hot in the brow, I backed away, my tongue fat within my mouth, obscene.

Stu, at first, said nothing. We turned and walked toward home. But then, as we waited for a light to go to green, he scuffed the curb, and said, "I know. I think about it, too. Ours would be exactly that same age."

He didn't sound angry, but only sad and stranded—and I had to accept that as improvement.

Also, he had called the baby *ours*.

Why have we stuck it out? Why does any couple? Danny and Debora have split, it seems. Rina and Richard, too. Thousands of marriages, every day, dissolve. But here we are, Stu and I, still . . .

Still a *we*.

Last week I received a long letter from Susan Blandon, my old creative-writing teacher from college. For years, we've traded letters—actual paper letters—hers typed on a Royal, mine in cursive. Our subject's usually poetry (the sudden fad for ghazals; Cavafy's unfinished drafts finally rendered into English), but personal life can poke its head in, too. Susan's been with Ned, her archivist husband, for forty years. They renovated a succession of old homesteads in Vermont, raised three kids who have their own kids now. A foursquare man, is Ned. I've always liked him.

I never would have guessed what Susan wrote me in her latest, that she and Ned are getting a divorce. There isn't any scandal, she assured me; they're still friendly. "But, well, what can I tell you?" she wrote. "We were steering for a harbor that turned out not to be there."

I wonder, sometimes, if Stu's and my disaster was what saved us. Whatever happens now, we think: *It's not as bad as* that *was*. There was no one day when we said, "Oh, thank God, it's over." It isn't over, maybe. Maybe what has happened is that we have gotten past the thought that what we tore wide ever could be closed. The opening means that further pain could enter, but so could progress.

Everyone knows the riddle about the boundaries of personhood: how can I ever know if the blue you see is just like mine? With Stu I've learned that even if our *seeing* is not the same—and his blue, I'm sure, is two or three shades darker—it doesn't matter, as long as we're committed to *being* together.

The harbor we were steering for was not where we'd expected. Perhaps it never existed, in the first place. But I'm more sure than ever, now, that Stu—Stu and no one else—is the person I will always steer with.

Today's the Fourth of July. A difficult day for us. Especially in D.C., with its massive celebration, tourists pouring in for the parade, the Capitol show. Even out here, at Friendship Heights, our Metro stop gets swarmed: families carrying picnic baskets and opera glasses and blankets, heading to the Mall to stake out seats.

The only way to avoid all the hoopla is to stay at home, and so we do, the whole day long: just us two, in the condo. We order food from Lucky Wok and bring it to the balcony, and sit here in our lawn chairs, sharing crab rangoon, staring out at the GEICO building's roof. Washington, as most people know, is built upon a swamp; in summer it's a hazy, humid fug. But once in a while, after a rain, the air goes clear and crystalline: a swift, capricious rinsing of creation. Today's that way, the sky like a massive flag's blue background, waiting to be endowed with sewn-on stars.

Mostly we don't talk, just take in all that blueness, the impotent pops of cherry bombs exploding in the distance.

Stu gives me a soy sauce kiss. "Happy Independence Day."

"Yes," I tell him. "Happy Independence."

I picture, as I often do on rinsed-off days like this, the lucid sky that spreads across Rio Grande do Norte: the almost-purest air on all the earth. Below its blue, the white, white dunes, like brilliant sugar mountains. *Genipabu.* I hear Deb say the name.

I'd like to share my vision with Stu, but I'm not sure I should. Maybe next year.

Next year, yes, I will.

See Deb at the summit, in the beaming new dune buggy? See the boy she's hugging in her lap? (A boy is my unjustified assumption.) Three years old, with green-flecked eyes, a forceful Nadler nose. His mother's arms, around him, make the world's securest seat belt.

"With emotion, or without?" she asks.

He squeals and shivers. "With."

She tells the driver, who hits the gas—sand spits from the tires—and oh! Here they go! They're flying!

acknowledgments

For support during the writing of this book, I am indebted to the MacDowell Colony, the Instituto Sacatar (especially Augusto Albuquerque, Mitch Loch, and Taylor Van Horne), and James Duggins. For help with various drafts, I thank Carrie Bjerke, Brian Bouldrey, Cathy Chung, Bernard Cooper, David Elliott, Elinor Lipman, David Long, Bill Lychack, Fiona McCrae, and Heidi Pitlor, with special gratitude to Hester Kaplan and Vestal McIntyre. Boundless thanks also to my agent, Mitchell Waters; my editor, Raphael Kadushin; and the staff of the University of Wisconsin Press. Finally, thanks and love to all my family, especially Janet Lowenthal and Jim Pines, Abraham Lowenthal and Jane Jaquette, Linda Lowenthal and Chris Johnson, and Scott Heim.